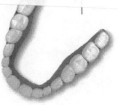

ADVENTURES OF THE OLD BLUES
BOOK 2

Da Broad SQUAD

CHRIS LEGROW

OMAHA, NEBRASKA

Omaha, Nebraska

DA BROAD SQUAD: ADVENTURES OF THE OLD BLUES - BOOK 2

CL1557 Publishing, LLC books may be ordered
from your favorite bookseller.

www.SenileSquad.com

CL1557 Publishing, LLC
4822 South 133rd Street
Omaha, NE 68137

Paperback: 978-0-9977036-5-8
Mobi: 978-0-9977036-6-5
EPUB: 978-0-9977036-7-2

Library of Congress Cataloging Number and
Library of Congress Cataloging-in-Publication data on file with the publisher.

PRODUCTION, DISTRIBUTION AND MARKETING:
Concierge Publishing Services, www.ConciergeMarketing.com

Printed in the USA

10 9 8 7 6 5 4 3 2 1

To my wife Kara, kids and grandkids.

Sorry Papa had to spend so much time at the computer.

PROLOGUE

The mist that enveloped her conscious thought was starting to lift. A slow but constant thump forced her to focus on the sound and the strange feeling in her head each time she heard it. Gradually the sound and sensation became familiar. She realized that her head was bumping against the window of some sort of vehicle. Then there was one big thump as the van hit a slight dip in the road, jolting her awake.

Amanda Crantz sat up and looked around, recognizing the van that had transported her from one foster home to another, one temporary placement to another, one adolescent treatment center to another, and finally to juvenile probation. At almost eighteen years old, she had spent half her life in some type of placement. Each placement started out well, but something always happened at school or with the other kids. She would get angry, aggressive, and often violent. It did not take long for therapists to recommend medications, and unfortunately, it was easy to get prescriptions for mood swings, attention deficit, or any number of diagnoses for her behavior.

Taking pills became as normal to Amanda as drinking water. Soon she began running away from her placements and her problems. She would hook up with people who were willing to provide drugs and shelter to a pretty, petite brunette.

"What day is it?" she asked the man driving the van. He glanced at her in the rearview mirror, clearly startled that she had woken up. After realizing what the girl was asking, he gruffly answered in a strange accent, "Vensday." Amanda shook her head and realized that she could not remember anything since Sunday. All the other times she had run away, she could at least remember something about her partying blitz. This time was different—she recalled nothing, absolutely nothing.

Amanda gazed up to the ceiling of the van and said, "That must have been some party."

A female voice with an accent similar to the driver's responded, "Why do ju say that?"

Amanda's eyes quickly found the woman sitting to the far right on the same bench seat she was on. "What? Oh, I didn't even see you," Amanda said with a startled chuckle. She then looked hard at the woman, trying to determine who she was. It didn't take Amanda long to decide that the woman was probably some sort of Health and Human Services contractor who transported state ward youth to wherever their caseworkers told them to deliver the child until a decision was made for their next placement.

"Well, ju did it this time, Amanda—got kicked out of another program."

Amanda frowned and said, "I don't even remember what happened. Where am I going this time?"

With a smile the woman asked, "Ju don't remember anything?"

Amanda shook her head. The woman smiled and said, "Never mind, ju must be thirsty. Here." The woman raised a clear water bottle to Amanda's lips. Amanda tried to reach for the bottle but realized that she was handcuffed to a large leather belt that was around her midsection.

The woman smiled and repeated, "Ju really don't remember anything, do ju?"

Amanda looked at her hands, shrugged, and said, "Must have been a great party."

As the woman raised the plastic water bottle to Amanda's mouth, Amanda noticed a tattoo of a star on the inside of the woman's right wrist. "Nice tat," Amanda said. The woman seemed startled that this young woman had noticed her tattoo, but she quickly recovered from her surprise and said, "Here, have some water."

Amanda drank to the sound of the plastic collapsing. The popping sound increased as she swallowed. Then the van hit a bump and the bottle fell to floor, spilling the remainder of its contents.

She sat back in her seat, looked at the handcuffs, and said, "Must have really been a wild night." After about ten minutes, Amanda started to get dizzy again. Within twenty minutes she was unconscious.

The woman on the seat next to Amanda smiled and said to the driver, "This one will bring a good price. Make sure ju don't beat her about the face."

Amanda was a constant runaway, near adult age, and there would be little, if any, effort to find her. She had never imagined that living life in the fast lane would drive her straight into the dark and unforgiving world of human trafficking.

Abducted runaways like Amanda were taken to a secret location and injected with heroin or some other mind-destroying drug for about two weeks. By that time they were addicted and willing to do anything to get another "hit" so they could avoid undergoing withdrawal. To cope, they mentally went to another place while their bodies were abused by unscrupulous men and women. After a couple of years of abuse, they would be discarded. Another rebellious runaway was soon found to replace them.

The woman in the van picked up her phone and placed a call as the driver eyed her through the rearview mirror. When her call was answered, she said, "The package will be delivered soon. She woke up for a few minutes and said that she doesn't remember anything. I gave her another drink with the drug provided by our friend, the Chemist. She is now unconscious and should arrive at his home in about an hour or two."

The voice at the other end of the line responded, "Good. After the Chemist is finished with her, call me when she is taken to the Omaha house and is secure. We'll take care of her from there. I will have another pickup for you soon." Then the line went dead.

The woman who had given the final instructions smiled, then looked at the calendar on her desk. *It's Friday. Nobody is even going to bother looking for Amanda because she'll be eighteen in a couple of weeks, an adult. The state has too many other children to worry about.*

"Too easy," she said as she looked at her phone. Her sleeve pulled away from her wrist to reveal a portion of a tattooed star.

CHAPTER 1

The Old Blues Precinct was a beehive of activity. The old officers were walking around in their police hats and shirts, clad in "hospital gown indignity bottoms" (as they called them) from the waist down. Each wore patent leather shoes with black socks held up by sock suspenders. Many sported adult diapers, while others wore white boxers with a catheter connected to a piss pack attached to their leg. Unlike other nursing homes, this police retirement home was specifically designed to maintain the facade of a 1950s police precinct with a geriatric twist. The officers played their roles to perfection to hide their actual crime-fighting activities from the public, the medical staff, and the local police.

The Sarge was in his office behind a closed door. He was on the phone, waiting for an opportunity to get a word in edgewise. He held the phone next to his ear with his right hand while holding his unlit cigar between the index and middle fingers of his left hand. His forehead was in the palm of his left hand, and both elbows were planted on his desk. Sarge looked like he was completely exhausted from the conversation.

The voice on the phone growled, "You're not fooling me, Sarge! I heard what's going on there and I want in. I busted my keister for twenty-seven years in the department. You know I put up with more abuse than any of those other diaper-wearing geezers. I deserve it, and you know it."

Sarge waited as the person on the other end had a long coughing spell. Then he asked, "How soon can you get here?"

The answer was brief: "I'll be there in two days, and there will be others. You can count on it. Sarge, you know the department owes us."

Sarge sat back in his chair, put his cigar in his mouth, and said, "You're right, Crantz. See you in two days."

∽

Two days later, Boss Nurse Betsy looked up from her computer and told the student nurse, "There will be two new patients this morning. Remember, just wheel them into the Precinct, then stop and let them look around and take it all in. Sometimes it's quite a shock for them to see that old police room for the first time. We want them to calmly reminisce at their own pace. The other 'patients,'" she said with emphasis, "will help them socialize and feel at home." Boss Nurse looked back at her screen and mumbled to herself, "Why we call these guys 'patients' is beyond me; they think they run the place."

As the two new patients were wheeled into the giant facility, they could see that this building was much more than a simple retirement and nursing home. It housed a branch of the Nebraska Department of Health and Human Services as well as educational, medical, and mental health staff. All of these divisions, including a corridor that led to a supply room, could be accessed from a large central lobby. Each doorway had an old-fashioned brass engraved sign identifying the hallway's destination. There was a large double-wide brass door below a prominent sign labeled "The Precinct." The young student nurse smiled at her patients as she pressed the button opening the broad doors granting entrance to the nostalgic main office reminiscent of a 1950s police headquarters. As the doors opened there was the unmistakable sound of typewriters tapping away, creating reports for dissemination to officers assigned to various hot spots in the city.

One of the retired cops said, "Oh my," and the other remarked, "I don't believe my eyes." The student nurse said, "We get that a lot here. Would you two like to sit for a while and take this in? I can come back in ten or fifteen minutes if you would like?" One of the patients gently patted the trainee's hand and said, "Thank you, child." With an understanding smile, the student nurse left the two to their memories as she closed the doors behind her.

The first officer said to the other, "Thought she'd never leave." The other officer spoke with a raspy voice, "Yeah, she's a sweet kid, but for crying out loud, leave us be." The new officers' brief conversation was cut short by the booming voice of the Sarge.

"'Bout time you two got here." Sarge's voice echoed throughout the Precinct. That got the attention of all the officers in the room. As they looked at the two new officers, the typing abruptly stopped.

"What the… Oh, no!" gulped Benson. Then Big Al Afasa, the giant Samoan nicknamed "Tink," recognized the new officers. His eyes widened as he gasped, "Holy moly, dat's gonna be trouble."

Behind Benson and Tink there were similar grumblings, and one Ol' Blue was heard to say, "Not broads! Especially not *that* broad!" Sarge smiled and quietly chuckled to himself.

Agnes Crantz tossed the blanket off her lap and strained to stand up as straight as her seventy-eight-year-old frame would allow. She pulled the nasal cannula oxygen tubes from her nose and moved them to her forehead like many people do with sunglasses. Then she put a cigarette in her mouth and lit it. Her eyes squinted as the smoke surrounded her face. She took a long drag as she slowly panned the Precinct as if sizing up the officers who were all quietly staring at her. The men slowly stepped back, anticipating some sort of explosion from the oxygen being so close to the cigarette. Agnes Crantz pulled the cigarette from her mouth, blew the smoke into the air, and announced, "That's right, boys, it's Da Broad Squad. Now shut up!"

As if on cue, all of the men looked down and started to type or pretend to be busy doing something, anything, that would let them escape Agnes Crantz's deadly stare.

A satisfied grin edged the tips of Agnes's tight lips. The sound of Sarge's muffled chuckle drew her attention to him.

"Are you finished?" he quietly asked. She looked at him and said, "Not yet," then quickly jerked her head toward the men in the Precinct who had started to look up. They immediately jerked their heads back to their tasks. The right edge of her mouth twitched with satisfaction as she announced, "*Now* I'm finished."

"Good," Sarge replied. "The trainee nurse should be back any time now. Let her take you to your room. Once you're settled in, I want to meet with you two in my office."

Without looking up, one of the Blues murmured out of the corner of his mouth to Officer Harry Benson, "Who is the other broad?" Harry kept his head down for fear Agnes Crantz might still be looking at him. "Don't you remember Mary Blanch?" The Blue's eyes widened, but he was also afraid to look up. "You don't mean Meter Maid Mary!"

"Got a problem with that, bub?" Both Blues jolted their heads up in a startled response to the question coming from a woman with curly purple hair and huge glasses that made her green eyes look like they filled the entire lens. Mary resembled a great horned owl with glasses and purple hair. She sat slumped in her customized electric wheelchair. The motor was so quiet that she had been able to cruise right up to the two Blues without being heard.

For years Mary Blanch had driven a three-wheeled meter maid scooter through the streets of Omaha. She recognized every make and model of vehicle on the roads, and to this day her sharp mind could identify the type of vehicle from the sound of its engine. Nobody weaseled their way out a ticket with her. Then, near the end of her twenty-five years of service, she was hit by a drunk driver. Mary had to have three vertebrae of her neck fused. Her head barely moved, but her huge eyes moved from side to side and she didn't miss much. When she needed to look around, she moved her joystick and the wheelchair her nephew had made for her would quietly pivot in any direction she wanted. And it was fast—capable of reaching twenty-five miles per hour. Zipping along in her wheelchair was her main thrill in life, but she indulged her need for speed only when her family wasn't around. If they had known she could go that fast, they would have thrown a fit.

For the moment, however, she stared steely-eyed at the two Blues and waited for an answer. They stared back at Mary, glanced quickly at each other, then looked back at her and muttered, "Nope." Without another word, Meter Maid Mary pivoted her wheelchair and quietly rejoined Agnes Crantz. As if on cue, the nursing student walked into the Precinct and cheerfully asked, "Would you like to see your rooms?" The duo smiled as the student took Agnes's wheelchair by the handles and steered it toward the hallway to the patient rooms. Mary quietly followed, stopped, and then pivoted toward the two Blues she had just talked to and said, "This ain't no boys' club anymore." She said it like it was a threat, then quickly caught up with the student nurse and exited the Precinct.

As the two women were escorted out of the Precinct, one Ol' Blue bleakly sighed, "There goes the department."

About an hour later, the Sarge was sitting at his desk waiting to brief the latest additions to the Precinct. He reflected on how women had been treated in the old days. Back then, the women played a supportive role. Even though they were officers, they were expected to get coffee for the male officers, wear skirts instead of pants, and do the mundane daily activities that the male officers didn't want to do. What would be denounced as sexual discrimination today had been an unavoidable annoyance for those women. A lot had changed since then, but Agnes, Mary, and others had paved the way for additional female police officers.

As Mary Blanch quietly rolled into the office, the Sarge waited for Agnes Crantz to follow. Agnes's entrance was heralded by a constant squeak of the wheels of her oxygen tank holder. It stood about three feet tall, had two wheels and a tubular cage-like apparatus that held a small green oxygen tank. Agnes shuffled her feet as she walked, but her movements were accompanied by the unmistakable chirping sound of her oxygen carrier. From now on it was going to be a warning chirp to alert the Ol' Blues that Agnes was coming.

Once they were both in the Sarge's office, he motioned for Agnes to take a seat. Mary folded her hands on her lap as she waited to hear what the Sarge had to say.

They were a crusty pair of retired cops, but they also understood the importance of keeping the police department running efficiently. That meant following orders. They both knew and respected the Sarge. That's why both of them were eager to be part of what he and the Ol' Blues were doing. Both Agnes and Mary knew that some sort of crime fighting was going on. They didn't know the details, but they wanted to find out.

"What on earth are those geezers working on out there?" Agnes said as she pointed with her thumb towards the Precinct office. "Don't tell me that those wrinkled old cops are actually working cases." The Sarge looked at Mary and then back to Agnes. He pulled the unlit cigar from his mouth and leaned forward, resting his forearms on his desk. "Blues," the Sarge said, as if to correct Agnes and let her know that he didn't like the derogatory tone she used in reference to his officers. "Each of them picked by me." He sat back in his chair to let that sink in, making sure that both Agnes and Mary understood that he ran things around here and had a good reason for everything he did.

Agnes cocked her head to the right and gave the Sarge a surprised look. *There is something wrong with her face,* the Sarge thought as Agnes took a short drag on her half-smoked cigarette. She softened her tone and said, "Sorry, Sarge, I know you paid your dues and you were one of the best sergeants the department ever had. But for the love of Pete, two of those Blues out there threw me in the trunk of their cruiser and drove around the city for about an hour while I kicked and screamed. They thought it was funny. Do you know how hard it was for women to be coppers in the old days?"

"You two really had it tough," Sarge agreed. "I should have contacted you and a few other women officers when we started our little operation here. That is an oversight I plan on rectifying soon."

Agnes smiled, and with the same hand her cigarette was in, pulled the oxygen nasal tubes from her nose. The burning ash of her smoke got close to the oxygen flowing from the tube in the cannula, and a flame popped to life close to her forehead. Startled, the Sarge blurted, "Watch it, Agnes! You'll burn your eye… " The Sarge stopped and realized what was wrong with her face. "Agnes, you don't have any eyebrows!" He leaned a little closer, "No eyelashes either."

Agnes noticed the flame coming from her smoke and nonchalantly blew it out as if she had done it a thousand times before. The effort caused a short coughing fit as she tried to talk. "I'm a lady, *cough,* I can paint 'em on," she pointed out, then coughed some more. "I can also stick eyelashes on that I got on sale from the beauty salon."

Mary chimed in, "Oh, the purple ones? Those are my favorite, Agnes; they really make your eyes dance." This brought a confused stare from the Sarge. Agnes looked back to him after her coughing subsided and said, "All right, Sarge, tell us about this place."

The Sarge explained that what the public sees is the Ol' Blue Precinct conducting investigations for nuisance-type civil matters and acting as advisors to the local crime prevention organizations in the city.

"The Chief decided that using us for these community matters will free up his officers for working the streets. This works out fine, because whenever the media or any guests tour the Precinct, they see what you see…a bunch of old officers still trying to serve the citizens of Omaha as best they can. The public loves it, and the work provides a cover for all the secret operations we carry out." Both women perked up at that last statement. Agnes looked at Mary and then at the Sarge, and with the cigarette bouncing in her mouth as she spoke, said, "What do you mean, secret operations?"

Sitting back in his chair, the Sarge smiled and pulled the cigar from his mouth. The computer screen on his desk provided a quick view of the various surveillance cameras in the area around the Ol' Blue Precinct. He quickly checked to make sure that none of the nurses, especially Boss Nurse Betsy, were making any kind of rounds that might result in a nurse overhearing what he was about to tell the newest members of the Ol' Blue Unit.

Satisfied that the coast was clear, the Sarge leaned forward and explained that below the main floor of the entire facility were tunnels, research and development labs, and a crack bunch of scientists who could make just about anything happen with computers. They were able to create all kinds of crime-fighting gizmos that could stun, subdue, or generally make any criminal's life miserable. The door that led to this incredible labyrinth of crime-fighting technology and weaponry was carefully guarded by the boys. It was located inside an unexpected place: the supply room.

Agnes and Mary felt lucky to be sitting when they heard this news. They both were shocked and amazed by what the Sarge had told them. Mary stared at him in disbelief and Agnes was speechless. Finally, she muttered, "I... I can't believe it. All of this is right below us?"

The Sarge popped the cigar back into his mouth and pointed downward. "Wait 'til you see it. If you think the Precinct is amazing, what's below us is inspiring."

"What makes it work is the Precinct," the Sarge added, pointing to the officers scampering about in the vintage 1950s-era police headquarters.

Agnes squinted and said, "But they're just doing busy work, nuisance-type stuff, not real kick 'em where it hurts police work."

The Sarge almost cut her off, saying, "Exactly, and that is what we want the whole world to think is going on here. We want the outside world to see just what you did when you first walked into the Precinct, and nothing more."

Pointing at Agnes, Sarge said, "I want you to make sure that the Precinct functions as a police precinct should. I don't want people to suspect that these old coppers are anything but a little senile and reliving their youthful lives. The public thinks it's adorable that these old guys think they are still cops, and we want them to go right on thinking just that. Got it, Agnes?"

Agnes sat back in her chair and took another long drag on her smoke. She smiled and asked, "Do I get to be Lead Officer in this little precinct of yours?" The Sarge liked the tone of Agnes's question.

"Only if you think you can handle it," he replied. Agnes moved the nasal cannula back to her nostrils and took a deep breath. After a couple of coughs, she smiled and said, "It will be good to boss these Old Blues around again. I miss kicking keisters."

Mary raised her finger in the air, asking, "What about me?"

The Sarge again checked his computer monitor to make sure no nurses were entering the Precinct.

"Glad you asked," he said as he pulled a map of the entire facility from a drawer in his desk. He spread it out and said, "We need a set of eyes outside guarding the perimeter of the buildings. Video surveillance is good, but if there is a nurse or doctor walking around, we can't very well be seen reviewing the grounds. So, Mary, I want you to motor around in that chair of yours and patrol the parking lot and the outside of the entire building. I hear that thing really moves." Mary smiled and nodded.

Then the Sarge pointed to his hearing aid and explained, "These hearing aids are also communication devices. You touch the back of the device and start talking. Those of us who monitor the radio will hear you. You can give us a heads up when people are entering the building. That way we can get our canned speeches ready for any impromptu tours that the Mayor or other dignitary wants to give to VIPs.

"That's all you need to know for now," Sarge concluded. "Remember, we're cops playing like we're cops while actually being cops. We're pretty good at it, and after a week or two, I'm sure you two will fit right in."

Agnes and Mary started to leave the Sarge's office. Just before Agnes reached the door she paused and asked, "How about finding lost kids?"

ᘒ

Thane Jared, the red-headed, freckle-faced computer genius for the Precinct, was sharpening his skills in the Ol' Blue lab with the computer system he had designed. He zoomed in and out of various companies, banks, and government offices without the security systems knowing what was going on. Thane especially enjoyed seeing what supervisors were doing in the building's government offices. He was so engrossed in his monitor that he didn't hear the door open behind him.

"Thanerboy!" The unmistakable bellow of the Sarge jolted Thane out of his chair. He quickly bent over and typed a command into his computer so that his work would not be jeopardized.

"Sarge, how many times do I have to tell you not to do that to me? You know I'm working." The Sarge took the stogie out of his mouth and blew Thane's statement off with a "Yeah, yeah, you're Thane, the fancy schmancy computer gadget king. You playing some game or something?"

Thane looked over his glasses at the Sarge and knew that trying to explain what he was doing would be like speaking another language. The Sarge would nod and smile, pretending he understood everything Thane said.

"Yep, just playing computer games, Sarge."

"Got a job for ya, Thane. One of the new Blues, Agnes Crantz, has a granddaughter that's been in foster care for most of her life."

Thane interrupted, "A woman Old Blue? I thought you old men were the cops back in your day."

The Sarge shrugged and said, "It was mostly men, but the women who took this job in those days were as tough as they come. Don't mess with 'em."

"This particular Blue, Agnes, is a no-nonsense, hard-nosed broad who could work circles around most of the men up there." The Sarge pointed to the ceiling where the Precinct was located.

"Now that her granddaughter Amanda Crantz is almost eighteen and getting out of the system, she wants to help the girl out. The problem is, the kid has run away again from her latest placement and Agnes doesn't think there will be much effort to find her. Agnes says she was reported missing about two days ago. Here's her information. See what you can find out." The Sarge put a piece of paper on Thane's desk and started to walk out.

Thane watched the Sarge take a step towards the door as he re-opened the Health and Human Services database system he had just happened to be investigating when the Sarge barged into his office. Thane quickly located Amanda's caseworker, and in short order Amanda's file filled his computer screen.

"Three days ago." Thane pushed his glasses higher on his nose and shot a quick *"Ain't I good?"* look toward the boss. This caused the Sarge to jerk to a halt like he had just stepped in something disgusting.

The Sarge slowly turned around with his cigar hanging from the side of his mouth. Thane wondered what kept it from falling. The clearly dazzled Sarge pointed to the computer and said, "How did you... "

Thane grinned and said, "She was reported missing three days ago. Hey, she is on probation with a GPS ankle bracelet. This kid really gets around. I see about six different placements in the last year or so."

The Sarge perked up. "Bracelet—you mean one of those tracking things?"

Thane didn't look up as he continued, "Yep, she'll be easy to find. All we have to do is... " Thane gazed into his monitor and just said, "Nuts."

Sarge's eyes darted from the monitor to Thane as he said, "What?"

Thane sat back and said, "The bracelet has been cut off. The probation officer found the bracelet at a country barn outside of Norfolk. Must have been one of those rave parties."

The Sarge straightened and sighed, "There are so many of those barns out in rural Nebraska. I hear those parties get pretty wild."

Thane scrolled through the information about the probation officer's findings. There was Amanda Crantz's history and a list of behaviors of concern. The Sarge's eyes narrowed as he read the behaviors that were of concern to Amanda's probation officer. "Look at all the stuff on this kid's record: numerous runaways, drug usage, lack of parental involvement, criminal activity, defiance of any authority, and no after-care plans. She's just a throw-away kid."

The Sarge elbowed Thane in the shoulder and said, "Send all of this information up to my computer." The jolt sent Thane's glasses down to the end of his nose. He pushed them back and uttered, "Sure, Sarge."

Thane accessed the photos of the scene taken by a deputy who had accompanied the probation officer and been assigned to investigate the runaway juvenile. The deputy had dutifully recorded the last known whereabouts of Amanda Crantz. Photos included the exterior views of the weathered, abandoned barn, trashed with beer cans and various bottles of liquor scattered around the once-beautiful symbol of the American farmer. Interior photos showed discarded clothing and some scattered pills spilled onto the ground during the night of music, dancing, and foolishly toying with the deadly barbed hooks of addiction. The last photo showed a GPS ankle bracelet on the ground. The deputy could easily see it in the middle of the floor while looking through the large barn doors.

Thane copied all the information from the investigation, including the photos, and sent everything to the Sarge's computer.

౭ﻭ

While Amanda was trapped in a drug-induced sleep, she was being taken to the first stop on the dark trail of human trafficking. She would not know what had happened to her afterward, nor would she remember much of anything that she saw during times of momentary consciousness. That was how the man who was called *"the Chemist"* liked his victims. The chemical concoction he added to the water given to the girls was designed to do just that. The van was on its way to the Chemist's home. The driver, Victor, a portly bald man who was about fifty pounds overweight and always seemed to need a shave, looked into the rear-view mirror and waited for his cousin Sasha to look up and meet his eyes in the mirror.

"Call the Chemist and let him know we will be there shortly," Victor said. Sasha nodded and dialed her phone.

The man receiving Sasha's call looked at his phone and smiled, realizing who was calling. He then looked around the service desk at a customer and told an old woman, "I have to check the inventory; I'll be right back." He retreated to the storage room, his favorite place to go when he got a call from this Sasha woman. It was dark, quiet, and no one could see him. It was the perfect place as he discreetly conversed with those who paid him for his special chemical concoction. He would be paid in cash and given the use of an unconscious young woman. When he finished with her, the girl was taken away. To where? He didn't really care.

"An hour or two—that should work," the Chemist said. "Make sure the garage doors are completely closed behind you, then leave her in the bedroom. Don't get nosy; just come back and pick her up tomorrow morning. Got it?"

Sasha assured the Chemist that she understood his instructions, just as she had told him a couple of dozen times before, then hung up.

Sasha told Victor, "The Chemist keeps every aspect of this routine to the letter. He wants the garage closed, the girl taken to the bedroom, and then we leave without even seeing him. Have you ever seen him, Victor?"

Victor shook his head and said, "No, and that's how he likes it. If you know what is good for you, you never will." Sasha nodded and put her phone away.

The man on the other end of the line quietly hung up his phone. He could not keep from smiling as he thought about the complete power he had over the young women who were brought to him... and the fact that they never knew who he was. To him it was like a chemical mask cloaking both his identity and his cowardly actions.

When the Chemist was finished with the girls, they would be taken to a house somewhere in Omaha, drugged to the point of addiction, and then transported to wherever business was good for the human trafficking trade. If the girls somehow were able to contact the police, all they would be able to say was that something had happened, but they would not remember exactly what it was. The cops would probably think the girl was crazy, or the girl would think she was going crazy.

Within seventy-two hours the drug was out of the girl's system. That was another of the drug's benefits. It was all too easy for "the Chemist." The victim didn't really know she was a victim, the drug was out of her system after a short time, and the Chemist just faded back into the cover of his day job. He would wait for the next girl. Given her height and weight information, he would formulate the memory-erasing drink and start the routine again.

Though he looked every bit the stereotypical geek, Thane Jared was an absolute warrior with a computer. The funding that the Bureau of billionaires had provided to the specially designed police retirement home gave Thane the means to develop and implement computer applications that he had only dreamed of when he was in college.

As a student, Thane had quickly surpassed his instructors and become bored with school. It didn't take people long to recognize Thane's genius, and he was offered a position in one of the Bureau members' companies. Thane was quietly recruited to lead the cyber policing unit in the secret research and development lab under the Ol' Blues Unit. Thane never really did anything people would consider "manly," but working with the cops appealed to his desire to be some sort of hero like the old guys in the nursing home.

Thane's computer system was a couple of steps ahead of what the world calls "state of the art." He had all the upgrades that were available to the powers that be in society, plus the programming that he was able to create with the funding provided to the police retirement home.

When Thane "hacked" into a network or company, he went directly to the IT branch of the corporation. That gave him access to many more avenues and much more information regarding the business or agency network. Not only could he get into the IT section, he had developed a way to escape detection, by routing his computer infiltrations through various cities, countries, and even other businesses. Thane's cloaking expertise caused the targeted corporation to invest precious time tracing the source of the breach. Thane made his escape in the form of a circle. As the IT computer security personnel traced his routing, he did so in a way that repeated one IP address to another, thus causing what cyber security usually sees as a zigzag of cyber routes bouncing from one side of the world to another. Thane called his technique the "Big O." Before cyber security knew it, they were in a continuing circle of repeating IP addresses. On a digital map, it looked like a large circle with no beginning and no end. Impossible to trace.

Suddenly the monitor that Thane was using to investigate the missing girl had a word flash in red, like a warning: "ANJATEL!" Thane lurched forward to his keypad. He knew that someone other than him was monitoring this Health and Human Services computer from outside the network. This same someone had given some sort of warning to a person inside the government agency, and Thane could tell that this same agency worker was trying frantically to get the computer to shut down. Thane had already retrieved the needed information on the missing girl but could see that something he did had caused some sort of alarm. Possibly he had stayed too long or accessed something with a trigger alert.

Thane instantly remembered that when the Sarge had burst into his office his train of thought had gone from his surveillance of the Health and Human Services computers to finding out what the Sarge wanted. Whatever had happened, someone could tell that there was something going on with the Health and Human Services computer. Then that same someone decided to warn rather than investigate further. It was clear to Thane that whatever was being done from this computer in the Health and Human Services Department must be something very big to have an outside person monitor what was being discussed from this site.

Thane's eyes transformed from the initial widened surprise to a determined glare when he realized that someone had sounded an alarm. He didn't want to make another knee-jerk reaction that might give away his presence, so he slowly and methodically withdrew from the computer with the additional outside computer monitor, making a mental note to determine who it belonged to. Thane came back to the IT computer systems and decided that he would start his search from there. He smiled and quietly said to himself, "Now let's see why someone would want to have an outside monitor over a State computer."

⚬

The Sarge sat at his desk as the information on Agnes's granddaughter arrived at his computer. He tapped a small button on his hearing aid and said over the communication network (or "earcoms," as the Ol' Blues called them), "Smitty, I need you in my office pronto."

Smitty was in his apartment and had just attached his colostomy bag to his side. The Sarge's voice came over Smitty's earcoms and he got all giddy when the Sarge ordered him to his office. He had never lost that quick jolt of energy cops get when they hear their call sign on the radio and know that they are about to get a dispatch.

"On my way, Sarge" was his quick and excited reply. Smitty loved the fact that his skills were still needed, and he jumped at every opportunity to use his special ability to observe crime scenes and see things that other officers missed.

Smitty pulled his police uniform shirt on over his hospital gown, strapped his black socks to his leg suspenders, and tied his black patent leather shoes. As he rushed out of his apartment, he grabbed his Omaha police hat and closed the door behind him. He shuttled up the hallway toward the doors that had the words "*The Precinct*" over them.

As he moved between desks and through the sound of snapping typewriters, Smitty was jolted to a stop by the unmistakable raspy voice of Agnes Crantz: "Hold it right there, Officer Smitty!" As if a neck collar with a chain attached had just been pulled to its limit, Smitty stopped dead in mid-stride. He slowly looked to the desk from which the voice had emanated.

Smitty blinked as he focused on who was talking to him. Sitting behind her desk, facing him, sat Lead Officer Agnes Crantz. She was slightly slouched forward, with her right elbow on her desk and her right hand holding a lit cigarette. Smitty's eyes followed the swirling smoke from the cigarette as it seemed to slither around Agnes's light purple hair. She peered over her bifocal glasses and glared straight at Smitty, who returned her glare with a confused expression on his face.

Before Smitty could say anything, Agnes gestured toward the back doors that Smitty had just used to enter the Precinct. "Next time you walk through my precinct, your uniform had better be regulation."

Smitty was still perplexed as he tried to formulate a response. There was only a brief pause in Lead Officer Crantz's rant as she took a drag on her smoke and coughed, forcing the smoke out her nose past her nasal oxygen tubes and her mouth as she spoke.

"Next time, I want that colostomy crap catcher on your side worn per regulation. I don't like the way the food around here looks before I eat it, so what makes you think I want to see what it looks like after it's strained through your guts?" Agnes pointed to Smitty's colostomy bag, which had somehow worked its way out from under his shirt and was partially visible.

Smitty did some quick blinks as he tried to comprehend what was happening to him. He looked down to his side, pulled his uniform shirt over his crap catcher, and muttered, "Sorry."

The Lead Officer's smoking fingers then pointed towards the Sarge's office as Agnes said, "I believe you were called into my precinct for a reason. Now get your fart flapper in there."

ۀ

The Sarge sat at his desk and looked up as Smitty walked into his office and quickly shut the door as if to keep someone from following him in. Smitty looked shell-shocked.

"Smitty?" the Sarge prompted, waiting for an explanation. Smitty looked toward the ceiling and said, "Why did you put that woman in the Precinct?" Then he looked directly at the Sarge and blurted, "Lead Officer? What were you thinking?"

The Sarge smiled and said, "Oh, run into Agnes Crantz, did ya?" The Sarge then pointed to a chair in front of his desk. As Smitty walked toward the chair, the Sarge stated, "She put her time in just like we did. As a matter of fact, she and the women that came on with her during those early days had to put up with more harassment and belittlement than you or any other officer back then. Crantz, and any other woman who was a cop, deserves to be here just as much, if not more than some of the other guys out there." He pointed toward door to the Precinct.

Shifting to a different topic, the Sarge turned his computer monitor toward Smitty and said, "We've got a situation with a missing foster care kid. This was one of those rave parties which the reports say was the last place the girl was seen. Here is the report."

Smitty was studying the monitor photos as the Sarge spoke. Without looking up, Smitty said, "Her history, and all other reports on the girl." The Sarge knew that if Smitty wanted all that information, he would get it. The Sarge pulled his unlit cigar out of his mouth and muttered, "I'll have her records brought up here for you. It's about time for my bath. I don't want Boss Nurse to come and drag me out of here, so I'll leave you be." Smitty acknowledged the Sarge with a nod and continued to stare at the photos.

The Sarge turned the knob to his office door but didn't open it for fear of other Ol' Blues hearing what he was about to say. "We got this case as a special request. The girl's name is Amanda Crantz."

The last name made Smitty freeze. Making the connection, he said, "You mean this girl is…" Smitty was cut off by the Sarge saying "Yep" as he popped the cigar back into his mouth and continued, "She is Agnes Crantz's granddaughter." The Sarge didn't bother monitoring Smitty's response to the realization that he would have to talk to Lead Officer Crantz throughout the investigation.

Smitty looked at the floor and muttered, "I hope she doesn't remember me and Benson stuffing her into the trunk of our cruiser." The Sarge was halfway out the door as he froze, his eyes widened, and he uttered under his breath, "Smitty's screwed."

⚬⚭

Lois Luka was a forty-five-year-old Armenian immigrant who stood five foot seven and weighed about two hundred fifty pounds. Poorly groomed, she wore an unsightly scowl that made people tend to avoid her. Lois had been working in the public sector for over ten years and had quickly learned that her line of work had a high burnout and turnover rate due to low pay, mountains of paperwork, and being hated by everyone who was investigated, supervised, or removed from a home.

She was unconcerned by the drawbacks of her job because her motivation for leaving her Armenian homeland had been to learn all she could about the American system of dealing with children who had become wards of the state. She was part of a group who planned to tap into this growing population of young women.

Whenever Lois looked at her wrist, the tattoo of a green star reminded her of the only family she had in Armenia and the criminal empire they were building. They were a Mafia cartel who made their money by trafficking young women in the countries of the former Soviet Union. These countries were relatively poor, so coming to the United States offered the opportunity to chase the real money.

Lois had been sent to America to learn to tap into the plethora of rebellious teenagers who were prime targets for American pimps grooming them for prostitution. She had chosen to work in Nebraska because it didn't have the huge populations of other states. This resulted in less funding for government offices. With the high burnout rate among caseworkers, Lois recognized an opportunity to move to a supervisory position rapidly, and she capitalized on it.

She had learned quickly that if she just kept working, she would be promoted continually due to worker attrition. In her current position as a mid-level supervisor, she controlled the reports from the field caseworkers and determined what information would be sent up the chain of command to the upper-level bureaucrats. With the older teens, Lois forwarded just enough information to let the bureaucrats know that another runaway was about to age out of the system. This often put them on low priority status, which set up the next part of the plan.

Lois remained emotionally detached from her coworkers and the kids she was supposed to serve as a state worker. She actually despised them.

She was in a position ideal for her family's needs. She had two transportation workers sent over from Armenia. She used them to pick up the runaways and deliver them to the safe house located in Omaha. In the safe house the girls were usually given enough doses of heroin to make them addicted. Once the drug had strangled a girl's ability to resist, she would easily do whatever she was told. Resistance resulted in beatings and denial of the drug, which caused withdrawal symptoms so severe that the girl begged for more of the drug and would do anything to get it.

The only person involved in this scheme who was outside Lois's direct control was the man they called "the Chemist"—a pharmacist who provided the cocktail that rendered the young women unconscious. That's what Lois really prized, because the drug caused the girls to have a significant loss of memory of what had happened to them prior to being stored in the safe house. The Cartel family had blackmailed the pharmacist when he was traveling in Armenia a couple of years earlier. He had fallen to the temptation of a prostitute who belonged to Lois's family. He drank too much and as a result talked too much. The prostitute had taken him to a special room where the blackmail of this traveling American was filmed. All the activities he engaged in were documented and shown to him afterwards. He was ruined. He knew that all of his years of schooling and work would be gone if he didn't do what the Armenian mafia wanted.

At first, the Chemist had to be reminded of the evidence the Cartel had on him if he didn't cooperate. However, as time went on, he was given the opportunity to abuse the young women who were kidnapped, as long as he didn't injure their faces. He enjoyed being in control.

The Armenian Cartel didn't realize that the Chemist had a long history of abusing women. He was smart, and school was no problem for him. He mastered everything he decided to put his mind to. Women, however, were a different story. He often became frustrated when a woman wouldn't do what he wanted. In response, he concocted a date rape drug. Toying with the women he met, drugging and abusing them, brought excitement and power to an otherwise pathetic individual. The police had even questioned him a few times, but they had never been able to find enough evidence to arrest him.

Lois's computer was monitored by her brother in Armenia so the family could keep track of what she was doing in the land of Nebraska. Their plan was perfect. Lois's family had received a couple of dozen young girls over the last two years, which provided the Cartel with hundreds of thousands of dollars for each of the girls who were used and abused. Lois had become very comfortable in her position, and then suddenly she was thrown off balance when a warning flashed on her computer: "*Anjatel.*"

Lois was startled. She immediately adjusted the monitor. Clearly her brother was sending an urgent message. She picked up her phone and called him.

"*Aziz, what are you doing? Why are you telling me this?*" Lois asked in Armenian. Her brother responded, "*You shut your computer off, yes?*" Lois frowned, "*Not yet, I don't...*" A scream cut her off: "*Fool! Someone has downloaded some information from your computer. Shut it off now!*"

Aziz did not need to say anything else. Lois knew that the intercepted information involved the girl that Victor and Sasha had just picked up. She had been delivered to the Chemist's house by now.

Lois's mind raced, and she knew she had to act fast. Failure by a member of the Cartel was dealt with in a swift and deadly fashion. If Lois's operation was discovered by the American police, the blame would be hers. Her brother Aziz was not only the person who monitored her computer but also the person who would carry out any punishment for failure. Aziz was a ruthless, sadistic killer who dished out the punishment, torture, and execution of people whom the Cartel determined to be a threat, or even worse, a disgrace to the Order of the Star. Lois knew her failure would be considered a disgrace, and Aziz would consider it dishonorable to him as her brother. He would not hesitate to slit her throat with a look of satisfaction on his face.

The same fate awaited those who failed along with her. Everyone in the Cartel knew that Aziz was unstoppable.

As Lois listened, her back stiffened in fear when she heard Aziz utter the words, *"This better not be a problem, Lois. You know this is the biggest shipment the Cartel has ever had. If it fails, you will be blamed."* Lois regained her composure and replied, *"Not to worry, Aziz, this is a periodic audit of the system. They do it all the time."* She lied, then thought of a way to appease him and simultaneously buy some time to figure out what was actually going on.

Lois stated calmly, *"It is not a problem at all. However, since this audit seems to include my wing of the department, you must not monitor my computer for a couple of weeks. Your diligence, Aziz, has been a great help to our operation. You have made me aware of the audit. Now I can make sure there is nothing that can be detected that is out of the ordinary so everything will go as planned. Aziz, remember: Do not interfere or monitor anything until I let you know that there is no threat."*

Lois hoped the compliment and her lie would placate Aziz. A brief silence told her that Aziz had muted his line while speaking to someone else. Any change in procedure for an operation this big would have to be approved by one of the leaders of the Cartel.

After a few moments, Aziz came back on the line. *"Two weeks. Do not fail us, Lois."*

As Lois hung up, she noticed that she had been sweating. After surveying the mess that had been her workstation, she disconnected every cord she could find from the wall or surge protector. Quietly, she said to herself, *"Let's see what is happening here."*

Smitty slowly opened the door from the Sarge's office and peeked out to see if Agnes Crantz was still in the Precinct. He spotted her sitting at her desk about twenty feet from him, with her elbow still planted on top of the desk and her hand pointing upward with a lit cigarette between her index and middle finger.

The smoke whimsically danced around her purple hair. "Nuts," he said to himself. Then he looked around to see if the Sarge was within earshot. Smitty didn't see him.

Remembering his new hearing aid communicator, Smitty reached up and touched the button on the device. It was instantly ready to transmit a signal.

"Sarge, this is Smitty. If you're done with your bath, I've got something for you regarding the photos of the runaway girl."

The Sarge answered, "Getting dressed now. I'll be there in about ten minutes. Over." Satisfied, Smitty closed the Sarge's door and walked back to the monitor he was viewing. Then a raspy, unmistakable voice chimed in, "I'll be there too," followed by a coughing fit. Smitty knew Lead Officer Crantz heard everything he said, and he shivered at the thought of being in the same room with her. "Absofreakinglutely great," he muttered.

Smitty looked up as the Sarge entered the office and held the door open. There was a slow, rhythmic squeaking sound as Lead Officer Agnes Crantz shuffled into the room. She glared at Smitty, who involuntarily checked to see if his poop bag was tucked under his shirt. She clearly didn't share the Sarge's opinion of Smitty's ability to review cases. She sat down, moved her oxygen tube to her forehead, and lit a cigarette.

Sarge watched for a moment, anticipating a flameout. When it didn't happen, he looked at Smitty and said, "What d' ya got?" Smitty showed the photos of the barnyard and said, "This is the aftermath of what clearly was some sort of party."

Agnes coughed, then pointed to Smitty and said to the Sarge, "Wow, he really is some sort of Einstein! His observation skills are clearly beyond what any other officer... "

She was cut off by the Sarge, who said, "Agnes, why don't you relax and listen to what Smitty has to say?" She rolled her eyes as she took a drag from her cigarette and blew the smoke into the air.

Smitty was annoyed but continued. "This was a runaway report, and I think Amanda Crantz probably did run away. However, even though her ankle tracking device was there, I don't think she was at this barn party."

Agnes sat up abruptly and barked, "What the...what do you mean she wasn't at the party? The kid's a chronic runaway and partier, her ankle tracker is at the barn, and the case worker says she was there. What else do you need?" Agnes had obviously seen the report.

The Sarge looked like he was watching a tennis match as he looked back and forth between Smitty and Crantz. After Agnes decided to make the mistake of trying to insult Smitty with the obvious, he knew Smitty was going to shove it right back in her face.

"Of course that is what the report says!" Smitty spat, then pointed to the computer screen with the photos. "Any idiot could see that! I believe she did run away, but all the other times she ran away she was gone for about a week and never really made any effort to cut her little party trip short. She recently got this ankle tracking device. She's a smart kid, and she knew that as soon as she cut it off, some alarm somewhere was going to go off, right?" Sarge and Agnes nodded.

Smitty continued, "If you were going on a party spree and didn't want to get caught, would you tell your caseworker where you were on the first day you took off?" Smitty didn't wait for an answer. He went on, "If you were then going to cut off that same ankle bracelet and you knew it would set off some sort of alarm which marked your location, wouldn't you throw the thing in a field, down a storm drain or something?"

The Sarge nodded, and then Agnes closed her mouth and gave Smitty a focused stare. Again, Smitty pointed to the barn floor. "Look at the inside of this barn: it's a disheveled mess. Yet, right in the middle of the floor as the officer opened the barn door was the ankle bracelet. This was not inadvertently left there; someone opened the door and tossed the bracelet right where they knew it would be easily found."

Smitty then looked at Agnes and said, "I don't care what the report says. This was no ordinary runaway." Smitty's eyes narrowed as he glared at Agnes. "I think someone *did* find her and then made it look like she was at some wild party by cutting off the bracelet and tossing it into the barn. Since she is almost eighteen years old, it looks like our little Amanda has hit the road, never to be found again."

Agnes sat back in her chair and took a long drag on her cigarette. She stood up, and as the inhaled smoke billowed from her mouth and nostrils, she looked at the Sarge and grumbled, "You're right, this guy is a freaking genius."

Smitty's mouth dropped open. Agnes rolled her eyes and headed for the door. Her oxygen tank chirped as she shuffled. Without looking back, she said, "Keep digging, Smitty."

Sasha and Victor had taken the girl to the Chemist's house in the country. They opened the garage door using the code that had previously been provided, then closed the garage door before getting out of their van. Once everything was secure, Victor carried the semi-conscious girl into the bedroom and left her on the bed as instructed, not knowing they were being watched.

There were video cameras in and around the home. Parked a mile away, the Chemist watched them carry out his instructions from his cell phone.

Sasha inadvertently glanced around the house while following Victor to the bedroom. Her phone rang, and a male voice sternly said, "Just drop the girl off and leave." Sasha knew that there must be some sort of surveillance camera watching their movements. She quickly caught up with Victor, and after the girl was placed on the bed, both of them left the house.

"Sasha, who called while we were in the house?" Victor asked.

"I'm pretty sure it was the Chemist," Sasha replied. "He told me to drop the girl off and leave."

Victor's eyes widened, and he stared at Sasha. "What were you doing behind me?"

Sasha shrugged and stated, "I was just looking around as we walked to the bedroom. He must have some sort of video cameras set up. He didn't seem to like that I was looking around the house."

Victor spat, "Idiot! Do not get him angry. If Lois finds out, you could end up dead. He is very important to the organization." Then Victor quietly added, "You are not." Victor's warning was understood.

They drove for about twenty minutes before stopping in one of Nebraska's numerous small towns. Victor parked in front of a bar and told Sasha, "I'm going to get a drink. Since we have some time, go back to that gas station that we passed before getting to town and get some gas." Sasha knew that when Victor wanted to drink, she had better let him.

The town they were in was very small. The gas station was a co-op used by farmers and townsfolk, and it was located between the town and the Chemist's house.

As Sasha started to fill the tank, her phone rang. She answered, "Hel..." but she was cut off.

"Get the girl and get her to the house in Omaha now!" Sasha recognized Lois's voice.

"I'm getting gas. Victor is in the town, I'll get him..." She was cut off again.

"Did you hear me Sasha? Get the girl now!" Sasha knew something was wrong. She stopped what she was doing and got back into the van. Something was very wrong, but she knew better than to ask questions. She would pick Victor up after getting the girl.

The Chemist smiled while glancing at the girl lying on his bed. He looked at himself in the mirror, then reached for a puka shell necklace he kept next to his high school picture on the dresser. After placing it on his neck, he reached into his closet for the silk shirt that had been fashionable when he was younger. His pants dropped to the floor, exposing his silk leopard-print briefs. He walked toward the defenseless girl, whose name he didn't care to know. If his drug had been administered correctly, it would ensure that his face would remain only a faint memory that was dimly perceived at the back of her mind.

Handcuffed at her wrists, the girl was wearing a watch that briefly caught his attention. There was something familiar about it. However, the sight of her on his bed overwhelmed his momentary curiosity about her watch.

Grinning triumphantly, the Chemist rubbed his hands together. "Let's see what we have here," he whispered to himself.

"Funny undies," the girl said with a raspy voice. Then she started to giggle. She clearly was drifting in and out of consciousness yet appeared to be momentarily aware of her surroundings.

Her giggling reminded the Chemist of all the women who had humiliated him throughout his life. Rage consumed him as he glared at her through narrowed, furious eyes and inadvertently clenched his fists. Like a crazed animal, he lurched toward the girl's throat.

As he squeezed her neck with both hands, Amanda's eyes suddenly burst wide open with shock that people often exhibit at the realization that they can't breathe. Kicking her feet, she looked directly into the eyes of the man choking her. The terror in her eyes made him start to smile. Now he had complete control over the girl because he could determine whether she lived or died.

Suddenly a familiar sound made him release his stranglehold and jump up. The garage door was opening. Amanda gasped for air and then was once again lost in the chemically induced mist in her mind.

The Chemist stepped out of his bedroom at the same time that the door between the kitchen and garage burst open. A woman ran toward him. He recognized her as the woman who had brought the girl to his house.

"Something's gone wrong," she yelled. "I don't know what it is, but I've got to get this girl out of here!"

She ran up to him as he stood shocked and frozen. Sasha stopped and was also shocked at the sight of this skinny man standing in a silly shirt and leopard-print briefs staring back at her. She inadvertently looked him up and down and started to laugh. The Chemist quickly covered himself as he noticed that the woman was looking at his face. He swiftly put one hand to his face, used the other hand to cover his spotted undies, and yelled, "Get out!"

Sasha grabbed the girl by her handcuffs and dragged her off the bed and out of the room. The jolt of landing on the floor caused the girl to awaken and she started to look around, trying to see through the cloud that partially covered her mind. With some effort, Sasha was able to get the girl back to the van. Once they were inside the van, she headed back to town to get Victor.

∽

"What happened?" the Chemist said out loud while briefly looking into his rearview mirror at his mother's home. *Something got screwed up, and that stupid Armenian delivery girl saw me.* He was embarrassed and humiliated at the memory of the Armenian walking in and seeing him in his "special underwear." This fueled his anger.

He called the only Armenian who knew his identity and worked at the Health and Human Services state office. When Lois answered, he screamed into his phone, "What is going on? That stupid delivery woman just burst into the house and dragged the girl out of here. She saw me, Lois! Do you hear me? She saw me! What are you going to do about this?"

Lois was still trying to recover from the news that her brother Aziz had told her about someone hacking into her computer. Now the Chemist, an essential part of the Cartel's operation, had just been exposed. Lois calmed herself, then said matter-of-factly, "Don't worry, we will take care of everything. Just go back to your normal activities."

The Chemist's voice became almost a shrill scream. "Don't worry? That woman saw me, Lois! We have a deal. What are you—"

Lois interrupted "Calm down. I will personally make sure everything is taken care of. You must go back to your normal activities and get ahold of yourself. Our friends in Armenia would not like it if they heard that you panicked and did something stupid, no?"

The Chemist went silent. He was afraid of being seen but even more terrified of what the Armenians would do to him if he jeopardized their operation. "No, I didn't mean…um, well… just make sure this problem goes away." Then he hung up.

"Sniveling coward," Lois commented after hanging up her phone. "If we didn't need him, I would have him cut to pieces and fed to pigs."

From about a block away Sasha saw Victor standing outside the bar.

As he waited, Victor's phone rang. He looked at the caller ID and saw that it was Lois calling. He answered, and she said, "That idiot Sasha just walked into the Chemist's house and saw him." Victor froze with the realization. Lois continued, "You know what that means? No one can see him but me. That was the deal we made with him." Victor's voice turned cold and resolute as he responded, "I will take care of it."

As Sasha stopped at the curb, she opened the passenger side window and said, "I don't know what happened, but Lois told me to get the girl. I think something has gone wrong."

Victor shrugged and said, "It's no problem. We will drive her to the safe house in Omaha. Take the country roads. I'm not sure what happened either."

The man known as "the Chemist" spent most of his time living a lie. The public saw a polite pharmacist, a man whom people could trust with their lives on a daily basis. He would ask about the well-being of his customers' families and answer their questions about the medication he dispensed. He was far from a handsome man, with thinning and receding black hair framing a protruding forehead. His eyes were dark brown, almost black, looking even darker against his pale white skin. Thin, blue blood vessels coursed over his arms and legs.

When he was a young man, his lack of good looks and socially awkward mannerisms had pretty much guaranteed that he had no luck with women. As compensation, his brilliant scientific mind provided him the satisfaction of always feeling superior to everyone around him. That same superiority spawned disdain for those who mocked him, especially young women. He wore glasses with thick black frames, which helped him feel as though those who talked to him saw only the façade he had worked so hard to develop to shield his dark, predatory nature.

He enjoyed making some of the young women he targeted his personal play toys, like a cat with a captured mouse or bird. Cats often play with their prey by pawing at it and knocking it to the ground over and over again. This exhausts the prey to the point that it no longer fights back. This also makes it safe for the cat when it makes its final pounce.

When the Chemist disliked a specific woman, he would mentally paw at her. At first it was nothing really obvious. Sometimes weeks before attacking a woman, he would start tightening a mental noose around her mind by simply moving small objects out of place in her home or slightly turning the outside faucet on, just enough for a large puddle of water around her driveway to be found when she returned from school or work. This caused the woman to start questioning herself: "Did I leave that faucet on?" or "Jeez, I don't remember putting that there." For some reason, he felt empowered by making them feel stupid without saying a word.

The Chemist often used various drugs on the girls, then assaulted them. It was his way of getting back at all the women who had rejected him when he was young.

There had been a brief suspension of his predation when he suffered a bout of cancer that required a bone marrow transplant. Eventually he was able to finish pharmacy school and resume his pattern of periodically punishing an unsuspecting girl for the perceived wrongs inflicted on him by those who shared her gender. He was smart enough to avoid being arrested for the rapes, even though he was questioned a couple of times by the police. They could never accumulate enough information to charge him.

All of that had taken place when he was a younger man. Now a few years had passed, and scientific advances had given the Chemist a way to avoid having to answer for his past crimes. Thinking about it always made the Chemist feel proud of being able to outsmart women and evade the police.

Now, with the help of the Armenians, he was able to punish young women by having them delivered to his mother's house in a little town north of Omaha called Kennard. His mother was in a nursing home, which left the house empty, so he would justify going to the house to make sure everything was all right. When he finished with the young women, the Armenians took them away. He provided the chemicals, and the Armenians provided the girls. The Chemist was able to partially satisfy his cravings.

&

The Chemist worked at a neighborhood pharmacy as well as one of Omaha's hospital pharmacies. The first job helped him maintain his façade, while the second allowed him to feed his predatory side. Working at the hospital pharmacy gave him access to medications used in surgery, one of which was Midazolam. This medication was used for sedation prior to surgeries, and it had the additional effect of causing amnesia.

This drug was what was provided to the Armenians for use on abducted girls. The pharmaceutical manufacturers dispensed the medication in small glass vials. These are commonly seen when medical personnel hold a vial upside down and stick a syringe needle into the rubber lid to withdraw the needed dosage for a patient. These medications are strictly monitored by the hospital, and one could not take a couple of cc's out of a bottle and put it back on the shelf without detection. Once the bottles were used up, they would be destroyed.

The Chemist had discovered and profited from a weakness in this system. The pharmaceutical companies always put a little extra medication in each vial to make up for losses that would naturally occur when the medication was being sucked out by the syringe. The Chemist simply harvested that extra medication before destroying the vials, then pocketed it. At his home he mixed the proper formulation based on the girl's body weight to create the chemical cocktail that the Armenians used to sedate young women.

&

After driving for about an hour, Victor pulled up to the safe house. The only other person in the van was a semi-conscious young girl. Sasha's body had been dumped in a small ditch in an unpopulated, wooded area in the Nebraska countryside. Her neck was broken and all of her identification gone. Victor had chosen to dump her body in an isolated spot where scavenger animals would quickly make it difficult for anyone to identify her.

Soon the Armenians would send someone to replace Sasha. Lois could easily create the required documentation for the Department of Health and Human Services to contract with a new "transporting agent" to pick up and deliver juveniles to various parts of the state.

Victor smiled when he thought about how easy it was to leverage the American system once the right person was in the right place within the bureaucracy. The Armenian organization was making hundreds of thousands of dollars of profit from each of the young women he transported to the safe house.

&

The Sarge's hearing aid made a small chirping sound to alert him that an incoming radio message was strictly for him, not the general body of Ol' Blues. The Sarge touched his hearing aid and responded, "Sarge here."

"I did some searching on the computer that I was monitoring. Looks like it was definitely from the Department of Health and Human Services. However, there was something very strange about it. Why don't you and any other officer that is going to be assigned to this case come down here and I'll show you what I found."

The Sarge recognized Thane's voice and told him, "I'll get Smitty and Crantz. We'll be down in about ten minutes."

Smitty and Agnes were summoned by the Sarge, and the three of them walked to the area marked, "Supply Room." As Agnes shuffled between her two male counterparts, she inquired, "What are we doing? Out of paper clips?" Smitty smirked as he remembered that Agnes had not been through the supply room initiation yet.

When they entered the supply room, Agnes's eyes lit up when she recognized Papps and Jerry. The two men had managed the police supply room for so many years that she couldn't remember a time when they had not been the guardians of all police equipment.

Papps immediately recognized Agnes and hit Jerry on the arm, commenting, "Look! The guys upstairs brought us an intern."

Jerry crossed his arms and then stroked his chin, saying, "I don't think she has enough experience to even make it as an intern."

Sarge and Smitty exchanged a glance, knowing that Papps and Jerry were about to touch the door to what looked like a high-voltage room and pretend to get shocked. The door actually led to the conference area, research and development labs, and the tunnels underneath the retirement home. The Ol' Blues loved using the tunnels to sneak out and go on missions without the medical staff knowing what they were up to.

Agnes gazed at the two supply room workers. Her eyes squinted as she took a drag from her cigarette and remarked, "The day I'm interned anywhere, it will be in a casket."

Papps and Jerry chuckled, then Papps gave Agnes the supply room standard warning: "Nothing goes in or out without the proper paperwork. Jerry and I work very hard to maintain…"

Agnes cut him off by waving her smoke in the air. "Yeah, I know you two tunnel rats live down here and make sure everything runs smoothly."

Papps appeared irritated at being cut off and gave the Sarge a frustrated look. Eager to give Agnes a scare, Smitty asked in off-handed manner, "What is that electrical room over there?" Papps turned to the door marked "High Voltage" and said, "Well you've got to be careful when you open these doors, because by touching... "

Papps grabbed a lever and sparks shot into the air. Papps screamed, and then Sarge and Smitty let out fearful yells. Jerry bolted from his seat, grabbed Papps, and started screaming too.

During the electrical shower and screaming show, the men gradually realized that Agnes had remained unperturbed. She stood silently with her left arm crossed over her stomach, her right elbow resting in her left hand, and her right arm holding her cigarette by her index and middle fingers next to her right ear. The men's screaming faded as Agnes nonchalantly looked at her smoke and flicked the filter part with her thumb, breaking off some ashes onto the floor.

"You putzes about finished?" she inquired. "I got reports to take care of upstairs."

The men looked at each other in astonishment. Agnes added, "Is this why these two saggy derrieres are kept down here? To scare defenseless old women out of their compression knee highs?"

The Sarge turned to Papps and said, "Open the door, we got work to do."

∽

Thane sat at his desk and heard the Sarge blurt his usual greeting, "Thanerboy! Whatyagot?"

Thane looked up and recognized the Sarge and Smitty but was somewhat shocked to see a woman with purple hair wearing the Ol' Blue uniform. Standing up, Thane introduced himself. "Hello, I'm Thane."

Agnes was actually taken aback. "Manners? I haven't had a young man stand when a woman entered the room and introduce himself in years."

Thane smiled and said, "My mother insisted on it. She told me that good manners would cover many social shortcomings. I'm not very graceful socially," he confessed, gesturing toward the many computers and gizmos in the room. As Agnes smiled, both Smitty and Sarge took notice. Smitty whispered to the Sarge, "Ever see her smile?" Sarge replied, "Never."

Agnes stated, "I'm Agnes Crantz. I hear you may have some information on a young lady who is missing. She's my granddaughter, Amanda Crantz."

Thane looked surprised. "I didn't know, Agnes. May I call you Agnes?"

Again Agnes smiled, charmed with Thane's manners. "Of course you can, young man." The smile disappeared as she added, "The rest of these putzes call me Lead Officer Crantz."

Thane smiled and gave the Sarge a sheepish grin. The Sarge pointed to the computers and said, "You called us down here for a reason."

Thane blinked and refocused on the matter at hand. "Yes, sorry. There was a very interesting development as I was monitoring a computer in the Department of Health and Human Services. It seems that someone in that office has an outside computer tech monitoring their computer."

Smitty asked, "Is that normal?"

Thane shook his head and replied, "Absolutely not." Then he gazed intently at his monitor.

"The only reason for an outside party to monitor a state computer would be to know everything that was going on." Thane frowned. "I just can't imagine why. I mean, this is not some state revenue site where someone could hack into the State's money."

Smitty's mind was racing, and he asked, "Whose department is this?"

Without looking up, Thane responded, "It's child welfare, state wards, and foster care. Why would someone want to monitor this?"

The Sarge added, "Unless you were trying to find a particular kid. Maybe some parent was trying to find their child and go abduct them. That happens a lot."

Thane leaned back in his chair and said, "I don't know why someone would do it, but after I started to download information, they sounded some sort of alarm. Flashing in capital letters was the word 'Anjatel.' I've been trying to figure out what this word means."

He quickly typed the word into various search engines, finding nothing. Then Thane tilted his head and said, "I wonder if it's just a foreign word." He typed the word into a translation web site and his eyes opened wide.

"Turn off! *Anjatel* is Armenian for 'Turn off'! That's the first thing that makes sense. Somebody who speaks Armenian saw that a download was taking place and tried to warn the State worker to turn off the computer."

Thane smiled and concluded, "Good, but not good enough. I downloaded a lot of data from that computer, but I really don't know what to search for among all the information."

Looking at the computer, Smitty said, "Send everything you have on this upstairs and I'll go through it."

Thane answered, "You got it." Without looking up, he clicked his mouse and said, "Done."

Smitty looked at the monitor and quickly headed for the door leading back to the Precinct.

Agnes tapped Thane on the shoulder and said, "Thanks for everything you've done." Without looking up from his computer, Thane replied, "I'm not done yet. I want to know whose computer this is and why an Armenian is nosing around a computer for kids that are state wards."

The safe house for the Armenians was located in an older neighborhood in Omaha. The trees were full grown, and most of the residents were older folks who pretty much kept to themselves. There were a few families with children. The kids often rode their bikes, drew on sidewalks, and got into various sorts of mischief together.

Victor pushed the button on his sun visor that opened the garage door. He drove the van with his doped-up passenger completely into the bay and closed the door behind him, shielding his activities from any curious eyes. As he carried the young woman into the house, he heard the familiar voice of his cousin Vladimir: "Ah, so this is the new one that caused so much trouble for the Chemist."

Victor looked at his cousin and flatly stated, "She also caused a problem for Sasha."

Vladimir sighed and without emotion uttered, "Yes, unfortunate, but necessary. You took care of the body?"

Still carrying the girl in his arms, Victor shrugged his large, meaty shoulders, saying, "There is so much back country in this Nebraska, I simply found a wooded area. The animals will take care of the body."

Vladimir clapped his hands, "Yes, well now for this one. Put her in the bedroom at the end of the hall that makes us full. These girls will make us a fortune."

Victor carried the girl toward the back bedroom. While walking through the hallway, he could see into each of the bedrooms along the way. Each one contained a couple of young women sprawled on a filthy mattress in the middle of the room. No other furniture was needed. For the last few weeks each had been drugged with heroin to a semi-conscious state. They were brought dangerously close to death, receiving enough of the drug to bind them deeply in addiction.

Once their bodies craved the heroin, the withdrawal symptoms caused by the addiction made them beg for another fix. They screamed in pain and kicked their feet in the air, flailing with their arms and bodies. Heroin withdrawal is horrible to see and even worse to experience. That's why keeping the girls addicted made them very compliant prostitutes. No need for the Chemist once they were hooked.

Victor had a satisfied smirk on his face. He knew that as soon as Vladimir finished with this new girl, she and the others would be sent to Armenia. Once the girls were securely in the grip of the Armenian Cartel, they would continue to be useful for a few years. Eventually their bodies would become so ravaged by the men in various cities that the Cartel wouldn't get top dollar for them anymore. Once that happened, the girls were transferred to mining, logging, or other work areas where men were less picky about what a woman looked like.

The hopeless isolation and constant threat of violence makes the needle and drug the only source of relief. It also ensures that the girls will continue doing what they are told. When they are no longer of use to the Cartel... "*Well*," Victor thought, "*we just get another stupid girl to take her place.*" He shrugged his large shoulders, then dropped the girl onto the mattress, ignoring the sound of her body landing on the mattress and her head hitting the floor.

૭૮

Smitty's daughter Brittany walked into the Ol' Blue Precinct. Though she knew what the geezers were really up to, she was in awe of the authentic- looking precinct. All of the officers were busy typing, talking on the phone to community crime watch groups, and diligently maintaining the façade of a bunch of retired officers in a therapeutic environment.

The public only saw little old men in police hats, shirts, and those awful hospital gowns from the waist down. Brittany had recently been drafted as an *Ol' Blue* when she inadvertently walked into one of their meetings and discovered the secret geriatric crime-fighting unit. Nobody, not even the Omaha Police Department, had any idea what was going on here.

Brittany had always brought cookies, a cheery smile, and a listening ear to the Blues whenever she visited as a civilian. After becoming a Blue herself, each time she walked into the Precinct she was greeted with winks, nods and a knowing look from the fellow Blues.

"I still can't believe what these guys do here," she quietly said to herself as she made her way to the Sarge's office. Her train of thought was derailed by a raspy female voice commanding, "Hold it right there, young lady."

Brittany's head quickly turned to locate the source of the voice. She blinked as she took in the sight of a woman sitting at a desk outside the Sarge's office. The wiry-looking older woman was wearing a policeman's hat that partially covered curly light purple hair. Cigarette smoke swirled around her head, caressing her skin and sifting through the largest purple eyelashes Brittany had ever seen. The woman took a long drag from her cigarette, and as she exhaled, she pulled her oxygen nasal cannula down from her forehead, inserting it into her nose. Brittany's mouth dropped open as she gasped and attempted to comprehend what she was seeing.

"The name is Lead Officer Crantz, Sweetie. Anyone coming into the Precinct comes through me first. Then when I decide…" The Sarge's door opened, and he interrupted, "It's okay, Agnes, she works for me. She's an Ol' Blue; as a matter of fact, she's Smitty's daughter."

Agnes's penciled-in brows raised at that bit of information.

"Brittany, this is my new Lead Officer, Agnes Crantz," the Sarge announced. "One of the first female cops in the Department. Also one of the best cops you'll ever meet."

Agnes tilted her head and eyed Brittany with a suspicious glance. Brittany closed her mouth and then perked up. "Oh, you're Mrs. Crantz! My friend Thane down in the research lab told me all about you. He told me you were a welcome addition to the Blues."

At the sound of Thane's name and his kind words about her, Agnes seemed to melt a little. A smile spread across her face as she said, "Oh, Thane is a sweet young man. If he is your friend, you must be on the level… even if you're related to that clown with the crap catcher on his hip."

Brittany blurted out a startled laugh before regaining her composure. She had never heard anyone describe her father in such a colorful way. All of the other cops always conveyed a healthy respect for her dad. This lady seemed like just the one to keep him in his place.

"If you two are finished, we need to talk," Sarge said. "I asked Brittany to join us in my office while we discuss your granddaughter, Agnes."

Agnes's face returned to its natural scowl. With her cigarette between her index and middle finger she waved Brittany toward the Sarge's office. "If you say so, Sarge. From what I hear she's a pretty sharp piece of work herself."

Brittany gave a polite smile and nod to Agnes as she walked to the Sarge's office. She stayed a couple of feet away from Agnes's desk while walking by, as one would keep a distance from a chained, growling Pit Bull.

As Brittany closed the Sarge's door, she gave him a confused look. He easily read the look on her face and explained, "She, young lady, is one of the toughest broads you'll ever meet."

Brittany blinked a couple times and said, "You don't need to explain that to me, but I like her."

The Sarge smiled and then opened his desk drawer and twisted the handle, causing a computer screen to pop up.

Thane's face appeared on the screen. "Hey, Sarge! Oh, Brittany, how ya doing?" Brittany smiled and waved. The Sarge tapped his hearing aid to send a broadcast to the Old Blue Precinct: "Smitty and Agnes, could you come into my office, please."

Smitty jumped up from his chair and instinctively bolted towards the Sarge's office upon hearing his name called. When he heard the name Agnes, he inadvertently looked down to make sure his colostomy bag was covered by his shirt, per regulation. He then quickly walked into the Sarge's office.

Once everyone was settled in, the Sarge asked, "Well, Thanerboy, whatyagot?"

"I'm still trying to figure out why an Armenian was monitoring the Nebraska Foster Care system," Thane reported.

The Sarge looked up. "How about you, Smitty? Anything else from the reports?"

Smitty shook his head and said, "Not much more than my original observation that this was some sort of setup. I went through Amanda's property inventory and she really didn't have anything that someone would want to steal. She had the usual girl stuff like earrings and hair supplies. There was also a Securo Gips watch."

Brittany gave her dad a quizzical look.

"A *what* watch?" Brittany said.

Thane, the only other person in the meeting who was younger than sixty, also chimed in. "I've never heard of that brand of watch."

Smitty looked at his notes and said, "That's the brand, Securo."

Thane was typing the information as he talked. "Securo. Well, here is the…" There was a pause as Thane quickly read about the company. Everyone in the Sarge's office started to look at each other, then back to the Sarge and the computer monitor. Thane was looking at another screen, and his eyes suddenly got wide. He looked back at the screen to see Smitty. "How is that watch model spelled?"

Smitty looked again at his notes: "Um, S-e-c… "

Thane interrupted, "No, not the company Securo, the model of the watch."

Smitty looked puzzled and then consulted his notes again. "Just as I said: Gips."

"Spell it!" blasted from the monitor. Smitty said, "G-P-S."

Brittany's eyes widened. Then the speakers on the computer monitor almost blew up as Thane yelled, "GPS! That's not a name; it's an acronym! It means Global Positioning System!"

Brittany stood up and said, "That's great!"

Thane added, "This changes everything if she's wearing it."

The Sarge, Smitty, and Agnes looked back and forth between Brittany and Thane, then at each other. Agnes shrugged and said, "Well, she may need some money, so she could have pawned it a day or two ago. How is checking pawn shops going to tell us where she is?" Smitty and Sarge nodded in agreement. This time Brittany and Thane gave each other quizzical looks.

Thane, staring into his monitor at the clueless geriatrics in the room, opened his mouth but nothing came out. Brittany said, "Not to pawn; that watch must be for some sort of medical alert."

Thane could finally speak: "Yes, yes! Agnes said that Amanda has a mild case of epilepsy. These watches are given to people with these kinds of conditions in case they have a seizure. Then the company Securo is made aware and through GPS can pinpoint where Amanda is located."

Agnes looked at Brittany and asked, "But how?"

Exasperated, Thane sat tapping his mouse on his desk and shaking his head. Brittany explained, "Satellites that orbit the earth track the positions of certain devices and can tell us where Amanda's watch is located anywhere in the world."

Agnes's cigarette drooped from her lips as she said, "You mean in outer space?" A clunking sound came from the monitor. Brittany smiled to herself as she pictured a red-headed computer geek thumping his forehead on his desk.

෬

"Careful with that one, Victor. Lois said that she will bring us the most money; she is a pretty one. Don't just throw her around like that. We would not want to damage the goods," Vladimir said.

Victor smirked, shrugged, and with an air of indifference, jested, "To me they are all the same: stupid American girls that are good for nothing but to make money for...." A thumping sound caused Victor to abruptly cut his boast short. Vladimir stood and looked past Victor to the room where the new girl had just been tossed. Victor simultaneously turned to look as well. Both men froze at the sight of the girl's feet, the only part of the girl they could see through the doorway. Dangling off the end of the mattress, they were shaking in a most peculiar, spastic manner.

Both men briefly looked at each other and simultaneously hurried to the bedroom. Upon entry the men saw Amanda shaking and convulsing on the mattress, with her head thumping repeatedly on the floor. "Grab her head, Victor!" Vladimir shouted, and then muttered with a fearful tone, "Or we will both end up like Sasha."

Once the girl stopped convulsing, Victor pulled out his phone.

"What do you mean she had a shaking fit?" Lois spat into the phone. "Don't do anything to hurt her. I've already told Aziz about this one, and they are expecting to make a great deal of money with her."

Lois listened for a moment to Victor's explanation of what had happened and screamed, "Hit her head? Is she still breathing?"

Again, she listened. When she was satisfied, she ordered, "Don't let Vladimir do anything to her with the drugs. Just keep her bound for now."

Lois gritted her teeth and hissed, "Don't let anything happen to this girl, Victor. You are easily replaced!" After her threat, Lois lowered her voice and added, "I may have another girl for you to pick up. Be ready to leave when I call." The line went dead.

♋

The nurses' lounge at the Old Blues Retirement Home is the place where students and staff take their breaks, catch up on reports, or relax for a minute. It's also where they work together to figure out what to do with these Ol' Blues who just can't accept the fact that they are patients.

On this particular day, about eight people including nurses, students, and a couple of mental health specialists were talking and watching television. Against a wall with her back to the main lounge area was Boss Nurse Betsy, studying reports on her computer.

Suddenly there was a loud slam as a young nurse walked into the lounge looking completely disheveled and screamed, "Whose bright idea was it to take those old cops on field trips through their old beats?" Everyone but Boss Nurse looked at the obviously stressed-out woman. Her hair was a mess, her blouse was soaked in sweat, and her hands were shaking.

One of the mental health specialists spoke. "The mental health staff suggested that periodically going through the areas where they used to work as young men would provide them with meaningful memories of their youth and... " She was cut off by the nurse extending both of her arms, palms facing outward, like she was stopping all the traffic at an intersection.

"Tell those specialists to *BITE ME*! I took six of those *sweet- little- old- men*" she said with pointed emphasis, "... on a ride to their old beat or whatever they call it. I stopped at a light, looked to my left and saw that there were some young thugs on the corner. Well, those old cops saw them too. They started yelling at them. I could not believe what I was hearing. All of the old cops came to the driver's side of the transportation van and stuck their heads out the windows."

The nurse then tried to imitate various old men. "I see ya, hood! Don't even think about touching that woman's purse, I'll crack your skull wide open!"

The nurse's hands started to shake again, and she said, "The leader of the hoods"—she paused, thinking *I can't believe I'm talking like them*—"anyway, the leader started to walk toward me yelling all kinds of threats. My window was open and I...I just froze. I didn't know what to do."

The women in the lounge gave each other incredulous looks as the stressed-out nurse continued. "As the hood—*Oh, jeez, I did it again*—well, he got about a step away from me," she blinked and took a quick breath, "and then he got cracked upside the face by some slimy dentures. The guy just froze with his hand on the side of his face and stared wide-eyed toward the ground as the teeth landed at his feet. Then," she gulped, "I looked up at the big rear-facing mirror and one of the cops yelled, *PUNCH IT, SISTER!*"

One of the other nurses yelled, "Holy crap, what did you do?"

The nurse caught her breath and blurted, "I screamed and punched it! I drove right through the red light, barely missing about four cars. Horns were shrieking, I was screaming, and after about a block I heard a police siren behind me. I thought I was in big trouble until I looked in my mirror and saw one of those old cops with his head out the window and his mouth wide open, screaming like a police car. He didn't have his teeth in. They were still at the feet of that punk at the intersection. You should have seen it; his whole mouth was flapping in the wind. I didn't know what else to do, so I just got back to the home as fast as I could. Those old farts are crazy."

The winded nurse flopped down on a chair and looked up at the ceiling and in a gasping tone said, "I still have four hours left on my shift."

At the back of the room sat Boss Nurse Betsy. She didn't even look away from her computer monitor. She just spoke out loud for everyone to hear. "Next time, make sure you take a 44-ounce soda pop with you, and make sure there's a lot of ice in it." The exhausted nurse stopped staring at the ceiling, looked at Boss Nurse, and said, "What the…did you listen to a word I said?"

Boss Nurse just kept looking at her monitor and talking without responding to anything that was said.

"When you're driving and they pull that screaming siren on you, just throw the full cup of soda out your window. That cold pop hits them right in the face and shuts 'em up quick."

Boss Nurse got up from her computer and walked toward the door as all of the eyes in the room followed her. Then she turned and softly added, "You'll have to get the van washed, but no more sirens." She smirked and left the room, allowing the door to slowly close behind her.

The Old Market in downtown Omaha is one of the most unusual and captivating shopping areas in the Midwest.

In the early 1900s, Omaha was in its prime as a great railroad center connecting the East Coast with the wide-open West. Paved in red brick, the area was the epicenter of the agricultural industry of America and the railroad. The streets were filled with produce dealers, buyers, and transporters.

The huge warehouse buildings in the Old Market reflect the type of business this industry represented, with red brick, extra-thick walls that are generally four to six stories high. As time went on, markets changed and the country grew. Modern shipping made it possible to distribute the centers of the agricultural industry throughout the country.

Omaha was stuck with these mammoth brick buildings. Demolition seemed to be the only option. Then a man named Samuel Mercer decided that the area could be saved. Over a period of about a decade in the 1960s he bought the old buildings and began to convert them to a shopping area. Nowadays thousands of people visit the Old Market to shop and enjoy the retrofitted monuments of a bygone agricultural era. The former industrial epicenter of the Midwest is now a unique shopping venue that one has to experience to appreciate.

That is precisely why the Omaha Police Department makes the area a priority: to ensure that those who come to this shopping mecca enjoy a safe sojourn.

Unfortunately, there are always a small percentage of people who look for ways to exploit such venues for criminal purposes. An uptick in robberies, thefts, and other nefarious activities had recently caught the attention of the Gang Unit.

Undercover officers had spent weeks stationed throughout the Old Market. Sergeant Scott was sitting in an unmarked surveillance vehicle monitoring security cameras and looking for known gang members. It didn't take him long to spot a lone young man wearing colors typically worn by one of the older gangs in Omaha.

"Turley, do you see the guy with the bandana walking down the middle of 12th Street?"

There was a short pause as Turley pointed the banger out to a new officer. "Hard to miss him. I think he's actually flashing signs. What a stupid moron; he's got to know we're working the Market."

The new officer blurted into his radio, "I'll nab him."

Turley grabbed the officer's arm just as the Sergeant responded, "Don't, he's frontin'."

Turley stopped abruptly, hitting the back of the officer's head with the palm of his hand, and said, "Look, he's baiting to see who will approach him."

The other officer who was still learning how to police bangers asked, "What's the deal? Why don't we nab him?"

Turley looked about to make sure they weren't drawing any attention, then quietly said. "They conduct surveillance just like we do. Doesn't this guy look very obvious, like he's daring us to nab him?"

"Yeah, so he's a stupid prick daring us. I say we get him," the officer responded.

Turley stopped looking around to see if anyone noticed him. Then he began looking for people watching the obvious gang banger walking down the middle of the street.

He quietly uttered to the newbie, "It takes a while to look around at nothing in particular but spot exactly what you're looking for."

The newbie's head cocked sideways as he looked at Turley quizzically and asked, "What are you talking…"

"Got him," Turley said, ignoring the new officer. He keyed his microphone and told the Sarge, "I've got four guys, two on each side of 12th Street, slowly walking and watching the moron." Turley described the men he had spotted. He then looked over at the newbie with an obvious eye-roll.

"This is a Market, look what everybody is doing… " He didn't wait for a response and quickly added, "They're talking, looking at the windows, the shops, and up at the flowers hanging from the awnings."

Discreetly gesturing toward two sets of guys ranging from sixteen to twenty years old, Turley explained, "Those are bangers from the same G. They aren't looking around at the shops or talking much; they're all looking at the moron flashing gang signs in the street. Once one of us approaches the guy in the street he'll start running. His plan is to get every undercover officer to chase him. Once the other bangers see you chasing their homie, you're made, and your undercover status is flushed down the toilet."

Turley keyed his microphone. "Sarge, I've made five, looks like they all belong to Fourth Street."

Sergeant Scott answered, "Follow 'em. Give their description and position to the uniformed officers. If they bolt, we may have to try to nab 'em all. Then take them to Central for interviews."

Turley provided the location of the suspects to the uniformed officers stationed throughout the Old Market. As the officers started to converge on the bangers, they quickly determined that they had been made and all started to run in the same direction. They had a pretty good lead on the uniforms, who found it odd that they were all heading to the same partially developed warehouse. Turley watched the bangers run into the building, then commented, "They usually scatter." He laughed and radioed to all the officers to surround the building. "These guys are stuck."

Once the building was sufficiently covered, an entry team was formed and the search of the building began. "Police. Sound off now, show your hands, and come out where we can see you."

No response.

"This doesn't make sense," Turley said. "Why are they hiding? We didn't catch these guys really doing anything. I could see them hiding if they stole a car and led us on a pursuit. I don't understand this."

The entry team finished inspecting each of the three stories in the building and found nothing. The lead officer of the search team keyed his microphone and reported, "Empty. No sign of the suspects."

"They couldn't have gotten out of the building that fast. We had it surrounded," Turley said. After searching the building with the newbie, Turley shook his head in confusion.

Sergeant Scott arrived on the scene, and Turley shrugged. "I don't know how they did it, but they're gone."

Over the next couple of weeks this scenario would repeat itself four times. After the fourth time, Sergeant Scott and the Gang Unit decided this was no coincidence.

෨

The Sarge's office was abuzz with excitement. Thane was figuring out how to get into the Securo's database and Amanda's folder. His concentration was interrupted as he scrolled through her information. In his headset he could hear the excited voice of Lead Officer Crantz exclaiming, "Cripes, Sarge, this all makes sense now. Thane said something about Armenians. The Armenians used to be with the Red Commie Rooskies. Those sneaky Commies launched Sputnik 1, then later Sputnik 2 with the dog and a bunch of spy gizmos."

Smitty's mouth dropped wide open. Baffled, he asked Agnes, "What's that got to do with anything?"

Agnes picked up her cigarette and pointed it at Smitty. "Do you have a knot in that crap bag of yours? It's right in front of you, like Boss Nurse's giant keister. The Rooskies launched the Sputniks, we thought it was just a bunch of radio pings when it passed over us, but now the Rooskies' old friends, the Armenians, are using the Sputniks to track my Amanda."

Brittany's head was moving back and forth as she followed the conversation between her father and Agnes. When she heard Agnes's conclusion that the Armenians were using Sputnik satellites to track her granddaughter, she tried not to burst out laughing. She held it in pretty well until she heard the thudding sound from the computer monitor again.

In an exasperated tone, Thane's voice blurted over the speaker, "Sarge, I've got Amanda's file now and there is actually about a month's worth of data that I'll have to go through, but... " Thane's words came to an abrupt halt.

"Wait." He paused and read the latest information. "She is having a seizure right now!"

Brittany perked up and asked, "Do you have a fix on her location?"

Thane glared into his monitor. "Got it. She's in the older part of South Omaha not far from the Missouri River. Here's the address."

As the Sarge bolted into action, his quick movements startled Brittany. He tapped his hearing aid and ordered, "Benson, you there?"

There was a small pause, and then Benson answered, "Here, Sarge. What do you need?"

The Sarge said, "I want you and Smitty to hightail it for a surveillance mission. Get your civvies on, then the two of you get to the supply room and get a pair of ball drums. Smitty will fill you in on your way to the mark. Got it?"

Benson quickly replied, "Roger, Sarge."

Agnes looked at Brittany and asked, "Ball drums?"

Brittany smiled and leaned toward Agnes, explaining, "Those research guys in the basement have special glasses that can record audio and visual, then send the information to the computer guys downstairs. The Blues call them eyeballs and eardrums—'ball drums' for short."

Agnes tilted her head and acknowledged this information with an "Oh," acted like she knew what Brittany was talking about, then took a drag from her smoke.

Brittany smiled, adding, "Don't ask me what civvies are. I have no idea." Agnes, looking at her below raised eyebrows, explained, "Civilian clothes, honey, civilian clothes."

Within the hour Smitty and Benson were dressed in civilian clothes and had been hooked up to their ball drums in the research and development section of the Precinct. The supply room façade couldn't have been a more perfect way to hide what the Ol' Blues were doing in plain sight.

After being fitted with their gear, the two cops were escorted out through sewer line access tunnels that had been built especially for the Blues—tunnels that were wide enough to allow two golf carts to drive side-by-side. Smitty and Benson were driven to an old mechanic shed on the south side of the facility where they got into what looked like a regular delivery van and were off to the house where Amanda Crantz's watch had sent out a signal.

❧

"You will get both of us killed, you idiot!" Vladimir spat out as he slapped Victor on the back of his head. "You threw that stupid girl on the mattress, and she ended up hitting her head and having a seizure. We're both lucky she is still alive."

Two girls in one of the rooms started to moan. "Ahhh," Vladimir gasped, "With all of this confusion we haven't been drugging the other girls. We've got to keep a small dosage of heroin in their systems or they will start to have withdrawal fits. Help me, Victor. The dosage is already measured in the syringe. Just add it to the I.V. in the girl's arm, like this." Vladimir showed Victor how to inject the drug into the intravenous setup that each girl had hooked up to her arm. One by one the needle was inserted and the heroin was released to enslave another young girl to this horrible addiction.

After about an hour of drugging each of the young women in the safe house, both Vladimir and Victor sat in the living room drinking.

Vladimir drained his glass. "American vodka, how do they drink this bottled piss? It's nothing like the good stuff in Armenia."

Victor nodded in agreement, and as he tilted his head back to finish his drink, he gazed through the living room window to the street in front of the safe house. Three young boys were riding bikes around the cul-de-sac. This was not unusual; in fact, the presence of families was one of the reasons the house had been chosen. Kids playing in a neighborhood gave the appearance that there was nothing suspicious going on. One of the boys was accompanied by a younger boy, probably his little brother, who was running behind the bike and trying to keep up.

Then Victor noticed two old men who appeared to be cheering on the boys as they showed off the tricks they could do on their bikes. One of the men had a cane, the other a walker. Victor had never seen these men in the neighborhood before. After studying them for a few moments, he dismissed their presence, saying, "Hrumph, pour me another glass of that piss."

"Looks like he sees us, Smitty," Benson said while he tried to act interested in the boys riding their bikes while simultaneously keeping his glasses pointed toward the large living room window.

"Keep looking at the window, Benson. The laser in your glasses picks up the vibrations they make when they speak," Thane instructed as he monitored the information transmitted from the ball drums.

"Listen, computer kid, the last thing you want to do is let your mark make you," Benson growled, then added, "Watch and learn, Junior." While holding onto his walker for support, Benson dropped to one knee and called the youngest boy to him. He pointed to a spot for the boy to stand, which placed the lad between him and the mark. "Come here, young fella. Don't you have a bike of your own?"

Thane's monitor was filled with the face of a little boy who smiled and said, "I'm too little to ride yet."

Thane started to tap the mouse on his desk, muttering, "What are you doing, I only see that…"

Thane's rant was cut short as the image on his screen slowly moved to the right and directly toward the target window. Thane realized that by kneeling down and appearing to talk to the young boy, Benson was able to slowly direct his gaze toward the window. He appeared to be looking at the boy as he spoke to him, exactly what he wanted the mark to think was happening. "Are you getting this, kid?" Benson inquired.

Thane nodded in quiet admiration. "Yes, getting it loud and clear."

Benson kept smiling at the little boy, then said to Thane, "You spend too much time looking into a computer monitor that doesn't look back at you. Remember, kid, the key to surveillance is never letting the mark know he's being watched."

❧

"*Let the heroin work its magic. These girls will do whatever is asked of them for more—umm, what do they call it here—heroin fix.*" Vladimir said the last two words in English, then made a toasting gesture with his glass and continued in Armenian, *"Very soon we'll be ready to get these girls out of here. I'm glad because this is the most we've had yet."*

Victor nodded and was about to speak when his phone rang. He stood up when he saw that the caller was Lois. While Victor was intently listening to the voice on the other end of the call, his sleeve moved up his arm, exposing a green star tattoo on his wrist. Victor didn't know his Cartel mark had been exposed, but Smitty did.

After being instructed about another girl to be picked up, Victor responded, "Got it" and hung up. He turned to Vladimir and said, "I go to pick up one more girl. This one is south of Lincoln. It will be a few hours before I get back with her."

⁂

The Sarge walked into Thane's workspace with Agnes's portable oxygen tank squeaking along behind him. "Well, Thanerboy, whatya... " The Sarge was cut short when Thane's hand shot up for silence.

"Heroin fix?" Thane said with a questioning tone. "These two brutes were speaking some language, and I'll bet it's Armenian. Then one of them raised his glass, and it sounded like he said 'heroin fix.'" The squeaking behind Sarge stopped and Agnes gasped, "Dear God, no."

"I can't stay on my knee any longer." Benson sounded like he was straining to get up. "Hope you got what you needed. If we stay here much longer, they'll get wise to us."

Smitty's hand grabbed Benson's arm to help him up. Smitty touched his hearing aid and said to Thane, "Did you see the tat that guy had on his wrist when he was talking on the phone?"

Thane looked confused. "What's a tat?"

The Sarge and Agnes simultaneously said, "Tattoo." Thane looked around quickly, feeling like he was the only one who didn't get it, which he was. "Oh, well... ah, no, but when we review the tape, we'll check it out. I will have the guys in research work on translating the surveillance video."

"Roger that. Wait, the garage is opening up," Smitty said. Smitty and Benson slowly walked away from the house, waving at the boys on their bikes as they did so. A van was backing out, and Smitty and Benson waved at the driver as he drove past without acknowledging them.

"Ball drums still recording?" Smitty asked, "cuz I got the plate in my sight."

"Sure is, Smitty," the Sarge replied. "You two stay in sight of that house. I'm making a call to police headquarters. Let's see if we can get the one-knock wonder boys up there to kick that door in."

Smitty and Benson looked at each other and smiled.

Thane looked at Sarge and Agnes with a questioning expression on his face.

"I gotta make a call" was all Thane could hear as the Sarge hurried out of the room.

۶ؙ

For the last year, Jake Mitchell had been working as the Public Information Officer for the Omaha Police Department. He and his lieutenant reported directly to the Chief of Police. Things had gone great for the first few months, and Jake seemed to be a natural. He had learned to handle the press like a master, and the Chief valued his opinion when the realities of law enforcement in a free society hit the fan. No matter how hard the police throughout the country tried, there were always incidents that caused a social uproar. Omaha was no exception. The Chief knew that the media could make things worse if situations were not handled with care and professionalism, so having someone like Jake Mitchell on his team was a must.

Jake loved his job at OPD. He had been a detective in the Salt Lake City Police Department for a few years until he lost his wife and daughter to a terrible car accident. Wanting to be near family, he had moved to Omaha where his brother Ben Mitchell lived.

Ben had built quite a financial empire. Jake later learned that his brother was the man behind the Ol' Blues Retirement Home, with its secret crime-fighting unit the likes of which the world had never seen. Jake had fallen in love with Smitty's daughter, Brittany, and eventually found out about this geriatric crime-fighting organization that operated under the radar of the police, the medical staff, and the public at large.

Jake had to admit the covert operation was brilliant. That is why, when he found out that those Ol' Blue geezers had gone rogue, he didn't expose the whole operation. Jake realized that with his position in the Chief's office he could be a valuable asset to the Ol' Blues and the public. He clearly understood that he couldn't share what he'd learned with anyone who wasn't aware of it, especially anyone in the police department.

Right after arriving at work each day, Jake went over the morning reports from the previous night's police calls. Then he reviewed the Crime Stoppers tip line. He especially hunted for tips from the Ol' Blues under some false name. Those tips got top priority. Jake knew that information gathered by the Blues was always top intelligence, and when they took the time to call it to his attention on the tip line it meant something big was going down. That is why when his personal phone rang, he was surprised to see that the call was directly from the Sarge. Jake looked around to make sure he was alone.

"This is Jake. What's up, Sarge?"

The voice on the phone said, "Are you able to talk?" Jake knew this was big, so he checked again to make sure nobody could hear him. Then he said, "We're good, Sarge" and listened intently.

"Jake, we've got a situation," Sarge said. "How fast can the SWAT team be roused up? It looks like we discovered some sort of drug house, and we need it hit as soon as possible."

Jake was confused. "A drug house? I can let Narcotics know about it, but I doubt they would hit it with a SWAT team. They'll watch it for a while, then... "

"Jake, we think some Slavic Eastern European foreigners are selling out of the home at this address."

Jake wrote down the information. Then the Sarge's tone of voice became more urgent. "Jake, one of the Blues' granddaughters is at the drug house and could be in trouble."

Jake let out a quick breath. "One of their granddaughters? Jeez, Sarge, I don't know what I could do to make the Narcotic Unit push for some SWAT overtime, but I'll...."

Jake thought for a second about something the Sarge said about Eastern foreigners. Then he said, "Drugs being sold from possible foreign nationals... wait a minute, you think guys from an old Soviet bloc country are trafficking drugs in Omaha?"

The Sarge stretched the truth a little. "That's what it looks like, and we need SWAT to hit the place as soon as possible, Jake."

Suddenly Jake's voice changed an octave or two. "I've got it. Since there may be foreigners involved in this, that makes it international. I'll notify the FBI. Once the Narcotics guys hear that the FBI may jump on this, they'll want a piece of it as well. They'll activate the joint task force to hit the place. I'll make the calls."

The Sarge hung up the phone. "Jake is gold," he thought to himself.

CHAPTER 3

A few hours had passed since Victor left to pick up the last girl. Vladimir slouched in his armchair in the living room. He, like Victor, was bald, sporting a three-day growth of black beard. His short-sleeved shirt was unbuttoned, revealing a dirty sleeveless undershirt that cops refer to as a "wife beater."

To Vladimir's left was an old mirror that had been left by the previous owners of the house. Aesthetics and upgrades were not the reasons the house was purchased. Vladimir threw his head back to toss down his fourth shot of vodka. "To the girls," he chuckled, holding his glass like he was making a toast to his reflection in the dirty mirror. He had the thickly muscled shoulders and large gut typical if thugs from the former Soviet Union. Vladimir knew he was no lady's man, but it didn't matter to him. He, like Victor, relished seeing fear in the eyes of the people they victimized… especially these young American girls.

Once they learned that defiance earned a fast slap to the back of the head or punch to the stomach, the girls quickly obeyed when Vladimir simply gave them his threatening wide-eyed stare. Usually that look was followed by a punch to the stomach. This form of punishment ensured that the girl's face was not marked. It was extremely painful for an hour or two afterward as they struggled to breathe. Once the heroin had been injected, painful punishments were no longer necessary. To avoid withdrawal symptoms, the girls would do anything to get that next dose.

When the girls' bodies were controlled by the drug, they offered no resistance and Vladimir could have his way with them. As long as he didn't damage them, nobody cared. Vladimir smiled to himself and quietly said, "Nobody can stop me." The vodka started to loosen his thoughts, and Vladimir began to focus on the pretty new girl. He grinned, deciding that the new girl would provide him some pleasure.

"Time for some fun." He clapped his hands together, then stood up. Vladimir's eye caught something different when he looked out the window. "No kids out there," he noted as he glanced toward the street. He looked at his watch and realized that it was almost 4:30 p.m. *Mothers must have called them home for dinner,* Vladimir thought. "Humph," he belched as he grabbed the bottle of vodka by the neck and headed down the hallway that led to the room where Amanda's feet could still be seen in the doorway.

The fog of Amanda's mind was starting to clear. This was nothing new to her. She slowly realized that she was coming out of a seizure. Her eyes began to open, and she started to control her breathing. She heard an unmistakable sound of a bottle being slammed on a wooden table, in this case a small wooden nightstand next to the mattress she was lying on. The noise helped jolt her to consciousness enough to lick her dry lips and swallow normally. Her eyes opened but she could only make out the silhouette of a large figure standing over her. This had happened to her before when she had run away from one of the many foster homes of which she had been placed. She had known men who provided shelter in return for *services*, and in her mind she thought that she was awakening to another of those situations.

"Look, man, I really don't feel… *pahawwh!*" was the sound she made as her breath was knocked out of her. Pain shot through her midsection, and she was unable to inhale.

Amanda's eyes flashed wide open, and suddenly the entire room came into focus. A strange, smiling man was glaring at her through dark, piercing eyes. He pointed his finger and shook it as one would tell a small child "No, no, no."

"You shut your mouth, stupid girl, or..." Vladimir made a fist and motioned like he was going to hit her again. Amanda's hands instantly shot forward as if she was begging not to be hit again, but she could not utter a sound. Vladimir stood up straight and said, "That's better." Then he gave her a perverse, controlling smile. Amanda knew there was nothing she could do to stop this man from doing whatever he wanted to her. She knew there were men who victimized women like this, but she had never actually been with one.

What Amanda didn't know was that there were also men who went above and beyond their already stressful occupation of policing to specialize in very high risk and dangerous situations within law enforcement. These were the men of the Special Weapons and Tactics Units (SWAT) of the Omaha Police Department and the FBI's Critical Incident Response Group (CIRG). These units periodically train together and provide support and cooperation in crisis or high-risk situations. These men were ready to do harm to those who victimized the innocent.

What Vladimir didn't know was that these men had just cleared the streets of the children outside the safe house and were armed, determined, and coming for him.

⁓

A single helicopter hovered above the safe house neighborhood. The copter was equipped with advanced telescopic observation equipment and nighttime Infrared (IR) optics. The pilot and co-pilot were trying to maneuver in a way that would allow them to maintain visual contact with the Special Ops Units as Alpha Unit took the back door and Bravo Unit approached the front. Both of these units were slowly closing in on the house below them. The pilot noticed some power lines directly in front of him. He quickly corrected his course by pulling a sharp right turn. When a helicopter makes a turn like that, one can hear the beating of the rotor blades with a loud "whop, whop, whop" until the helicopter has finished its turn.

Vladimir's large hands were gripping Amanda's neck when he felt the house seem to shake with a loud, rapid thudding sound. He paused for a moment and Amanda gasped for air. She started to cough and even heave like she was about to vomit. Vladimir backed off for a moment in case the girl puked. He reached over to the vodka bottle and started to take large gulps that sloppily dripped down his face onto his undershirt. "I don't want this piece of trash hurling her guts all over me," he said quietly to himself. "It might ruin the moment." He laughed and took another sloppy swig.

⟋

The two six-man teams, Alpha and Bravo, approached their objectives. Bravo team briskly walked up the driveway toward the front door. Bravo would make the initial breach into the house while Alpha secured the outer perimeter in case the suspects inside the house decided to jump out the windows or flee through the back door. The Alpha team would rejoin Bravo once the house was secure.

The Bravo Unit started quickening their pace following the lead officer who was holding a ballistic shield with a small window made of bullet-proof glass. The shield allowed him to see where he was going as he led the team up the driveway. He was followed closely by another officer holding a battering ram to break down the door. Each of the other officers had one hand on his weapon and the other on the shoulder or back of one of his fellow officers. This allowed each officer to know the position of the others.

The boss for the Bravo Unit was Sergeant Tatum Morgan, a twenty-year police veteran who had spent years with the Army Ranger Special Forces before joining OPD. He knew his mission: breach the entry, search, detain, and secure the scene so the follow-up detectives could do their work. So far things had worked perfectly until...

Over the radio all the officers suddenly heard the voice of the spotter in the helicopter. "Bravo Unit…ah…check your six." Sergeant Morgan immediately knew that something had gone wrong behind his unit. He quickly looked back and his eyes widened as he mouthed, "What the...?" After years of seeing and overcoming practically every obstacle to maintain a tactical advantage, what he saw made him stop his unit with a quick fist pump into the air. The team froze and quickly glanced toward the house to see if a threat was coming from the target.

Sergeant Morgan's mouth quivered as he tried to think of something to say. His men immediately knew something was wrong and darted their eyes toward their sergeant. Then in unison they followed his stare, and every mouth dropped as they focused on a small old man following them with a walker. The man stopped as he realized that six large, heavily armed men had just halted and were staring at him.

"How are ya?" Benson said in a cheerful voice.

The sergeant, coming to grips with the situation, quickly slapped one of his men on the shoulder, pointed to the old man, and motioned with his thumb. That officer let his rifle down on its sling, which freed his hands. He quickly grabbed the old man around the waist and without any effort picked him up.

"What the...? Whoa!" Benson gasped as he and his walker were quickly whisked away by a huge SWAT officer and moved to the sidewalk.

"Get over there, sir, now!" The officer pointed to the house across the street. The officer then turned around and quickly joined the approach formation, and Bravo Unit was back on track heading for the door.

⁓

Unbeknownst to everybody on the driveway, a terrified red-headed computer geek was staring in horror as his monitor showed Benson waddling up behind the SWAT team. When the entire special unit of very intimidating men turned and stared at Benson, Thane felt as though they were glaring through his monitor at him. He started to sweat profusely and sat transfixed, leaning back in his chair. He didn't blink until he heard the big man say, "Get over there, sir, now!"

Thane tried to talk but was only able to mutter, "B-B-Benson. W-What were you doing?"

Smitty was across the street watching the helicopter and didn't witness the stunt that Benson had just pulled. He looked down to see Benson waddling as fast as he could with his walker towards him.

"What happened?"

Benson didn't answer Smitty's question. He just exclaimed, "Cripes, did you see the size of those guys? Were we ever that big?"

Thane's voice chimed into Smitty's earpiece, "Benson decided to join the SWAT team when they weren't looking."

Smitty held his hand to his earpiece, then gave Benson a stern look.

"I couldn't help it," Benson explained. "For a moment I felt like we were raiding the gambling joints down on 16th Street. I just needed to help, to go with 'em."

Smitty shook his head, but he understood Benson's reaction perfectly after spending his life watching the backs of brother officers during dangerous calls.

"It's instinctual, kid, I'll try to explain when…" Smitty's comment to Thane was cut off in mid-sentence as a thunderous voice bellowed, "*Police! Search Warrant*," followed by the crash as the breaching tool smashed the front door into pieces. In less than two seconds, the heavily armed men charged through the doorway into the house across the street from where the two Ol' Blues were standing.

Once inside, shouts of "Police! On the Ground!" were heard as the men of the SWAT team charged throughout the house, not knowing what was around each corner or in every room. The house was quickly being cleared and secured.

Benson grabbed Smitty's arm and said, "We gotta help 'em, Smitty, come on." With an understanding look, Smitty put his hand on Benson's chest and quietly yet firmly said, "We can't. Our time is past. It's up to them now."

Releasing his walker and grabbing Smitty's arm, Benson said through quivering lips, "We gotta, Smitty. We gotta help 'em. They're so young."

Smitty clenched his fist, wadding Benson's shirt between his fingers. "I know. Look at me," he ordered.

Benson couldn't pull his eyes away from the commotion across the street, Smitty saw a tear streaming down Benson's face as he repeated, "They're so young, Smitty, we gotta..."

BOOM! The shockwave knocked the Ol' Blues backward onto a lawn.

As Sergeant Tatum Morgan led his men through the house, all of his senses were sending information to his brain at an incredible rate. Men yelling, dust in the air from the shattered door. The sounds, smells, and sights were overwhelming, but his biggest concern was what he couldn't see or hear.

Over the radio he heard his men clear a room and then call for a squad for one young female after another. He could not understand why all these women were in this house, but he would worry about that after the residence was secure.

Suddenly a large shadow quickly passed across the doorway in the last room at the end of the hall. Instinctively Morgan threw a flash bang ("stun grenade") into the room. The grenade bounced off the man's thigh and exploded in mid-air, shattering the bedroom window and spewing shredded glass onto the front lawn. The intense heat from the grenade flash burned the neck, shoulder, and arm of the big man. His scream of pain was cut short by a kick to the stomach by Sergeant Morgan. As additional officers stormed the bedroom, the large bald man being cuffed continued screaming through the searing pain of his burns combined with having the wind knocked out of him.

Once the other team members of the Bravo team could hear again, the unmistakable sound of a young woman screaming caught their attention. She was lying on a mattress like the other girls, but there was no I.V. hooked up to her arm. The Alpha team entered the house, and after a few minutes the eerie quiet that follows such an intense action settled in. Narcotics and FBI officers followed and soon were able to piece together what was going on. Drugs were being used but not sold here.

One of the detectives said, "Trafficking... this bald slob is drugging up these girls for trafficking." After the officers and paramedics heard what was going on, the usual gentleness that the paramedics used when treating burn victims disappeared.

Vladimir screamed in pain and shouted in some unknown language as he was moved around in preparation to being taken to the hospital. Seeing that he could walk, some of the SWAT team members marched him outside. "Due to the smoke and glass," they told the paramedics. Somehow Vladimir's burnt shoulder bumped every corner while he was being escorted to the front yard and plopped onto a gurney. Sergeant Morgan pointed to the bald guy and said, "Call command, this guy will have a hospital guard on him until he is released from treatment."

⟋

"What was that?" Benson asked as he struggled to stand up.

"I think it was one of those stun bombs. In our day, all we had was a revolver and a club," Smitty said as he stood and brushed himself off.

Smitty touched his earcom and said, "Thane, we're done here. Have the van pick us... what the... for the love of Pete, Benson!"

Thane studied the monitor as Smitty and Benson looked at each other and Smitty shouted, "You idiot, you landed on me and plastered my crap catcher."

Benson looked down at himself and realized that his stomach and legs were covered with last night's dinner.

Thane quietly asked, "You two aren't coming through the lab when you return, are ya?"

Smitty and Benson said in unison, "Shut up, Thane." Then both the Ol' Blues froze, looking at each other as they simultaneously recognized the sound of raspy laughter, followed by the familiar croaking of a smoker's coughing fit.

Smitty touched his hearing aid and said, "Thane, tell the Sarge that it looks like the SWAT team got here in time."

Smitty looked across the street where young girls were being wheeled out of the home and placed in ambulances. One of the girls was walking on her own with a white blanket wrapped around her.

Thane watched the procession of what appeared to have been about a dozen girls. Behind his right shoulder Thane heard the unmistakable scratchy voice of Lead Officer Crantz explaining, "The one walking on her own, that's my Amanda."

✺

Victor had narrowly missed being caught up in the disaster. As he approached the cul de sac, he saw that it had been blocked off and a number of ambulances were speeding toward him. He pulled over and let them pass.

Victor watched in disbelief as one by one, the ambulances turned toward the safe house. He grabbed his phone and called Lois as he drove past the cul de sac. He was able to see what he had feared: cops, lots of them, surrounding the house.

Victor told Lois, "I was thirty seconds away from the safe house when I saw what was going on. There are police everywhere! Even a helicopter and ambulances are rolling up. I've got to get out of here."

Lois's mouth dropped as she realized that the largest group of girls that they'd ever had—the group that was going to bring the Cartel millions of dollars—had just been discovered.

"What do I do, Lois?"

There was a pause as Lois processed the fact that the discovery of the safe house would be viewed in Armenia as her failure, and she would have to pay.

"Are you there?" Victor shouted into his phone.

Lois was good at what she did and had tried to prepare for what she would do if her operation was discovered. She calmly said, "Easy, Victor, you still have the new girl with you, yes?"

"Yes, yes, I do, but Lois, what about…"

Again, with a calm voice, Lois directed Victor to take the girl back to the small Nebraska town where she had been reported as a runaway, bringing her to the local police.

"Do this just as you would take a girl back while contracting with the State to provide transportation. Victor, you must act as though this was just another assignment. Drop her off. I will call ahead and make arrangements with the local authorities. I'll let them know the girl was found in Omaha, and you are simply returning her to her foster parents. We must not change what we want everyone to think of this little operation. I will talk to you after the girl is returned. Trust me, Victor. Soon—I give it two weeks—the Cartel will learn about what happened. We will be blamed, and you know what that means, yes?"

With a sigh, Victor replied, "Yes, I know."

"Good, Victor, call me when you're finished, and I will tell you how we will avoid getting our throats slashed. There is more than one cartel in this world." *Click.*

GS

"Agnes… Agnes, you copy?"

This was the third attempt of Meter Maid Mary to contact Agnes Crantz. Finally, after the sound of coughing, laughing, and trying to catch her breath, Lead Officer Crantz came onto the communications system.

"Crantz here. What ya got, Mary?"

There was a pause, then a loud rebuke: "Been trying to reach you, thought something happened. You all right?"

"Oh sure, just had the laugh of my life. You'll never believe what I just saw! Smitty and Benson got knocked into each other, and Smitty's crap-catching colostomy bag blew up."

There was a cough and a laugh, then Agnes added, "The both of them are covered with everything Smitty has been eating for the last 24 hours. I'm having that computer kid make some copies for the Christmas party this year."

There was another pause.

"Well, you better get back to your desk. I just stopped an uppity-type gent out here who tried to park in the staff parking lot. I told him to move the car or I'd tow it. The guy gives me the *'Don't you know who I am?'* line."

There was a slight pause again as Mary took a breath.

"So I point to his chest and say, 'I suppose you pay my salary, know the Mayor, and probably know the Governor.'

"The guy steps back a little, looks around, and says, 'Actually, I do. I am Dr. Nathan Baggaley, the Director of Health and Human Services for the State of Nebraska. I don't know what kind of retirement home this is, but I'm going to make sure its policies and procedures conform to state regulations or heads are going to roll.'

"Then he asks me if I'm a patient here, and I tell him, 'Don't worry who or what I am, fancy pants. I make sure the laws are obeyed here, and you're not staff, so move that car or pick it up later from the impound lot.'

"Next, he tries to butter me up so I won't have his car towed, but I tell him, 'Watch it, Bub, making sweet talk with me won't work. I've been propositioned by men better looking than you.'

"He's on his way over here now," Mary concluded. "He's the type that wears his pants too high, likes to hear himself talk, and thinks everyone should bow down and kiss his feet. I'd say he could be jolted by questioning his manhood."

Agnes smiled and looked around the Precinct to all the Blues who were listening in on the channel. There were winks and nods.

"Copy that, Mary. Good work."

❧

A nurse tried to keep up with the Director of Health and Human Services as he strode through the main entrance of the Ol' Blues Retirement Home.

"Dr. Baggaley, are you sure you wouldn't want to wait for an administrator to meet with you prior to touring the facility?" the nurse half asked, half pleaded.

"No," he replied. "I've sent three administrators here over the last month, and each came back with the most ridiculous reports. This time I decided to come over so I could see for myself exactly what's going on here." He crossed his arms in a condescending gesture.

"Look, Nurse Whoever-You-Are, I've been made aware of how this... *facility*," he continued as he pointed toward nothing in particular, "has been operating without due regard for the regulations of my department. Those regulations are made for the safety of the patients, which, if I've been informed correctly, seems to be more of a suggestion around here. I've come to put a stop to this and make sure the patients are in a safe and nurturing environment."

Dr. Baggaley raised his voice to make sure all the staff heard and feared him. "Now, I want to know where this facility's main police room, or whatever it's called, is located, and I want to know now. I also want to see the patients, each and every one of them. Do you understand me?"

The young nurse pointed toward the large wooden doors under a brass sign that said, "The Precinct." The other nurses in the area stopped what they were doing and stared in disbelief.

Dr. Baggaley was emboldened by the attention he received from everyone except one very large nurse who was sipping a soda and looking at some notes on her desk. He started to strut towards the wooden doors, and the nurse who had given him directions asked sheepishly, "Are you going in there, sir?"

Dr. Baggaley proclaimed, "Young lady, I am the Director of Nebraska Health and Human Services. I go where I want, when I want, and I don't need anyone's permission to do so. Do you understand that?"

The young nurse pointed apprehensively to the Precinct doors and asked, "Even in there?"

Almost yelling, Dr. Baggaley blurted, "Of course I can go in there!"

A voice from one of the other nurses in the lobby exclaimed in disbelief, "Without an appointment?"

Dr. Baggaley looked in the general direction of the voice and bellowed, "What do you mean, *an appointment?* I don't need an appointment. Just get out of my way." He turned his back on the nurses, who stared wide-eyed at him, then glanced at Boss Nurse. She quickly grabbed her soda and said, "This is gonna be good." She started a long, slow slurp through her straw.

The doors to the Precinct slowly opened as Dr. Baggaley, aware that the medical staff was watching him from behind, arrogantly stuck his chin out and strutted through the threshold. He had only taken a step or two when he came to a complete stop. His eyes repeatedly darted from left to right, then slowly up and down as he scanned the ceiling and then the floor. He felt as though he had gone back in time fifty years. There was the tapping sound of typewriters, the whir of desk fans, and the room was lit with incandescent bulbs that gave off a strange golden hue.

One of the fans had a rhythmic squeak as a single blade brushed against the metal casing. A couple of dozen men were sitting at desks, examining neighborhood maps of the city and arguing about various topics that Dr. Baggaley couldn't make out from the other side of the huge room.

The background noise was suddenly pierced by the sound of an actual metal ringer on a phone that caused it to bounce all over a desk. As the phone rang, a police officer limped toward it. "I can't believe this."

Baggaley said out loud, "There are actual police officers here and..." Suddenly he got a better look at the officer approaching the telephone. "Hey, n-n-no pants" was all that came out of his mouth as he pointed to the officer's hospital gown. The officer looked at Dr. Baggaley and matter-of-factly explained, "Indignity bottoms. This is regulation uniform for this precinct. Have a seat, and an officer will be with you shortly."

The officer picked up the hand piece of the phone and before answering, he raised his voice and said, "Did you hear me, Slick? Park it right over there and an officer will be with you shortly." He pointed to a couch against a wall, above which was a sign which read, "Waiting Area."

Dr. Baggaley's ire rose as he responded in a condescending tone, "Sir, I'm Dr. Nathan Baggaley, the Director for the State of Nebraska's Health…."

He was cut off by a raspy female voice saying, "Lose the introduction, Baggs. The officer just told you to park your toilet seat warmer on the couch and an officer will be with you shortly. Now plant it, Bub."

Clearly shocked at being interrupted so rudely, Dr. Baggaley was incensed to hear the disrespectful verbal directives that were being slung at him, punctuated with an annoying squeaking sound.

Unbeknownst to Dr. Baggaley, approximately ten feet behind him the large wooden doors had been wedged open as ten nurses tried to maneuver around each other for better views. Everything in their world had come to a screeching halt. The gathering of healthcare providers had become a bunch of awestruck onlookers at what would go down in the annals of Ol' Blue history as "*The Baggaley Butt Kicking.*"

Dr. Baggaley slowly turned toward the sound of the squeaky wheel, as if making a grand gesture. He placed his hands on his hips, tightened his lips, and announced, "Now, see here. I determine how nursing and retirement homes are to be run in this state. I don't wait to be served; I tell people how to serve." He raised his voice so that everyone in the Precinct could hear: "Is that clear?"

He then lowered his gaze to identify the source of the squeaking sound, which became louder as a woman shuffled toward him. A pair of bright, angry eyes peered over spectacles hanging on the end of her nose, braced by a nasal cannula oxygen tube in her nostrils. Curly purple hair spilled out from under a blue police cap. Like the male officers, the woman wore a blue police shirt and hospital gown. Knee-high stockings and thin, wrinkly thighs were exposed as the gown snagged on the handle of the oxygen tank holder that produced the bothersome squeak.

Dr. Baggaley blinked a couple of times as his mouth dropped open in complete shock. The woman puffed a cigarette as she shuffled, and the ember glowed as she inhaled directly under the tube that pumped oxygen into her nose. Seemingly on cue, Lead Officer Crantz grabbed the smoke with her index and editorial middle finger and the glowing ember burst into a small flame. Agnes glanced at the flame and then blew it out and coughed.

Agnes decided it was time to fish out something that would jolt his manhood. She pointed her cigarette at Dr. Baggaley's nose and started to probe.

"Listen to me, Baggs. You're pretty tough with those nurses out there, and you seem to like throwing your voice around so that everyone hears you."

Dr. Baggaley glared silently at her.

"I don't know how many fart clappers you had to kiss to get to your high and lofty position," she said as Baggaley rolled his eyes, "or how many dogs you had to kick out of your way as you marched through the capital." This time Dr. Baggaley gasped in shock. *GOT YA!* Agnes said to herself. Cops have a way of drilling in when they are interrogating until they strike a nerve.

"At the capital, you are known as Dr. High and Mighty Baggaley, but in here you're Baggs, and as far as I'm concerned, you're Baggs-O'-Crap Baggaley… probably one of those perverts who likes spending too much time with his dog."

Dr. Baggaley jolted his head back in shock. Before he could say anything, Agnes poured it on by yelling to the Ol' Blues, "Remember those sickos we would catch at the stockyards doing all kinds of disgusting things to the cattle? I think we got one of those perverts right here." She shook her finger, causing ashes to fall to the ground.

In his most indignant tone, Dr. Baggaley almost shouted, "I beg your pardon!"

Now it was time for the Ol' Blues to get their digs in. From the right of Baggaley was yelled, "Don't even think about doing anything disgusting around here, you degenerate."

Before Baggaley could locate the source of the remark, from behind him another Ol' Blue yelled, "Let me guess—you own a wiener dog, don't ya? Pervert."

Dr. Baggaley's head swiveled toward the second accuser.

"I … I would never, ever…."

Agnes added the finishing touch: "As a kid you probably snuck into the 4-H fairs with the sheep. You were one of those wooly weirdos, weren't ya, Baggs?"

All of the Blues stared at Dr. Baggaley as he tried to organize his disheveled thoughts. There were three to five seconds of quick blinking and absolute silence.

Suddenly the air was filled with the sound of a soda cup being sucked dry. Everyone in the Precinct turned toward the open doors filled with the shocked faces of nurses and Boss Nurse Betsy, who suddenly realized that she was the source of the slurping sound. She quickly put the cup behind her back. She looked at the nurses holding the doors open and motioned with her head to close them. The doors slowly drew together as the nurses stared and Dr. Baggaley stared back. The awkward stillness was broken by the sharp click of the solid brass latch.

"Back to your stations, y'all!" Nurse Betsy blurted, and like mice the staff scattered. Boss Nurse bounded to her desk and sat down. At that moment the doors opened and Dr. Baggaley took three quick steps outside the Precinct as he tried to calm himself down.

As the doors slowly closed behind him, he took a deep breath and announced, "I have been nothing but a responsible owner for my poodles." From the Precinct one of the Blues could be heard saying, "Poodles! I knew it! Ha-ha!" A chorus of jeers followed until the brass latch clicked again.

Dr. Baggaley quickly marched out of the Ol' Blues Retirement Home. Once outside, he tried to control his breathing and regain his composure. He stopped at the staff parking lot just in time to see his vehicle on the back of a tow truck leaving the parking lot.

"Thought I was joking, didn't ya, sweetie pie?"

Dr. Baggaley turned and looked as the owl-eyed woman pivoted in her mechanized chair. He stared at her as he tried to regain his composure and figure out what had just happened to him. He was unaccustomed to being treated with anything but respect. Nothing about this Ol' Blues Home conformed to his rigid ideas about how a retirement home should be run. He looked back at the massive building. "Well, now, I'll just have to look into some way to deal with these Blues."

His focus returned to the owl-eyed lady who quietly scooted away.

"I will not be treated like this," Dr. Baggaley said as he pointed to Meter Maid Mary. She didn't bother to return his gaze. As her chair quietly glided away, Dr. Baggaley thought he heard the woman making barking noises.

෬

The Chemist enjoyed the protective cover that being a pharmacist provided. He relished talking to customers and padding his reputation as a simple man who provided the trusted service of filling prescriptions for those who were suffering some sort of ailment.

"How's your mother doing?" the drugstore's cashier asked.

"The same," he replied. "She's still at the nursing home, and as old as she is, there really isn't much hope that she'll ever go home."

The cashier smiled. "It's nice that you take care of her house for her. I'm sure she is grateful to have you."

With a charlatan's grin, the Chemist walked back to the pharmacy desk at the rear of the drugstore and grinned at the thought of how his mother's home was actually utilized. In her vegetative state, she would never know that young women were being violated in a drug-induced, semi-comatose state with the chemical he designed. It was the perfect setup for his debauchery.

A snide smirk could be detected in his reflection as he walked past the mirrors in the cosmetics section of the drugstore.

"No one will ever know," he snickered to himself, "not even those stupid young…"

He took a step onto the elevated drugstore pharmacy desk and paused as he noticed a pop-up advertisement sitting on the table for the customers to see. There was a picture of a young woman being hugged by her parents, accompanied by the words, "Always know where your loved ones are and keep them safe." The young girl was looking away from her parents and holding up her hand. As he noticed what was on the girl's wrist, the Chemist froze in place.

The advertisement was for a Global Positioning System designed to track the location of children with debilitating conditions. The girl in the photo was wearing a GPS watch. His brain seemed to fire an electric shock through his body as he realized that the watch was identical to the one worn by the last girl who had been brought to him. The watch could record the locations of that girl for more than a month.

Suddenly, the Chemist's mind was flooded with various ways police could track the girl to his mother's house. After that, it wouldn't take long for them to connect the house to him. He stared transfixed at the photo, and as he did so, saliva started to drip from his lip and run down his chin. This snapped him out of his shock. At the same time, the vague sound of words started to penetrate his stupor. An old woman's voice shrilled, "Young man, young man, do you hear me?"

He wiped his chin and focused on the old woman who was shaking a box of laxative suppositories at him.

"Will these pills work gently, or will I have to stay close to the bathroom all night?"

He blinked a couple of times and looked at the saliva on his wrist, then noticed that he was sweating profusely.

"Young man?"

Annoyed at being interrupted while he was trying to concentrate, the Chemist blurted, "I don't care! Cram one up your butt and swallow the rest."

The woman stopped talking, winced, and attempted to read the fine print on the box.

Another pharmacist's voice came from behind him. "Whoa there! He was just joking. Insert one of those at bedtime; they are pretty gentle." The old woman gave him a disgusted look and walked away.

The other pharmacist, a young man named Jared, had just started working at the drugstore a couple of months earlier. He inquired, "Hey, you all right?"

Snapping out of his haze, the Chemist controlled his emotions and said, "I don't feel well; I think I'll go home."

There was sudden sensation to his shoulder as Jared touched him, which caused him to jump. Jared pulled back his hand and said, "Hey there, guy, you don't look so good. Maybe you should go home. I'll take care of things here. It should be a slow night."

"Uh, yeah. Good idea."

The Chemist grabbed a tissue from a box on the desk and wiped his sweating upper lip.

"Umm, goodbye" he blurted, then hurriedly walked back through the drugstore. As he passed the cosmetics counter, the mirrors reflected the face of a terrified man who was about to be exposed for what he truly was: a spineless, despicable sexual predator.

♎

"It's simple, Victor, we'll have about two weeks for the organization to realize what has happened. There is no forgiveness for this. They will send someone to kill us."

Victor sat back in the seat of his van, which was now parked along one of the many country roads in Nebraska. He looked at his phone and exclaimed, "We're dead... walking corpses."

"Foolish one, do you think I got to this position without keeping my options open?"

Victor sat up, looked at his phone, then put it back to his ear and asked, "What do you mean, *options*?"

There was a slight pause. Then Lois said, "You certainly don't think all the cartels are in the East, do you? People with our skills can be very marketable to the cartels of the South. The trafficking market may even be easier with the Southern border as open as it is. We will contact them and offer our services. I will close down operations here in my office. Gather what money you can and I'll..."

Lois stopped talking when she realized that someone was standing in the doorway of her office. She put the phone down. "Who are you? What are..."

She glanced at the small man wearing glasses, a silly-looking police shirt, and a hospital gown from his hips to his black shoes.

"...you doing here?"

The man replied, "Taking Boomer for a walk" and pointed downward.

"Victor, I'll have to call you back. One of those old men from the home just wandered into my office."

Lois hung up her phone and stood up. Then she commanded, "You get back to your bed before I have the nurses put you in a crib."

Her desk had been blocking what the man was pointing at. She looked down at it and her eyes opened wider. "What is that?"

"Boomer" was the little man's response, "the best K-9 the department ever had."

The man had a stuffed German Shepherd that looked as if it was lying down, only it was on a small platform with wheels on it. The animal's face looked contorted, and its eyes were crossed. The lip flaps on the animal were curled back, its tongue hung from the right side of its mouth, and its front paws were curled inward.

"Charlie! How did you get in here?"

The voice of a young nurse was heard from the receptionist desk of the Health and Human Services wing.

"How do you always find a way out of your wing?" the young nurse asked, with an understanding smile and her hands on her hips.

"Get this old goat out of my office!" Lois barked.

The nurse looked startled, as if she hadn't expected anyone to be in the offices at that time of day.

"The Blues just finished dinner. I'm so sorry; I didn't know there was anyone here."

Pointing her finger at the animal, Lois demanded, "What is that thing?"

"Boomer!" Charlie said.

The nurse tried to explain, "This is the K-9 dog that Officer Charlie had when he retired."

"Boomer, sit," Charlie ordered.

Lois shook her head. "That thing looks hideous. What is wrong with it?"

The nurse stroked the stuffed animal and explained, "Poor Boomer fell into a chemical container while chasing a crook through the old tannery building. By the time the other officers arrived, it was too late. They pulled Boomer out of the tanning chemicals and he looked like this. Officer Charlie had him preserved."

The nurse looked at Lois and mouthed the word *stuffed*. Then she commented, more for Officer Charlie than for Lois, "Officer Charlie takes Boomer everywhere he goes." She looked at Boomer and patted his head. "You're a good boy, Boomer."

Lois blinked her eyes trying to understand what she was hearing. She finally shook her head and yelled, "I don't care about this Charlie and his stupid dog."

"Boomer," Charlie pointed to Lois, "Sic 'em!"

The nurse gasped as if Boomer was about to jump into action.

Lois jumped, bracing herself as if the animal was going to charge at her. Then she realized the absurdity of the situation and pointed toward the Ol' Blues Home.

"Get him and that thing out of here!"

"Down, Boomer." Officer Charlie was led away by the nurse. Lois didn't look too closely at the nurse as she tried to comprehend what had just happened. If she had, she would have noticed the rather large black-framed eyeglasses and strands of red hair stuffed into a large headband.

"How was that, Thane?"

"Nice job, guys" came the reply. "Looks like we have the face that goes to that suspicious computer."

The commotion caught the attention of everyone in the commons area of the Health and Human Services offices, including a still-frazzled Dr. Nathan Baggaley who was trying to get a ride to the impound lot.

"Well, now," Dr. Baggaley said to himself, "Lois Luka seems to have problems with these Ol' Blue patients."

Dr. Baggaley had despised Lois for quite some time. She had union protections and she also had what Dr. Baggaley felt was an arrogant contempt for him and his position.

"Ms. Luka."

Lois jumped at the voice of the Director of NHHS. She detested the man because on more than one occasion he had stuck his nose into her activities and almost exposed her operation.

The last thing she needed was Baggaley nosing around. She needed another week to get her operation moved out of this office and to have things in order for contacting the Southern Cartels. She needed to stay calm and keep Dr. Baggaley from discovering her efforts to conceal incriminating information about her operation.

In a low voice Lois responded, "Well, Dr. Baggaley, what can I do for you?"

Dr. Baggaley ordered, "You can start with making sure this nurse and these patients are treated with respect." He pointed to Brittany and Charlie with his stuffed dog.

Then he turned to Brittany and said, "Please inform your supervisor that in appreciation for this facility donating offices for my staff, Lois here will be happy to assist you with anything you need. Is that clear, Ms. Luka?"

Brittany could sense the animosity between these two people. She would make sure that the Sarge was informed that the woman who owned the suspect computer has been instructed to provide any service the Ol' Blues may need. This could come in handy.

"Of course, Dr. Baggaley. I'm more than happy to help out." Lois almost choked on her words.

This is the last thing I need," she thought to herself, but she could not jeopardize her plans. *"I'll do what I must, then move the operation to the South."*

Dr. Baggaley smiled complacently, knowing that he had just made Lois's life miserable. A sense of satisfaction eased his animosity toward the old cops. He walked back to the office common area to find a ride to the impound lot.

⸎

Pheasant hunting in rural Nebraska was a favorite pastime of brothers Scott and Kasey Tucker. Working with Scott's trained dogs to flush the game birds was something Kasey always enjoyed. Driving from Omaha to his brother's farm was always a nice break, and watching Scott work the fields with his dogs was fascinating. The dogs' bloodlines gave them an irresistible urge to seek, point, and retrieve game. The large male Black Labs, who were named Buddy and Macie, knew that whenever Kasey was visiting, they were going hunting.

When Scott and Kasey emerged from Scott's farmhouse, Buddy and Macie were waiting in the bed of Scott's pickup. They were barking and jumping in anticipation of unleashing their generational bloodlines of hunting instinct which bonded them to their human master in a way only hunters understand.

On this occasion they were working a field that had a lot of trees and vegetation around the farm grounds. The dogs would sweep right, then look back to Scott for instructions. Scott would give a quick whistle and point to the left. The dogs darted towards a thickly wooded area, and both of the Black Labradors came to a complete stop.

Kasey said, "They're on to something."

Scott agreed, but he noticed something different about how his dogs were pointing. Instead of standing motionless and looking toward a spot where a pheasant was hiding, the dogs were restless with excitement. Their tails were excitedly whipping back and forth as the dogs pawed eagerly at the ground as if they were waiting for a command to sprint forward. They were well trained, disciplined dogs, and Scott told Kasey, "Something is wrong."

The dogs quickly jerked their heads back to look at Scott. "Let's get over there!" Scott yelled, and both men ran to within ten yards of the dogs.

Suddenly eight coyotes sprang up from the thick growth and charged at the Labs. There was no command Scott could give now. The Labs stood their ground in a defensive posture and responded with loud barks and growls. The coyotes, working as a pack of killers, darted back and forth surrounding the Labs. Scott and Kasey came to a stop and started to yell. Three of the coyotes, which would normally flee at the sight of a human, were now full of snarling fight as they darted toward the men.

The dogs saw the coyotes charging their master, and their protective instincts fueled every muscle of their bodies. Now the Black Labs were full of protective fight and they went on the offensive, charging at the coyotes that were attacking Scott and Kasey. The wild animals were fast and elusive, but with their attention on the two men, they didn't see Buddy and Macie charge them from behind. Buddy bit hard into the upper hind leg of one of the attackers and violently shook the animal off its feet. It screamed and tried to bite back at the larger Lab. Simultaneously, Macie clamped his jaws around the back of the neck of a coyote that had stopped a few feet from Scott. A few vicious shakes snapped the coyote's neck.

The dogs' attack gave Scott and Kasey the needed couple of seconds to respond. The third coyote backed off as two members of his pack were being ravaged by the Black Labs. Scott and Kasey let loose a volley of shots, killing two of the animals and wounding a third as the rest frantically fled. One final shot pulverized the animal Buddy had injured.

"Do you believe that?" Kasey almost yelled. "Coyotes *never* attack like that."

Scott wiped sweat from his forehead with his sleeve and looked at his brother.

"Never seen anything like that. It was as if they were defending a kill from other predators."

Both men looked at each other as they realized why the coyotes had acted so aggressively. Simultaneously they gazed toward the brush from which the coyotes had sprung. As they walked toward the area, the pungent smell of some sort of carcass got stronger. Suddenly Scott stopped and pointed, "There... oh, dear God!"

On the ground was the half-devoured remains of what looked like a woman. The animals had consumed most of her torso. Kasey pulled his phone from his pocket and called 911.

"Send the Sheriff."

Kasey then described the area where the body was located. "Doesn't look like she's been here too long, but some coyotes were feeding on her. Yes, we'll wait and watch for you." As he hung up the phone, he looked at the body and noticed that the dead woman had a star tattooed on her wrist.

Jake Mitchell showed up at the Ol' Blues Precinct for his weekly meeting with the Blues. After the meeting he would return to Central Headquarters and tell the Chief about the public services the retired officers were providing and how they were continuing to serve as advisers to neighborhood groups. It looked good for the Department, plus it allowed the regular officers to focus on answering calls for help rather than getting involved in community activities.

When Jake had fallen in love with Smitty's daughter Brittany, it was only a matter of time before he figured out what the Ol' Blues were actually up to. Now he was the inside man at headquarters and the Crime Stoppers anonymous tip line specialist. Jake's position made it easy for the Blues to feed tips to various units in the police department.

Jake's access to the Chief's Office and every unit in the department also meant he could gain intel for the Blues. This week Jake sat in the Sarge's office and thought to himself, *"Whatever these geezers wanted to go after, they would. They could stick their noses into ongoing investigations without the knowledge of cops or crooks. Set the criminals up for a sting and waddle out without anyone knowing... freaking genius."*

The door opened and Sarge walked in.

"Hey, Jake, good to see ya. What's the latest from headquarters?"

Jake stood and shook Sarge's hand. "Well, the Chief wanted me to thank you guys for the work you're doing. The fact that his main line officers don't have to address simple complaints like"—Jake started to count off on his fingers—"barking dogs, nosy neighbors, kids that won't stay off people's grass, and a bunch of other nuisance calls that I don't have enough fingers for, makes him very happy to have you guys around. It keeps his cops on the street answering calls for help, the response times are faster, and the public seems to be happy with it. Of course, this bunch of innocent old men playing like they are still cops are the darlings of the city. Believe it or not, the public likes you guys much more now than when you were on duty... officially." That remark got a rare, large smile from the Sarge.

The conversation was interrupted by a couple of knocks at the Sarge's door.

"Yeah," was all he said in response.

The door opened and a large puff of smoke preceded a sight that shocked Jake: a woman shuffled into Sarge's office. Jake was taken aback because he had never seen a female Blue.

"Sarge, I just came from the supply room and wanted to touch base with you about... Oh!" Agnes was startled.

Jake stood as the Sarge took his chewed-up cigar out of his mouth and said, "Jake, this is my new lead officer, Agnes Crantz. Agnes, this is Jake Mitchell, the Public Information Officer for the Chief of Police."

Agnes gave the Sarge a questioning look. "He's one of us, Agnes. We're lucky to have him."

Agnes turned and gave Jake the sizing-up look she gave every new Blue she met. She took a long drag on her smoke and spoke with the cigarette wedged between her lips: "How did we land this guy into this little boys' club?"

Jake had never smoked a cigarette and was in awe of how this woman could inhale so deeply, then speak while smoke rushed from her nose and mouth. Agnes studied Jake thoroughly with squinted eyes.

The Sarge declared, "Well, Agnes, the young man before you is one of the luckiest guys you'll ever meet. It turns out that Smitty's daughter Brittany is sweet on him, and the two of them are soon to be married. Not long ago he figured out what we do here and after a bit of persuasion decided that being part of our 'little boys club'..." he said with emphasis, "...would be the best thing he could do for the department."

The prospect of future nuptials sparked a pleasant gleam in Agnes's eye.

"A wedding, how wonderful."

The smile disappeared from her face as she added, "Smitty as a father-in-law... you unlucky schmuck."

Agnes did a small U-turn with her squeaky wheel behind her.

"I'll check with you later, Sarge."

She looked at Jake, smoke billowing from her mouth as she spoke.

"We got a guy in the Chief's Office... nice touch," she told the Sarge, who acknowledged the compliment with a nod of his head.

"When you're done talkin' to the Sarge here, stop by my desk," Agnes added. "Got a favor to ask."

Jake smiled. "Sure thing."

Her only response was a wave of her hand holding the cigarette as she shuffled out the door. As it closed, Jake's eyes were wide as he looked toward the Sarge for an explanation.

"Toughest broad you'll ever meet."

Looking confused, Jake asked, "Broad?"

"Your generation doesn't use that term now, but when we were young that was a term for a woman." Sarge pointed to the door and said, "When a woman like that came around, she was referred to as 'one tough broad'—the kind of woman you just didn't mess with. She was on the force when female cops were considered uniformed secretaries, and she would have none of it. More than once she dumped coffee onto the laps of coppers who made the mistake of telling her to grab them a cup, and not once did a cop ever make that mistake again."

Jakes hands went up as if in surrendered. "If you say so, Sarge, that's good enough for me. Anyway, there's not much to report right now. I've only got some strange reports about gang thugs slipping into the Old Market, causing all kinds of problems, and getting away. The Gang Unit is having fits over this bunch. I'll try to find out more for you, and maybe some Ol' Blues downtown could help nab these turds."

Suddenly Sarge's eyes were drawn to the television in a corner of his office. He turned up the volume as a serious-looking reporter was streamed live to the anchor newscasters at the TV station.

"*Breaking news: A body was found about five miles northwest of Omaha in a wooded area.*"

This announcement drew the attention of Jake and the Sarge.

"*The County Sheriff's office was called to this remote location by hunters who discovered the body. At this point in the investigation, the Sheriff's Department is not giving a statement but has promised to do so as the investigation unfolds.*"

The Sarge looked at Jake, "Any missing persons of note?"

Jake shook his head. "Not that I can think of. That area is remote, with nothing but old farms. Ten to one, that body was dumped. When I get back to Headquarters I'll try to find out a little more."

Jake stood, shook the Sarge's hand, and said, "Don't tell Brittany about me meeting up with Agnes. Might make her jealous." Then Jake winked.

"I won't, but don't expect me to keep your secret for long," the Sarge said with a smile. "Agnes probably wants you to check in on the girls who were taken at that drug house. One of them is her granddaughter."

Jake snapped his fingers. "Oh, yeah, but that was no drug house, Sarge. Turns out there was an international aspect to what was going on there, but it wasn't drugs, it was actually the girls."

The Sarge's eyebrows scrunched down as he said, "I don't follow you. What do you mean, *the girls?*"

Jake reached into his pocket pulled out a small note pad.

"This was a safe house, not a drug house. The girls were being drugged up on heroin until they were junkies, then dragged into the sex trade. Somehow they were stowed away and taken to some country..."

Jake thumbed through his notes, muttering, "What country was it?"

The Sarge took his cigar out of his mouth, leaned forward with his forearms on his desk, and almost growled, "Armenia. Our computer guy downstairs thinks he's traced a connection with these girls who are runaways from our own Department of Health and Human Services in Nebraska to some Armenians."

"Ah..." Jake muttered. "Were you going to share this information with the rest of us?"

"Of course, Jake, as soon as we had enough intel. I think this is enough to put together a task force. What are you doing about 2:00 tomorrow morning?"

Jake cocked his head back, confused.

Sarge explained, "That's when we have meetings for big investigations, develop a plan of action, and execute it. The midnight nurses like it quiet, and they think we're all in our beds sleeping. It's perfect. A lot of us take naps during the day, so it's not like we're missing sleep. I'll put together a task force and contact you with the details in about two hours."

As the Sarge checked the time, Jake noticed that he wore his watch on his left wrist so that the clock face was on the underside, next to the palm of his hand. His grandfather did the same thing because back in the day, the watch faces were made of glass that broke easily if bumped.

"Holy crap!" the Sarge almost yelled. "You get out there with Agnes. I've got to go; it's time for my bath. Nurse Betsy will come in here and drag me in if I don't show up on time."

Jake just shook his head. "Yeah, fine, Sarge, I'll wait for your call."

゜

"What can I do for you, Officer Crantz?" Jake asked as the Sarge's door closed behind him.

The Lead Officer didn't look up at Jake, just pulled the cigarette from her mouth and gestured toward a chair in front of her desk. "Park your vertical smile right there, Junior."

Jake snickered at the reference to his backside as he settled into the chair. He couldn't overcome his amazement at how the smoke curled through Agnes's purple hair and wafted into the air.

"Thanks for calling the cavalry for my Amanda," Agnes said.

"No problem. Turns out it was not a drug house," Jake replied.

Agnes's painted eyebrows lifted at that bit of information. Jake could tell she wanted to know what was going on.

"Your granddaughter almost got sucked into an international human trafficking ring. A day or two more and she would have been gone. Looks like they were on the way to possibly Armenia."

Agnes sat back at the realization that her granddaughter had come very close to a life of absolute hell where she probably would never have been heard from again.

"Armenia—that word has been tossed around a lot lately." Agnes's voice got low and started to fade as she growled, "Dirty commie pinkos."

Jake was a little confused by the "commie" reference but impressed by the determined look in the eyes of the woman in front of him. He now understood what the Sarge had said about this woman.

"*She is a tough broad,*" Jake thought to himself. Then he said, "The Sarge is setting up a task force tonight to—"

"Payback!" Agnes announced. "Those Armenian pricks tried to take my Amanda. It's payback."

Jake could tell that Agnes was deep in thought about what could have happened to her granddaughter. He said, "I'll see you tonight at the task force meeting."

Still gazing at nothing in particular, Agnes dismissed Jake with a wave of her hand. Her cigarette left a trail in the air.

ↁ

Sergeant Scott was determined to catch the bangers who were causing problems in the Old Market.

"Need I remind you, guys, there's been three robberies, five assaults, numerous fights, and two instances of shots being fired into the air. This sent hundreds of people running for safety and caused all kinds of trouble for the businesses down here," Sergeant Scott told the Gang Unit as they prepared to hit the streets again looking for this phantom gang. "Looks like the shots into the air were to help them make their escape by causing panic, which gave them cover to disappear… again."

Detective Turley added, "We're pretty sure they've made about five of us during the last few run-ins, so we won't have to worry about snooping around so as not to be seen."

Sergeant Scott pointed to an overhead map of the Old Market. "We've got a pair of cruisers at every corner that leads to the Market. We have a pretty good idea what these guys look like, so this should deter them from getting into the area. If we can't catch 'em, we'll keep them from getting in. Any questions?"

Nothing was said.

"Move out."

ↁ

"There's coppers all over the Market, Sarge," Tony Chelini reported into his earpiece communicator.

As Pauli and Tony Chelini walked around the Old Market, they could see a police cruiser parked at each corner that led to the Market. They were easily able to spot the undercover cops scattered about. "I'd say there are at least ten guys undercover," Pauli noted.

The Sarge listened to the intel coming from the Chelini brothers and replied, "Sheesh, there's no way those punks are getting away from that many officers. As a matter of fact, I don't see how they can even get into the Market with a cop at every corner."

"Sarge," Tony Chelini said, "It's about closing time. We're pretty sure this is a waste of our efforts. When the punks see all the cops..."

They were cut short by the sound of shattering glass as a brick was hurled through a large café window. The noise directed everybody's attention to the far east side of the Market area. A crowd moved en masse toward the sound of the aftermath as chunks of glass still clinging to the top of the window frame fell to the ground. Even the undercover cops, who had been working the area for hours, jumped and ran to the eastern part of the Market.

"Jeez, Sarge, someone just broke one of those huge storefront windows. It's on the east side, close to 10th Street. We're heading over there now," Pauli said.

The Sarge could hear the commotion of numerous people in the background. Agnes had entered the Sarge's office as the Chelini brothers were reporting in. The Sarge pointed to a chair, and she shuffled slowly, followed by her squeaky oxygen tank holder. She honed into the voices on the radio as she sat.

"What kind of idiot would break one of those big windows? Must be a drunk; it's about time for the shops to close up for the night," the Sarge wondered out loud.

Agnes's eyes squinted in thought as she took a drag from her cigarette and then spoke with a matter-of-fact tone.

"Closing time, huh? Good time to hit the bagman with the night's sales money."

The Sarge's eyes widened as he realized what Agnes was suspecting. Then he sat up and yelled into his microphone, "Don't go toward the commotion. I want you two to head west, away from crowd."

The Chelini brothers both keyed the microphones on their earpieces.

"What are you talking about, Sarge?" Pauli asked.

The Sarge and Agnes yelled in unison, "Distraction!"

A simultaneous roar belched from Sergeant Scott's radio, stopping all the undercover cops dead in their tracks. Sergeant

Scott yelled again into the microphone, "It's a distraction! Stop what you're doing and..."

The alarm tone on all the police radios screamed into the officers' ears, and the Sarge could hear the tone from his police scanner. "*Robbery, party down behind Amber's Waggly Tongue Bar in the alley area of 12th and Farnam.*"

Officer Turley clenched his fists. "We've been had. It was a set-up. That bar is two blocks away. By the time we get there... Nuts, they had us. Sergeant Scott, they set us up good."

As Turley had feared, by the time the winded officers arrived, bar owner Amber Hunter was being attended to by medics. She had a nasty gash on her forehead.

Amber looked at the officers and said, "All of it... they got my night's earnings, almost five thousand. We had a huge crowd tonight. The guy must have been watching for me as I took the night's take in the bank bag. I went through the kitchen area to the office safe. He was on me before the door swung closed. He hit me with something metal across my face as I looked back at him. I tried to hold onto the bag, but he just dragged me out the back door. There was another guy outside and the two of them ripped the bag from my hands and ran. It happened so fast that I couldn't get a good look at their faces."

She pointed towards some old, undeveloped buildings. "That way—they ran that way."

Turley whispered to another officer, "About fifteen minutes ago, long gone, but let's head that way anyhow. Maybe they dropped something."

⌘

"Woman wouldn't let go. Pistol-whipped her face and dragged her; she wouldn't let go," one of the robbers said to the other as they ran toward a group of undeveloped warehouses.

"Don't matter, we got it. Now, where's that kid?" the other asked, referring to the young wannabe gangster who had thrown a brick through a window to lure the cops away from the planned robbery. "He should have caught up with us by now."

Pauli and Tony Chelini were about fifty yards behind the two fleeing robbers.

"There they go," Pauli transmitted. "Just like you said, Sarge, that broken window was a set-up. We can see the two hoods running towards some old buildings off Twelfth and Jackson. Don't know why they'd run that way unless there's a car hidden for their getaway. No way we can catch 'em."

Over the Chelini brothers' ear microphones came the unmistakable sound of Sarge's voice.

"Eyeball 'em as best you can. They may have the other member of their little band heading your way. From the chatter on the radio scanner, they didn't catch the one that broke the window."

"There!" Tony said, hitting Pauli on the arm. "That young kid running at us." Sure enough, Tony spotted a young boy with a huge smile running in the same direction as the two robbers. The Chelini brothers were standing in the shadows shielded from the streetlight just a few yards away. After decades of surveillance, staying hidden was natural for them.

"Nobody catching me!" the boy thought as he congratulated himself for slipping away from all those cops. He peered at the buildings where he was supposed to meet the other guys and smiled again. *"There it is. All I gotta..."*

KA-BITH!! Something slapped and burst all over the boy's chest. The wind was knocked out of him, and fluid was all over his chest and throat. The boy stopped cold and fell to his hands and knees gasping for air. This is when he realized that his eyes were burning and a horrible stench of foul urine was all over him. It was thick and hot; the smell was so bad that he started gagging. Desperately trying to inhale after getting the wind knocked out of him made it worse. His body started to spasm for lack of air, but when he tried to breathe, he got a lungful of that awful, putrid stench. His stomach lurched to puke.

"You're too young to be with the likes of those hoods, young fella."

The boy looked up to see an old man standing alone in the middle of the street with his hands on his hips.

"They'll just use you until you get caught, then find another young kid to do their dirty work. Don't you see that?"

"We're Demons," the young lad spat as he almost choked out the words. "We won't get caught; we fade into the night." Then he threw up. "What is this SHI…"

"SHUT UP!" Tony Chelini cut the kid off in mid-curse. "Look how easy it was for me to catch you. You're no good at this, kid. Stop now; just go home."

The boy's eyes burned with rage as he ripped his splattered shirt off and threw it at Tony. "Demons, we Demons!" he yelled.

"So are we, punk."

Tony pointed to the shadows where Pauli was standing. Pauli moved his face forward just enough for his nose to appear out of the darkness. Then he flapped his false teeth halfway out of his mouth. The streetlight lit up his teeth, and then he gummed down on them. Tony had to admit it was a scary sight. Pauli's nose and teeth looked as if they were appearing out of a dark cave. Then Pauli widened his eyes and jerked his face forward. The face made the kid scream and step back. Pauli then sucked his teeth back into his mouth with a loud *clack* as he bit down to put them into place.

"We're the original Demons, kid. We've seen hundreds of boys just like you. Stop now or we'll come after you." The boy's eyes widened and he let slip part of a question: "You know about the…?" Then he stopped talking as if he had said too much. The boy turned and ran… away from the warehouses.

"Don't forget us, kid… Original Demons!"

Tony turned to Pauli, who was now out of the shadows completely.

"That was the scariest face I've ever seen. Where did you think of that?"

Pauli shrugged. "I saw an old Mexican death mask at the Day of the Dead Festival when we worked South Omaha. It gave me the shakes, so I thought it might do the same to that kid. Pretty good, huh?" Pauli smiled.

"Absotively brilliant," Tony agreed. "Hopefully the kid's pants are covered with piss, too."

Tony and Pauli simultaneously turned at the sound of two men walking. As they watched them approach, Tony commented, "The way they're walking and looking around, they gotta be coppers trailing the hoods that ran to the warehouse."

The Ol' Blues faded into the shadows as they watched and listened to the gang officers.

Detective Turley pointed toward the undeveloped buildings.

"Right towards the warehouses again. How many times have we chased them to that row of undeveloped buildings over the past few weeks? Can't figure it out. They just disappear. Jeez! Do you smell that?"

The pungent odor of the piss pack that Tony had pelted the kid with seemed to seethe throughout the alley.

"This is worse than the sewer water treatment beat," the newbie agreed. "Let's get outta here."

Pauli whispered to Tony, "How long has that piss pack been stored? It really is ripe."

Tony shrugged. "Filled my urine bag a couple of weeks back. We haven't been out on an assignment for a while. Let's get back to the Precinct. The Sarge will want a briefing. There is something strange about those old buildings; these coppers are having all kinds of problems with them. Did you hear what that kid said about us knowing about something? Then it looked like he caught himself mid-sentence."

"Do we have anyone that used to work the old Warehouse District at the Precinct?" Pauli looked at the string of warehouses, rubbing his chin in thought. "Logan... Detective Jack Logan."

Tony almost dismissed his brother's statement. "He's in his upper nineties, the nursing wing, and from what everyone says could die any day. Old Jack Logan was a good cop, but he doesn't have the strength to do nothin' much anymore. The Sarge will want to hear about everything that happened tonight. Call for the van to come get us."

The Sarge and Agnes listened to the report from the Chelini brothers, who were at a loss to understand how the hoods had seemingly vanished.

Pauli added, "Jack Logan worked that area for years, back in the fifties. He might know something about the area."

The Sarge leaned forward and said, "Detective Logan… he's about at the end of his shift, isn't he?"

Agnes gave the Sarge a questioning look.

"Here, that means he's about to die."

Agnes's eyebrows lifted in recognition as Sarge explained the Precinct jargon. She moved her oxygen tube with her thumb, simultaneously taking a drag from the cigarette clasped between the index and editorial fingers of her left hand.

Pauli pointed in the direction of the nursing wing and said, "That guy worked that warehouse area longer than anyone I've ever known. If there's something worth knowing about, Logan would know it."

At the rear of the Precinct were the doors that led to the various living areas of the Old Blues Retirement Home. On the other side of the doors, one hallway led to the private living quarters for those Blues who could take care of themselves with minimal assistance from the nursing staff. Another hallway led to the assisted living area, and a third hallway led to the nursing wing where the officers who were near "end of shift" were cared for.

A number of student nurses were working in the nursing wing this evening. A training nurse explained the procedures in this area. She also discussed the challenges of working with this particular bunch of special patients.

"You see, this facility is like no other in the world. You've seen 'The Precinct,' which looks like a police office of the 1950s because it's supposed to help the patients…" She stopped abruptly as she noticed a silver-haired Ol' Blue walking directly into a treatment room of one of the patients. He had three stripes on his shoulders and seemed to act as if he had every right to walk right into the patient's room.

"Sir, you can't just walk into a patient's room in this ward," the training nurse said.

All of the students turned to see the Ol' Blue answer without looking at the nurse.

"He's one of my men, and I need to see him about a case. I won't be long."

The students' heads moved in unison as they turned back to look at their teacher.

"This is what I mean," she explained. "No other facility has a bunch of old cops that still think they're on the job."

The students looked at each other in disbelief.

"Sir, stop right now or I'll…"

The nurse was stopped cold by an old-school power point. The Sarge's left hand was extended and he was pointing right at the training nurse's face.

"Watch it, sister, this is police business," the Sarge said. "If you interfere, I'll clamp on the silver bracelets and you can spend the weekend in the can."

The training nurse's mouth dropped open and she was about to stop the Sarge when a squeaking sound at the entryway was heard and a raspy voice said, "He means it, sister. If the Sarge needs to talk to one of his officers, I suggest you stay out of his way."

The training nurse's neck was now red with anger at the prospect of looking weak in front of the students.

"Just a minute—this is my ward, and I will not…"

The sound of a lighter flicking to life with the flame set on high interrupted the training nurse's protest. She looked at the old female standing in the doorway with a police hat covering curly purple hair. The woman's oxygen nasal cannula pulled up to her forehead, and a six-inch flame burst to life in front of the police shirt she was wearing.

Agnes purposely moved the flame closer to her cigarette as she spoke. The cigarette bounced around as her lips moved, and she moved the flame around as if trying to catch the end of it.

"You can't smoke in here!" the training nurse yelled.

The nurses could hear the sound of a lighter cap being snapped shut after the cigarette burst into the glowing red signal that Agnes was inhaling her smoke.

"Really, sweetie, why don't you and your candy stripers come take it from me?"

Incensed, the training nurse forgot about the Sarge and marched directly toward the skinny female officer standing in the doorway.

"There's oxygen in use throughout this area," the nurse announced.

"What do you think is in my tube here, Miss Nightingale? I haven't had to pluck my eyebrows in years."

The nurse started lecturing Agnes about how dangerous it was for her to have flames around oxygen. Agnes laughed and sparked her lighter, which shot a stream of flame in front of Agnes's face. With her other hand Agnes pulled her nasal cannula out of her nose, and there was a small explosion blowing towards the nurse's face.

The Sarge smiled in appreciation, realizing that Agnes had distracted the nurse to buy him some time to slip into Jack Logan's room.

After entering the room, the Sarge pulled the door shut to silence the noise in the reception area of the nursing wing. Detective Jack Logan was motionless in the bed. Wires were connected to his chest, his eyes were partially closed, and the slow beep of his heart monitor changed ever so slightly with each of Logan's breaths.

The Sarge knew time was short for Logan because he looked so weak and tired. Logan didn't look like he had the strength to talk. There was only one thing that the Sarge could say that would possibly get a response from Logan.

"Detective Logan."

The sound of the title he had earned and loved for over thirty years caused Logan to stir and open his eyes. The beep on the monitor quickened.

"Detective Logan, this is Sergeant Martinez. I need your help with a case we're working."

Detective Logan took a deep breath, looked at the Sarge, and smiled weakly.

"H-hey, S-sarge," he whispered, and then he motioned with his hand for the Sarge to continue.

The Sarge briefed Logan on the warehouse situation and the hoods that kept eluding the cops. Logan pointed his finger as if he understood and struggled to speak. The Sarge leaned over to put his ear closer to Logan's mouth.

"Boot," Logan breathed out with difficulty, then tried to speak again.

"What are you doing to my patient? You'll have to leave now."

The Sarge knew from the tone of the nurse's voice that he would have to leave. He figured there wasn't much use trying to talk to Detective Logan. The poor guy just didn't have enough strength to speak.

As he straightened, the Sarge felt a light touch of Logan grabbing his hand. The Sarge looked down at Logan, who forced out the word, "Leggers." Then Logan's hand dropped to his chest. The beeping of the monitor had doubled its cadence and the nurse stood at the door pointing to the ward's exit.

The Sarge started to walk away from Detective Logan. He didn't realize that Detective Logan was desperately reaching for the Sarge's arm but unable to grasp it.

As the Sarge walked past Agnes, he noticed that her left eyebrow was gone. He decided not to say anything and just walk away clean.

He walked out of the ward. Upon meeting up with Agnes, whose cigarette had been snapped in two by the irate nurse, the Sarge told her, "Didn't say much, just two words: Boot and Leggers."

Agnes shrugged. "Worth a try. That poor Ol' Blue still thinks he's chasing old-time mobsters."

ᕲᕲ

Brittany and her soon-to-be-husband Jake Mitchell were enjoying their weekly dinner together. Being on call whenever something big happened in Omaha kept Jake attached to his office cell phone most of the time. Tonight Jake's lieutenant had agreed to take his calls so Jake could spend some precious time with the redhead who was able to fill the void left in his heart from the death of his wife and daughter in a horrible canyon crash a few years earlier. Having time off from phone duty also meant that he could attend some special task force meetings with the Ol' Blues.

Jake loved just looking at Brittany when he didn't think she was aware of it. Brittany loved the way he looked at her when she pretended not to know he was doing just that.

"Have you even looked at the menu yet, Jake?" she said without glancing up from her own menu.

A startled "Oh" escaped Jake's mouth. "Umm, yeah, I'll have a burger."

Brittany gave a small snicker and pointed to Jake's menu. "Quit looking at the main course of your life." She held up her ring finger with a beautiful engagement ring. "I don't think a burger is an option at the House of Quang's." She gave Jake a knowing smile, then reached over and took the menu from his hand. She turned to the waiter that Jake hadn't noticed was next to their table and said, "We'll take the #3 dinner for two."

Embarrassed, Jake had just been blindsided in three ways: (1) being a cop and not seeing that the waiter had walked up to their table, and (2) realizing that Brittany was aware of the loving gaze he thought he'd stolen without her knowledge, and (3) for ordering a stupid burger in a Chinese restaurant.

Jake rested his elbows on the table and covered his face with his hands, moaning, "Look what you've done to me, Britz. When I'm around you, nothing between my ears works."

She smiled and murmured, "Don't worry, I'll cover for you as long as I know your heart belongs to me. I'll also cover for the brain clog you seem to get when you are staring at me. By the way, I like the way you stare."

Jake took her hand, smiled, and said, "I'm a lucky guy."

"You better believe it." She fluttered her eyes. "You get me and my twenty uncles who are sneaking all over town throwing their piss packs at unsuspecting thugs."

Jake laughed and then looked at his watch. "Oh, that reminds me, I'm supposed to go to some sort of task force meeting tonight."

Brittany perked up. "Oh, Jake, get ready for the weirdest meeting of your life."

Jake's face displayed his confusion.

Brittany explained, "I went to one of those zero two hundred hours meetings a few months ago. Remember the night you came over for dinner and a movie and I had to leave? I told you my dad needed his medicine?"

Jake frowned and said, "You left me alone in your apartment with the dishes. How could I forget?"

Brittany smiled and quickly added, "That was so sweet of you to do the dishes. Next time make sure the dishwasher is full before you start it."

Jake rolled his eyes.

Brittany continued, "I was almost late; my dad would have been furious if I wasn't ready to go when the meeting started. Those geezers take that stuff seriously."

Brittany looked around to make sure no one else could hear, then leaned forward and attempted to whisper. However, her excitement was hard to suppress and anyone who was eavesdropping could have heard her without much effort.

"First, they have you meet them in the maintenance garage at the back of eastern part of the grounds."

"Yeah, that is weird," Jake agreed, "and I'm supposed to just wait there."

Brittany's eyes were wide as she listened to the instructions that the Sarge had given to Jake.

Her childlike excitement caused Jake to smile at the sight of Brittany anticipating his every word about this middle-of-the-night meeting.

"What are you so excited about?" he asked.

"Wait 'til the Blue turns the oil can—you'll freak! Then once you get to the secret meeting area, which is also below the Precinct, you won't believe what's in there. Surveillance screens for the entire Ol' Blue facility. Those guys will know when the nurses start nosing around, and they actually have some of their guys stationed at every hallway that leads to the conference room. If a nurse or doctor or other 'unauthorized personnel'," Brittany said, making air quotes with her finger, "walks too close, the guys have all sorts of signals they use to…" She counted on her fingers: "Identify a threat, determine the nature of the subject, and find out what their apparent intentions are." She tried to imitate her father.

Brittany's animation increased as she relived the experience in her mind and tried to put it into words.

"On the monitors I could see the Blue they call Speedy Benjamin in a hallway. Boss Nurse Betsy decided to make a surprise round. One of the sentinels sounded some sort of alarm, and the next thing I knew, Benjamin flipped off his hospital gown so he was completely naked except for his tennis shoes and a grin. He looked at one of the hidden cameras—I guess he knew the Blues in the conference room were watching—and gave a thumbs up. Then his naked wrinkly butt was shuffling down the hallway and he started yelling like he was in a foot chase with some crook.

"Boss Nurse saw him and started chasing him. She must have some sort of alarm, because within a few seconds about four student nurses fell in behind her."

Tears started to stream down Brittany's cheeks as she remembered the Blues at the table laughing and leaning from side to side like they were on a roller coaster ride, leaning to the left then to the right with each of Benjamin's turns.

Jake tried to suppress his urge to burst out laughing at the story and the sight of Brittany so engrossed in her account that she was crying and laughing at the same time.

"F-Finally Benjamin burst into the female staff's locker room and scared a poor young student intern who had just stepped out of the shower. I swear the sight must have scared a year of nursing school out of her. Benjamin stopped, Boss Nurse stopped by grabbing the door frame with both hands, and the student nurses bounced off her giant fanny and onto the floor in a tangle of legs, arms, and stethoscopes."

Brittany folded her arms on the table and put her forehead down as if exhausted from the story. "I was laughing so hard I had to cross my legs to keep from peeing."

"Do you want more food or some dessert?" a short, thin, and rather confused waiter tentatively asked. Brittany was startled out of her uproarious memory and sat straight up as if she had been caught by her dad sneaking out of the house.

Jake couldn't hold back his laughter any longer.

"I've had more than enough," he blurted, "and we'd like our check, please." His laughter was cut short as Brittany's napkin hit him in the face.

෴

Sunlight poured through the window, interrupting Amanda's slumber. She opened her eyes, looked around the room, and said, "Crap, I'm still alive."

Amanda and the other girls in the safe house had been sent to a residential drug rehab center. Throughout the last couple of days Amanda had listened to the tortured screams of the other girls as they suffered the agony of withdrawal from the drugs that Vladimir had put into their veins.

Amanda didn't really know what was causing all the screaming; she only knew that she wasn't sick like the other girls. She tried to remember what had happened over the last couple of days, but she could only recall strange, disconnected images.

The rehab center was nice enough. There were the usual bedrooms, cafeteria, and commons areas for recreation and group therapy. Amanda's room had French doors that opened up to beautiful grounds at the rear of the building. There was a large cement deck where she could stand and feel the warming rays of sunshine on her face. From the time she was a little girl, she had always enjoyed feeling the sun on her face.

The sunlight warmed her closed eyelids, and she took a deep breath of the morning air. She paused in mid breath, recognizing something familiar in the air she inhaled. She opened her eyes and sniffed like a dog sifting the air for a special scent. Amanda took a few short whiffs and knew that she had smelled something like that smell many times when she was young, but she could not remember exactly what it was.

From behind her a familiar, raspy voice said, "You always loved to stand outside and breathe the morning air as a child."

Amanda jumped at the realization that someone was behind her. She quickly turned and tried to focus on who was standing on the deck with her. The smile, the face, and the smell of the cigarette suddenly struck a chord in Amanda's mind.

"Nana?" she asked tentatively. "It's me, little Manda-Cakes," using the sweet nickname Agnes had given Amanda when she was young.

Amanda had been removed from her home after her mother had gotten mixed up with drug users. Any relationship she could have had with her policewoman Nana was nixed for years. In the years that followed, Amanda had bounced from foster home to youth facility to other foster homes so frequently that she rarely had contact with anyone in her biological family. After Amanda turned fifteen, her mother was no longer part of her life.

Standing about four feet away was a frail woman with purple hair and an oxygen tank with a hose running to her face. She was wearing some sort of police shirt with a hospital gown for pants.

Officer Crantz must have recognized that Amanda as trying to comprehend who was standing in front of her. She smiled and said, "Don't let the clothes fool ya; it's what we wear at the old folks' home where I live. You, young lady, have been a hard person to find." Agnes then bitterly muttered, "Stinking commie pinkos."

"How did you find me, Nana?"

Agnes smiled and said, "Hey, I'm an old cop; we have ways of finding things. I know you've been through a lot in the last few days. Let's go inside and talk."

Amanda didn't hesitate. The familiar sound of her Nana's voice was a comfort she hadn't felt in years, and she was immediately drawn to it. She walked to her Nana, who took her by the forearm and shuffled next to her as they entered the room.

"We have a lot to talk about, Manda-Cakes," Agnes said.

5

CHAPTER

"What! Are you out of your mind? How on earth will that ever work?" the Sarge blurted to Agnes. "You're telling me that you want to have that young lady move in with you?"

Agnes tried to give the Sarge a stern look as she countered, "It's my apartment. Why can't I have my grandchild live with me, at least 'til she can get out on her own?"

"With all we have here?" The Sarge started pointing in different directions from his office. "All of this, the officers, the work we do, the lives we save? You want me to just act like that doesn't matter and take care of a young girl who could jeopardize our entire operation by moving in with you?"

The debate continued for about thirty minutes. Agnes's arguments and periodic coughing fits eventually subsided as one reason after another was shot down by the Sarge. Finally she stopped arguing and quietly uttered, "I'm all she's got, Sarge."

Something in Agnes's tone caused the Sarge to calm himself and slowly sit down in his chair.

"Her mother never let me see her, she grew up in terrible circumstances, and, she… had… nobody," Agnes added.

The Sarge looked at Agnes, and his mouth dropped open as he noticed a tear slowly forming at the corner of her eye. Agnes leaned forward, placed an elbow on the Sarge's desk, and let her forehead fall onto the palm of her hand. Her cigarette came dangerously close to the curls of her purple hair. The pressure to her cheek caused the forming tear to drop onto the Sarge's desk, reinforcing Agnes's silent, desperate plea to care for her granddaughter.

The Sarge had known Agnes for decades and had never seen her cry. He was helpless to reject the quiet dignity with which Agnes pleaded for her grandchild.

Finally he exhaled loudly, leaned forward, and rested his forearms on his desk.

"Does the kid like applesauce? It's served every night. You know the nurses expect us to eat all our dinner."

As Agnes's eyes opened in surprise, she realized she was staring down her elbow at the Sarge's desk. She sat up and quickly wiped the tear's trail from her cheek. She squinted and took a long drag from her smoke, then replied, "She'll learn to love it."

The Sarge pointed to Agnes and sternly announced, "She's your responsibility, Agnes. Keep her busy up here in the Precinct. There's always dozens of things going on."

Smiling slowly, the Sarge added, "If you ask nicely, I'm sure some of the Blues will help you."

This suggestion drew a scowl from Agnes. Then, as if resigning herself to the reality of her situation, she blew smoke into the air and simultaneously growled, "We'll see."

⁊

Vladimir winced as he climbed into the van. Then he looked at Victor and smiled through the pain of his burned shoulder and neck.

"My lawyer told me that he did a lot of work for people who are in the country illegally," Vladimir remarked. "He said he knew a judge who doesn't like the ICE agency. So I was able to get the bail and leave without them being contacted. If they had been told, I never would have gotten out."

"You have the devil's luck, cousin," Victor said as he shook his head. "Let's get out of here before someone tells ICE that the judge gave you bail."

After Vladimir closed the door, the van pulled away from the Douglas County Jail.

Lois hung up the phone and sat back in her chair. "Unbelievable!"

She looked down at her desk, amazed by her good fortune. She had listened quietly as Victor told her how Vladimir had appeared before a judge who didn't like the way the country deported people, so the judge simply didn't cooperate with the federal authorities.

Now she had both Victor and Vladimir back and was in the process of gathering all of the evidence that could be used against her—all of her personal files, records, letters, and lists of girls who had disappeared. Everything was going as smoothly as she had planned. Everything that was incriminating at her apartment and office had been destroyed.

She glanced around her office and then froze when she looked at her computer. The one thing she could not control was the information that had been acquired by her brother Aziz in Armenia. He had monitored her computer and undoubtedly downloaded all of the information for his own records. Once the Cartel figured out that something had gone terribly wrong with their biggest haul of young girls, swift punishment would be administered to her, Vladimir, and Victor.

Lois leaned forward and stared at her computer. With all that had been going on, she had failed to analyze what had gone wrong with her operation.

"*How did the police discover the safe house? Someone had downloaded information from my computer. An old cop just popped into my office followed by one of the nurses. Then I was ordered to provide any assistance I can to those old officers. Just, how do they say in English, 'Out of the blue.'*"

Lois looked toward the door where the old man and his K-9 stuffed dog had stood. Then she inadvertently spoke out loud.

"The download of information, cops at the safe house, the cops arrest Vladimir, a cop at my office with that hideous dog."

As Lois realized what had happened to her operation, her fists clenched. She decided then and there that before she left this facility, she was going to get revenge. The only person, the only piece of this puzzle that led to the discovery and downfall of her scheme… was Dr. Baggaley.

&

Every nursing home or assisted living center has patients who seem to just sit in hallways all day. Unresponsive to what is going on around them, they seem to be waiting to die. The nurses and staff get used to these patients.

Officer Tucker Preston was one of those patients. All day, every day he sat in his wheelchair, staring into space without really looking at anything.

The nurses kept an eye on him and moved him from one nursing station to another just to give him a change of scenery each day. Before Brittany became an honorary Ol' Blue, she brought cookies to the Blues and always made a point of offering one to Officer Preston. She tried to make eye contact with him, hoping to find some spark of life. Tucker Preston always seemed to be looking past her, not at her. Brittany remembered a time when he did seem to look her in the eye for a few moments. Hoping that she had connected with him on some level, she left an oatmeal raisin cookie in the palm of his hand before moving on.

Today Brittany walked past the nursing station and saw Officer Preston sitting and staring. "Hi, Tucker!" she said cheerfully, hoping for a response but not expecting one.

After walking into the Precinct and winking at the greeting officer, she stopped at Lead Officer Crantz's desk.

"Officer Crantz, I'm here to see Sarge," Brittany said with an almost official tone.

"I'll let him know you're here. Oh, by the way, this is my granddaughter Amanda," Agnes responded.

Brittany looked up to see the back of a young girl filing papers in a cabinet. The girl turned around slowly, looking bored out of her mind.

"Hey", she said with a wave of her hand.

"She'll be staying with me for a while," Agnes uttered and looked to Brittany as if to say, "*Please talk to her.*"

Brittany caught the vibe from Agnes. She pointed to Amanda and said, "You and I have something in common." Amanda gave her a questioning look. "Both of us have relatives who think they're still cops in this crazy little Precinct of theirs." This brought a slight snicker from Amanda, along with a smile.

"I've got some things to do with Sarge for now, but..." she pointed to Amanda, "you and me, we gotta stick together. Especially after what you've been through. I'll call you later."

Amanda's eyebrows raised in joyful surprise. Then Brittany added, "I've got to go for now, but we got business, sister—we're going shopping."

As Brittany gave a thumbs up, Amanda's smile widened. Brittany winked at Agnes, who smiled and winked back.

The Sarge was standing at his doorway and caught the last part of the conversation. Brittany walked past him as she entered his office.

"That's twice." The Sarge almost gasped in amazement at seeing Agnes smile.

"Agnes's granddaughter is a beautiful girl," Brittany said as she sat down in the Sarge's office.

Looking confused, the Sarge asked, "What did you say to her?"

"Oh, I told Amanda that we were going shopping later, and..."

"No!" The Sarge cut her off, "What did you say to make my Lead Officer smile?"

Brittany smirked shook her head and replied, "Sarge, I told Amanda we were going shopping."

The Sarge was still confused.

"Girl stuff, Sarge, something rather lacking in this little geezer crime squad of yours."

The Sarge shrugged, still not completely understanding. "Oh."

"Don't bother trying to figure it out, I'll take care of her. This is not exactly a place a young woman gets accustomed to overnight," Brittany said.

"Anyway," she added, "I've come over to see if we got any other information on this lady in the government office—the one whose computer Thane hacked and got the information on Amanda."

The Sarge nodded. "Yeah, because of Thane's work we found a flaw in our intelligence-gathering ability. We've got cameras, all sorts of gadgets down in the research lab. We can find out all kinds of intel all over the city. Problem was, we didn't think we'd need it in the government offices outside the Blues area. The education wing and Health and Human Services wing are our focus for improvement right now."

The Sarge leaned forward and pressed his intercom button. "Lead Officer Crantz, could you have Cadet Amanda wheel Officer Preston into my office, please."

"Right away, Sarge," came the reply.

Amanda heard the intercom and rolled her eyes at the sound of her title, "Cadet Amanda."

"I'll go get him," she sighed.

Brittany gave the Sarge a questioning look.

He explained, "We've always had some sort of intel gathering around the nursing stations. They do a lot of talking, and we learn a great deal about what's going on facility wide from their conversations among themselves."

Brittany sat back in her chair, crossed her arms, and asked, "Why on earth are you bringing him in here?"

The answer had to wait as Cadet Amanda knocked at the door.

"Enter!" the Sarge bellowed. Cadet Amanda wheeled Officer Preston into the Sarge's office and put him in front of the Sarge's desk. "Thank you, Cadet, that will be all." She rolled her eyes at Brittany, who smiled and mouthed the word "Salute," trying to discreetly put her hand to her brow. Amanda smiled and gave a crisp salute to the Sarge. When she turned to leave, she gave Brittany a mischievous smile as if the two of them had a private antic going on with these old cops.

"Send Lead Officer Crantz in please."

Again, Amanda smiled and replied, "Yes, sir!"

Agnes waddled into the Sarge's office. After the door was closed, she eased into her chair.

"What's up, Sarge?"

"I want us all to be on the same page with the latest intel regarding this Lois Luka," Sarge explained.

Officer Preston reported, "The nurses hate her, and she hates everyone, especially..."

"Whoa, hey!" Brittany jumped out of her chair. "He can talk!" she blurted, pointing to Officer Preston. Brittany continued, "I've been in and out of this place for months, and he has never uttered a word or looked at me when I tried to talk to him."

Agnes chimed in, "The best surveillance officer on the force, Officer Tucker Preston. The guy is a legend."

Brittany looked back at Sarge, still blinking quickly as her mind tried to wrap around the realization that the Ol' Blue that she thought was practically comatose was now talking.

To prove her point, Agnes added, "Remember the Napper Mortuary caper?"

"Oh yes," Sarge replied and pointed to the officer. "That man, Tucker Preston played dead in a mortuary for a week to catch a crook who was taking jewelry from the dead bodies. Nobody else has ever had surveillance skills like this guy."

Brittany glanced over at Officer Preston, who looked at her and said, "It was Napper's wife. You should have heard her scream when I grabbed her arm as she tried to take my watch."

Officer Preston imitated a woman's scream, then added, "She fainted and pissed all over herself." He chuckled, and Sarge and Agnes joined in the laughter.

Brittany sat down, shaking her head and thinking, "*These geezers did it to me again. Just how many tricks do they have?*"

"As I was saying," Officer Preston continued, "the nurses talk about this Lois and her absolute loathing for Dr. Baggaley."

Brittany chimed in, "Maybe that was why he told her to do whatever she could to be of service to us. I thought it was kinda strange. He must have heard how she yelled at Charlie and his dog Boomer."

The Sarge rubbed his chin. "That info may be handy. We don't have any surveillance set up in *Lois*'s area yet, but maybe we can change that… with her assistance."

The Sarge smiled as he picked up his phone and called the lab. "This is Sarge. I want you to get together some of your wonder boys. We need a surveillance tool put together."

"I'll be down in the lab. Thanks for stopping by, Brittany."

The Sarge stood and wheeled Officer Preston to the door. As they went by Brittany, Officer Preston put his hand on Brittany's arm and said, "I really like your oatmeal raisin cookies."

Brittany smiled and nodded. "Noted."

Then Officer Preston smiled, then stared straight ahead as his face appeared to go numb. He was once again wearing his "surveillance face" as the Sarge wheeled him back to the nurses' station.

"This place is still full of surprises," Brittany sighed.

Agnes nodded. "Tell me about it. I didn't know Tucker Preston liked oatmeal raisin cookies."

6✑

"So, what do ya need on this thing, Thanerboy?" the Sarge asked as if he was talking about equipment on a new car.

"Well, it will have to be able to transmit video and audio like the ball drums. It would be nice if I could remotely make it move and face different directions, in case I need to focus our attention on other areas in and around Lois's office and the surrounding wing of the building. That's about it. Are you sure this is gonna work, Sarge? I mean, look at this thing."

The elevator chime sounded. Sarge looked over and told Thane, "That should be the gizmo guys in the white research coats." Sarge and Thane watched as the doors opened to reveal an Ol' Blue. His police hat was too big for his little head, covering the upper half of his ears. Even his police shirt looked two to three sizes too large. In his trembling hands he held what looked like a couple of oversized test tubes.

The Sarge smiled and said, "Hi ya, Shakey." The man looked toward the sound of the person calling his name.

"Oh! How ya doin', Sarge" The man didn't move.

"I was expecting a couple of research and development guys," the Sarge remarked.

Shakey got a sour look on his face. "Those white-coated wimps are back there." He motioned with his head. Sarge looked past Shakey and saw two men forcing themselves against the farthest corner of the elevator. They were clearly terrified. Their eyes were wide open and sweat was dripping from their faces. Shakey shuffled to the left, looked back at the pair, and said, "Scram." Both bolted from the elevator and ran toward the Sarge.

"He's crazy!" shrieked Karew, a brilliant audiovisual engineer from India. He was a thin, humble man with dark hair who spoke with a delightful Indian accent. Abinya, a Nigerian computer/robotics specialist, was equally gifted. He was a small man with an absolute love of making things work with technology. Abinya was a tinkering genius.

"That man is going to kill us all" Abinya said, pointing to Shakey. Sarge looked over at the elevator. Shakey's hands, per his nickname, were quivering uncontrollably. The fluids in the test tubes were violently bubbling.

"Ya little babies, you have to mix the two substances for it to explode. Sheesh!" Shakey looked at the Sarge and said, I'll be down later to take a look at your little project."

"Sure thing, Shakey," Sarge said with a wave. The elevator doors closed, but not before Shakey had glared in disdain at the two terrified scientists.

Thane looked quizzically at Sarge, who motioned with his thumb toward the elevator. "Officer Mel Emery was the best bomb tech we ever had. Served in Korea, Vietnam, and did some covert work for the CIA. We're lucky to have him. As the years came and went, his hands shook so bad the brass had to let him go. Here at the Precinct I hired him and gave him the nickname Shakey."

Thane didn't understand old-school reasoning. "Why would you make fun of his disability? I mean, the man's hands were his livelihood. Don't you think you're hurting his feelings?"

The Sarge smiled and gave Thane a pat on the back. "Men like us give a nickname to other fellas which may relate to something like Shakey's hands. It means we know what's going on with him and we want him anyway. It makes a man feel accepted. It also means you're in; you're one of us."

Thane thought he understood, but it would take time for him to get used to the seemingly derogatory nicknames used by the Ol' Blues.

A strained Indian voice yelled, "Are you out of your mind? That lunatic comes down here wanting to see what new adaptations we are working on for the Blues upstairs. He always wants to expand the blast radius of weapons that aren't even supposed to explode."

The Sarge calmed the two men by changing the subject. "Here's the problem. We need to place a device in the State offices that has audio and visual capabilities and can be mobile if needed. The cameras need to be able to adjust to different conditions, such as different lighting or environments, in case it gets moved around. It also must transmit the information to Thane here. Do you two think you can manage it?"

Karew's eyes widened as he said, "This is going to be very challenging."

Abinya smiled and then blurted, "I love it. Let's get started."

❦

Victor, Vladimir, and Lois were in the final stages of erasing all evidence of their trafficking operation.

"Make sure there is nothing left to connect us to the girls," Victor said with beads of sweat forming on his forehead.

Lois glared at him. "Don't you think I know that, fool? I've been preparing for this day for over a year. I know what needs to be done. But since the FBI got involved, we must be very careful. Any of the girls' records after they ran away must be destroyed. Nothing can connect their disappearance to us. The last thing the Southern Cartels will want is for us to show up being tailed by the FBI. I've also been ignoring calls from Aziz. I'm sure the Armenian Cartel must be suspicious by now."

There was a knock at the door.

"Excuse me, Ms. Lois."

The voice shattered the intense conversation. All three Armenians jumped and looked at Lois's office door. Lois recognized the large woman standing at her doorway as the Head Nurse from the police retirement home.

"What is that thing?" Victor spat, pointing at what was staring into Lois's office from behind the woman's legs.

"K-9 Officer Charlie had to go for medical treatment for a couple days," Boss Nurse Betsy explained. "He said that you were supposed to help us at the retirement home with whatever we needed."

Lois's back stiffened as she remembered the instructions and condescending look Dr. Baggaley had given her when he told her to provide any assistance those old goats needed.

"Officer Charlie specifically asked to have you look after his dog while he's gone," Nurse Betsy continued.

Lois looked at the big nurse and said, "You can't just..."

She was cut off.

"Bring in Boomer," the nurse said, ignoring Lois's objection. Boomer was pushed into the office by a young female staff member from the retirement home.

"That thing's hideous!" Victor blurted as Boomer was wheeled into the office. Lois, always the cool one, composed herself to avoid bringing any unnecessary attention to her office. She pointed to a couch where Vladimir was standing. "Put it over there and get out; I'm very busy." The young assistant to the big nurse wheeled Boomer to the area where Lois was pointing.

Vladimir's mouth dropped open as the assistant stopped pushing the large, deformed stuffed dog and stood staring back at him. The girl tilted her head as if trying to remember something familiar about Vladimir's face. The big man with his arm in a sling turned away from her and looked wide-eyed at Lois. Her attention was focused on the disgusting stuffed animal in her office.

"Nice tat," the girl said to Lois. "I've seen one of those wrist star tats before… somewhere," the young girl said as if trying to retrieve a distant memory. "Where was it?"

Victor and Vladimir quickly pulled their sleeves over the green star tattoos on their wrists.

The large nurse's voice broke the silence that followed as Lois, Vladimir, and Victor looked at each other and back at the young girl.

"We better go. I don't know why Officer Charlie likes you, but for whatever reason he only wanted you to have his dog… something about what Dr. Baggaley said about you."

Lois was jolted by the realization that the young woman had noticed the star tattoo on her wrist. She quickly dropped her hand to her side.

Standing in her office was the last girl who had been kidnapped and taken to the safe house—the girl who could connect all of them to her kidnapping and expose their entire operation… *Amanda.*

As the young woman turned to follow Boss Nurse out of the office, she placed her left hand on the doorframe and froze. With her right hand she rubbed her stomach; then she quickly turned her head for a final look at Vladimir. They locked eyes for only a second or two, but it seemed much longer.

"Gotta make my rounds," Boss Nurse said over her shoulder. "Come on, Cadet," she chided with a chuckle. This broke Amanda's gaze at one of the bald men in the room.

⤶

"Did you see that?" an excited Smitty almost yelled. He pointed to Thane's computer screen and started shaking his finger. Sarge, Agnes, and Thane all jumped at Smitty's outburst.

"Her wrist! Did you see her wrist? That's the same tattoo the guy had at the house me and Benson were watching."

Smitty slapped Thane on the back, "Son, those cameras are great. The pictures are so clear. Wait, get a shot of the two guys in the office."

⟡

The two men and Lois spoke in a language that the Sarge and the others didn't understand.

"*What is that girl doing here?*" Vladimir spat. "*Did you see her look at me? She must remember something.*"

Lois rubbed her chin. "*It must have been Dr. Baggaley. Somehow, he has figured out what we were doing. He must have been the one that hacked into my computer. Then with that information, he was able to somehow figure out what we were doing with the girls. Next, he called the FBI on us and they raided the safe house.*"

Victor chimed in, "*How could he have known about our plans?*"

Lois smiled and said, "*He must not know all the details. Otherwise he would have had the police all over us. He must have had the girl placed here to see our reaction. This Dr. Baggaley is a smooth one. I have underestimated him. From now on we will be much more careful.*"

"*That animal is disgusting. Why is it here?*" Victor said with a queasy look on his face. "*I've never seen such a distorted animal. Was it hit by a car or something?*"

Lois waved her hand in the air and stated, "*It fell into some chemicals during a police chase. The crazy old cop had it stuffed and walks around with it like it's alive. That pompous Dr. Baggaley told me to provide any service these old goats needed. Baggaley must like this old guy and his filthy dog. When we've finished mopping up our operation, I'll take care of that thing.*"

Vladimir winced and almost whispered, *"Its eyes... they seem to follow me."*

Lois spat, *"Oh, shut up, idiot. Grab that box of papers and load them into the van."*

⁊

"You can make the eyes move?" Smitty was almost giddy. "This is fantastic. The research guys put cameras in the dog's eyes, wow!"

Without looking away from his computer screen, Thane explained, "That's not all we can move. I can even point each eye in different directions."

Smitty looked at the two men. "Sarge, you're not going to believe this."

Sarge, Thane, and Agnes looked questioningly at Smitty.

"Those are the same two guys at the house we had the SWAT team raid. Didn't Amanda just say something about a tattoo?"

Thane immediately started to tap away on his keyboard. He brought up the video at the house Smitty and Benson had surveilled and got the screen shot of Victor in the window speaking on the phone. Thane zoomed in to the man's wrist as he held his phone to his ear. Then Thane got the video from the Boomer cam. He zoomed the video to Lois Luka's wrist, where Amanda had pointed out a tattoo. Thane pasted the photos next to each other and turned the screen so that the Ol' Blues could see.

Smitty smiled. "Well, now, matching tattoos on the wrist. Gotta be some sort of gang."

Thane tapped his monitor. "I'll bet it's an Armenian crime bunch."

Smitty added, "I'll also lay odds that the other bald guy with the sling has the same tattoo."

⁊

Jake Mitchell stretched out on his bed. "Do I have time for a nap?" he asked himself as he glanced over at his alarm clock. "Eleven. Well, that's two hours to snooze."

Before he realized it, his alarm was sending shockwaves down his spinal cord.

"Jeez, did I even sleep at all?" He reached over to silence the noise. "One in the morning. I can't believe I'm doing this." Jake forced himself out of bed, took a quick shower, and got dressed. "Okay, let's see what this middle-of-the-night meeting is all about."

Jake drove to the maintenance building located behind the large retirement home, parked his car, and walked into the large garage area. There were vehicles in various stages of repair, including one that was on a lift.

"You're almost late there, Junior."

Jake jumped at the sound and instinctively reached for his pistol.

"Easy there, young buck!" A Blue folded his newspaper and slowly stood.

Jake shook his head. "Dude! Don't jolt a guy like that."

The Ol' Blue shrugged and said, "Sorry, young fella. The Sarge said that I'm to escort you to the meeting. Been waiting here for about twenty minutes." The Blue stood and reached for an oil can on the shelf above his head. He turned it slightly to the left. This caused a hissing sound, and Jake expected the vehicle to lower on the lift. He did a double take when he realized that the vehicle on the hoist hadn't moved. The floor under the vehicle started to move up, and after about 15 seconds an elevator came to a stop at the bottom of the hoisted vehicle. Jake gave an incredulous gasp as the elevator doors opened. "Wow" came out of his mouth. Brittany had told him about this, but actually seeing the incredible hidden elevator was impressive.

"After you," the Blue said as the doors opened.

Jake stepped in, and as the doors closed, the Blue said, "There are Blues stationed at various windows and lookout points throughout the facility."

Jake snapped his fingers. "That's right; Brittany told me about that. She said that some of the Blues are stationed in the building in case a nurse or an unauthorized person wanders toward the conference area."

The doors opened; a golf cart was waiting. They climbed aboard, and as they drove through the tunnel leading to the conference area Jake's mouth was open in admiration as he realized, "*These geezers have thought of everything.*"

A few minutes later, the golf cart came to a stop. Jake was still rubber- necking to take in the details of the amazing tunnel.

"Ready to head up?" the Blue asked. Expecting some special hidden lever to expose a hidden entrance, Jake looked around.

The Blue sensed that Jake seemed to be glancing everywhere but the obvious. "Just push the button by the door, Junior."

Jake rolled his eyes. Right in front of him was a normal button next to the elevator doors. "Oh, yeah. Sorry."

Jake stepped out of the elevator and found himself standing in a very modern office-like area. He walked through a lounge and saw a video screen which read, "*Task force meeting conference room #1.*"

"Guess that's me."

From his right he heard, "You guessed right." The voice of the Sarge was unmistakable.

Jake's head snapped to his right; standing in the doorway was the Sarge. Behind him was a large door with #1 written on it. "We're ready to start, Jake. Come on in."

The modern-looking conference room was equipped with the usual large table with comfortable chairs surrounding it. On the wall opposite the doorway were three large surveillance monitors. Each monitor displayed six screens showing various parts of the facility. Jake remembered Brittany giving a description of this room, and he realized that she had not done it justice. Jake noticed that about half of the smaller screens showed Ol' Blues looking up and down the hallways. Each would look quickly at a hidden camera and give the *thumbs up*. This place was incredible.

The Sarge, the Chelini brothers, Smitty, Benson, Agnes, and Thane were all present. Sarge gazed at the screens, satisfied with the signals from the look-outs. Then he started the meeting.

"All right, now that everyone's here, let's review what we got. First, Amanda and those poor girls are safe. Jake, thanks for moving so fast with the SWAT teams. Their rapid response saved all those girls from a horrible fate." The members of *Taskforce Amanda* gave Jake an appreciative nod. Jake thought Agnes almost smiled.

"Second, we identified the suspect in Health and Human Services who seems to have been getting information from the State's computers about Amanda."

Thane chimed in, "Also on the other girls that were in the house. Turns out they were runaways from all over the state. This Lois Luka had all their information at her fingertips. I'm still researching her, but we know Lois has been working in social services for close to twenty years. She has been a supervisor for about four years. This placed her in a perfect position to identify these young girls. From the intel we gained from Smitty and Benson when they surveilled the safe house, we know that there's an Armenian Cartel connection."

Thane looked at the Sarge and added, "I've done some research and found that there are a bunch of these sex trafficking cartels throughout the ex-Soviet Bloc. Earlier today we did find a possible clue. When we placed Boomer Cam in Lois's office, we found out that she had a star tattoo on her wrist. Smitty spotted the same tattoo on one of those bald guys while watching him through a window at the safe house."

"I'll bet that other goon has the same tattoo," Smitty added. Thane displayed photos of Lois and one of the bald goons on the monitor. The green star tattoos were unmistakable.

"That's where we stand at this point in the investigation," the Sarge stated. "Thane is backtracking the information from Amanda's outer space watch." Thane rolled his eyes.

"Once we have established what happened to Amanda, we should have a clearer idea about this Armenian bunch."

Thane said, "We've translated what we could pick up at the house where the girls were rescued. The bald goons are Victor and Vladimir. They talked about the Armenian Cartel and Lois. Then they made reference to someone they called "*the Chemist*" and something about Sasha seeing him. They also made some statement about the same thing happening to them as what happened to Sasha if they failed to bring these girls to the Cartel."

"Looks like they failed," stated Tony Chelini.

His brother Pauli pointed to the pictures of Lois, Victor, and Vladimir. "If the Armenians are anything like the Italian mafia, they're gonna get whacked."

Agnes blew smoke into the air as she spoke. "If they know their toast, my guess is they are trying to clean up shop and skedaddle. To catch this bunch we're gonna need to know what they're planning. I say we keep Boomer recording everything they are doing. Maybe we'll get lucky."

Jake watched in awe as the old officers took intel and quickly developed a plan of action.

The Sarge got everybody's attention and told them, "We still need to know who this Chemist and Sasha are, but…"

An alarm sounded and a red light started to blink on the wall. All eyes looked at the light and then the surveillance monitors. Speedy Benjamin's face was looking back at them via the monitor. He had been alerted to some sort of threat to the meeting being discovered. Speedy had a rather confused look on his face as he pointed down a long hallway. He looked into the camera, gave an "*I don't know*" shrug, and took off toward the sound of some sort of disturbance.

Jake blurted, "What's going on?"

"Speedy is on to something." The Sarge keyed a button on his earpiece. "What ya got, Speedy?"

There was a short pause, and Speedy responded as he ran. "Not sure, Sarge. There is some kind of commotion down the hallway; some nurses are running back and forth. Looks like something big."

The taskforce watched in fascination as Speedy ran up behind four nurses heading toward the Specialized Care Unit. They didn't even notice him.

"One of the short-timers must have died," Smitty quietly muttered.

The Sarge keyed his earpiece again. "Back off, Speedy, looks like they're heading to the Intensive Care Unit. One of the Ol' Blues must be end of tour."

Jake gave Smitty a questioning look. Smitty leaned over to translate: "Died."

Speedy slowed down. As he began heading back to his post, he looked down an adjacent hallway and stopped in his tracks. He keyed his earpiece as he looked up at an exit sign that he knew was also a surveillance camera. He pointed excitedly down the hallway to his right and said, "Jack! It's Jack Logan."

The Sarge responded, "Ol' Detective Logan died."

There was a brief pause, and then Speedy announced, "No! He's face down on a gurney, but his feet are on the floor. He's pushing the gurney down a hallway towards the Precinct."

Speedy ran up to Detective Logan, who had tubes dangling from his chest and arms. His back was exposed from the hospital gown, and the only covering he had was his adult diaper.

Speedy saw that Detective Logan had blood on his arms where it looked like IV needles had been pulled out. Speedy immediately knew that the nurses were frantically looking for Jack Logan.

"Jack, what are you doing? We gotta get you back..."

Speedy was cut off by Logan pointing to the doors of the Precinct. "Sarge... gotta tell him."

Both men looked up as the thundering voice of Boss Nurse echoed down the hallway.

"I got him. He's heading towards the Precinct. Detective Logan, what are you...? Benjamin! What are you doing out of your...? I swear these geezers are gonna be the death of me."

Detective Logan started to slide off the end of the gurney. Boss Nurse rushed up and wrapped her arm around his waist and effortlessly lifted him back onto the gurney. With her other arm, she pointed in the direction of Speedy's room and commanded, "You get back to your room right now, Officer Benjamin. I'll talk to you later."

Speedy paused, thinking his robe was caught on the gurney. He looked down and saw that Detective Logan was holding onto it with the last of his strength. Speedy locked onto Detective Logan's eyes and could see the strain in his face as the word, "Tunnels" wheezed from Detective Logan's lips.

Detective Logan's grip dropped as Boss Nurse wheeled the gurney back to the Intensive Care Unit. He didn't make it back alive. He had answered the call of his duty by making his final report at his *end of tour*... another cop living true to the code of Ol' Blue.

෮

"What do you mean, I'm on my own? We had a deal, Lois." The Chemist's voice became more and more agitated as he spoke.

"I would suggest you calm yourself down. It looks like we are going to leave the state and go somewhere warmer." Lois's voice had a threatening edge to it. "I suggest you go back to your little pharmacy and contain those urges you have for unconscious women. Our friends in Armenia will be coming to America soon, and they will not be happy. They don't accept failure without punishment. Like it or not, *you*..." Lois emphasized, "are part of that failure."

The Chemist almost threw himself back in his chair. The realization of his predicament felt like a slap in the face.

Lois sensed that her veiled threat had hit its mark.

"Now my associates and I are moving on to some different opportunities. I suggest you keep a low profile. If things work out with our new employers, perhaps I will contact you. It will be difficult for the Cartel to find you, but remember, I have all your information. If you keep to yourself and continue to conceal our arrangement from the authorities, you won't have anything to worry about. If you don't, the Armenians will want to know where to find you."

There was a short pause.

"Do you understand?"

The intense expression on the Chemist's face faded to a blank stare. He responded, "I understand." Lois hung up.

"*Why don't we just kill him?*" Vladimir asked.

"*We may need him in the near future,*" Lois responded. "*The Cartel in Armenia will want to dish out punishment. They may be satisfied if we offer him. And if all goes well with the Mexican Cartels, we may want his services. Either way, our little Chemist may come in handy.*"

Vladimir mumbled, "I swear that filthy dog is looking at me."

⤳

The following morning Jake Mitchell attended his chief's briefing. The Omaha Police Chief, FBI representative, and the sheriffs of the neighboring counties met weekly to discuss various issues such as cross-boundary crime sprees, to exchange various alerts, and to bounce difficult cases off each other.

Since the Crime Stopper tip line was utilized by all of the agencies involved, and since Jake was responsible for the tip line, he played a valuable role with each of the agencies.

Once the common interests of the participants had been discussed, the sheriff from a county just north of Omaha placed a folder on the large, round conference table.

"We've got a body of a female that was found in the countryside, and we're at a complete loss. A couple of hunters found her. Animals, including a pack of coyotes, had consumed much of the body. The woman's teeth had been knocked out and her fingers cut off."

Jake spoke the obvious: "Someone didn't want that body found or identified." Acknowledging nods came from all around the table.

The sheriff continued, "We sent the photos to the Feds." He pointed to the FBI liaison agent. The agent reciprocated by holding up photos of the crime scene. Then he punched some keys on his laptop, and images from the scene started to flash onto a screen on the far side of the conference room.

As the photos of the immediate area surrounding the crime scene were displayed, the sheriff and FBI agent described what they had determined to this point.

"The body was placed in a very secluded area. We figure after the suspect performed the dental and manicure job on the woman, she was dropped about twenty-five yards off the old gravel road. Whoever did this must have known that the animals in the area would find and devour the body. We were lucky that those hunters were in the area. The dogs they had with them helped find the body. Another couple of days and the animals would have torn it to pieces and scattered it throughout the area. Odds are we never would have found her."

With a tone of frustration, the sheriff added, "The weather made it difficult to get any tread marks on the gravel and dirt. We took photos of what we think were possible tire marks but nothing we could really make out. The coroner thinks the woman was strangled and her neck was possibly broken, but it's inconclusive due to the animals."

The FBI officer chimed in as the photos went from the surrounding scene to the immediate area around the body. After discussing the specifics of the body, the agent said, "Whoever did this forgot one thing about the victim which would help us identify her. There's a tattoo on her wrist, and our lab has been able to analyze it." He displayed the photo of the green star.

The agent continued, "This tattoo originates from a crime family in..." Jake immediately recognized the tattoo as the same one that he had seen just a few hours earlier in the Ol' Blues task force meeting and inadvertently blurted, "Armenia!"

The FBI agent's mouth dropped open. "Uh, yeah." In unison, the Chief of Police and all the officers turned and stared at Jake.

Jake knew that everyone in the room was about to drill him on how on earth he knew about the tattoo. Thinking fast, he pointed to the photo of the tattoo with his pen and said, "Winter Olympics 2002. I was on the threat assessment task force for my previous department, the Salt Lake City PD."

Then Jake turned to the FBI agent and added, "You're right, there are a lot of crime cartels from Armenia. Tattooing is one of the red flags we utilized in determining what we were dealing with."

The FBI agent acknowledged the accuracy of Jake's information in front of the other attendees, and everyone seemed satisfied with Jake's response. To pad his answer, Jake added some cop jargon for big cases: "Lotta overtime on that one."

The questioning looks turned to nods and smiles. Meeting adjourned. Jake sat back and discreetly exhaled the breath he had been unaware that he was holding.

◈

"There is no way these banger pricks are doing this without some kind of help," Sergeant Scott barked.

Detective Turley shook his head. "There must be a car or van or something we're missing. I've reviewed every surveillance camera surrounding those old buildings. I can't figure it out."

Sergeant Scott looked at the pile of surveillance videos Detective Turley had gone through over and over. "We're missing something. This just doesn't happen. We couldn't even see them walking into the Old Market. Let's set up again for this evening. This time, as soon as we spot some of the bangers, I don't want them followed, I want them detained immediately. Run them for warrants. Maybe we'll get lucky and arrest a couple. Perhaps we'll get one to talk."

Tony and Pauli Chelini were back at the Old Market as well.

"They set up a little different this time. The coppers don't seem to be hiding like they have before. Wonder why?" Pauli asked.

"Let's find out. Remember, nobody sees the little old men," Tony said with a smile. The two old men walked up to a couple of officers and conducted some of their own surveillance. The officers didn't give the old men a second glance, because they weren't a threat.

"Just nab'em?" one officer said to the other.

"That's right," the other officer replied. "Don't follow, don't watch them, just detain and run for warrants. The Gang Sergeant wants to nab one with warrants and see if he can get information out of him at headquarters."

Tony leaned towards Pauli's ear. "They are getting desperate."

Then Tony touched his earpiece. "Hey, Sarge, looks like the Gang Unit is just gonna try to nab and grab, then sweat the guy at headquarters. Get him to spill his guts about the disappearing act these hoods perform."

The Sarge responded, "You're right, it's a risky strategy. They're just fishing, hoping to find one that will talk. Can't blame them for trying. Just stay on your beat and check in with any information."

&

Agnes walked into the Sarge's office and said, "Holy cow, Boss Nurse had been giving it to Speedy Benjamin. I went by his room and I could hear her down the hallway."

The Sarge smiled. "Boss Nurse has been chasing him around for a couple of years now, but she never catches him. She always gives him a good shakedown the following day. I think Speedy is used to it."

&

"I've worked graveyard shift for twenty years," Speedy said. "Nobody is gonna tell me how and where the hot spots are on my beat."

Boss Nurse rolled her eyes. "There are no hot spots; the entire building is secure. Now, if I find you scrambling around here in the middle of the night one more time, I'm gonna restrict you to your room."

Speedy stood up and pointed to his uniform, which had been draped over the small couch in his living room. "I've never been stuck on desk duty, and I'm not about to start now. When I hit the streets, the hoods know it and my beat stays clean."

"You don't have any stripes on your shoulders, and I won't take orders from a civilian who has no idea how to collar the crooks on my beat," Speedy added. "Like it or not, I'm here to stay, and nothing gets by me. As a matter of fact, I have some ideas that I'm going to bounce off the Sarge about tightening security at the outer perimeter---"

Boss Nurse threw her hands in the air. "I swear, you bunch of nutty cops are gonna be the death of me. When you talk to the Sarge, tell him you want to work the day shift."

Boss Nurse walked out of Speedy's apartment shaking her head and muttering, "The death of me, every last one of these cops."

Once the door had closed, Speedy keyed the microphone in his hearing aid. "Officer Benjamin calling Sarge."

After a second he heard the response, "Go ahead Speedy." "

"Got a minute? I'd like to give you my report from my patrol."

The Sarge responded, "I'm clear on that, Speedy, come to my office."

⟨⟩

"Tunnels? Detective Logan escapes the ICU by shuffling himself on a gurney and all he has to say is 'tunnels'?" The Sarge took the unlit cigar from his mouth and scratched his head. "That doesn't make any sense."

Speedy shrugged and said, "Seems to me it was pretty important. He grabbed onto my robe and tried to pull me close to him. He knew exactly what he was doing. His eyes were clear and determined. I tell ya, Sarge, Old Logan needed to say that. Maybe it makes sense to you."

The Sarge sat forward and thanked Speedy. "Go on back to your place and get some shut eye."

As Speedy turned to leave, he was stopped by a jolting, raspy voice. "Get that diaper changed. You're sagging. Get it to regulation. You're a police officer, not a plumber."

Speedy cringed and looked back at the Sarge, who in turn shrugged. "She's probably right."

Agnes gave the Sarge a stern look, and he corrected himself.

"She's right. I'd suggest changing it before she conducts some sort of inspection."

Speedy agreed, "Sure thing, Sarge," then pulled his indignity bottoms together and shuffled out the door.

⟆

"First things first," Brittany said to Amanda. "The Old Market has some of the cutest shops around. There's food, great clothes shops, and just about anything else you can think of. However, like I said, first things first—ice cream."

Amanda allowed herself to relax. Brittany seemed like the perfect person to help her make sense of her crazy life.

"Cookies 'n' Cream always seems to solve whatever is bothering me," Brittany said as she bit into the delicious treat. "It's chocolate for me, any kind of chocolate."

Brittany leaned forward and with a smile said, "I've been visiting with these Ol' Blues since this home for old cops opened. I know these guys can be a bit difficult—"

Amanda seemed like a shaken soda bottle. Her emotions were ready to burst out as soon as there was an opening.

"Who put all these guys together? They're all nuts. They think they are actually still cops. I mean, they talk like they are actually still working the streets or their beat or whatever they call it. My grandmother acts like she is some sort of supervisor, and I have to salute, and they made me some sort of cadet. My life is so weird."

She flopped back into her chair, and after a second or two the expression on her face suggested that she had suddenly remembered something very important. Amanda straightened up with eyes wide open and tried to yell and whisper at the same time. "What's up with all the farting?"

Brittany burst into laughter while swallowing a mouthful of ice cream, which ended up shooting out of her mouth and nose. Then they both enjoyed a long laugh as they thought of the chorus of flatulence the Ol' Blues could produce at a moment's notice. Brittany tried to control her ice cream from going everywhere but her mouth.

Amanda saw the difficulty Brittany was having, so she quickly grabbed a bunch of napkins and tried to help her. But trying to help someone in Brittany's condition while at the same time laughing uncontrollably herself made her efforts sweet but pointless. Once the two of them were able to regain some degree of composure, they spoke for about an hour about what Amanda had been going through during the last few years of her life. Amanda was surprised by how comfortable she felt talking to her new friend on such a personal level.

Brittany told Amanda about her life as a missionary in Africa and her amazement at how the Sudanese were able to be such good people after their lives had been ravaged by war and terrorism.

"The experience taught me a lot," Brittany concluded. She looked up as a senior citizen walked by. "Now I'm working with my dad and these geezers who treat me like a bunch of my favorite uncles... in diapers." This time, the ice cream came out of Amanda's nose.

Brittany laughed at Amanda's expense. Then she happened to glance through the large window at the front of the store and see the Chelini brothers walking by. Her momentary look of surprise caused Amanda to follow her gaze. Brittany quickly grabbed a bunch of napkins and slapped them over Amanda's face, catching the ice cream and temporarily blindfolding her until the two Ol' Blues were clear of the window.

"Hey, the face is clean already!" Amanda blurted.

The two of them decided it was time to go, and they picked up the mess of napkins and walked by the cashier, who smiled at the young women who had evidently had a nice time in her shop.

"Whatta ya say we go look around the old warehouses?" suggested Tony. "We're only walking around here doing nothing. I say we should take a look. The coppers always lose the punks when they run into those buildings."

Tony pointed to the group of three empty red brick structures dating back to a time when Omaha was the epicenter of agriculture for America's growing population.

"Might be a good idea." Pauli scratched his chin. "If something goes down, maybe this time we will be in the building and we can nab the hoods."

"They don't make 'em like this anymore," Tony commented, stating the obvious. The old warehouses had been used to transfer thousands of cattle, pigs, and other animals from the stockyards to trains for distribution throughout the country. The streetlights from the Old Market provided enough illumination to see the dangling pulleys and chains that had been used to pick up and move heavy loads.

Hitting the wall with his walker, Tony said, "The walls look like they're two to three feet thick." The giant beams of wood above the Chelini brothers' heads had been built to support the building and carry the weight of a hungry nation.

"Jeez, will ya look at the floors?" Tony pointed down. The uneven, thick timbers which made the foundations for each floor of these buildings contributed to the fort-like superstructure.

Pauli nudged his brother, saying, "I don't think they could make these buildings again even if they wanted to.

Suddenly they heard footsteps, and both of the cops instinctively crouched down and looked toward the sound. The two brothers tried to move quietly, but Tony's walker made an unavoidable sound as he moved. Pauli tried to make Tony stop moving by frantically waving at him. When Tony saw Pauli's signals, he immediately froze. The footsteps were getting louder. Tony backed up to the darkest corner he could find and stood quietly. Pauli listened; from the sounds he could tell they were almost upon them.

The Sarge's voice crackled in his earpiece. "Hey, Tony 'n' Pauli, there was a robbery in the market."

Pauli quickly responded, "We're in the warehouse. The punks are running right at—*Hold it right there! Grab some sky, ya stinkin' hoods!*"

Three bangers dressed in dark pants and hooded sweatshirts jolted to a stop ten feet from Pauli. They were breathing heavily, and their hands shot up into the air. The leader, a brute about six feet tall, looked to his left where the command to stop had come from. What he saw made him drop his hands so quickly they slapped onto his thighs. An old man was pointing his index finger at him with his thumb up.

"What the… put your hands down," he told the others. "It's a homeless dude, and he's pointing his finger. Ain't no gun."

The second banger was shorter, stockier, and breathing heavily. "Yo, pop a cap in dis guy." He pulled up his sweatshirt to reveal the handle of a pistol.

The old man yelled, "Try it, punk, and I'll drop you where you stand!" Pauli pointed at the banger.

The first thug slapped the stocky one on the chest. "Shoot a gun in here? The cops will know where we are." Just then they heard the unmistakable sound of police outside the warehouse: "Set a perimeter! Call for back-up; they ran into this building."

The group's leader said, "Hit the hole." Then he pointed to the third and smallest of the three. "Jack this guy so he doesn't follow us, then catch up."

Two of the bangers started to run toward a flight of stairs that appeared to go to the basement of the building. The third gave the old man a threatening stare. *Knucks,* short for Knuckles, was his moniker among the Demons because of his fondness for beating people up. The thug relished seeing terror in the faces of his victims.

As the others ran, Knucks stepped toward the old man. His movement was cut short by an unsettling sight. The old man didn't utter the words, *"Please don't hurt me"* or *"No!"* He didn't show the typical terrified response of hands extending forward, a natural defensive stance that Knucks would slap away before beating his victims to a bloody mess.

"This old guy ain't scared. He's just staring right back at me." Knucks said to himself. *"He looks like he's snarling."* Knucks's surprise turned to shock when the old man threatened him.

"You're nothing, punk. Your two little girlfriends can't help you now." The air was filled with a ripping sound. *Phifft-Phifft* .

Knucks's world came to a jolting stop as two taser darts shot from Tony's walker struck the goon—one to the chest, the other to the groin. 50,000 volts ripped from his upper chest to his nether region. For five seconds Knucks felt his muscles cramp to the point of breaking his ribs. Then he collapsed forward, hitting the hard, wooden floor face first. He tried to scream, but unintelligible gibberish was the only sound the Chelinis could hear. Then there was an electrical combustion erupting between Knucks's legs. Knucks felt like his testicles had been welded together.

Tony pointed to the hood and spoke out loud. "The boys in the Precinct lab tried to explain how these zappers worked when they put 'em in our walkers. Remember, Pauli?"

Pauli started to laugh. "We thought they were stupid." Then he pointed to the punk at his feet. "Looks like they work pretty good to me."

Tony chimed in, "They didn't tell us anything about catching a zapper to the nuts. We'll have to brief them when we get back."

Pauli stood over the thug as he rolled onto his back, convulsing in agony. The pain to his chest ceased as the five-second shock stopped. Pauli asked, "Aren't they supposed to snap out of it after five seconds? I guess that's the added benefit of 50,000 volts to the twins."

Pauli grabbed Knucks by the hair and turned his head so that he was staring right into the punk's eyes. "Remember the time your momma said, '*One of these days you'll mess with the wrong guy*'?" Pauli gave Knucks a little shake to his head to make sure he was listening. "You just messed with him."

The Chelini brothers looked up at the sound of officers entering the building yelling, "Police! Come out where we can see you." Tony looked at Pauli and smiled. "This will make sure he doesn't scram before they catch him."

Tony pushed a button on his walker and released another 50,000 volts. Knucks started flopping again and making weird sounds. "He won't run now. Pull the darts, and let's get outta here."

Sergeant Scott made his way to the interrogation room. He was giddy with excitement but trying not to show it.

"Finally caught one of those pricks" he thought to himself as he walked. Before talking to the suspect, he wanted to find out who he was dealing with. As he walked down a hallway, he crossed paths with Jake Mitchell.

"Hey, Sarge, heard your peeps caught one of those bangers in the Old Market, nice work," Jake said.

Sergeant Scott replied, "Been hoping to get one of these guys. I'm on my way to interrogation now. Want to join me?"

Jake looked at his watch. "I've got some time."

The two men walked together to the interrogation rooms.

Outside the rooms there were computers for the detectives to utilize prior to interviewing suspects. Detective Turley was reviewing the suspect's history and researching intel on him.

"Talk to me," Sergeant Scott said as he approached Detective Turley.

"Tatum Madison," Turley reported. "He goes by Knucks, and he's a thumper. Just turned eighteen, and his juvenile record is full of assaults, robberies, burglaries. Our intelligence lists him as a documented Demon."

Sergeant Scott looked at the monitor. The hidden camera in the interrogation room was recording a young man who looked like he had been dragged through a Nebraska corn field.

"What happened to his face? Did he fight with you guys?"

Detective Turley shrugged and said, "Don't know. When we approached him, he tried to get up and run but kept making the weirdest noises and fell onto his face. He did that three times before we nabbed him. It was weird. We figured he was drunk."

"I'm about to talk to him." Turley started the recording video.

Sergeant Scott and Jake sat down and watched the monitor as Turley walked into the room with Knucks.

"Hi, Tatum, I'm Detective Turley. I understand you reported to the officers that you were assaulted by someone in that building."

The sergeant smiled. "Turley's letting this guy think that he's the victim of being assaulted... smart. This will get him talking, and we haven't even started to interview him about the crimes he may have committed. That way we don't have to read him his rights yet. If he thinks he's being interviewed as a victim, he's likely to talk. And if Turley can establish some sort of rapport, maybe he'll keep talking until he mentions his gang ties."

Jake had plenty of experience interviewing suspects and knew how difficult it was to get information. "Takes a good cop to do that."

Sergeant Scott agreed and pointed to the monitor. "Turley's the best."

"We've had problems with a couple of older guys in the area, and I'd like to catch this guy." Turley appeared concerned about Knucks's well-being. "Is there anything you can tell me about the guy?"

Knucks started to speak too quickly. "We thought he was just a homeless guy."

Turley mentally noted, "*You said 'we,' so there were others with you.*"

Knucks continued, "He was a homeless dude, but his clothes weren't all shabby."

Turley pretended to be interested. "Do you remember anything else about him that I could use to identify him for you? Anything you could think of would be helpful."

Knucks paused, thinking that he didn't want the detective to know what he was actually doing in that building.

"There was one thing." Knucks paused. "That dude wasn't afraid of us—" He stuttered, "Me... it seemed like the guy wanted to pick a fight with me. I mean, what kind of old guy stares at you like he wants to fight you?"

Jake suddenly sat up straighter in his chair. The suspect's comment had piqued his interest.

Sergeant Scott asked, "You all right?"

Jake tried to settle down. "Oh, yeah, just trying to hear what this guy is saying." Outwardly he looked calm, but he couldn't help but make the comparison to the Ol' Blues. *Those guys aren't afraid of anything. I'll bet the geezers were snooping around and found this guy.*

Wanting to maintain his rep as a fighter, Knucks tried to come across as a tough guy to the cops.

"I was gonna jack the dude, then I must have stepped on some wires or something because I got shocked up my legs." Without thinking, Knucks put his hands between his legs as if checking to make sure he still had his masculine equipment.

Detective Turley reached over and patted Knucks on the shoulder.

"I'm just glad you're okay. When we found you, I gotta tell ya, you really didn't look so good." Turley decided that this was a good time to start pushing some buttons by challenging Knucks's manhood, one of the easiest buttons to push with bangers. Inwardly Turley smiled.

"That old guy really pounded you good, dude. Your face was a mess. You couldn't even stand up when we got to ya. I honestly thought you were going to need the medics."

Knucks started to tense. He inhaled, straightened his back in the chair and inadvertently tightened his hands into fists.

Detective Turley's inward smile broadened. "Are you feeling all right? I can call a nurse for you if you would like."

Knucks almost yelled, "Don't need no nurse! I told you I stepped on some electric wire or something."

Sergeant Scott leaned over to Jake, saying, "Watch. Turley is going to get him now."

Detective Turley let his internal smile turn into a snickering trap. He laughed as he spoke.

"C'mon, Knucks, the old man busted you up. It's an old warehouse with no electricity!" Detective Turley let loose with a loud laugh. "You, my man, got a senior slap down. That old dude made a fool of you, then left you on the floor a bloody mess."

"*This banger ain't gonna let that stand*," Turley thought to himself. So, before Knocks jumped out of his skin to respond to the accusation, Turley interjected, "Oh wait. You know, I almost forgot… jeez, sorry, Tatum. Whenever I interview someone, I'm supposed to read them their rights. You know, like on TV."

Knocks raised his voice. "No, no, dude, that old man didn't jack me."

Again Turley's palms went up. "Okay, okay. You know you have the right to remain silent and not answer any of my questions."

Knocks stamped his foot. "Yeah, I know, and I have a right to an attorney? I know my rights. Let me talk, that old dude didn't…"

There was a slight uplift at the corner of Turley's mouth as he quickly glanced at one of the hidden cameras.

Sergeant Scott pointed to Turley's face on one of the monitors. "That's good enough, and Turley knows it."

Jake had to admit it—Detective Turley was good.

Jake looked back at the monitor and saw that the young banger was almost bursting with anger as he struggled to defend his reputation.

"Ain't no old man gonna jack me!"

There was a slight pause, and Turley tried to get Knocks to give away something incriminating. "I believe ya. Why were y'all running, anyway?"

Knocks blurted, "Just rolled a guy and were headed for the hole…"

Knocks's eyes widened. He looked at the detective and saw that he was smiling. Knocks knew he had just been had.

"I ain't sayin' nothing else!"

Detective Turley reached over and turned the doorknob, then with a slight flick of his wrist, opened the door to the interrogation room. Standing there was a man with a bandaged forehead.

"That's him; that's one of the guys that robbed me. He was the one that hit me in the face after I gave them my money."

Turley's smile was gone. He knew he couldn't ask any more questions. Now it was time to give some orders.

"Stand up and put your hands behind your back. You're under arrest for robbery. Stand up now!"

The detective applied the handcuffs with the usual clicking sound as the teeth of the cuffs tightened around Knucks's wrists. Detective Turley led Knucks by gripping his upper arm. While escorting Knucks to be booked, he smiled.

"I never really figured out what that old man did to you, but one thing is for sure—*you messed with the wrong guy.*"

Those words had already been burned into Knucks's mind. He let loose a string of curses about the cops and old men as the elevator doors opened.

Jake listened until the doors of the elevator shut. He shook his head and said to himself, *"I don't know how they did it, but I just know it was those geezers."*

CHAPTER 6

Agnes opened the door to the apartment she shared with her granddaughter. Amanda was watching television.

"Hey, Manda-Cakes, sorry I've been so busy. Did you have a nice time with Brittany?"

Amanda's face immediately brightened. "She is a hoot! We went to the Old Market and did some shopping. I've never really gone to the Old Market and just enjoyed myself so much. We laughed at these old guys and all the funny things they do."

This brought another smile to Agnes's face. "Yeah, I suppose these old putzes could be entertaining for you two."

Amanda added, "Brittany and I are gonna go out each week for our OFT." Agnes's squeaky oxygen tank holder came to a stop as she gave her granddaughter a questioning look.

"Old Fart Therapy."

Agnes threw her head back for a rare, all-out laugh, followed by a coughing fit.

There was a knock at the door. When Agnes opened it, she smiled broadly.

"Thane, how are you?"

Remembering that Amanda was in the room, she quickly cut Thane off from saying anything.

"Oh, you must meet my granddaughter. This is Amanda. Amanda, this is Thane. He works here at the retirement home as a… umm…"

Agnes didn't know what to call Thane. Sensing her confusion, Thane spoke up.

"I'm the I.T. guy for the building. It's nice to meet you, Amanda."

Thane looked at her cadet shirt. "Nice uniform. Are you part of this police group?"

Agnes interrupted, not wanting Thane to say too much.

"Not a full member, Thane. She is just staying here with me for a while."

Thane understood. "Oh, well, welcome. You're a nice addition here."

Amanda smiled at the compliment. Her smile dazzled Thane, who silently smiled back.

Agnes broke the silence. "What's an 'it' guy?"

Thane looked at Agnes in confusion. "It?"

Agnes nodded. "Yeah, i-t... it."

Thane shook his head. "What is it with you Blues and acronyms? It means Information Technology. You know, computer stuff."

Agnes threw up her hands. "I thought you were more building maintenance." She smiled. "You know, BM."

This brought out a chirp from Amanda as she tried to stifle an all-out belly laugh. Thane knew he'd been had, and he decided not to pursue a battle of wits with Agnes.

"Very funny."

He looked over at Amanda. "I get to work with this all day, and she is the sweetest one of them all."

Amanda let out a good laugh, and Thane was hooked.

"Thane, is this about the stuff we discussed with the Sarge?"

Thane looked away from Amanda... again.

"Oh, yeah." Thane realized Amanda wasn't part of the Blues. "Don't worry about it; I'll talk to him tomorrow. I should probably get going. It was really nice to meet you. Amanda."

"Same here," she replied with a smile.

Thane smiled back and stumbled as he turned toward the door.

"See ya tomorrow, Agnes. Bye, Amanda."

As the door closed behind him, Thane realized he had started to sweat with embarrassment at his stumbling. "Wow" was all he could say to himself as he walked back to his underground office.

"He seems nice… kinda clumsy but nice."

Agnes smiled. "Very nice young man." Not wanting to answer questions about Thane, Agnes turned the conversation back to Amanda and Brittany.

"I think it's great that you and Brittany go out like that. I think you two are perfect for each other. She's getting married soon. It's hard to believe she is the daughter of that dolt Smitty."

Agnes started to walk away towards the bathroom, muttering, "He thinks I forgot about him and Benson giving me a trunk jaunt."

Amanda gave her Nana a confused look.

"I'm gonna take a shower."

Amanda shrugged and turned her attention back to the television. The bathroom door was closed, and Amanda heard the shower being turned on.

About a minute later, Amanda noticed that the water had been shut off and her Nana was making some strange noises.

"Jehoshaphat! Mary and Joseph! Detective Logan! Whatta copper!"

The commotion behind the bathroom door caused Amanda to jump up from the couch.

"Nana? Are you okay?"

The bathroom door swung open and steam billowed out. Agnes was shaking as she attached the oxygen cannula to her nose and tugged her hospital gown over her shoulders. Her oxygen tank holder started its usual squeak as she tried to hurriedly shuffle out the door.

"Nana?" Amanda asked.

"Can't talk now, sweetie. Gotta get to the Sarge."

Moving faster than Amanda had ever seen her shuffle, Agnes headed for the door. The back of her hospital gown was not even tied together, and Amanda could clearly see that her Nana hadn't bothered to put on any underwear.

Agnes left the apartment before Amanda could voice her concern about her Nana's exposed backside. Shaking her head, she plopped down on the living room sofa, grabbed her phone and texted Brittany, "Can we move up R next OFT pls?"

∽

Big Brock and Benson were making their way to the cafeteria for a late-night snack.

"What do you feel like eating, Brock?"

"Don't know," was the reply. "Let's see what's left over from dinner."

"Outta the way, ya gorilla," the lead officer yelled as she barreled around the corner. Brock put his back to the wall, followed by Benson. Both Blues watched as Agnes shuffled by, explaining, "Gotta talk to the Sarge."

Brock and Benson looked at each other in shock and then simultaneously watched Agnes as she scooted away. Seeing Agnes's completely exposed, saggy backside, both Blues stood dumbfounded.

Without averting his stare, Brock mumbled, "Not hungry anymore."

Benson added, "Me either, and breakfast is questionable."

∽

With a white towel slung over his shoulder, Sarge was wearing only his red striped boxer underwear and black socks held up by straps below his knees. He had just finished brushing his teeth. Smiling into the mirror, he commented,

"Well, at least they're real. No smile in a glass each night for this guy."

He popped the unlit cigar back in his mouth and walked to his bedroom. On his dresser was a photo of his family. They all loved him but had never really understood this old cop. He smiled at the memories that accompanied each face in the photo. The Sarge looked toward the other side of his dresser and smiled at a photo of his departed wife, Jacquelin.

"Hi ya, Jackie." Sarge kissed his fingertips, touched the photo, and softly said, "You kept the family together. Without you I would have been nothing. You were the only one who really understood me."

Suddenly the Sarge's mind was flooded with memories of Jackie walking into emergency rooms shaking her head. Jackie used to scold him for getting hurt in street brawls with unruly drunks, and dozens of times she entered the ER as medical staff sewed up a wound or put a limb in a cast. Often there would be blood on his uniform, and once in a while the uniform had been completely cut off.

"I swear, George, if I get picked up by a police car and driven to the hospital one more time, I'll move to Oklahoma!"

Jackie knew how much the Nebraska-Oklahoma football rivalry meant to fans in the Husker State. This was no idle threat.

Jovially pleading, he would respond, "Oh, Jackie, please don't. It won't happen again... I swear." The doctors and nurses would laugh and make funny comments, and as they did so, the sounds in the room would be drowned out as Jackie's attention was focused on inspecting her husband to make sure he was really all right. She would always start with the injury, then after giving him the once over, their eyes would meet and Sarge's piercing yet soft gaze let her know once again that he was gonna be just fine.

Sarge's eyes were still piercing, but now they were surrounded by aging, wrinkled skin. His old eyes started to tear up at the memories of his Jackie.

His reminiscing was interrupted by someone banging on the door of his apartment. Sarge walked out of his bedroom as his front door was being pushed open.

He stared in shock at what was standing in his doorway. Agnes Crantz had pushed the door open and was leaning against the frame. Her breathing was labored, and her robe had fallen halfway off her right shoulder. Her hair was wet, and all the purple curls had straightened into long stringy strands over her face. Dark eye makeup was streaming down her cheeks. She appeared to have stepped off the set of a zombie movie.

The Sarge attempted to formulate a sentence that would make some sort of sense. All that would come out of his mouth was "Agg-nes... ah, what... what is this?" Her hand went up like she was signaling to the Sarge to wait as she tried to breathe. Then she started to cough and speak at the same time. It didn't work. She became more and more frustrated as she attempted to speak and her coughing simply would not let her make any coherent statements. She had to wait until the coughing spasms subsided.

Finally the Sarge couldn't take it anymore.

"Agnes, what's wrong? You look... horrible." During her final few coughs Agnes looked over the hand she was coughing into and rolled her eyes at Sarge.

She stood erect, and without invitation, walked into the Sarge's apartment.

"I've only had a few officers in my life that I thought stood out as terrific cops. Today I added the name of Detective Logan to that list," she announced.

As the Sarge waited for an explanation, suddenly Agnes realized that the man was standing in front of her in his underwear and socks. She froze, tilted her head, and said, "Stripes? Not quite regulation. However, you could probably pass for some sort of cupid."

"Agnes! What are you talking about?"

"Oh, yeah, Detective Logan, that magnificent Ol' Blue!"

The Sarge shrugged and responded, "He was a good cop but he was living in the past. Remember, he thought we were looking for bootleggers."

Agnes waved off the Sarge's statement. "Of course I remember what he said a few days ago. It's what he said right before he died! Don't you remember what Jack Logan said?"

The Sarge shrugged and replied, "Ah... he grabbed Benjamin's robe and only said *tunnel*."

Agnes became more animated, "Yes, that's right, I was in the shower when it hit me. Tunnels!"

Again, the Sarge just shrugged. Agnes stared straight into the Sarge's eyes and with her hands moving like she was cutting up bread, she said in a chopped sentence, "Boot—Leggers—Tunnels!"

The Sarge's eyes opened wide as he recalled something that only the old Omaha cops would remember.

Agnes became more animated as she explained, "Those old buildings were built in the early days of Omaha. The coppers nowadays wouldn't know there were numerous tunnels interconnecting the buildings, including some of the old neighborhoods... especially the really old neighborhoods that used to be lined with mansions."

The Sarge's mind began to race as he started making the connection between the gangs of today and the gangsters of the past. Suddenly the ambers of nearly a hundred-year battle between order and mayhem burst back into flames. The great-grandchildren of both sides were utilizing some of the same methods to commit and fight crime. The juxtaposition caused the Sarge to shake his head, and he inadvertently gazed past Agnes's right shoulder and saw Boss Nurse walking past his open door. Sarge noticed that she had stopped and was backing up to look into his doorway.

"This changes everything in the Old Market!" Agnes was almost giddy with excitement. "We just need to contact Jake... Mmmph!" Agnes's sentence was cut off by the Sarge grabbing her and planting a smooch right on her lips. Agnes's eyes popped wide open as her excited utterance was cut short.

Then the Sarge pulled back and yelled, "Hey! How about some privacy!"

Agnes turned her head to see what the Sarge was looking at. Standing in the doorway was the giant Boss Nurse staring at them in shock. Her hips almost touched both sides of the door frame, which she grasped as if to keep herself from falling backwards.

"I was just... ah..." Boss Nurse was at a loss for words. The scene before her was beyond any verbal description. The Sarge was wearing striped boxer underwear with silly little black suspenders holding up his black socks. His cigar was broken and hanging from the side of his mouth. But that was not what stunned her into silence. Between Boss Nurse and the Sarge was a woman wearing a hospital gown that wasn't tied. She had no underclothing on, and purple stringy wet hair hung straight down around her face. Her robe was hanging off her right shoulder and appeared ready to fall off at any moment. The woman quickly turned to look at Boss Nurse, and her face looked absolutely frightening. Her eye makeup was running down her cheeks. Her jaw line had a skid mark of pieces of the Sarge's cigar smeared from the side of her mouth to her left ear. She gave Boss Nurse a glare that made Boss Nurse feel like a child who had walked into her parents' bedroom at a very bad time.

"I just heard some talking about leaving the facility and going to the Old Market. I didn't know you two were, ah... ah..." Boss Nurse pulled her hands from the framework of the doorway and started fidgeting.

"Were what? Can't two people enjoy a little privacy?"

"Ah, sure, Sarge, I just didn't know... ahh... Is it hot in here? I'm gonna go check the thermostat. Bye." Boss Nurse left without another word, making sure to close the door behind her.

"Sorry, Agnes, she was at the door as you were talking."

"No need to explain." Agnes reached with her left hand to pull her robe back over her shoulder. "We got some good intel here, Sarge."

Nodding, the Sarge said, "Let's meet in my office tomorrow morning. We'll discuss our strategy then. You should probably get back to your apartment. Your granddaughter may be worried."

Agnes turned and started to walk toward the door. Her robe was still open in the back. Not wanting to say anything that might embarrass her, he remained silent. After all, he was standing in his living room in socks and skivvies.

As Agnes shuffled out the Sarge's door, she smiled and quietly said to herself, "*Wonder how long he's wanted to do that?*"

The two thugs had just rounded the bottom of the stairs.

"Where's Knucks? He should have caught up by now." The two stopped and listened. There was no sound of Knucks running up to them. Then there were the sounds of police entering the building.

"Police! Don't move. Over here! There's a guy on the ground."

"Sounds like they found the homeless dude. Knucks must have ran another way. Let's hit the hole."

The two ran over to a corner of the basement of the warehouse. They ran to what appeared to be a three-foot steel beam riveted to a brick wall, then pulled. A five-foot section of the wall opened with surprising ease, revealing a tunnel. The squeaking of pulleys with iron counterbalances caused the door to easily pivot on hinges placed on the tunnel side of the wall. Once inside there was another small steel beam riveted to the inside of the door. After the door was pulled closed, it was almost completely invisible to the naked eye, especially at night.

As the two ran, they heard only the sound of their own footsteps echoing off the walls.

"He has a phone. Can you call him from down here?"

The taller gang member pulled a phone out of his pocket to call Knucks. After three rings the phone was answered.

"Yeah," he said. "Where you at?"

There was a pause at the other end of the line, and then "Where you?" was the response.

"We just hit the hole and..." There was another pause.

The taller gang banger known as *Scat* immediately became suspicious, remembering that he had told Knucks where they were going when they left him with the homeless guy. The person on the other end of the call was Sergeant Scott, who informed Scat, "Your boy Knucks is with me now."

Scat looked at his phone in shock, knowing he was probably talking to a cop. He quickly ended the call.

Jake entered Sergeant Scott's office as he was jotting down the phone number on the Caller ID. Then the sergeant made another call, saying, "Dispatch, ping this phone number."

Jake gave the sergeant a questioning look.

"If we can locate his phone, we might just get lucky and catch this guy," Sergeant Scott explained.

The ping was successful.

"Good! The guy is only a few blocks away from the area he was last observed. These guys must not have a car; they are only a couple of blocks away and don't seem to be moving very fast."

The radio dispatched cruisers to the intersection of 7th and Farnam Streets. Officers in the area responded quickly.

"On location," the officer reported on the radio. Sergeant Scott picked up his radio.

"The ping came back to that location. Are there any parties in the area?"

"Nothing, will continue to search."

Sergeant Scott looked at Jake and said, "They're right on top of them. They've got to be there."

Jake listened for the response from the officers at the scene.

"No parties in the area."

Sergeant Scott shook his head and keyed his mike. "The guy must have ditched his phone."

Two officers were standing at the intersection. One said to the other, "That sergeant really wants this guy."

The other officer shook his head, "Can't believe we didn't catch him. He was right here, according to the radio." The officers didn't know that Skat and his companions were ten feet away from them—directly below, slipping away again.

᠂᠊᠊

The following morning, Thane was tapping away at his computer.

"This doesn't make sense," Thane said as he reviewed the history of Amanda's medical warning watch. "Why would she have been in Kennard? She was tracked moving through

Nebraska, and then all of the sudden she was in Kennard for an hour."

One of the technicians asked, "Who are you talking to?"

Irritated, Thane lifted his hand to silence the voice that was interrupting his train of thought. The tech took the hint and left the area.

Thane tapped out Sarge's phone number and started to speak.

"Just checking in, Sarge. I've been following up on the medical tracker on Amanda, and there is something really strange about the path that she took to the Armenian safe house. She stopped at a little town north of Omaha called Kennard and stayed there for about an hour. Then she was driven out into the countryside before going to the safe house."

The Sarge thought for a second. "Very well, Thanerboy. See if you can determine what was going on in Kennard. Thanks."

∾

Sarge let out a breath of air and looked at a piece of paper on his desk. Then he picked up a pencil and started to make a list of the current investigations his task force was working on.

"Let's see, I got Armenian sex traffickers in our building. An investigation going on to figure out why Agnes's granddaughter was in that little town for an hour. A bunch of gangsters utilizing the old bootleggers' tunnels."

He put the pencil down, placed both elbows on his desk, then rested his forehead on the palms of his hands. While looking down at his desk, he spoke again.

"Add to this little list of mine the fact that Boss Nurse thinks I was making out with a zombie last night and you've got the cherry on the hot fudge sundae of my day."

"Don't flatter yourself, Stripes," came a response from his doorway. "I got at least five marriage proposals and one offer to appear at a freak show on my way back to my apartment."

Agnes shuffled into the office. "Next time, take that filthy stogie out of your mouth before you plant one on me. Could have lost my eye. If that disgusting thing was lit, we both would have burst into flames." She tapped her oxygen tube.

Surprised, the Sarge responded, "Maybe next time a place less conspicuous, like the cafeteria during dinner."

Agnes chuckled, waved the lit cigarette in front of her face, and said, "All right, let's see how we can dig up those rats running through the town in those tunnels."

&

The Omaha Police Department provides ongoing training to develop the skills of its officers. Twenty hours are required each year, and additional training is encouraged.

Jake sat at his desk reviewing studies involving various types of crimes and criminals. He started to review a section on a topic that has consumed many social scientists, biologists, and psychiatrists: What motivates people to do horrible things to other human beings?

Serial criminals seem to have a common thread running through their lives. The development of their mindset in the early years of life is heavily influenced by several factors.

Lack of love and affection, or an inability to develop a sufficient degree of empathy, appear to influence whether this tendency manifests itself in criminal behavior. This, of course, is only part of a very complex explanation as to why some people turn into killers, rapists, pedophiles, and so on. Psychological, sociological, environmental, and biological theories have been offered to explain why some people are driven to commit violent acts on numerous victims. Add to these sources the influence of alcohol, drugs, violence, abuse, and a string of other social ills, and you have a favorable mental mindset for a criminal predator.

Jake closed his notebook, shook his head, and quietly said to himself, "How are we ever going to stop this?" His train of thought was jolted back to the present as his phone rang. "This is Jake."

The voice on the other end inquired, "Can you talk?"

Jake looked around to make sure there was nobody in earshot. "Yeah, we're good. What ya got, Sarge?"

"How about stopping by the Precinct in a little while?"

"Sure, Sarge, I can be there in about an hour."

"That's fine. See you then."

Jake hung up and looked at his phone. "Sarge doesn't just call and invite me to come by. He must have something good to pass along."

Jake placed his phone next to the notebook that he had been reading. He smiled and thought to himself, "*Not sure exactly how we can stop all this crime, but these geezers are definitely part of the solution.*"

ۃ

Jake walked through the Precinct doors and gave one of the officers a nod. The Blue returned the nod and pointed over his shoulder with his thumb toward the Sarge's office.

At her desk outside the Sarge's office, Lead Officer Crantz was looking at some papers in front of her. She had the usual cigarette between her fingers and her elbow planted on her desk. Without moving her head, her eyes locked onto Jake and she pointed with her cigarette towards the Sarge's office.

"Hey, Jake, how are ya?" The Sarge greeted him with a shockingly firm handshake and gestured toward a chair.

"Just fine, Sarge." Jake sat down. "Now why would I get a call to this secret geriatric crime fighting unit?"

The Sarge smiled at the friendly jibe. There was a single knock at the door, then it opened and Agnes Crantz shuffled in. The Sarge pointed to the sofa, and she sat down quietly.

"Well, Jake, I've got some good news for you and your gang squad."

He looked at Agnes. "Everything secure in the Precinct?"

With a nod, Agnes responded, "Yeah, the squad is on watch mode. If anyone comes into the Precinct, we'll get the signal to shut everything down."

The Sarge moved the thick Standard Operating Procedures manual on his desk. A light emanated from his desk and illuminated a blank wall across the room. A map of the Omaha downtown area was projected, with the Old Market highlighted.

"Turns out those thugs that have been giving your detectives the slip used an old trick... so old that only a few old coppers even know about it."

This comment piqued Jake's interest and he leaned forward.

"This is great news. The Gang Unit has been going crazy trying to catch 'em."

The Sarge looked at Agnes, and she smiled in response. "Well, it turns out..."

The Sarge paused for a moment to study the projected map. Agnes stopped smiling and gave Sarge a questioning look. The Sarge raised his index finger as he met her glance. Agnes knew the Sarge had something on his mind. She didn't know what it was, but it appeared that he didn't want to say something in front of Jake. She gave the Sarge a raised eyebrow and crossed her arms.

"Back when these buildings were in their prime, they had many uses."

Jake looked at the map and nodded in agreement. "Yeah, so?"

The Sarge smiled and stood, pointing his unlit cigar at the map of the Old Market.

"Well, for years during Prohibition days and during the gambling hubs, buildings all over town were used to hide what they called speakeasys—what you would call night clubs or bars today."

Jake sat back in his chair and motioned with his hand for the Sarge to continue.

"Well, these establishments weren't located on the corners or out in the open like they are today. They were hidden all over town in various businesses, buildings, and even in houses. The coppers had a hard time finding them because they were usually built behind a false wall or in the basement of the old buildings like we see here."

The Sarge again pointed to the warehouses. "Those thugs found one of the rooms in the basement of the warehouses. It was the same building where your officers caught that guy the other night."

Jake sat up straighter. "How did you know about that?"

Sarge smiled and told Jake about the Chelini brothers and how the hood had gotten on the wrong side of Tony Chelini and been blasted by the taser on his walker.

Jake was flabbergasted. "You mean those two Italians actually caught that guy?"

Sarge popped the stogie back into his mouth. "Yep, they were in the building and saw the punks as they ran. One of them spotted my officers and tried to rough 'em up."

The Sarge smiled and added, "Got a few thousand volts of electricity for his trouble. Actually, he got jolted a couple of times. Those Chelini brothers know how to teach thugs a lesson. After giving him an electric enema, they left him for the detectives and skedaddled. The hood must have looked pretty bad, because he plopped on his face a couple of times, poor baby."

Sarge again pointed to the projected map. "Once they closed the entrance to those secret rooms, they just sat back and waited for the heat to blow over, then popped out like gophers—or Demons, as these guys like to call themselves."

Again Jake blurted, "How did you know that? We interrogated that guy just the other night. There is no way you could have known that. Wait... do you have other officers in the Department that work with you?"

The Sarge removed the cigar from his mouth and used it to point at Jake for emphasis. "You're our guy, Jake. The Chelini brothers overheard the guys talking, that's all. They referred to themselves as Demons. Anyway, I'll talk to the Bureau and see if they can dig up some old designs in the city's archives and find out if there are any other suspicious additions to the old buildings in the Market."

Agnes wondered why the Sarge wasn't telling Jake about the tunnels. The speakeasy rooms were a good ruse, but she thought to herself, *There must be some reason behind what the Sarge is doing.* She decided to go along with it.

"Sure, as the years went by, those old buildings or houses were sold and the new owners sometimes stumbled onto these rooms. I'm sure they are still around in the old neighborhoods."

The Sarge gave Agnes a slight smile and a wink.

Agnes questioned, "The Bureau?"

Jake looked at her and explained, "They're the rich folks who put all this together. For some reason they thought a special Diaper/Denture Squad was a good idea. My brother is a member of that group. Gotta hand it to him; you guys really have come through for us."

Jake looked back at the Sarge. "Now, where exactly is this secret room?"

The Sarge shrugged and said, "Not really sure. Could be in the floor, a wall, or even what looks like a small closet. In the old days the gangsters were pretty clever. We only discovered a few of them. We'll get the researchers to work on it for a while, and we'll let you know what they find."

Jake threw his hands into the air. "All right, but make it quick."

With a smile, the Sarge winked and said, "We'll get right on…"

Suddenly both Sarge's and Agnes's hearing aids let out a warning signal. Jake looked back and forth between the two as their eyes widened in alarm and both put their hands to their ears to hear more clearly.

"Sarge, this is Mary. A news team just pulled up in front of the building. I heard the woman reporter say something about getting a live shot of the Precinct."

&

"Broadcasting throughout the greater Omaha area, it's today's Fox News," the announcer said as music played in the background. The camera at the local Fox News studio focused on a sharply dressed woman sitting at a news anchor desk. Her hair was perfect, and her makeup covered every blemish. As a matter of fact, she looked more like a brown-haired porcelain doll than a real human being.

"Good evening, and welcome to Fox News on the spot." She did a quarter turn to face another camera. "I'm Nicole Morgan, and here are today's headlines." The woman robotically read off some of the happenings of the day, both locally and nationally.

Ten minutes into the broadcast, she made an announcement. "After the break, we'll hear about a shake-up at the Precinct of the Old Blues Retirement Home. You don't want to miss this. That report will be coming live from the actual Old Blues Precinct for retired police officers after these messages."

Marching through the front entrance of the retirement home was a Fox News reporter who was scheduled to begin broadcasting live soon. She was looking into a compact mirror and fixing her hair as she walked.

"C'mon, Todd, we go live in ten minutes. I swear when we get back, I'm giving the producer an earful about you."

She continued to talk as she opened the door. Todd, the camera/sound man, was carrying his gear and trying desperately to keep up with her. She pulled the door open and walked through without holding it open for him.

The door closed, causing Todd's camera to hit the side of his head.

"How 'bout holding the door, Karen?" Todd complained as he rubbed his temple while trying not to drop anything.

Karen glanced in Todd's direction and spat, "Just get into that police room or Precinct or whatever they call it and get set up for the live feed."

Karen gave her full attention to her face in the small mirror as Todd scurried by and walked through the Precinct doors before any of the nurses could confront him.

The sound of the camera man walking into the Precinct drew the attention of Boss Nurse as well as an aide.

Karen viewed Omaha as a stepping stone to a larger metropolitan market. She was talking quietly to herself in a self-pitying tone.

"One more year and I'm outta this town. Kansas City, maybe St. Paul."

She focused on her nose. Satisfied, she gave one last look, then snapped her compact shut. Karen's eyes focused on a large woman standing in front of her with her hands on her hips. Startled, she jumped, then was annoyed because the woman was delaying the start of her live broadcast.

"Can I help you?" Boss Nurse bellowed as she cocked her head with an irked expression.

Karen composed herself. "Yeah, um," she said with a condescending tone. "Karen Madison, Fox News," she said this, expecting an adoring response.

Boss Nurse's expression and stance didn't change. "And?" was her response. Karen opened her purse and plopped the compact into it. Aggravated that she was not being treated as a celebrity, Karen condescendingly announced, "I'm here to do a live shot for this little old cop house. I don't have time to explain, and I doubt you'd understand if I did. So, take your little candy striper aide and please get out of my way. I've got to get into that Precinct and get this over with."

Boss Nurse's eyes narrowed at Karen's disrespectful tone. "Have you cleared this with the administration?"

Karen placed one hand on her hip. "Listen, I don't have time for this. We'll get our feel-good, fluffy little live shot of your old boys' and girls' club and get out of here. I'm sure your administration will appreciate the free publicity we'll get for them."

Boss Nurse's face remained expressionless. "So, you have not cleared this with anyone in the administration?"

"No," came the irritated reply, "and I don't need to. I'm going in there to talk to someone who hopefully isn't drooling, and then I'll get out of this place."

A mischievous grin started to form on Boss Nurse's face. The nurse's aide sheepishly chimed, "You mean you didn't call ahead to make an appoint—" Boss Nurse's hand shot up to silence the aide.

Karen barely glanced at the aide. "Look, you ladies just take care of these people's diapers and get out of my way."

Boss Nurse still didn't move.

"Hmmph," Karen grumbled as she stomped around the nurse and made her way toward the Precinct doors.

Boss Nurse smiled at the aide. "That little prima donna is about to get schooled. Let's go to the lounge and watch this live!"

As the door to the nurses' lounge burst open, five nurses sitting at a table jumped up from their chairs.

"Where's the remote? Turn it to Fox News," Boss Nurse commanded.

The nurses looked incredulously at each other, then Boss Nurse explained, "An uppity news reporter just walked into the Precinct without an appointment."

The nurses scrambled to find the remote.

~

"There's a cameraman setting up in the main walkway of the Precinct," the Sarge said as he looked at the surveillance video monitors that were hidden in his desk drawer. "Get rid of them," he added, looking at Agnes.

She gave him a half-smile and said, "I'll be back in a minute."

It was a good twenty yards from the Sarge's office to the spot where the cameraman and the blonde reporter stood. A bright light was turned on above the camera, and Todd announced, "We're on in thirty seconds."

Karen gave herself one last look over. Then she glanced over her shoulder and saw a woman in a silly police shirt and hat, wearing a hospital gown from the waist down, walking directly toward her.

"Oh look," she said to Todd. "There really are women here. Could you come here, ma'am?" She pointed to Agnes.

"Ten seconds," Todd said.

"Could you hurry it up? We're about to go live. I just need

you to stand next to me so that we get a shot of one of the female old cops who live here. Don't say anything; just nod your head and smile. Okay, sweetie, right here." Agnes saw the reporter point to a spot on the floor. "C'mon, we're going live."

Todd checked his audio. "There is a high-pitched chirp, and it's getting louder." Then his attention was drawn to a louder sound from the studio.

"Todd you're going live in 5, 4..." Todd looked at Karen and quickly said, "Karen! In 3, 2, 1," then pointed to Karen, whose face immediately transformed from an impatient, demanding reporter to a pretty, smiling celebrity looking into the camera.

"Yes, we're live here at the Old Blues Police Retirement Home. We had heard that there have been some additions to this Police Squad, and that there are now retired female cops here." Karen leaned toward Agnes and smiled. She didn't look at Agnes, just smiled at the camera and verbally acknowledged the woman standing next to her leaning on a walker.

Agnes immediately got irked at this pretty girl's flippant attitude. She looked at the woman talking, then at the camera. Sure enough, up went the nasal cannula. She shook a package of cigarettes until one emerged from the pack. She pulled a lighter from her uniform pocket and lit her smoke. The smoke was blown between the dolly girl and the camera.

Todd's eyes widened and he started to giggle. "*This is too good*," he thought. "*The spoiled brat is finally looking like an idiot on a live feed!*"

"Yes, it's true, these old gals are adding some class to these crusty old cops who like to pretend they are still police officers, by adding a feminine touch that..." Karen abruptly stopped speaking as she lost sight of the camera lens that was less than five feet away but now obscured by a curtain of smoke.

Suddenly Agnes looked past the reporter as if she wasn't there. "Benson! Brock! When am I going to get the reports on those dogs continually barking in the Kara Heights neighborhood? The people up there are furious about all the noise." Todd instinctively moved the camera to focus on the men that Agnes was addressing.

Benson and Big Brock were standing next to a bulletin board, and both simultaneously looked at Agnes with confused faces.

"Compare it to neighborhoods bordering Kara Heights. This may be some serial canines causing problems in the area." Benson and Big Brock continued to stare, dumbfounded.

"Make it fast. My Vickie's Secret brassiere keeps my ladies from drooping to my hips. I'd like those reports before they are knocking between my knees."

Simultaneously both officers' mouths dropped open in shock.

The camera swung back to the face of a completely stunned reporter. Agnes put her smoke back in her mouth and left the audience with the parting words, "Dis broad's feminine touch consists of a kick to the keister."

Agnes turned and shuffled away, leaving Karen staring at the camera wordlessly. The feed was cut and the anchor at the news studio had her hands over her mouth, laughing. "We... we will be right back after these messages."

Karen stormed out of the Precinct with Todd again trying to keep up. She came to an abrupt stop as her path to the main doors of the facility was blocked by the large nurse standing with her hands on her hips.

"Have a good time in our little boys' and girls' club?"

A chorus of laughter burst from a group of nurses standing outside the door of the nurses' lounge.

As Karen stomped around Boss Nurse and approached the door, Boss Nurse blurted, "Don't let the door hit ya where the good Lord split ya."

Todd was taking in all of this with satisfaction. As he walked out, he turned and said, "I'll make sure you all get a copy of this."

෴

"Did you see that?" Jake was hardly containing himself. "That's Karen Madison from the Fox channel. That woman can't walk past a mirror without admiring herself, and she never treats anyone like they have the right to exist in her little world. She's a 25-year-old brat."

Jake clapped his hands. "Agnes was great! That woman is incredible. She made that reporter look like a fool on a live feed. I loved every minute of it."

The Sarge chuckled and took his cigar from his mouth.

"Women like Agnes have had quite a life. Over the years they've been called Birds, Chicks, Honeys, Babes, Foxes—that one I never understood—Let's see… Chickas, Cuties, and a bunch of other names. But the women you never messed with were *da broads*. They could not only take whatever was thrown at them, they could chew it up, spit it back, and hit you in the face."

As the Sarge finished talking, the door opened and Agnes shuffled in.

Jake pointed to her from his chair. "You, Miss Congeniality, can handle my press conferences anytime."

Agnes gave a brief smile. "Anytime, especially with that little reporter. They think they're the center of the universe until they meet up with a real woman."

"Ah, yeah," Jake responded. "Well, Sarge, I'm going back to Central. Let me know when the research guys go through the blueprints of that building. When we find the secret room, I'm sure the Gang Sergeant will love to hear about it. I'll keep things under wraps until we get a better picture of the situation."

Sarge did a salute with his cigar. "You bet, Jake, I'll keep you informed."

Jake smiled and nodded to Agnes as he walked out of the Sarge's office. Once he was out of the room and halfway out of the Precinct, Agnes looked at the Sarge and said, "Secret room? Why didn't you tell him about the tunnels?"

Sitting back in his chair and popping the cigar back in his mouth, the Sarge studied the map that was projected on his wall. Then he expanded the map to include a lot of the older northern and southern parts of Omaha.

"If I recall, it wasn't just gangsters that used these tunnels," he said. "Many of the tunnels were built before the Prohibition days. The old Omaha money folks had their little mansions to the north and south of downtown Omaha. In those days it was all the rage to employ tunnel diggers so that the rich and powerful had secret entrances and exits to their estates."

Sarge picked up his phone and dialed a number that very few people had. With the phone at his ear, he looked at Agnes and a smile made its way from his cigar to his opposite ear.

"Makes one think, don't it?" he said.

Agnes shook her head in confusion. "Makes one think about what?"

Ben Mitchell, the driving force behind "the Bureau" and its primary contributor, hung up his phone and sat back in his large leather chair. Ben looked up at the ceiling and said out loud, "Those crazy old-timers are actually gonna pull this off."

He made a few calls, and a couple of hours later his special conference room was being filled by the other members of the Bureau—leaders of major industries in the Midwest. Construction, military technology, insurance, and even architecture. Ben himself was a captain of the telecommunications industry.

"They want us to upgrade those bootlegger tunnels for their use? Those old geezers are out of their minds," exclaimed Steve DeGoff, CEO of two multi-billion-dollar military defense corporations.

Dan Roberts, the architectural genius, rubbed his chin. "I'm thinking of a massive sewer renovation as a ruse. The Sarge said that some gang is using one of the tunnels to cause mayhem in the Old Market. Well, we will have to clear that tunnel, maybe even seal it so they can't use it anymore. If I remember my Omaha history right, there are numerous tunnels throughout the older areas where the high and mighty built their mansions."

Ben interjected, "They also want us to build a secret room in one of the warehouses in the Old Market. That way, the police will think the gangsters were hiding in a hidden room to escape from the pursuing cops and be none the wiser about the tunnels."

Ben scanned the room to make sure all eyes were on him. "I don't claim to understand all the crazy things these Blues have devised to stop so many crimes and bust so many criminals on our streets, but this much I know…"

He slapped the notebook in front of him.

"These Blues get results. Not in our wildest dreams when we started this little home for sweet little old retired coppers could we have imagined the magnitude of their abilities. They have exceeded our wildest expectations. They have vigorously pursued criminals, saved countless lives, and now are developing a plan to expand their expertise and abilities to our older, poorer communities. I say give them the tools they need and let them do the only thing they know, with a dedication I only wish I could have one day."

Steve exhaled and tapped a pen on the table as he talked. "We're going to have to create a reason to start constructing our own little sewer system."

Ben's brow furrowed in concentration. "Sewer… sulfur dioxide… just the smell of it will cause folks to demand action. Just pump some of it into the various sites. We'll get Al Long and his construction army to make plans to develop a sewer and tunnel complex like the one at the Old Blues facility, but this tunnel system will open up parts of the Omaha metro that were previously out of the reach of our precinct of geriatric crime fighters." Ben looked around the table to make sure everyone was on board.

Satisfied, he said, "It's settled, then. After there are some noticeable sewer smells in the city, I'll make some calls to the Mayor's office. Let's get this rolling. The Ol' Blues want this project going as soon as possible."

$\backsim$

The evening Fox News anchor looked into the camera and tried to show interest in something she couldn't care less about.

"In other news, the City of Omaha is announcing an upgrade to some of its sewer systems. Various neighborhoods have been complaining about a strong odor emanating from their sewers and storm drains. The Mayor's office in a statement explained that many of these upgrades have been in the planning stages for a while now. There will be minimal disruption of traffic due to most of the work being underground."

⁓

Thane had been looking at a map of Nebraska and had superimposed the route that was taken to Omaha. Each time there was no movement, there was a time stamp.

"Kennard... why in the world would they stay in Kennard for over an hour?" Thane asked as he tapped away at his keyboard.

A voice on his headphone interrupted his concentration.

"Hey, Thanerboy, whatta ya got?"

"Nothing much, Sarge, just doing my usual stuff, playing video games," Thane responded in a sarcastic tone.

"That's what I thought. It's a good thing I have your name on my itinerary on a daily basis. If not, you'd probably just be playing that ping-pong game all day."

With a shake of his head, Thane accepted the fact that he was talking to a man who was speaking of games that were thirty years old. Thane then informed the Sarge that he was looking over the route that Amanda's kidnappers had taken and was stumped about why they were in Kennard for over an hour.

"They stopped at an address on the outskirts of the town called Kennard on N. Pine Street. Amanda was at that address for about thirty minutes and was taken into the countryside northwest of Kennard. Her kidnappers then doubled back and headed to Omaha. Very strange."

Thane's work with the Ol' Blues had influenced him in many ways, one of which was a never-ending urge to pursue hunches and check out things that didn't make sense.

"Hmmph." Thane heard the Sarge make his usual sound when he was considering information presented to him.

As if reading the Sarge's mind, Thane said, "I'm checking it out now, Sarge."

Acknowledging Thane's remark, Sarge said, "Good, get me the addresses and we'll do some checking of our own."

The Sarge then turned his attention to his group of Blues. He walked to his office door, pulled the cigar out of his mouth, and yelled into the Precinct, "Benson, Brock!"

From somewhere in the Precinct came the responses, "Yo! Yeah Sarge."

"You two in my office for an assignment."

Benson and Brock exchanged a look of excitement. The thought of getting back out on the street shot waves of anticipation into their old yet eager hearts.

Benson and Big Brock quickly walked towards the Sarge's office. At approximately ten feet from the desk of Lead Officer Crantz, both officers instinctively gave themselves a visual and pat-down inspection to make sure their uniforms were regulation.

As they approached her desk, she eyed them over her reading glasses with her ever-present cigarette held in the fingers of her left hand and her cheek in the palm of the same hand. Her eyes gave both officers the once-over. Walking away, they started to exhale in relief at having passed Agnes's inspection.

Then the Lead Officer's voice rang out. "Brock, ya big palooka! It's about time for that fart muffler to get changed. You're sagging."

At six-foot-five, Big Brock had been a mountain of a man before years of working the streets had taken their toll. Intimidation by his mere presence made the common hood think twice about trying anything stupid like fighting with this cop. When he growled, "Move it!" there was rarely any debate. But gravity had pulled at Big Brock for decades without mercy. He had a bit of a bend in his spine and appeared to be slouching forward, but he could still give a warning look that made anyone on the receiving end of his glare stop whatever they were doing.

Given the fact that very few things intimidated this man, the Sarge was amused to see him try to straighten up without looking back at Lead Officer Crantz.

"I'll take care of it, Lead Officer."

Sarge closed the door. He could tell Big Brock was miffed about being scolded for his diaper sagging a bit. As he walked by the two Blues standing in front of his desk, he took an exaggerated look at both of their back sides.

"I've seen worse."

Brock smiled. "So have we. Agnes about ran over us on her way to your little rendezvous the other night. She didn't have the back of her robe tied. A sagging diaper can't compare to the drooping raisin butt cheeks we had to see when she scooted by. My mind's eye still burns when I think about it."

Benson laughed and added, "I saw a couple of dehydrated prunes next to each other on a plate in the cafeteria and 'bout yacked."

The Sarge tried to contain himself. "All right, you two. I have an assignment. Turns out before our little recruit Amanda ended up in that house of horrors, she was in a little town north of Omaha called Kennard."

"Yeah, I know the place," Benson responded. "Not much to it. My sister lived there for years. Mostly farmers and small-town workers live there."

Sarge suggested, "Might come in handy when you nose around at the address that Thane is tracking down for you. Small-town folks like to talk when you can drop a name of someone they know. If your sister lived there, odds are people would know her. Get some civilian clothes on. I should have the information for you by the time you change."

Benson and Big Brock were as giddy as little boys heading to their first baseball game. The golf cart ride in the tunnels leading to the garage/repair shop rekindled the excitement of heading for an undercover detail. They couldn't wait to hit the streets. They had to take Thane with them because he could not find an address for an area outside of town where Amanda's GPS watch showed that she had stopped for about thirty minutes.

"It's right up the street about a half a block. Belongs to an Ethel Kurt," Thane informed the driver.

"Drive past the house," Big Brock instructed in a tone that sounded like an order.

"Past the house? Why on earth would you want to do that?" Thane blurted.

"Don't ever drive up or walk up directly to your mark, kid," was Brock's reply. "Always get a look at what you are dealing with before you step into something you didn't expect. Many a copper has gotten hurt or killed walking up to what he thought was a simple look-see."

Thane had learned to shut up when a Blue was giving him field advice. *"Listen and learn,"* he told himself.

As the van went by the house, Thane leaned forward and was about to speak.

"Sit back, don't stare, just glance over and we go right by the place," Brock instructed. "That way, those inside won't think we are taking an interest in what is in that house."

Thane sat back and looked straight ahead. "Got it, sorry."

Big Brock let out a deep breath. "Feel like I'm field training a new recruit."

Benson nudged Brock to his side. "Not much in the field, but the kid knows his computer stuff. Sarge swears by him."

Big Brock's eyebrows lifted. "You don't say? High praise from the Sarge?" Then he turned his attention to the driver. "Go around the block. The place looked empty. Let's see what we can find out."

This time the transport van pulled up in front of the house. Benson and Big Brock glanced around and then acted like slow-moving old men, which wasn't hard for Benson to do since he used a walker. They talked about the trees, flowers, and things in general as their eyes searched for anything that might provide information about the people who lived in this house.

"Are you from the nursing home?" an old woman called to the men from her porch chair across the street. "Ethel hasn't been home in a while. Thought you men were lost when you drove past the house the first time."

Benson smiled and quietly commented to Big Brock, "Small towns... there's no fooling these folks. They know everything that goes on here. She made us right off the bat."

Benson thought he had better earn some quick trust. "We haven't seen Ethel for a while, so Brock and I decided to come visit her. My sister used to live over on 3rd Street. Maybe you knew her... Morgan Benson?"

The old woman threw her hands up. "Oh, yes, what a sweetheart she was. She used to be a wonderful baker."

Benson smiled and said, "She made the best strawberry rhubarb pie I've ever eaten. I used to visit her, but as I got older, I just didn't get out as much as I would have liked. You know how it is."

The woman smiled and nodded. "Time goes by, doesn't it?"

Both men smiled in agreement.

"My sister mentioned that Ethel moved to Kennard a few years back. After we hadn't seen her for a couple of months, me and Brock decided to stop by and say hello. You say she isn't here?" Benson asked.

The woman rested her hands on the apron that ladies of her generation always wore around the house. "Ethel only lived here for a few years, but I always liked her. Poor dear is in hospice care now. From what I hear she probably won't ever return to her home. It's a shame."

Benson looked at Brock, who acted surprised. "Well, that explains why we haven't seen her for so long." Benson figured that he had established enough trust with the woman. Brock quietly told him to find out if anyone else lived in the house.

"Does her family still live with her?"

"Oh no, nobody lives there now. Ethel's husband died about ten years ago. There's a lawn service that takes care of the yard."

Brock said quietly enough for only Benson to hear, "Looks like a dead end. Maybe Amanda was with those grounds crew guys. They would have been here an hour or two."

Benson shrugged and said, "Maybe." Then he looked at the yard. "Those lawn care people seem to do a good job," he commented. "Do you know which company it is?"

The woman shook her head. "No, seems to be a different outfit every few weeks. It's good that the house is kept up so well. Probably planning on selling it."

Benson waved. "Well, it's been nice talking to you, Miss... " She cut him off. "Mrs. Christopher Brimhall," she said with pride. Benson smiled and said to Brock, "Women of our day used to introduce themselves as Mrs. whatever their husband's name was."

Waving, Benson said, "Thank you, Mrs. Brimhall. It's so nice to meet someone who knew my sister. You have a nice day now."

Benson and Brock turned and started walking back to the van. Then, as small-town folks do, Mrs. Brimhall kept the conversation going while the men were walking away. "Her son stops by and checks on the house fairly often."

Both Blues stopped in their tracks and slowly looked at each other. "Her son?" Benson asked. "We didn't know Ethel had any other family."

I didn't really know him. He moved out before she moved into this house with her husband for their retirement home. He doesn't talk much. Coming from a big city, I guess they just come in and do what they gotta do, then leave. He would wave, but that's about it. Sometimes some friends in a van drive up and park in the garage. Must help him clean. I think he is in the medical field, so he's pretty busy. I never really knew his name. Kinda odd, don't you think?"

Benson shrugged. "City people, I guess, just don't know how to be neighborly. Well, thanks again, Mrs. Brimhall. It was so nice talking to you." She waved and smiled.

They were about three steps from the van when they were stopped again by Mrs. Brimhall's voice. "Last time he was here was a little over a month ago."

Again, both men turned. "What's that?"

She pointed to the garage. "Ethel's son came over, and a little while later his friends came by. A bald man and a woman in a van. Possibly their daughter in the back seat. Well, they went into the garage, and then a short time later drove into

CHRIS LEGROW | 175

town leaving their daughter there. Probably went to pick up some cleaning supplies. A little while later the woman came a rushin' back to the house and drove into the garage. She closed the garage door, then a few minutes later, the garage door opened up and she drove off by herself. Strange, isn't it?" She added. "I didn't see them after that, and I haven't seen them since. Just can't figure out city people. Her son has come by a couple of times, but that's about it."

Benson leaned on his walker and looked over at Big Brock. "Ten bucks says we don't make it back to the van before she starts up again."

Benson yelled, "Haven't seen them since then? That is odd, but the son still comes by. Well, nice to see he's taking care of the house. Thanks again, Mrs. Brimhall."

"So nice to talk to you. If you see Ethel, tell her I said Hey."

"We will. Bye now."

Thane could hear the conversation outside the van through his open window. He was amused that the woman seemed to want to carry the conversation on and on. It appeared that it was finally over as Big Brock and Benson came to the doors of the van.

"Watch out for the turkeys!" Mrs. Brimhall called out.

Both men looked at each other again, then back toward Mrs. Brimhall with questioning expressions.

"Horrible birds. They are big and mean out here. If you walk around the outskirts of town, you'll probably run into a bunch of those awful things."

Benson reached over and slapped Big Brock with his hand palm up and wiggled his fingers. Brock reached into his pocket and pulled out a wad of bills. He counted out ten bucks and slapped the money into Benson's hand.

Mrs. Brimhall continued, "A group of them chased the mailman all the way down the street last week. They got them big claws, and they jumped at the man as he ran. Cut his legs all up. There's a lot of 'em around here."

Thane remembered something he had seen on the Internet regarding turkeys. He quickly typed, "Turkey attacking people/video." To his horror, there were all kinds of videos of turkeys attacking people, chasing them, and cutting them with their talons.

"Holy smokes, those things are vicious," he said out loud.

"We'll keep an eye out for the turkeys. Thanks, Mrs. Brimhall." Again, Benson and Brock waved.

As they turned, they could hear the old woman continuing to talk. "Probably what killed that woman north of here. Foolish women running around in their ponytail hair and tight elastic clothes. Jogging all over the countryside. It's them turkeys; I just know it."

Once they got back into the van, Benson told the driver, "Time to head back to the Precinct."

As they were leaving Kennard, there were cornfields to the left of the road they were on. Sure enough, about fifteen turkeys walked out of the field and onto the road. Big Brock pointed. "Look, those are turkeys, just like that old woman said. I've never seen one in the wild. They're huge." Then Brock noticed their feet. "Claws! Look at their claws!"

Thane looked up from his laptop. "Talons, and they're sharp. Wow, they really are big. Gotta be three feet high."

The driver stopped as the monstrous birds waltzed onto the road like they owned it. The birds took an interest in the shuttle van and started to walk around it and peck at it. The driver laughed. Benson and Big Brock started to laugh too.

Then Thane held his laptop where both Blues could see the screen and started to play the video compilation of turkeys attacking people. Benson was amused, but Big Brock's eyes were wide in terror. Something about birds attacking people scared him to death. His eyes shifted from the video images of people screaming and running to huge birds that he thought were heavily clawed and ready to attack.

Brock's forehead touched the window as he looked at the big birds surrounding the van. He had never seen a turkey in the wild, only on a plate next to some mashed potatoes and gravy. One of the turkeys looked up at him and jumped toward his face. It spread its wings, making it look three times bigger than it actually was, and pecked on the window.

Thane, Benson, and the driver were jolted by a shrill scream from Big Brock. "Drive! Drive! Get outta here! Tried to eat my face!"

The driver was looking back into the passenger compartment. He jerked his body forward and started to drive slowly forward, trying not to drive over the turkeys in front of him.

Benson looked at Brock and then at Thane. Thane was already looking at Benson. Both men simultaneously looked at Big Brock, who had a horrified look on his face as sweat started to run down his forehead.

"Brock, what's wrong?"

Big Brock didn't say a word; he just put his hand on the headrest on top of the seat in front of him and twisted to look out the windows at the turkeys. He wailed, "Ahh, they're coming, they're chasing us!" Sure enough, the turkeys were running alongside the slow-moving van. One even flew up and hit the back window. Its huge wingspan blocked both windows.

Brock started screaming and banging his back against the back of his seat. "Faster! Faster! Ahhh!"

The driver was clear of the turkeys that had been in his path earlier, and he floored the accelerator. The birds tried feverishly to run after the van. It was a funny sight to everyone in the van. They were laughing and pointing at the birds as they gave chase for about twenty yards. Everyone but the largest, meanest man in the Precinct. Brock turned forward, sweating and breathing like he had just sprinted across a field. His hand was on his chest.

"Get me back to the city."

Benson started to laugh. "Brock, what's wrong with... "

"I said get me back to the city!" Brock reached into his pocket and pulled out a handkerchief. He wiped his face while looking up at the ceiling. "Lord, why'd you put them birds here?"

Benson looked at Thane and put his finger to his lips. "Don't laugh," he mouthed. This was more of a warning than an instruction. The ride back to the Precinct was quiet.

Thane periodically looked into the large mirror above his head and saw that Big Brock would sit quietly, then quickly look out the rear windows to check for any pursuing feathered hellions.

CHAPTER 7

As he spat a mouthful of toothpaste into the bathroom sink, he imagined spitting in the faces of all the women who had humiliated and degraded him over the years. As if he was watching a movie in fast-forward, he saw the faces of the women who had laughed at him, belittled his appearance, and mocked his awkwardness. He hated them, all of them, and craved the satisfaction of demeaning and dominating them.

The Armenians had provided a means of quenching his lust to dominate women without having to face any consequences. In exchange for a modest fee, he provided them with a concoction of chemicals mixed just right to invoke a mind- and body-numbing haze. The Armenians even delivered the women to him and then took them away after he had released his aggression on them.

He had to admit that this was a safe and convenient way to assault women, but he missed the satisfaction of manipulating women while they were awake. Prior to attacking each of his targets, he had enjoyed messing with the woman's mind. He would find out where she lived and then cause things to happen around her home that made her question her own sanity.

He would turn on an exterior water faucet during the night, just enough to leave a puddle waiting for her in the morning. He would let out the air from her tires bit by bit—not enough to make them flat, but just enough to cause problems driving. When she tried to get them fixed, the mechanic would tell her that there was nothing wrong with the tires. He would open gates and even move outdoor equipment like lawnmowers or tools from a backyard shed to another spot or even on the lawn. His goal was to make the woman think she was losing her mind. Each action was small, but gradually she would start doubting herself.

After a few days of causing what the woman thought were small mental lapses, he would start to tighten his grip on her mentally. He enjoyed stalking the woman and learning everything he could about her. Eventually he would figure out how to get into her home while she was away.

He knew that the mental stresses he had caused with his antics outside of her residence could now be focused on causing serious psychological effects inside the security of her home. All the little comforts of her home could be used against her to accomplish his designs.

He started with insignificant things like moving magazines from a coffee table to various other places in a living room. Then he found that interrupting a woman's daily routine had a profound effect on how she viewed her own mental state. From a hidden vantage point outside her home, he could observe her from a safe and discreet distance. Usually she would sit on her couch, then glance around with a confused look on her face. Then she would stand with her hands on her hips looking around for whatever he had hid or put in a different place.

Once the woman started to put the palm of her hand on her forehead and make some frustrated gestures, he knew that things were working out just as he wanted. In his final act of psychological assault, he would start moving the woman's personal items—things that were almost always put in the same place, such as her deodorant, toothbrush, underwear, and the utensils in her kitchen drawer. As he observed her from his concealed position, she would unknowingly provide him the sadistic entertainment that he craved.

Finally he would carry out the physical assault that sealed his vengeance. After covering his face, he drugged the woman and then assaulted her while she slept. When she woke up, the woman wouldn't even know what had happened to her and would feel dazed or confused. If she tried to get help, she might be hospitalized for mental exams and drug evaluation.

In the past the police had questioned him a couple of times, but they could never gather enough evidence to connect him to the crimes he had committed. The fact that the women all said that they thought they were losing their minds was problematic to the police investigation as well.

These assaults had taken place years ago. Despite advances in DNA testing, today's cops would still have a difficult time pinning any sexual assaults on him. He smiled as he reminded himself that if an investigation were to lead to his arrest, he could use a "get-out-of-jail-free" card that he kept quietly to himself.

The Chemist smiled and whispered to his reflected image, "I don't need the Armenians anymore."

Inside the Sarge's office, Thane, Benson, and Big Brock were almost dozing off as they sat waiting for the Sarge.

Thinking out loud, Benson said, "When the Sarge gets here, all we really have to report is that the woman who used to live in the house, Ethel Kurt, is in hospice care and probably won't come home. Second, her son, who is not identified, periodically comes to the house and stays inside. That neighborhood watch lady, Mrs. Brimhall, did say that every week or two a van drives into the garage and closes the door. After a couple of minutes, the garage door opens and the van leaves, only to return an hour or two later. Why do you think they do that? Something is strange here. Why would anyone drive a van into the garage, close the door, and then leave a while later? I think the people in that van are up to something. And this son of the lady that lives there...I'm sure something is going on."

Thane responded, "When I get back to my desk, I'll see what I can find."

Benson started to smile. He looked over to Big Brock who was in and out of his nap, snorting with a low snore. Benson's smile broadened.

The Sarge approached his office, giving a nod to Lead Officer Crantz. As he reached for his doorknob, he started to turn it when the most unusual sound emanated. Sarge pulled his door and the strange sound got louder and was joined by a loud screech from Big Brock.

The Sarge took one step into his office and froze at the sight of Brock waving his arms and wiping at his face.

"Brock, what the... "

Benson was blowing into what turned out to be a turkey caller. As the Sarge stepped into his office, Benson abruptly stopped blowing into the tormenting instrument.

Big Brock regained his composure, looked around and through labored breathing gasped, "Jumping at my face, my face."

Trying to grasp what he was seeing, the Sarge yelled, "What is going on?"

"Biggest birds you ever seen."

Big Brock looked terrified and beads of sweat started rolling down his face. "Jump right at you and rip your face off."

After a couple of seconds, Big Brock realized that Benson had been the cause of his near heart attack. He glared at Benson and promised, "We gonna talk later," then gave him a stare that Benson had seen for many years when the two of them had worked together.

"Don't give me that look, Brock," Benson said. "That was a good one and you know it. We'll just have to watch out for those killer cluckers when we go up to that town again."

"Are you two finished?" Sarge asked as he made his way to his desk. He sat with an old man groan, then pointed to Thane.

"Thanerboy, whattayagot?"

Thane looked up from his computer with his usual annoyance at his nickname. Then he provided the Sarge with the information they had found so far in their investigation. The Sarge leaned forward in his chair as Thane reported what the neighbor had said about the activity at the house.

"This last time it was a bald man and a woman. There was a young woman in the back seat when they pulled in, but she wasn't there when they left. They weren't gone too long when the woman came speeding up the street and into the garage again and then closed the door. She left about five to ten minutes later. Mrs. Brimhall said she thought the woman was alone in the van."

In a sarcastic tone, the Sarge said, "If I were the suspicious type, I would think they were bringing something to the house, dropping it off, and then coming back later to pick something up. Looks like they didn't want anyone to see what it was."

"I'd have closed those doors, too, with all them turkeys around," Brock quietly interjected.

"Will you stop with the stupid turkeys?" Benson didn't want Brock to get any angrier about those birds, so he was trying to avoid discussing them.

"Killed a woman out in the countryside few weeks back. That's what Mrs. Brimhall said. Right, Thane?" Brock spoke as if Benson wasn't in the room.

"She said that somebody found the body of a woman who was probably killed by a flock of those turkeys." Brock folded his arms as if the statement supported his newfound fear of the birds.

"Actually, they're called a rafter, not a flock," Thane interjected while pointing to his laptop.

"I knew it. Remember the dinosaur movie with them vanilla rafters? Those birds were just like 'em. Kill ya with their taloclaws."

Thane looked at Big Brock in confusion. "I think you mean velociraptor, and turkeys have talons, not claws."

Brock gave Thane the same look he had given Benson. Thane then added, "...but they are very sharp and can cut you pretty bad. I saw the pictures."

Satisfied that he'd made his point, Big Brock crossed his arms, leaned back in his chair, and looked at Benson out of the side of his eye. "I better not hear that turkey whistle again. Boss Nurse Betsy will be pulling it out of your diaper—just watch."

"If you're finished with the turkey lesson..." the Sarge said, "you jokers did manage to get us some intelligence we can work on. Thane, see if you can identify this Ethel Kurt's son. Give me a call when you find something."

Nodding at his crew, the Sarge concluded the meeting. As Thane and the Blues were exiting, the Sarge's mind caught hold of something that had been said during the meeting. "Wait, did you say a woman was killed outside that little town?"

Big Brock pulled his hands from his pockets. "That's right, them vicious birds killed a woman, according to that lady." He stated it in a matter-of-fact tone, again validating his newfound fear of the feathered beasts.

The Sarge's mind had begun searching for something he had heard recently about a woman's body being found in the countryside.

"All right, fine, dismissed."

He reached for his phone and started dialing as he sat back in his chair. "Jake. Can you talk? Remember that woman's body that was found in the countryside north of Omaha?"

∽

Lois was transferring computer files to thumb drives and then deleting the files from her hard disk. She needed to remove any evidence that could connect her to the missing young women.

Her mind raced as she tried to plan for her success and prevent any possible failure. The progress of her operation was monitored by her brother Aziz in Armenia. He in turn kept the Cartel informed of her activities so they would be able to determine what her operations would produce for them. The fact that she had not been checking in with Aziz as usual must be causing concern.

Lois knew that she could only delay the inevitable. She told Aziz lies about having to keep a low profile for a while. She said that the Director of Health and Human Services was conducting an audit of all the departments in her agency. This meant that her brother Aziz could not stick his prying eyes into her computer for fear of causing the discovery of the operation. This was an effective ruse, but even the best of plans could only last for a limited time.

Lois was putting the finishing touches on the inner workings of the operation from her office. She knew that when Aziz discovered her failure, he would not hesitate to have her killed. Brother or not, Aziz was devoted to the family business and would not tolerate failure.

A few other details needed to be wrapped up. She had to make sure that any records of the safe house could not be traced to her. She also had to remove any evidence of the network that had been employed to transfer the girls from Nebraska to Armenia. Anyone who knew of the connection to her and the girls would have to be eliminated. She kept Victor and Vladimir around to take care of any messes that came along with cleaning up her network.

At the sound of footsteps, Lois looked toward the door of her office.

"There, see, it's back," Vladimir pointed. "That disgusting animal is back. I pushed that thing into the hallway yesterday, and it's back."

Victor gave him an impatient look. "Stupid, they have cleaning people here every night, they probably put it back. All the people that work in these offices know Lois has to keep this animal for that old man."

"Yeeach, it makes me sick to my stomach when it looks at me."

Lois slapped her desk. "Will you two stop your talk with this dead dog? We have work to do. You're supposed to be workers helping me with upgrading my office. Start acting like it. Make sure you are speaking English when you talk. Americans don't like it when you speak another language in their presence. Makes them feel like you are talking about them."

Victor smiled, "We are." Both men laughed.

Walking into his computer lab, Thane came to an abrupt stop when he noticed a man sitting at a surveillance monitor. Thane wasn't accustomed to having anyone near his workstation. The man was listening intently and didn't notice Thane as he entered the room.

Thane looked the man over. This guy was in his late seventies, but Thane's experience with the Ol' Blues had taught him never to judge a man by looks alone. The man's hair was gray, and he appeared to have thick straight sections on his scalp that looked like scars. Thane could see that he must have been a huge man in his day. Even though his age was apparent, his shoulders were still broad. His skin was wrinkled and appeared to have been cracked by lots of time in the sun.

Before Thane announced his presence, he looked at the man's left hand resting on the arm of the chair. Thane cocked his head as he realized something wasn't right with the man's fingers. His eyebrows raised as he noticed that the man had scars where his fingernails used to be.

The stranger must have sensed that someone was close to him. With a jerk, he snapped his head around. Thane thought the man had an angry look on his face. Without uttering a word, Thane slowly raised his hand and meekly waved. The man appeared to relax as if he had determined that Thane wasn't a threat.

"You that red-headed keyboard jockey I've heard about?" the man almost growled.

Thane was terrified and realized that he was still waving at the man.

"Relax, kid, I already had my lunch, I ain't gonna eat ya."

Thane looked at his waving hand and quickly dropped it. "Uh, why are you in my work area?"

The man pointed to the surveillance video. "Steve DeGoff from your Bureau thought my services would be helpful with this little investigation you're doing. As a favor to him, I told him yes. This isn't my usual operations specialty. Looks like you need someone to interpret these Armenian goons," the man said as he gestured with his thumb over his shoulder at the monitor.

"I've been watching this Lois and the two baldies this morning. I don't know who the jokers were that placed your surveillance cameras, but they did a terrible job concealing them. They all keep looking right at the camera. You guys are gonna be made any minute. They also keep talking about a dog, but I don't see a dog in the office."

Thane smiled and pulled up a chair next to the man.

"They're talking about getting records out of the office and making some sort of change. Oh, now that guy is saying something about a dog again. What dog?"

⚬

"There are fifty cases here," Lois said. "Make sure they are kept together. These are girls that are about to turn eighteen. We may need this information to show our new contacts south of the border that we are ready to provide these girls as soon as we agree to terms. This will make us more worth the investment."

Vladimir blurted, "That dog's eyes are driving me crazy. I don't care what you say, I don't have to keep looking at it."

Vladimir put the box down and marched toward Boomer.

⚬

"What did I tell you? That guy is walking right to the camera," the man said to Thane. "I thought you guys were supposed to be working with a bunch of seasoned cops. They should have known where to place cameras."

Then the man tapped the monitor he was watching. "The guy is grabbing your camera and…"

Both Thane and the mystery man watched in silence as the camera seemed to spin around and was then focused on an outlet on a wall.

"What kind of camera did you mount? This is really weird."

Thane looked at the confused man and smiled.

"What are you smiling about?"

Thane explained the Boomer Cam and described the work that had gone into retrofitting the stuffed dog with cameras in its eyes and then getting it into Lois's office.

The man leaned back in his chair and threw his head back with a loud laugh. "Brilliant! Hah! I never would have figured to use a dead dog as a camera. Problem now is that they put his face against the wall. We can't... "

He paused as Thane held up his finger to ask for silence. Thane pushed a few buttons. The room with the woman and men again filled up the monitor along with sound. Thane looked at the man and then sat back in his chair with his arms crossed in satisfaction. He pointed to the monitor and smiled, explaining, "Anus cam."

"What?" The man bounced in his chair in disbelief. "Freaking genius; a camera pointing at them where they'll never find it. Anus cam! I abso-freaking love it. Kid, I'm gonna love working with ya."

Thane smiled and softly asked, "Who *are* you?"

&

A workman was scratching his head as he looked at the building.

"These buildings are relics. Are you sure the boss said to put a room here? I mean, this is an old building that isn't even in use anymore."

His supervisor smiled. "Since when could we figure out why the boss wants something done? As good as he treats us, I'll build anything anywhere the man says. When we're done here, we'll join the crew working the underground. It's gonna be like the one at the Old Cops' Home, only this time we go through different parts of town, separating the sewer from the tunnels."

The workman nodded. "I'm with ya. Whatever the man needs, I'll do it. Now, where does he want this hidden room?"

෨

As the Sarge had requested, Thane was working hard to track down the identity of the man who had been in and out of the house in Kennard. According to the GPS watch, Amanda had been there for about an hour before being driven out to the countryside north of town and eventually to the safe house in Omaha.

The Sarge was on the phone with Jake Mitchell. Something from his meeting with Benson, Brock, and Thane had caused him to remember hearing about a woman's body being found north of town in the countryside.

Jake listened to the Sarge and was about to tell him about the meeting he'd had with the Chief and the other agencies regarding the woman's body. "Yeah, I was in your office when the media reported it. Turns out..." Jake was cut short by one of the local reporters who go through the piles of police reports each day and then choose one for a story to air on the news.

"Officer Mitchell... Oh! Sorry, didn't know you were on the phone."

Jake raised his index finger up and said, "Give me a minute." Then he got back with the Sarge and said, "I can be there in an hour. Would that work? Okay, fine." Then he hung up.

He turned to the reporter and explained, "Sorry, I'm the liaison between the Chief's Office and the retired cops out at the Old Blues Retirement Home. They run the neighborhood programs."

"Wait, what did you need? I gotta leave, but if it's something quick I can help you."

The reporter held out a report. "Just need a mugshot of this guy that got arrested in the Old Market for robbery. The news desk wants to do a spot on the guy tonight."

Jake knew that there was an ongoing investigation. "The Gang Unit is still working on additional possible charges on him. They're showing his photo to other robbery victims. If we release his photo to the public before we show it to the other possible victims, it will ruin the case. So I can't release his photo just yet."

This reporter, Katie Niver, had been in the business for quite a few years. She knew a good story when she heard it.

"So, this guy may be responsible for numerous robberies." She smiled. "Okay, Jake, I'll hold off, but I get the exclusive when the investigation is over."

Jake smiled back. He didn't respect a lot of the reporters, but this one was different. She wasn't out to ruin investigations just to broadcast a story, and she was good at what she did. She could always spot something about an arrest and see that there was more to it.

"Katie, of all the reporters who knock on this door, you're my favorite snoop. I appreciate that you'll hold off, and you bet you get the exclusive when we finish the investigation into this guy. He goes by *Knucks,* short for 'Knuckles.' I think this will be a good story for you. Thanks for the cooperation."

Katie folded the report and stuck it in her purse. "Remember, Jake, I'll sit on this but only for a few days."

Jake pointed at Katie and winked. "You're the best. I gotta get going, and I'll be looking forward to that video."

෴

The Sarge's phone rang. He glanced at it and recognized the number.

"Well, Ben Mitchell, how are you?" While waiting for a response, Sarge sat back in his chair.

"Good, Sarge. Got some news on the progress on the tunnels. Moving faster than we thought. Turns out the more we explore down there, the more tunnels we find. So, rather than having to build new tunnels, the crews will just renovate the old ones. They separate the tunnels from the sewers, which relatively speaking is a fast job. The guys down there also have been exploring and mapping out the tunnels. So far, most have been sealed off at some point during the last seventy years. The crews are in the process of working out networks so there will be access to many points of the city—especially those parts with a high crime rate."

This information made the Sarge lean forward in his chair. "That's great news, Ben. How about the tunnel that those crooks were using in the Old Market?"

There was a chuckle in the response. "The guys found the entrance in a false wall—pretty genius. They're putting the finishing touches on it. They used the entrance of the tunnel, sealed it off and made it into a room. They've been setting up surveillance in the tunnel while they survey it in case those thugs come calling before we secure it. Do you remember Steve DeGoff?"

After a moment, the Sarge replied, "The military billionaire. Yeah, I remember him."

"DeGoff has some special operations guy that works for him. I don't know where he finds them."

Sarge's eyes widened.

"Wow, DeGoff has quite the network," Ben added. "Nice to have him on our side. By the way, DeGoff is sending over an expert to help out your guys downstairs. This guy is an expert in that old eastern bloc area of the world, and he offered to have him help out downstairs. As a matter of fact, he is downstairs now getting to know your guys."

The Sarge's brow furrowed. "I know that those guys are your part of this outfit, but I like to know when there is a change in personnel. Who is this guy?"

"The man was ex-military intelligence, CIA, and other organizations that officially don't exist," Ben explained. "He speaks a number of languages associated with the former Soviet Union. From what Steve DeGoff told me, there isn't much this guy doesn't know when it comes to that part of the world and the underworld over there. The government no longer recognizes him as an official agent. That's what happens when one president tells his agents to do something and then the next president condemns everything. Meanwhile, the poor guys who were doing what they were informed was their duty to the country ended up being cut off, pension and all. DeGoff knows about these guys and utilizes them when the CIA or Homeland Security need help quickly and without the rest of the world knowing about it. I really don't know much more about the guy, but if DeGoff trusts him, I trust him."

The Sarge pulled his cigar from his mouth. "Sounds like an interesting man. He might just fit in really well here. Listen, Ben, your brother Jake is on his way over here. I didn't tell him about the tunnel system idea at first, but if this works out, it will expand our capabilities for intelligence and surveillance tenfold. I'm also going down to the research lab to meet this new guy. I don't even know his name yet. I'll bring Jake down with me and fill him in on what's going on with the tunnels and our new personnel. I don't know what Jake's response will be, but I'm sure he'll grow into it. It represents a major change in our abilities. It is also going to be more for him to keep away from the media, the Chief, and the public. I'll talk to you later."

Immediately after the Sarge hung up, his hearing aid let out a tone.

"Sarge, this is Mary. A good-looking young fella is coming into the Precinct. Tried to tell me something about working for the Chief of Police. Don't know what his game is, but I told him I'd check him out. Name is Jake Mitchell."

The Sarge smiled, "Tail him, Mary, and don't let him sweet talk you."

A few minutes later, there was a knock at the Sarge's door.

"Enter," was Sarge's response.

In walked a rather upset Jake Mitchell.

"Who is that purple-haired, big-eyed woman in the wheelchair? She followed me all the way into the building and grilled me on who I was coming to see. Did I have an appointment? She wanted my police identification. I wasn't sure if she knew about my status in this geezer squad. When I tried to speak nicely to her, she thought I was asking her on a date."

Jake realized that the Sarge hadn't said anything and was smiling. Jake's hands went to his hips. "You pulling my chain again, Sarge? Who is she?"

From behind Jake a female voice replied, "Your worst nightmare, sweet cheeks."

Sarge let out a loud, crackling laugh. "Jake, meet Mary. Her and Agnes are a couple of the best officers this department ever produced. This lady can work security better than anyone I know."

He pulled the cigar from his mouth and used it to point to Mary. "Mary, this is Jake Mitchell, our liaison with the police department and an honorary Ol' Blue. Jake is an important part of our organization."

Mary crossed her arms and glanced at Jake. "I don't care who he is. If he tries to get fresh with me again, I'll give him the what-for." She pointed to Jake. "Better believe it, bub."

She backed out of the Sarge's office. Before the door closed, Jake and the Sarge heard her remark to Agnes: "The nerve of that guy, thinking I'd chance a date with him."

Jake looked at the Sarge with his mouth open and hands in the air. Once the door closed, he looked at Sarge and said, "You got me again."

"Only means I like ya, Jake. Now come with me down to the research lab. Got some updates about our organization and some new additions. Also, possibly some information about the woman that was killed up north in the countryside."

⌒

"Hey, Thanerboy, whattayagot?"

Thane didn't even look up. "Nothing, Sarge. Just playing ping pong video games."

"Thought so. Don't know why we keep you dweebs around here. Anything else?"

"Not much. Just been researching the woman who lives in that house in Kennard, trying to figure out who her son is. Also been keeping an eye on that woman Lois and her two goons. That part of our work has been moving much faster since the new guy started reviewing all the tapes."

The Sarge looked around the work area and noticed that the new guy wasn't around. "Well, that's the other reason I'm here. I want to meet this guy that the military mogul thinks will help us out."

"Call me Mac." The voice bellowed from behind the Sarge. "The Mogul thinks you guys are a pretty sharp bunch out here. Well, down here."

Mac glanced around him at the research and development area. "Very impressive. My new dweeb friend Thane tells me you have a guy that's pretty good with seeing things that others don't see. I'd like to meet with him."

Sarge gave Thane a questioning look.

"Smitty," Thane said, answering Sarge's unspoken question.

"You got it; I'll have him come down after his bath."

Mac looked confused. Thane smiled, "You'll get used to it."

Mac shrugged and extended his hand to Sarge. "I take it you're the Sarge I've heard so much about."

Meeting Mac's solid grip with one of his own, the Sarge smiled with the cigar in his mouth. "If your boss thinks you can provide some service to us, I'm glad to have you aboard."

"Don't really have bosses anymore. After working that old Soviet region for many years, I got to know quite a bit about their underworld. When I heard that this little squad of old-schoolers was investigating a human trafficking ring connected to the Armenians, I wanted in. I've seen what happens to these girls once they're sucked into that trafficking world over there. They dope 'em up and use the poor girls till their bodies are almost shredded, then throw them away like trash."

"You'll make a nice addition," Jake chimed in.

Mac looked over to the younger man. "You don't look like an old crusty."

With a smile, Jake pointed his thumb at the Sarge. "Not yet, but these geezers are aging me fast. I'm Jake Mitchell. My brother is Ben Mitchell of the Bureau." Mac acknowledged the reference to his brother.

Jake added, "I work for the Omaha Police Department as the Public Information Officer for the Chief. He doesn't know anything about this operation, and my job is to make sure he never does."

Pointing his cigar, the Sarge announced, "Jake is a major part of our operation. He gets our intelligence to the proper crime units and lets us know about the problem areas of the city. We quietly help out the current coppers without them knowing we were ever there. Just a bunch of sweet old guys in a retirement home. We'll give you the tour once you're settled in."

Mac smiled, acknowledged Jake, and added, "Well, if it's anything like this outfit down here, it must be something to see."

Thane chimed in, "You won't believe it."

Sarge looked at Thane. "Wrap up what you've got so far and get me a report within the hour. Welcome aboard, Mac. I'll get Smitty down here soon."

As they left the research area, Mac leaned over to Thane and quietly said, "Uh, he wasn't wearing any pants. Didn't want to say anything, but... "

Thane pointed up to the ceiling. When you get up there, you'll understand."

As Jake and the Sarge headed back to the Sarge's office, Jake said, "Oh, you wanted to know about the woman whose body was found in the countryside?"

The Sarge hit his forehead with the palm of his hand. "Yeah, thanks for reminding me. I sent some guys up to Kennard because Amanda's GPS outer space watch said that she had been at a residence there for about an hour. We're trying to put together what was going on, but at this point it turns out that the woman who lives there has been in hospice care for quite a while. The lady across the street mentioned that a woman had been killed north of Kennard. The lady thought it was wild turkeys that killed her."

Jake put his finger to his chin, deep in thought. "The FBI thinks the tattoo on the dead woman's wrist came from Armenia. That matches up with what Thane has found, so we're on the right track."

Sarge pushed the button on his hearing aid. "Smitty, can you meet me and Jake in my office?"

Smitty eagerly replied, "Got it, Sarge, be right there."

As they approached the Sarge's office, Sarge filled Jake in on the new tunnel system that was being developed. Astonished, Jake exclaimed, "You mean we're going to have these Ol' Blues popping up all over the city, then disappearing and scooting along underground highways and popping up back here in time for their strained peaches?"

Sarge shrugged. "This will expand our abilities in ways we can't even imagine. Give us some time to work on it."

Jake rolled his eyes. "I was hoping to change departments, start over, and maybe retire here in the quiet Midwest. Now I'm sucked into the service of this bunch of rogue geezers."

Sarge elbowed him and jested, "Well, it ain't all bad. Our little Brittany seems to be a nice perk."

Jake smiled. "The only thing in my life that makes sense."

Smitty beat Jake and Sarge to the Sarge's office. He stood outside the door because Lead Officer Crantz would not allow him in without authorization from the Sarge. Smitty's arms were crossed, and he was tapping his foot in frustration.

"Mr. Crappy Sack here says that he's supposed to meet with you in your office," Agnes announced. Holding her usual cigarette between her fingers, she pointed to Smitty as she spoke. "I don't see him on my schedule."

"It's all right Agnes, I called him."

Agnes rolled her eyes. "If you say so."

Once everyone was inside the office, the Sarge briefed Smitty on the findings so far in the investigation. Jake added what he could about the woman who had been killed, and Agnes sat quietly listening and allowing the smoke from her cigarette to do its usual slithering dance around her head.

Smitty leaned forward and stared at the map of Kennard. "So, Amanda's outer space watch says that she was there for about an hour. The woman who lived there has been in hospice care for months. She has a son that stops by and takes care of the place. The neighbor says that a van periodically stops at the house, drives inside the garage and closes the garage doors. If these were the good old days and this was a gambling joint, I'd think they were running bag money in and out of the place."

Eyebrows raised, Jake repeated, "Bag money?"

Agnes spoke up. "The bookies, gambling joints, and gangsters would try to keep their money, jewels, or whatever they had for their ill-gotten gains, moving it around so the coppers wouldn't find it. It would usually end up at a safe location where they would invest in their criminal empire."

Jake thought about what Agnes had said. "The same thing is done today, but it's moved around electronically or laundered through legitimate businesses. Then it gets re-invested into their enterprises."

When it was clear that Jake understood what he had described, Smitty continued talking. "Looks like whatever they were bringing to the house, they didn't want anyone knowing what it was. On the day that Amanda was there, a man and woman drove a van into the garage and brought a young woman with them. The man and woman left, and then the woman drove back by herself a short time later and closed the garage door, which the lady across the street said was unusual. A couple of minutes later, the woman left. Again unusual."

Smitty added, "This time, the woman appeared to be the only one in the van. The neighbor said that soon after that, a woman was found dead north of Kennard. If the younger woman was Amanda, hmmm."

Smitty went silent as his mind considered various scenarios that might explain the events that had been described to him. Agnes looked at Smitty and saw that he appeared to be lost in thought.

Frustrated with Smitty's silence, she pointed her cigarette at him. "Well, looks like he needs to empty his crap catcher."

Smitty was annoyed by Agnes's jibe, yet his mind kept racing despite the inference that he wasn't up to the task. Different explanations were racing through Smitty's mind.

"Well. I've seen enough for now." Agnes started to get up. "We can still keep trying to figure..."

Smitty clapped his hands together. The sound startled Agnes, and she quickly looked at Jake and Sarge.

As Smitty turned to face the trio behind him, his eyes had widened with excitement. "The van!" he shouted. The Sarge, Jake, and Agnes remained baffled.

Smitty said, "The van...that's what connects all these pieces." He began to pace back and forth. "Benson and I were at the house where the Armenians were keeping the young girls. Why didn't I see this before? There was a van that kept going in and out of the garage. When the bald guy left, he opened the garage door and closed it behind him."

The Sarge, Agnes, and Jake remained baffled until Smitty explained, "The bag money was the girls!"

The other three finally understood where Smitty had been heading with his train of thought.

The Sarge announced, "I had Thane get the license plates on that van. When I get the information, I'll let you know what I find."

The Sarge looked at Smitty and then Agnes. "Anything else you want to say?"

Agnes turned and headed for the door. "If anything else comes up, let me know." Above the sound of the squeaking wheel Agnes said in begrudging admiration to nobody in particular, "Freaking genius."

⚬

The police radio broadcast to the district officers, "One Baker Fifty-One, check the area of 9th and Jackson Street. A female walking the streets acting strangely. The caller states that the woman was confused as to where she was and could not answer the caller's question when he tried to help her. She is possibly overdosed on drugs."

The beat officer responded, "One Baker Fifty-One, clear on the overdose." The officer replaced the microphone and looked at his partner. "That's the second female overdosed this week. Remember the one we saw a couple of days ago?"

The other officer nodded. "The last woman didn't know where she was either. What is wrong with these people?"

☙

Sergeant Scott heard the familiar special tone blare from his command post radio. Each of the officers working the Old Market instinctively put up their hand to cover the ear that held their communication earpiece. They all knew the tone. A robbery had been committed. After the brief warning tone, they heard an announcement: "Robbery just occurred. Southwest corner of 8th and Leavenworth. Three males dressed in dark clothes took the victim's money and cell phone. A passerby found the victim and called police. Robbery occurred approximately ten minutes ago. Suspects ran eastbound from that location."

Sergeant Scott got onto the radio to his detectives: "Don't respond to that scene, let uniform take care of it. We know where they're heading. Get to those old warehouses. They got a ten-minute head start, but maybe we'll get lucky."

The Chelini brothers monitored the police radio and also heard the robbery tone and broadcast. "Looks like we'll have some company soon."

The doorway that used to lead to the tunnel was still intact, but now there were some hidden technological additions to the entryway. Tony Chelini pushed the button on his earpiece. His Italian accent got thicker when he was excited. "Thane, you dere?"

Thane replied, "Right here, Tony. What do you need?" With a smile, Tony looked at Pauli, who had a questioning look on his face.

"Open da door, Thane."

There was a quiet click and then the hidden entryway wall section separated to reveal a rather large room. Pauli asked, "Tony, what you-a doing? They'll be here any minute."

Tony smiled and reached into the covered basket on his walker. "I got this little surprise from Smitty." Tony pulled out a two-foot-long tubular plastic container. "He saved this up for me for a few days and packaged it up really nice. Here, put it in the hiding room."

It took Pauli a few seconds to realize what he was holding onto with both hands. He looked at Tony, who was almost giddy. "Go quickly in the room! In the room, but don't break it open."

Pauli followed Tony's instructions and then emerged from the room. He was about to ask for an explanation when they heard the familiar sound of multiple footsteps.

Tony hit his communicator and announced, "Thane, they are coming. Close the door."

The electronic door mechanism was an addition that was able to override the manual handle that the thugs had used to open the door. Tony and Pauli went to a hidden surveillance spot and listened as footsteps echoed through the large basement area of the building. As the three thugs approached the door, there were shouts of "Police! Sound off and keep your hands where I can see them."

Pauli whispered to Tony, "The coppers are close this time." As they had done many times before, the thugs went to the hidden lever pulled it open. "In! In! Hurry!" was heard as the two punks that Pauli and Tony recognized from their last encounter started into the doorway. The second thug reached back and grabbed a third younger-looking kid by the back of his black hooded sweatshirt, saying, "Get in now." They closed the door just as the gang detectives rushed into the basement. With the room flooded with six flashlights, Detective Turley almost shouted, "No freaking way. We saw them come in here." The other detectives were shaking their heads."

Pauli leaned over to Tony and murmured, "Recognize that young kid?"

Tony whispered in response, "Guess my dentures and death mask only scared him for a little while. Now we'll teach him a harder lesson."

Thane was observing his monitor, accompanied by Mac. A small man who walked with a very unsteady gait entered the work area and looked over Thane's shoulder. Mac watched as the man reached up and touched his earpiece, saying, "Tony, just say when." Thane looked away from his monitor at the same time he heard Tony say, "Now." Thane, Mac and all the detectives searching the large basement heard a loud but muffled *BOOM!*

Instinctively, the detectives ran to the large section of wall which shook and appeared to be where the sound had come from. Pauli touched his earpiece and said, "Okay, Thane open it up."

The electric latches opened, and to the astonishment of the detectives the wall slowly swung toward them. All of their flashlights were targeted on the opening, which revealed three terrified thugs surrounded by putrid-smelling smoke. Their shock-filled wide eyes stared toward the lights pointing at them as they stood frozen with their hands in the air.

The smoke cleared and the detectives tactically approached the men, guns drawn and yelling. It became apparent that the three were in shock. About three steps from the entrance, Detective Turley's breath was taken away. "What the..."

The flashlights could clearly pierce the darkness now that the smoke was clearing, and the entire hidden room and three terrified bangers were covered with the end result of Smitty's last six meals.

The tube had burst in such a way as to cover every square inch of the room, and its contents were dripping from the occupants' faces and clothes. Detective Turley, the lead officer of the unit, stepped back and yelled, "I've got cover, get them cuffed."

Then, with the satisfied look of a seasoned officer taking advantage of seniority, he smiled as the three putrid suspects were taken into custody. He quickly pulled out his phone and started taking pictures. "A little something for morale to display on the announcement board," he said quietly, snickering to himself.

"Like the old days," Shakey said out loud as he watched the monitor screen.

Thane and Mac looked at the man with the quivering hands and a big smile. "Placed a small charge at three points on a tubular container of a semi-liquid substance for excellent disbursement. Worked great with napalm. This fecal fuse is an application I had never considered." Shakey then turned and left the room.

Thane was still trying to grasp what he had just witnessed as Mac started slapping the desk and laughing so hard his eyes watered with delight.

"Oh, I'm gonna like it here," Mac announced.

CHAPTER 8

Lois was talking on the phone. As she glanced around the room, she realized that her office door was open. She pointed to it and motioned for Vladimir. Understanding what she needed, he turned and ambled with excitement toward the door.

Glancing at the stuffed dog he had pushed into a corner of the office, he did a double take. *Did that thing just move?* Vladimir thought he had seen a slight movement under the dog's tail. Rather than say anything about it to Lois and risk a verbal lashing, he just shook his head and mumbled, "Yeesh, that animal is disgusting."

He closed the door of the office and walked back to Lois's desk, not even chancing a gander at his stuffed nemesis for fear of being ridiculed by both Lois and Victor.

"If your previous employer doesn't want you anymore, what makes you think we would be interested?" The tone of the voice on the phone was direct, and the question left an opening that Lois had been waiting for.

"I know your organization specializes in getting people over the border, and the use of some of the females you transport is a very profitable venture. We can increase profits from young girls and you won't have to sneak them through tunnels, cross deserts, or incur the usual costs before you can put them to use.

"The girls you are transporting are usually sick and quite unsightly when they get here. I have a list of eighty young, healthy women right now that my organization can deliver much sooner than your usual methods with much less trouble."

There was silence for a few seconds, then a question. "You can guarantee this?" The voice on the other end of the line made the question sound like a threat.

"All we need from your organization is a couple of safe houses and sufficient heroin to make sure that the girls will do whatever is asked of them. It is interesting to see how motivated they become when they are properly prepared. Of course, we would require any protection needed to conduct our business."

"We will consider your offer. My employer does not like doing business with people outside our established organization. However, you may be able to provide a service to us that could prove useful. I am still concerned about the failure you had with the Armenians. My employer does not tolerate failure either." Again, the question was said as a threat.

"The Armenian operation was very complex, with many steps involved in acquiring, hiding, and preparing the girls before transporting them to their destinations," Lois said. "There was an operation to get them out of the state, then out of the country. It was just a matter of time before the FBI would have figured it out. Once the Armenians established their network, they would not be flexible. The need to break our ties with them was inevitable."

Lois paused to make sure that the person at the other end of the line comprehended and accepted her lie. "Working for your Cartel would eliminate the problem of smuggling anyone over borders. In America we can take the girls anywhere you want them. I just need some time to move my operation to an agreed-upon location."

Another pause, then a final statement: "We will contact you after considering your proposal."

"Good," Lois said, then hung up the phone. Victor and Vladimir were pacing back and forth in Lois's office as she spoke to the mysterious person on the phone. When Lois hung up, they both stopped pacing and looked to her, waiting for some guidance.

"Well?" Victor almost shouted.

⟡

"Well, now, this is interesting," Mac said as he leaned forward to scrutinize his monitor.

He had spoken briefly with Smitty before turning his attention to Lois's phone conversation. Smitty was in the lab talking to Thane about a van, but Mac wasn't listening. After monitoring numerous conversations between the Armenians, Mac had figured out that when they were speaking English, it was a ruse for anyone who might overhear their conversations. Now he knew who the players were.

Thane and Smitty turned their attention to Mac. "What's so interesting?" Thane asked.

"This Lois seems to be the boss here, and the two bald slobs seem to be her henchmen. One is Victor and the other Vladimir."

With a groan, Smitty put his hands on his hips. "Seriously, those are their names?" I'm surprised it's not Boris Badenoff and Natasha."

That comment got a chuckle from Mac and a confused look from Thane. "Rocky and Bullwinkle. Thane, didn't you watch cartoons when you were a kid?"

Thane shrugged. "Never heard of 'em."

Smitty shook his head, "Never mind."

Turning his attention back to Mac, Smitty asked, "What's up with the trio there?"

Mac sat back in his chair. "She just got off the phone with someone, and it sounded like she was giving some sort of job proposal. She was offering to provide girls in exchange for drugs, specifically heroin, some safe houses, and protection. My guess is that she was offering her services to some Latino group. They were talking about the problems that come with sneaking girls across the border or desert. She made a pitch that she could provide eighty girls when they were set up. Sounds like she is preparing to jump this ship."

Mac tapped his monitor. "Thane, rather than moving the camera, have the lens widen. I think this Vladimir caught a glimpse of movement in the Anus Cam. Can you do that?"

Thane replied with a thumbs up. Mac was impressed. Then his attention went back to the monitor. "They're speaking Armenian. Let's see what else is going on."

ᏮᏜ

"When I get back to my office, I'll send you the information that came from the scene where the woman's body was found," Jake said as he walked out of the Sarge's office. After the door closed, he noticed young Amanda walking through the Precinct. Brittany had taken her under her wing, and after a lot of adjustment, Amanda seemed to fit right in. She wore a light blue official-looking shirt with her name embroidered where a police badge would usually be. Underneath her name was written in red "Cadet."

From the back of the Precinct an Ol' Blue yelled, "Hey Cadet! Didn't I tell ya I needed that report on the Cloudy Hill neighborhood? Where is it?" Amanda turned and without hesitation announced, "It's on your desk!" Then she started walking toward the officer who was making the demands. She continued walking past him to the area where his desk was located.

"Look at this mess. No wonder you can't find anything," she commented.

In twenty seconds, Amanda had organized the Ol' Blue's desk and picked up the report as he slowly walked with a cane toward her. He reached out to take the report, but Amanda suddenly pulled it back, saying, "Don't come another step closer."

The officer stopped with a jolt.

"Did you have the applesauce at dinner last night?"

The Ol' Blue nodded. "Yeah, why?"

Amanda put her hand out like a traffic cop at an intersection. She put the report on the Ol' Blue's desk and pressed down on it with her index finger. "It's right here. Don't take another step until I'm outta here."

She started to walk away, leaving the Ol' Blue staring at her with a puzzled expression.

"You Blues walk more than ten steps and start your applesauce fart parties," Amanda said. She kept walking as the surrounding Blues burst out in laughter. As the Ol' Blue continued to walk to his desk, he let loose a fanny clapper that was loud enough for Jake to hear. The Blue leaned on his desk with his free hand and called out to nobody in particular, "Call a nurse; I just filled my diaper."

The laughter bounced off the walls of the Precinct as the Blues slapped each other on the back and poked fun at the stationary Blue who didn't want to make any sudden moves that might jeopardize the retaining ability of his adult disposable diaper.

Amanda didn't bat an eyelash. She threw her hands up like a touchdown had just been scored, then walked away as if the whole encounter was nothing unusual.

Jake smiled at the scene before him and then heard a peculiar laugh mixed with coughing. He turned to see the rare sight of lead officer Crantz throwing her head back to let loose a full gut laugh followed by a coughing fit. Jake shook his head and thought to himself, "*Sometimes you just have to surrender to the absurd.*"

⁂

"Sorry, Smitty, we've got a lot of things going on at once here," Thane said in an apologetic tone.

"Nothing to be sorry about. When there are so many aspects to a case and a bunch of officers working different angles, things don't get busy, they get exciting." Smitty's eyes gleamed with anticipation at the prospect of putting the next part of the puzzle into place.

"Remember the van at the house of those two bald guys? I need to know who that van was registered to. It could be a big break in this investigation."

Thane noticed how excited Smitty was about the van, but he didn't understand why. As he began tracking down the information Smitty had requested, he started to comprehend just how exciting it was when numerous streams of information from different sources started to converge to form what the Blues called *The Big Picture*.

"So you're Smitty."

Startled, Smitty looked toward the other end of the workstation as a man approached.

"Name's Mac. One of the Bureau guys, Steve DeGoff, sent me down to this fancy place to help you guys out with these Armenians. I did some military and government work in that part of the world for a few years."

Smitty quickly sized up the man as he spoke: confident, quick to let you know exactly who he was and what his plans were.

The two men shook hands in a way that Thane didn't understand. Thane had noticed that of all these men always shook hands and looked at each other for a couple of seconds before letting go. He shrugged and quietly said, "Must be an old guy thing."

"The van is registered to…" Thane stopped speaking as he read about the company. "Oh, this company provides transportation to the Department of Health and Human Services."

"Bingo!" Smitty almost yelled. "The van picks up the kids. The van went to the house in Kennard. The van drives to the safe house. Now if the van does all this transporting, someone has to send the van. That must be the supervisor upstairs—Lois— who oversees the foster kids. She knows which kids are close to eighteen years of age. The reports go to her when the kids are found by the police, family, or that outer space tracker."

Thane rolled his eyes at the "outer space" reference that Smitty and the other geezers kept using whenever they mentioned Amanda's GPS watch.

Smitty's mind was racing. "They must have had this system down pretty good. There were a lot of girls in that safe house. They were drugged and going to get shipped to Armenia. From what the lady in Kennard describes, the van stops by that house in Kennard somewhat often. Something unusual happened when Amanda was at the house across the street, and we still don't know why they were there. Something must have gone wrong with their normal routine."

Smitty started pacing and speaking out loud. "It could have been anything. We don't need to worry about that now. We have to focus on what we know. Hmmm…oh, the tattoos! Remember, Thane, I had you zoom in on the tattoos."

This comment caused Mac to stand up. "Tattoos?"

⌇

The doors to the drugstore opened automatically. With a confident stride, the Chemist wound his way through the drugstore. Strutting through the cosmetic section, he smiled at five reflections of his face in various mirrors. He noticed that the reflected images held a look of confidence and satisfaction that came from his latest vengeful attacks on unsuspecting women.

"Too easy," he said, whispering a bit too loudly and then looking around to see if anyone had heard him. Satisfied that the editorial comment about his latest conquest had not been overheard, he took a final glance at the reflected faces. He winked at them, smiled, and continued his stroll to the pharmacy desk.

After about an hour of filling prescriptions and answering the usual mundane questions about dosages, harmful interactions, and whether Vitamin C cured everything, his phone rang.

He reached into his pocket as he walked away from the service desk. His facial expression froze as his eyes focused on the phone number that was calling him. He quickly looked around until he was satisfied that nobody was looking at him. The phone continued to ring as he quickly shuffled to the storage room and closed the door behind him.

The voice in his ear caused a shiver down his spine. It was Lois. "It looks like you've been up to your old ways. I thought I told you to not draw attention to yourself."

Even though he was in the storage room by himself, the Chemist looked around nervously. "What makes you think…"

The voice cut him off. "I'm not stupid! Do you actually think that the police won't be able to see that various women walking the streets in some stupor might be related? I just read it in the paper and it is plain to see, you fool!"

Lois's voice calmed as she regained her composure. Standing in her office, she unclenched the fist that she had just slammed on her desk. Then she looked at Vladimir and snapped her finger while pointing at her office door. He knew he needed to hurry over and close it. As he did so, he looked out in the hallway and saw that a couple of the state workers were looking at Lois's office. Vladimir smiled and waved his hand to signal that everything was all right, then closed the door.

"Now, listen to me, you idiot," Lois said into the phone. "We are close to finalizing an agreement with our new partners. Control your urges until we are ready to implement our plans. We have a good system here, but your behavior is a threat to our plans. If I feel that you are becoming a liability, you will regret it. Understand?"

The Chemist swallowed as thoughts raced through his mind. He desperately yearned to return to his domination of women but feared what Lois and her new Cartel could do to him.

"Do you understand?" Lois demanded.

Snapped back to his current predicament, the Chemist stuttered, "Y-yes, I-I do."

"Good. We'll be in touch." The line went dead.

After a few moments, the Chemist regained his composure. He walked back to the pharmacy service desk and noticed that there were three people in line.

"I'm so sorry, folks. Who was next?" He took a prescription from an older woman, and as he turned to fill it he froze. The advertising photo of the young girl wearing the GPS locator watch caught his eye. A crucial component of his control over women involved making sure they could not identify him. The GPS watch was a threat to his cherished anonymity. The girl who had been wearing it could inadvertently shine a spotlight on him. She could illuminate and destroy his ability to hide in the shadows of his victims' memories.

"Sir, what about my ointment?" a customer asked.

♋

Thane noticed that Mac's demeanor had switched from a good-natured guy with a loud and confident laugh to a stern-sounding and determined professional. The abrupt transformation gave Thane pause.

"What tattoos?" Mac asked in a tone that was more demanding than questioning.

Smitty looked to Thane. "Remember when I had you zoom in on his wrist?'"

Again, Mac's voice was stern and direct. "On the wrist?"

Making eye contact with Mac, Smitty explained, "Yeah, from the outside we saw that one of those goons in the safe house had a tattoo on the underside of his wrist."

At that statement, Mac's interest grew. He listened intently as Smitty continued to talk and Thane opened files on his computer containing the video.

Thane talked as he typed. "Let's see, that guy was at the window and drinking something, then he answered his phone. The tattoo looked green."

Mac looked over Thane's shoulder at the monitor. Thane quit typing when he got a call in his headphone from the Sarge.

"Thanerboy, Jake just sent me some photos of that woman who was found dead up by Kennard. I'm trying to forward them to you. How do I do it?"

Thane gave a few instructions and then gave up the effort. "Forget it, Sarge, I'll get it from your computer myself."

Mac became increasingly impatient as Thane spoke. "Yes, I can do that. I'm networked into all the computers in the Precinct.

No, Sarge, I don't copy everything, I can just download what I need. Just... just keep your hand off the mouse and don't touch the keyboard for few seconds, okay?" Thane was experiencing his usual frustration and stress when he tried to talk computers to the clueless Blues. "There, it's done. You don't need to do anything; I have it. Sarge, I'll let you know what I find as soon as I'm finished going through it. Okay?"

"Yeah, over and out."

Thane rolled his eyes at the Blues radio talk.

Smitty was watching Mac as Thane described what he could remember about the tattoos. With each detail Thane remembered about the tattoo, Mac seemed to become more and more interested in what Thane was saying.

"Okay, here we go."

One by one Thane started to paste screen shots of the photos of the wrists of the goon at the safe house, then those taken from the Boomer cam in Lois's office. Finally, he displayed the photo taken at the crime scene of the dead woman.

Smitty noticed that Mac had turned away from Thane's monitor and was staring at the wall behind Thane. It appeared that Mac was looking through the walls and into some distant memory. Very deep in thought. Mac started to rub his left hand in an odd way, pausing at the ends of the fingers on his left hand. Smitty squinted his eyes as he realized that Mac didn't have any fingernails on that hand—just scar tissue where his fingernails used to be.

Thane pointed to his monitor and simultaneously glanced over at Smitty, inviting him to look.

"See? Lois, the goons, and the dead lady's wrist... all have tattoos, all of them are green, and all of them are of a..." Thane got cut off.

"*Star,*" Mac growled as he looked at his left hand for a moment and then put his hand in his pocket to avoid drawing attention to it.

Thane was oblivious to what Mac was doing, but Smitty understood immediately. Reflexively, he put his left hand on his lower abdomen and his right hand on his colostomy bag.

Mac's mind had quickly relived something very traumatic, and only Smitty understood what that was like. He decided to stop by later and spend some time with Mac.

9 CHAPTER

The room in the border town of Meghri was a common meeting place for the five original members of the Green Star. Each member had the same tattoo on their wrist, and each had worked to establish the Cartel. For years they had made inroads with local government officials and various private businesses in the southern region of Armenia.

Human trafficking was a very lucrative business, especially in the border towns. To the west was Turkey, and in Armenia itself the large mining industry provided plenty of business for the Armenian Cartel's specialty of providing young women for a price. However, Armenia's southern border had the potential to be most lucrative. There was a shared pipeline for oil and natural gas. At the points where the pipelines and roadways crossed the border there would be a number of customers who wanted what the Cartel had to offer. But the main reason was the recent addition of a new product.

These women were different from the women that these men were accustomed to. They were willing to pay three times the usual price because the women were Americans. If anyone was caught abusing an American woman, the authorities would be unlikely to charge them with any crimes. The hatred felt by these men toward "the great Satan" America was so intense that trafficking in American women might even be excused or applauded.

The country on the southern border of Armenia is Iran.

The founding members of the Cartel understood why American women were sought after, and that was why they had agreed to invest in Lois and her operation. Lois and those she worked with had been supplying young women for a couple of years. The initial numbers had been fairly small, but the newest group of women was going to be the largest and most profitable.

Aziz stood guard at the door to the conference room. At 6'3" and 250 pounds, his physical presence was intimidating in itself. In addition, his reputation for torturing anyone who threatened their organization made him feared and respected throughout the Cartel.

The five members of the Cartel met regularly to discuss operations in various areas of the country. Aziz was a trusted member of the Cartel, and as the enforcer he played a crucial role in making sure the desires of the five were carried out. However, only the original five sat at the table.

Once the local issues had been discussed, attention turned to the American operation. All five members focused on Aziz.

"*What is the status of the American operation, Aziz?*" one of the five asked. Aziz took a couple of steps from the door toward the conference table.

"*The safe house has the largest number of women to date. The women are in the process of being prepared. They are all young and healthy. When I spoke to Lois, they were in the process of adding a few more before shipment. They will make us millions of Drams.*"

The news was received with smiles and nods of approval. "*Are there any concerns?*"

Aziz took another step closer to the table. "*While monitoring Lois's computer I observed that her computer was one of the subjects of an unannounced audit that the state offices were conducting, which included Lois's department.*"

The smiles disappeared. "*Lois's computer was shut off. She assured me that periodic audits are normal in the state offices. She also said that she would take the necessary precautions to avoid any possible detection of our project.*"

This assurance did not appear to satisfy the five. *"So, you are telling us that Lois may have exposed our operation?"*

Aziz shook his head. *"I am not saying that. She assured me that there was no threat of exposure. Lois said that we must not monitor her computer for at least two weeks. Once the audit is over, we will be able to go back to normal."*

Now the table was surrounded by men displaying concern and anger. *"This is too important to us, Aziz. I don't care if she is your sister; you know how we deal with failure."*

Aziz's voice grew stern while remaining respectful. *"I am well aware, and I will be the one that will punish those that fail us."*

The five exchanged looks, and then one member spoke.

"So our schedule is delayed for two weeks. I don't like it; something is wrong in the Nebraska. Aziz, wait in the lounge. We will discuss this situation."

Aziz turned and exited the conference room. After a few minutes he was summoned back to the conference room.

"You will go to this Nebraska State. You will learn what is actually going on. You will contact us on a daily basis and update us on the actual progress of the operation. If Lois has things under control, you will assist her and make sure the operation runs smoothly. If you find that Lois and the others have failed us, you will eliminate them. We will alert the rest of the operation to expect the delay."

Aziz did not answer. He acknowledged the instructions by bowing his head, then turned and walked out the door. He would soon be in the Nebraska.

6☙

Mac was focusing intently on the surveillance video from the Boomer cam. His headphones prevented him from hearing the sound of footsteps approaching, but he noticed a change in the brightness of the light at the doorway leading to the workspace that he shared with Thane. Mac instinctively turned to see what had caused the change and saw that Smitty was standing about ten feet away. Smitty stood still. He knew not to walk directly up to Mac and surprise him. Smitty waited until Mac had acknowledged that he was there.

Mac reached up and took the headphones from his ears. "You know how to approach an old war dog."

Smitty acknowledged the statement. "Didn't serve in the military, but worked for years on the streets. Never liked anyone approaching me from behind. My family knew never to surprise or scare me because I would react without thinking. I figure you'd do the same."

Mac nodded and motioned for Smitty to have a seat. "So, you Old Blues actually still find ways of busting crooks. From what I hear and see in this lab you guys got lots of equipment, but because you're retired old goats nobody gives you a second look. I haven't seen you guys in action yet, but what I've seen so far is pretty impressive."

Mac pointed upward toward the main floor of the building. "You guys really dress in police shirts with hospital gowns in a recreated police precinct from the old days?"

Smitty smiled and replied, "The Precinct gives us a place where we can conduct operations without anyone knowing about it. The public only sees a bunch of Old Blues getting to act like they were cops again. The therapists think that having us in the old precinct is good for us because it makes us feel needed and important instead of being depressed about wasting away in a nursing home waiting to die. I gotta admit that it does bring back memories and I do feel needed again."

Smitty pulled his shirt up to reveal his crap catcher. "The memories are good and bad. I caught a bullet in the gut when I was chasing a punk through an alley. I saw the bullet ricochet off the ground with a spark, and it ripped through my stomach and gut pretty bad. Had this bag attached ever since."

He paused a minute and then said, "When something reminds me of that night, I catch myself holding my stomach as I did that night laying on the ground hoping the other cops would find me. I had to crawl out of that filthy alley to a main street in hopes that someone would see me. It was a long wait, and

I barely made it. Ended up working a desk for years, shuffling papers and feeling worthless. If it wasn't for the Sarge asking for my assistance on tough cases, I probably would have eventually eaten my gun."

Mac's eyebrows went up as he realized what Smitty had been through.

"I guess it's a normal way of remembering those kinds of events in our lives." Smitty pointed to Mac's left hand. "Noticed you rubbing your fingers when we talked about this Green Star bunch. From the looks of your hand, I'd say you have a pretty good idea of what goes through my mind when I'm reminded of that night."

Mac's initial reaction was to cover his hand as he had done for years. But with this old cop he stopped, held his hand up, and looked at it. "That obvious, was it?"

Smitty smiled. "Not to the others, but for someone who understands, couldn't miss it. From what I've been able to observe, I'd say you had quite the run-in with this Green Star bunch. My guess is that there was a lot more damaged than your fingernails."

Mac knew that Smitty was older than him but had recognized something that a series of psychiatrists and therapists had barely understood. Smitty had cut right through the wall that Mac had used to protect his sanity and showed him how Smitty and the other residents of this so-called *"Retirement Home"* had dealt with the sense of worthlessness that haunts people who feel they are not needed anymore.

"You're among friends here, Mac," Smitty said. "I'll show you around a bit and you'll see what I mean. Afterwards I'd like you to give us a briefing of your findings from listening in on these Armenians."

᷍

Lunch at Brittany's apartment was something Jake always looked forward to. She had called him at work that morning and found that they both had a free hour for lunch. Jake knocked on her door, then turned the doorknob and stuck his head in. He looked around and saw that Brittany was on the phone. She motioned for him to come in and pointed to the table already set for two.

Brittany was laughing as she ended the call, saying, "Hang in there, Recruit." She pushed the button on her phone and looked over to Jake. "That was Amanda."

Jake smiled and replied, "You should see how she handles those Blues. It's hysterical; she's becoming some sort of boss in there. I swear I almost burst out laughing this morning after watching her deal with those guys and their antics."

"You're not going to believe this, but the Sarge just gave her a promotion."

Jake gave Brittany a questioning look.

"She has been promoted from Cadet to Recruit, and get this—it's a paid position."

Jake smiled. "The Sarge knows how to treat her. Whoever can put up with those guys like she does deserves a good salary."

Brittany crossed her arms, "Then I should be a millionaire by now." Jake laughed and got a hot pad thrown at him.

"You know those guys adore you, Brittany. You would not believe the love advice they give me whenever I'm there."

Brittany gave a short laugh. "Like those old crusties are love experts."

Jake reached into his blazer pocket. "I was told that what girls really like are, *Da lotions and da creams for their skin.*" Jake set two small bottles on the table: hand cream and body lotion. "Does this win your heart?"

Brittany smirked and then turned to a cabinet. She looked at Jake, reached up and with a flick of her wrist opened the cabinet door to show him a cabinet full of lotions and creams. "If that was all it took, I would have married any one of twenty of those Blues."

Jake's laugh was cut off by his phone ringing.

"Jake, this is Sarge. We're going to have an update on the Armenians in about an hour. Can you come?"

Jake responded, "Of course. Brittany is with me. Can she come, too? Got it, we'll be there."

Turning to Brittany, he said, "Well, looks like it's gonna be a short lunch. Is this what our life is gonna be like after we're married?"

Brittany thought for a second and pointed to Jake. "Worse, because you'll be related to them."

Jake responded, "Oh, that's great. Let's eat and then find out what these future relatives of mine have for us."

ᏀᏕ

From his job at the pharmacy it was only about a forty-minute drive to his mother's house in Kennard. The Chemist thought about numerous things as he drove. There was Lois and those two henchmen who worked for her. The young girl who got away from him. The stupid woman who barged in and interrupted him before he could get his full revenge against the girl who was laughing when she saw him in his special underwear. The fact that the woman had seen him was a breach of the deal he had with Lois. She told him she would take care of it. Soon afterwards there was a report of a woman's body found in the countryside. Without asking Lois, he presumed that the body was that woman.

The Chemist stared at the eyes looking back at him in the rear-view mirror. He noticed that those eyes seemed to be expressing concern. Out loud, he spoke to the reflection, "Let's just get this house on the market. Once it's sold, I can decide if whatever Lois is working on is something that I want to be part of or if I want to take whatever money I make from the sale and move somewhere else where I can..." he smiled at the reflection, "set up my own little operation."

As he approached the driveway, he looked over the house from the outside. "Looks like it's ready to go on the market now," he said out loud in a confident tone.

After pulling into the driveway, he got out of his car and stood for a couple of moments with his hands on his hips. Satisfied, he started to walk toward the front door. A voice from across the street broke his train of thought. "Hey, young fella, did your mother's friends find you?"

He froze and turned toward the sound of the old woman's voice. "I beg your pardon?" he shouted.

"Two friends of your mother. They came by and were asking about her. Older gentlemen from a retirement home. Oh, what was it called? Oh yes! It was written on the side of their van: The Old Blues Retirement Home. They also asked about the house. They seemed interested to know that you were taking care of it. I'm sorry we haven't met. I'm Mrs. Christopher Brimhall, and you are...?" The Chemist's mind was racing as he realized, "*Some men came to the house asking about me.*"

He looked over at the woman as she waited for an answer. The Chemist seemed irritated by her question about who he was. He waved his hand and snapped, "Very busy," then walked quickly back to his car. Without acknowledging the woman across the street, he backed out of the driveway and drove away. This time he looked at the reflection in the mirror and said out loud, "Someone is looking for me. I need to get to Lois and hear what kind of plan she has."

&

Agnes was sitting in the Sarge's office as the two of them discussed the human trafficking operation that the Armenians had been doing right under the noses of the government in the offices adjacent to the Old Blues Precinct.

"I hope this guy the Bureau bigwig sent over is worth his salt." The words seemed to ride the smoke streaming from Agnes's mouth as she spoke.

The Sarge replied, "Seems like he knows his stuff. I met him downstairs. If the Bureau likes him, I'll use him... especially if he can help us out with these Armenians."

The door to the Sarge's office opened, then Mac and Smitty walked in. With a hearty laugh, Mac blurted, "So you guys were cops but aren't cops anymore, and you're playing like you're cops for the public but actually being cops! The only other people who know about this wrinkled-butt brigade are Steve DeGoff and the bunch at the Bureau. Oh, and those two jokers guarding the research lab. Freaking stroke of genius."

"Glad you approve," Agnes commented. The fact that she and the Sarge were in the office had gone unnoticed by Mac and Smitty.

"Oh, sorry, Sarge. You remember Mac?" Smitty said.

The Sarge nodded.

Smitty's tone deepened. "Oh, and this is Lead Officer Agnes Crantz," he told Mac.

Agnes responded with a wave of her cigarette.

"Agnes's granddaughter was one of the girls who were rescued from the Armenians," Smitty explained.

"That must be Amanda," Mac noted.

Agnes was surprised that Mac knew her granddaughter's name.

"Thane talks about her a lot," Mac explained. "If I didn't know better, I'd think he had a particular interest in Amanda."

Agnes smiled. The thought of Thane being interested in Amanda warmed her heart. "She's a special young lady. That's why I'd like to give these goons my personal attention."

Mac gave Agnes a look of comradery. "You and I have some business with this Green Star bunch from Armenia."

Agnes gazed over at the Sarge and winked. "He'll do."

There was a knock at the door. "Enter," the Sarge stated. The door opened and Brittany and Jake walked in.

"Are we late? Dad goes nuts when I'm late," Brittany said.

The Sarge pointed to the couch for them to be seated, then touched his earpiece. "Hey Thanerboy, we're ready to start."

Mac elbowed Smitty in the arm. "Is that one of the radio earpieces you were telling me about?"

Smitty nodded. "Between that and the dog cam, the CIA has nothing on this place."

The monitor on the Sarge's desk came to life, showing Thane's face as he looked around the room. "Hey, Brittany! Jake. Oh! Hi, Ms. Agnes."

Melted by Thane's manners, Agnes smiled and waved. Mac waved at Thane and then said to Jake, "So Smitty here is gonna be your father-in-law." From the other side of the office a raspy voice quietly commented, "Poor schmuck."

Thane began providing information from the Boomer cam surveillance videos. "To tell the truth, Sarge, we were trying to put together what we had, and Mac made the pieces fit."

The Sarge looked over to Mac. "Would you fill us in?"

Mac stood and told Thane to put the photos of the tattoos up on the screen. "Each of the members of this particular cartel have the same tattoo of a green star on their wrist. The five-pointed star stands for the five original members who still run the organization. They deal in many of the usual things associated with these groups—some drugs, extortion, but this group specializes in prostitution. They are headquartered in the southern region of Armenia. The women make them a lot of money in the bigger cities. Then, when the girls are not as attractive from being used and abused, they just ship them to the mining operations and other areas by the borders... places where the men will pay for the girls because it's harder to find prostitutes in countries like Turkey and Iran.

"From what I've learned about this safe house you guys broke up, this was a shipment of American girls," Mac said, rubbing his chin. "My guess is that they were planning to take advantage of the ethnic and religious hatred from Iran and those in Turkey who identify with the ideology of the radical elements of Iran. I'll bet they were gonna charge big money for a chance to abuse an American girl. I think it was around a couple of dozen girls, right?"

There were nods.

"That would have been huge money for the Green Star Cartel. When the Cartel realizes that this operation has fallen apart, they will punish those who were responsible. This explains what we've seen and heard on the surveillance videos of this lady—Lois—and the goons Vladimir and Victor. From what I've been able to figure out, they are trying to pack up their operation and skedaddle. She's downloading a bunch of stuff from her computer and packing up a lot of records. She seems to think that somebody named Dr. Baggaley is doing some sort of audit of the unit. She really doesn't like the guy very much. Knowing what I do about the Green Star Cartel, if I were them I'd be getting out of town too."

Brittany asked, "Isn't the green star gang in Armenia? What can they do from there to make Lois and the others move?"

Mac became deadly serious. "They'll send someone to punish them. Probably kill them, and I know who they'll send."

Smitty noticed that Mac had put his left hand in his pocket.

Mac said, "Thane, put up the photo I sent you, please."

After a couple of clicks from Thane's mouse, the monitor displayed a photo of a large man standing outside the door of a building.

"This is Aziz Luka. He is the enforcer for the Cartel. He personally punishes anyone in the organization who fails their assignments or who is a threat to them. Looks like this little trio failed on a massive scale."

Mac pointed to the photo for emphasis. "That's the guy they'll send."

The Sarge told Thane, "Make sure we get copies of this photo. Agnes, give Mary a copy. If this guy shows up, she'll know who to watch for so she can warn us."

Sarge turned to Mac and asked, "Any clue when this guy Aziz will be here?"

Mac shrugged. "My guess is that Lois has been stalling him somehow. By now they must know something has gone wrong. He's probably on his way."

In a serious tone, Mac said, "This is a very dangerous man, Sarge. Do not approach him without me. As a matter of fact, we've got to plan nabbing this guy very carefully."

Agnes broke the momentary silence. "I'm thinking this Aziz is part of the special business you spoke about."

Mac stared into space for a couple of seconds, rubbing his hands together.

"He is."

"Good to know, Mac. Anything else?" the Sarge asked.

"Oh, there is someone else that they keep talking about. They call him 'the Chemist.' From the way they talk about him, it sounds like they don't like him, but they need him. They even mentioned killing him or offering him to the Cartel as a scapegoat if the operation went south. Well, it seems like things really did go south."

After a pause, Mac explained, "I know these people; they won't be satisfied with this Chemist. All of them will be killed. Lois and her goons know it."

Jake spoke up. "Maybe they could make some deal with the Feds."

Mac shook his head. "No way they would go to the authorities. Anyone deep enough in this organization to be trusted to head an operation this big is a solid believer in their code. They won't make any deals. The only people they would trust would be..." Mac stopped talking and clapped his hands together as a thought struck him. "Another cartel. I'll need some more time to catch up on their conversations and see if I can figure out what their next move will be."

The Sarge stood. "Good. Just keep me informed. Once you've got a grasp on our Armenians we'll get back together and work on a plan for these green stars."

꙰

In her motorized wheelchair, Meter Maid Mary was doing her usual patrol of the perimeter of the massive complex that housed the Ol' Blue Precinct and the residential facility. The same huge building contained the school of nursing and numerous business offices of the Nebraska Department of Health and Human Services for the City of Omaha and surrounding counties. The parking lots for the branches in the complex were located adjacent to each set of offices.

In the DHHS parking lot Mary spotted a blue PT Cruiser sitting in a parking space with its engine running. The driver seemed unsure whether to stay in the vehicle or turn off the engine and walk into the building. Mary noted that the man kept looking at the DHHS front doors, then checking his rear-view mirrors and looking around. He was unaware of Mary because in her wheelchair she was just barely above the hoods of the vehicles parked around her.

Mary muttered to herself, "If that guy was going into the Precinct, I'd sure let the Sarge know about him. He looks really nervous." Sizing up situations is a habit that lifelong cops just can't shake. If something looks wrong, they have to check it out. "There is definitely something wrong with this fella," Mary whispered. Without realizing it, she started to move toward the nervous man.

The Chemist looked up into his rear-view mirror. The eyes looking back at him definitely appeared worried. Lois had told him to lay low—actually, she had threatened him. *"But there were two men at my house who said they were looking for Mother,"* he said to the eyes in the mirror. *"No... there is no way someone just happened to pick this time to check on my mother after she has been in the home for so many months."* He glared at the eyes in the mirror. *"They were looking for me. That girl's watch must have left a digital trail to be followed."*

As if he had finally talked himself into it, he looked once more at the mirror. *"I need to talk directly to Lois; she needs to know about this. I'm not just gonna wait around to be called and told what to do. I'm gonna get in there..."*

He didn't realize his window was open. Suddenly a voice interrupted his thoughts.

"Are you waiting for someone or going into the building? This parking lot is for the Department of Health and Human Services."

The old woman's voice startled the Chemist. His hand hit the horn and his foot pressed down on the accelerator, causing the engine to race. Luckily the vehicle was in Park.

The Chemist looked over his shoulder to see a woman with huge eyes looking at him as she sat in some sort of specialized wheelchair.

"Jeez, Lady! You scared me to death. What do you want?"

"You just seemed a little confused, so I thought I'd check on you," Mary said sweetly.

The Chemist exhaled quickly as he realized that it was only an old woman talking to him. As he looked back at her, he noticed a few people walking to and from the building. The commotion caused a sting of fear to shiver down his spine. He felt exposed, out of the comfort of the shadows, as people looked at him and the lady outside his driver's side door.

"Well, what's your business here, young man?" Mary inquired.

With a stutter, the Chemist replied, "Oh, I'm a pharmacist and I come by and check with the caseworkers and make sure there are no problems getting the medications to their clients."

With a suspicious tilt of her head, Mary pressed harder, commenting, "I've never seen you here before." Her statement sounded more like a question.

"Oh, my pharmacy is trying to get a contract with DHHS to supply medications. This is my first time here."

Mary remained suspicious. "The government offices are that way." She pointed, then pivoted her wheelchair and left.

The Chemist noticed how quiet her wheelchair was and mentally kicked himself for allowing her to sneak up on him like that. He noticed that he was sweating as he looked around the parking lot. The people who had been looking at him as he spoke to the woman were now getting into their cars or entering the government offices.

"I'd better just get in there and get this over with. I need some answers."

⌒

"Are you sure this is allowed?" Amanda asked Big Brock and the Chelini brothers.

"Oh, sure, they take us on drives all the time. They say it's… ah… What do they call it, Tony?" Pauli asked.

Unsure of the word, Tony shrugged.

"Therapeutic," Big Brock flatly stated. "It's supposed to be good for us to drive around our old beats."

Amanda seemed satisfied with the answer and got into the transport van. "Well, get in, I've got about an hour before I have to be back."

Mischievous grins and looks were quickly exchanged among the Blues as they climbed into the van.

Amanda started to drive from the retirement home parking lot to the shared main drive that led to a city street north of the facility where the government offices were located. She noticed a rather thin man walking on the sidewalk toward the building. He had very pale skin and an unusually high forehead that even protruded a little. As she drove toward the man, she suddenly realized that she recognized him from somewhere.

The man looked at the van as it drove toward him, and he noticed the words "Old Blues Retirement Home" on the side. He stopped walking and froze as he stared at the van. His shocked expression caused Amanda to almost scream out loud. She didn't, but she let out a loud gasp and all the Blues heard her. She slammed on the brakes and stared directly into the man's startled face. She had definitely seen that man with the same shocked expression before. She knew it, and it scared her, but she didn't know why.

The sudden stop of the van caused the Chemist to stop looking at the words on its side—the same words that the neighbor in Kennard had mentioned when she told him about the people who were looking for him. The Blues were all thrown forward in their seats, yelling and cursing at the recruit for her driving.

The Chemist shifted his stare from the van to its driver, instantly recognizing her. He stared into the eyes of the girl he had tried to strangle not long ago in his mother's house for laughing at him, and a surge of anger flowed through his body.

If rage could actually be projected as a visual image, the Chemist was doing it now. Amanda had a clear picture of the furious man in her mind as she involuntarily placed both hands on her throat. The horrible fear of being strangled was relived in a terrible flashback.

The spell the man was seemingly casting at her was broken by the deep voice of Big Brock as he kneeled next to the gasping Amanda.

"Are you all right, Amanda?... Amanda!" The sound broke the emotional freeze that had engulfed her emotions. Big Brock recognized the fear and immediately stood up to block the line of sight between Amanda and the man on the sidewalk.

Big Brock pulled the lever opening the van's doors and stepped out, wearing his police shirt and hospital gown. Despite his silly appearance, Big Brock was able to drill into someone's soul with his eyes. The glare from the burly old man struck fear into the Chemist like a focused beam of bright light on a cockroach. The Chemist flinched, taking two steps backward. Then the thunderous voice of a man who knew exactly how to pierce the nerves of any street thug rumbled, "What you lookin' at, punk?"

The Chemist was almost knocked backward as the volume and ferocity of the voice caused him to shake uncontrollably. "Nothing! I... I've gotta... " Unable to finish his sentence, he ran toward the building.

The once-indomitable Big Brock mentally relived the years when he had sent troublemakers scurrying away to avoid facing what was sure to be a losing battle. As he did so, he felt his breath shorten. He reached up and grasped the handle next to the door for support.

"You all right, Brock?" Tony asked.

"Been awhile" was all the Ol' Blue could say as he got back into the shuttle van and placed his hands-on Amanda's shoulders. She was shaking.

"Who was that man, Amanda?"

She shook her head. "I'm not sure, but... I-I'm just not sure."

Again, Big Brock's deep, comforting voice felt like a warm blanket to Amanda. "Don't you worry, young lady, we're right here. Turn this van around and let's get you back to your room."

⁂

Big Brock's bellowing had not gone unnoticed by Mary. She spun her wheelchair around and caught the tail end of the confrontation between the man she had spoken to and Brock. She watched as the man ran into the Health and Human Services building.

"Think I'll take another look at that car of his," Mary muttered to herself.

The commotion had also been noticed by someone else. Across the street in a gray rented vehicle, a large Armenian man sat watching the government building. The man's attention was drawn to the commotion.

"*Well, now,*" Aziz quietly said out loud. "*That looks like my little Chemist friend. He is not supposed to be showing his face, especially at Lois's office. There is something wrong here.*"

"If you say one more thing about that stupid dead dog, I will slap you!" Lois pointed to Vladimir.

He responded by throwing his arms into the air in frustration. "I'm only saying that it's... " His words were cut off by Lois's door being pushed open by someone who didn't knock. As the door banged against the wall, Victor jumped to his feet and was ready to fight the man.

"Stop, Victor." Lois tried to control herself. Turning to her uninvited visitor, she said, "Well, now, what do we have here? I thought I told you to quietly go about your business and not draw any attention to yourself. Now I see you in my office."

Victor and Vladimir looked at each other and then back at Lois for an explanation. Lois said, "Please come in and close the door." The man did so. He walked across the office towards Lois's desk. She said, "Gentlemen, may I present our old friend, the Chemist."

The goons gave Lois a surprised look, then in unison looked at the man who for so long they had been forbidden to even see. If they had actually looked at him just a few hours ago, they would have been killed.

"There were men at my house, Lois. Men asking about me, and they were in a van with the words Old Blues Retirement Home on it." The Chemist pointed toward the side of the facility where the Ol' Blues lived. "Why would men from a retirement home be at my house?"

Lois was silent.

"On my way in here I saw the last girl," the Chemist added. "She was driving one of their shuttles. She recognized me, Lois! Nobody is supposed to know who I am. There has to be some kind of connection; she must have driven the old guys out there."

The Chemist put his hand to his forehead. "But how would she know to drive her little shuttle bus out to my mother's house? Then why would she bring some old men out with her?"

Lois placed her elbows on her desk and leaned forward, then rubbed her temples to fend off a headache. "I have no idea...wait—we don't even know if she was the one that drove them out there."

"Victor, was she given the proper amount of the drug?"

Victor shrugged and replied, "Sasha gave her the water. I don't know if she gave her enough. Then later she went back and got her out of the house."

"I know that!" spat the Chemist. The faces of that Sasha woman and the girl he had just seen in the parking lot—both of whom had laughed at him—were seared into his memory.

The Chemist put his hands on his hips. "She could not have found her way back to my house. There had to have been some kind of help. Those men that asked about me, who could they have been?"

Lois leaned back in her chair. "They were probably the old guys at..." Lois paused. "The Old Blues Retirement Home." She leaned forward in her chair and placed her hands flat on her desk. "The retirement home for old police officers."

Lois stood. "You don't think those old goats were helping her, do you?" She thought for a second. The Chemist started to sweat at the mention of police officers at his house.

He repeated, "Do you think these old cops are helping her?"

Lois let out a breath of air and replied, "I...I don't know. They are so old, and one of them walks around with that stuffed dog over there." She pointed to Boomer in the corner.

The Chemist looked confused. Lois explained, "That old man thinks the dog is alive and walks around with it. He talks to it and even tried to sic it on me."

"Not all of them would have dementia," the Chemist mused. "If I knew what kind of medications they were receiving, that would help me determine who would be able to actually help her out. All of these guys are probably on Medicare, and I can access their records on our computer to see what medications they're taking. I'll just need a list of names. Could you get them for me?"

Lois thought for a couple of seconds, then said, "I'll see what I can do. That's not my department, but I'll see what I can access."

The Chemist almost exploded. "You'll see! We need to know *now*, Lois. Get me that list! They probably know who I am. We've got to do something about this!"

Then the Chemist stood up. "Get me those names and I'll know who has the ability to actually help her. I'll also know what to do about them. Oh, and get me the information on that girl. I need to know who I'm dealing with." Drops of sweat were beading up on the Chemist's forehead and starting to trickle down the sides of his face. He was clearly on the verge of a panic attack.

"Just shut up, you sniveling twit." Lois sat up and gestured toward a chair. "Sit down."

Vladimir moved the chair closer to the man as he stood shocked at the tone Lois was using with him. The Chemist had always gotten a bit of a rush from knowing that he had special status with the Cartel. But now that status seemed to have disappeared.

"We have been in the process of cleaning up our operation, and I have been making plans for the girl—the one person who can connect us with the safe house and you. Everything was going smoothly until you decided to barge in here and draw attention to yourself." Lois pointed to the Chemist in a threatening manner. "From now on you will do as you are told, or these two men will beat you to death. Do I make myself clear?"

The Chemist sat back in his chair and quietly responded, "Yes."

"Good," Lois snapped flatly. "Now go to your little pharmacy and I'll send you whatever information I can find."

Agnes had just hung up her police hat and was shuffling over to her recliner to relax. Suddenly the door of her apartment burst open, and in walked Big Brock, the Chelini brothers, and the Sarge, who was holding Amanda by the hand. Sarge led her to the couch in the living room.

Amanda sat down and began to speak, but her throat was so tight that her words were high-pitched. "I really don't know what happened. When I saw that man..." She paused as she tried to calm down. "He looked at me, and I had all these images shoot through my mind. I've seen him before, and..." She attempted to swallow, but her throat seemed to spasm.

"Sweetie?" Agnes brushed past Big Brock and sat next to her granddaughter. "Just relax; I'm right here, and you're among good friends." Agnes gently moved Amanda's hair away from her face and caressed her cheek with the back of her hand. "Tell me, sweetie... tell me about this man." Agnes turned to Brock and commanded, "Don't just stand there, ya putz, get her some water."

Brock quickly entered the kitchen. Agnes rolled her eyes at the sound of him opening and shutting her cabinets looking for glasses. "The cabinet door by the fridge," Agnes said, not bothering to look at him.

"Got 'em." Brock returned to the living room and handed Amanda a glass of water. She took a sip, and the cool water soothed her throat.

She took a deep breath and looked at the Sarge. Then she looked at everyone in the room. Agnes noticed that Amanda's countenance had transformed from a scared girl to a young woman who was trying to figure out why the encounter with the man in the parking lot had affected her so strongly.

"I know I've seen that man before," she stated. "That man's face was staring at me. His eyes were staring at me with the most hateful gaze."

The Sarge grabbed a chair and sat down. As a sergeant, he knew how to convey a sense of confidence that would calm victims down. He knew how to assure a victim that they were talking to someone who could help them.

"Amanda, I know you can't get his eyes out of your head, but I want you to widen your memory's view of him. Tell me about what else you remember," the Sarge said.

Amanda shook her head slowly from side to side. "It doesn't make sense, but..." She looked at the Sarge and then into the faces of all those around her. These weren't just cops. Her grandmother and the other Old Blues were tenderly supporting her. From their expressions, she knew they wanted to find the guy and beat him to a pulp.

Amanda felt a cloak of security around her. She felt calm enough now to allow her mind to search through memories that had been pushed to a subconscious level.

"Okay, this is gonna sound weird. I remember laughing at that guy because was wearing a funny-looking puka shell necklace, a cheesy silk shirt, and leopard-skin underwear. Then there was this weight on top of me, and..." She grabbed her throat. "Choking me. He was on top of me, choking me. Staring at me with furious eyes and kinda smiling at me while he was doing it." She pointed toward the parking lot.

"When he looked at me today, he seemed to recognize me and he gave me that same look. Then Big Brock yelled at him and he ran off."

Amanda looked at Big Brock and gave him a grateful smile. She noticed that everyone in the room was listening closely to every word she said. Amanda had never seen such intense expressions on the faces of these old people before. She didn't realize it, but all of them were busy compiling and analyzing evidence. A couple of times she noticed that the Sarge and the others in the room were exchanging looks that suggested her story was making sense to them.

"Is there anything else, sweetie?" Agnes asked.

"There was something that made him stop and he got off me." She struggled to focus her foggy memory. "A woman! A woman yelled something and came in and dragged me out of the room." Amanda tried to focus on the woman. "Tattoo... I remember a tattoo star on her wrist."

As Amanda's memories gradually became more clear she shouted, "Hey, one of those guys with Charlie's dog Boomer had a green star tattoo. Isn't that weird?"

Agnes looked over at the Sarge and said, "Maybe we should give her a break for a while."

The Sarge nodded. "Well, Recruit Amanda, you've been able to provide some much-needed evidence. Nice work." Amanda didn't really comprehend what the Sarge meant, but she knew that a compliment from the Sarge was something special.

"Thanks, I think."

With that, the Sarge stood and motioned to the others that it was time to leave Amanda with her grandmother. The men offered caring looks and reassuring smiles as they left the apartment.

Agnes sat back in her chair, pulled up the nasal cannula and lit another cigarette. She blew the smoke into the air and said to her granddaughter, "You, my dear, are in the midst of a bunch of old men that seem to have adopted you. I'd say anybody that threatens you from now on is gonna get a fanny whackin' the likes of which they've never had before."

Amanda smiled. "For as old as those guys are, it's nice to know that they would protect me if they could."

Agnes looked up at the ceiling and let out a laughing cough that confused Amanda. "You'd be surprised sweetie. These old geezers know things that the thugs today couldn't even imagine. Always remember," she pointed to Amanda for emphasis, "Age and treachery will trounce youth and skill every time."

&

As only those who have endured a traumatic event can do, Smitty and Mac took a few minutes to talk about their lives. They talked about everything except for the actual events that had hurt them so.

Many modern therapists try to focus those who suffer from post-traumatic stress on the incident that caused the deep emotional scars. It's a difficult but necessary means of addressing the issue. However, those who suffer from the effects of such pain need to start by talking to others, not so much about what happened, which will eventually come up. These people need to discuss how they have been doing since the traumatic event—how they struggled and eventually were successful in making a life for themselves. Sometimes just hearing from others who can still function in spite of the terrible things they've been through is exactly what they need to heal, cope, and enjoy some degree of normalcy.

Smitty and Mac talked of loves gained and lost… of how they had struggled to function in a society that could not fully understand them yet needed them. For men like these, the need to be needed gave them purpose in life. For them, a life without purpose is no life at all. It's meaningless.

After talking, laughing, and even shedding a tear or two, the two old warriors shared their determination to make these Armenians suffer for what they had done. The comradery of their shared pursuit of these green stars sent new energy flowing through their old bodies.

"Remember, Smitty, these Armenians play for keeps, so we'll have to stay one step ahead of them," Mac cautioned.

Smitty responded, "At our age, staying one step ahead is what we do best, even if we need a walker to do it." He gave Mac a wink and a smile.

CHAPTER 10

Sitting on the couch at her apartment, Brittany thought about how much her life had changed over the last couple of years. When the Old Blues Retirement Home had opened and her father had moved in, she had expected him to relax and enjoy his golden years among his old buddies.

Looking up at the ceiling, she said to herself with a smile, "I had such a simple life. Now here I am a special agent with this troop of old-timers. My life was turned upside down, and I'm some kind of crime fighter with guys who wear diapers and carry taser canes."

Then her smile broadened. "But I did get Jake as a result of this crazy situation." She looked at the engagement ring on her finger. "After we get married..." She started to giggle like a young, excited schoolgirl. "I love saying I'm getting married." Then the smile left her face as she looked across the room to a photo of her father, Sarge, and a few other Ol' Blues. "I don't think Jake realizes just what kind of package deal he's stuck with."

Her phone rang, "Hi ya, Britz, this is Agnes."

Brittany sat up. "Oh, hello, Agnes. How are you?" There was a pause.

"I'm fine, but Amanda had a bit of a scare today. We think she was confronted by one of the men that abducted her."

Brittany stood up. "Holy crap! Did he hurt her?" Again there was a pause as Agnes looked around to make sure Amanda wasn't close enough to hear her.

"We think he was meeting with the lady in Health and Human Services. The reason I called was to ask you for a favor. Do you think Amanda could stay with you for a couple of days?"

Without hesitation, Brittany responded, "Of course she can. I think getting away from there would be a good idea. Especially since those two bald bruisers are at the government building next to your wing. I hope the dog camera thing is getting good information."

Agnes smiled at Brittany's willingness to help. "There's a new guy named Mac. I don't know his last name, but one of the guys on the bureau sent him over to help with these Armenians. Anyway, spending time with you would really help Amanda. Thank you, Britz."

Brittany's response was upbeat and reassuring. "Don't worry about a thing, Agnes. Does she have to put in for time off or something?"

Agnes laughed. "I think I can arrange for a couple of days of annual leave."

"Sounds good, Agnes. I'll be there in about an hour. Oh, and make it a week. Let's give her a real break."

Agnes thought for a second. "Listen, if she is going to be there for a week, I'll call the pharmacy and have her epilepsy medications refilled. They will deliver them." Brittany provided her address, and arrangements were made for the delivery.

Agnes hung up the phone. "Britz is such a doll. Hard to believe she's the daughter of that putz with the bowel balloon."

The medication station for the Ol' Blues was staffed by the nurses who didn't want to work the night shift. There were also a small number of student nurses who were ever-present for various rotations. Many of the medications were sent directly from a pharmacy. There were also numerous medications on site in case a patient needed medication changes before the pharmacy could fulfill a prescription.

The student nurses reviewed the medications for the Blues and got them ready for their late-afternoon dosages. They were supervised by a regular nurse.

"Wow," the student said. "A bunch of these guys must have sleeping problems." She was looking at the computer with the names and lists of medications that each patient needed.

The regular nurse looked up from what she was doing. "Must have been because of the problem the night shift has been having with these old guys running around in the middle of the night and early morning hours. I heard it gets crazy sometimes. One guy got out of intensive care and pushed himself on a gurney. The guy didn't have much longer to live, but him getting up and out of the I.C.U. sure didn't help him. He died that night."

The student looked at the list of medications again and said, "I'm glad they come pre-packaged. It would be a pain to have to individually get the dosages for each patient. They are all on something."

She looked again at the computer. "So we just add whatever additional medications are prescribed from our med locker here, correct?"

The older nurse didn't look up. She just nodded and said, "Uh-huh. It's pretty easy. Double-check the additional prescribed medication and make sure it is put in with their usual medication and in the little plastic cups. Any other questions?" The older nurse said that in a tone that the student understood to mean, "*It's pretty simple; just do it.*"

"These guys must really have problems sleeping," the student muttered to herself. "Temazepam, Zolpidem… these are some pretty strong sleep medications. These guys must really cause all kinds of problems for the night shift." She added the medications to about ten of the patients' normal evening meds.

"Do all these guys have problems with blood clots?" the student asked another student. She didn't want another grumpy answer from the regular staff nurse.

"Makes sense," the other student nurse responded. "With guys this old, they must have so many ailments that trying to keep up on their prescriptions is a nightmare. Let's get these meds administered."

At dosing time, each of the Ol' Blues would be handed a small plastic cup containing the prescribed medications. They would simply do a "bottoms up" with the cup holding all their meds, then follow it up with a drink of water. The old coppers were so accustomed to taking their meds this way that they didn't even give their pills a second look.

∽

The Sarge was sitting at his desk. Agnes had just told him that Amanda would be staying with Brittany for a while.

"She picked up Amanda about an hour ago," Agnes commented. "She's such a sweet kid."

Sarge struggled to pay attention to what Agnes was saying. A tone in his ear signaled that someone was trying to call him.

"Sarge, this is Mary."

The Sarge sat up straighter. "I've got Agnes here with me. What's going on?"

"I caught the shouting barrage that Big Brock gave that guy in the parking lot. That same guy was acting really nervous before getting out of his car. I asked him if he needed anything, and he brushed me off. After Brock got through with him and he ran into the government section of the building, I decided to check out his car. There was a white overcoat on his passenger seat, kinda like what you see doctors wear. There was a name tag on it. I couldn't make out the smaller writing, but the name on the tag said *Monte*. I've got the license plate number so we can have Thane run it for registration and maybe get an address."

The Sarge sat quietly and felt strange for a few seconds.

"Does that sound all right to you, Sarge?"

Shaking his head a little, Sarge replied, "Oh yeah, Mary, that will be fine. Let me know what you find out."

"Roger that, Sarge. Oh, by the way, there's a man in what looks like a rental car that's making me a bit suspicious. He sits for a while, and then an hour or two later he's at another location. If I didn't know better, I'd say he was doing some kind of surveillance of our building. I'll keep looking around and see if he pops up again."

The Sarge looked at Agnes, who had been listening to the conversation on her hearing aid. She gave the Sarge a questioning look. "Do you think Jake would know if there was some sort of police stakeout going on? Maybe he passed something along regarding the Health and Human Services Office."

Sarge shook his head. "I don't think so. Jake would have told me about something like that."

⚬⟋

Boss Nurse Betsy walked through the Precinct giving everyone a visual once over. She heard the various officers on phones and typing away with those noisy old typewriters. Some were even arguing with people who were calling for police services.

"Look, lady, we can't send officers to your house because your son won't vacuum his room! Yes, yes, I know the term *Protect and Serve*. For crying out loud, lady, I was there when we came up with that slogan. But it doesn't say *Protect and Babysit*. Now grab that little twerp by the ear and pull him into his room. If he still won't do it, pull that ear 'til he does. Now I got other calls to answer, lady."

Boss Nurse chuckled softly. "Some of that old-school parenting might be just what today's kids need," she muttered to herself.

Big Brock had his back to her and was leaning on a desk. "Officer Brock, when was the last time your diaper was changed? It looks like it's really sagging."

Big Brock didn't really respond; he just seemed to lean a little more on the desk.

"Hey, Officer Brock, what about your diaper?" Nurse Betsy walked up behind Brock, who still hadn't turned to look at her when she had spoken to him. She tapped Big Brock on the shoulder, and as he straightened up and turned toward her, she noticed that his eyes seemed unable to focus. He towered over her by a foot. Suddenly Boss Nurse noticed his eyes roll back.

"Officer Brock? Whoa, now…What?"

The big man's head went the way of his eyes, and he started to fall down on Boss Nurse. She instinctively reached for him but ended up in a bear hug as she fell backwards under the big man's weight.

The combined weight of these two massive bodies created an unstoppable human avalanche. They landed on a desk, which collapsed under their weight as the typewriter that had been on the desktop was catapulted into the air. The Ol' Blue who had been typing didn't know what was going on because things had happened so fast. He was looking at the report he was updating. As he reached for the return lever, he realized that both the desk and typewriter were gone. He looked toward the sound of the typewriter's bell and watched as the machine flew through the air. He continued to watch in stunned silence as the airborne typewriter with his report still partially in the roller streaked through the air and made a strange flapping sound. The Ol' Blue admired how strangely graceful his typewriter looked in mid-air. Other Blues looked up and watched the soaring typing instrument. One elbowed another, pointed, and said, "Look, air mail!"

Everything in the Precinct came to a stop, and the atmosphere seemed strangely quiet until the Sarge's window was shattered. At the same time, Boss Nurse's voice pierced the confusion, yelling, "Get him off of me!"

In Sarge's office, Sarge had been pointing to Agnes and saying, "Make sure that photo of the Armenian enforcer gets distributed…." The horrible sound of the office window shattering cut his statement short. The Sarge and Agnes looked out of the broken window in shock. The Blue who was using the typewriter that had gone airborne was still in his chair. Sarge looked at him, and the puzzled Blue shrugged and offered the only excuse he could think of: "I was just double spacing."

The main doors burst open as nurses responding to the noise ran into the Precinct. The first nurse stopped and tried to figure out what had happened. Through the shattered window, she could see the stunned faces of Officer Agnes and the Sarge. The other Blues were moving around making sure everybody was okay.

The nurse looked to her left and saw a desk lying on its side. Next to it, the Blue who had been typing was still in his chair. He looked at the nurse, shrugged, then pointed toward the floor to his left. The nurse couldn't see what he was pointing at because the other desks were blocking her view.

Suddenly Boss Nurse's voice bellowed, "Get him off of me, then call a squad. Brock has collapsed."

Once Agnes and the Sarge heard that Brock had collapsed, they looked at each other in panic. All of the nurses ran toward the sound of Boss Nurse's voice. It took four of the nurses to get Brock off Boss Nurse, but they could only roll him over to his back.

One tended to Brock while the other three struggled to help Boss Nurse get up from the floor. Once Boss Nurse got a hold of her senses, she took over.

"Check Brock's vitals."

She pointed to another nurse. "Call 911 and get a squad here pronto. Then we need housekeeping in here to..."

She was cut off by the sound of Benson collapsing while standing with his walker. He and the walker hit the ground pretty hard. The back of his head was cut and bleeding. One of the nurses ran over to Benson and saw that he was unconscious and bleeding from the back of his head.

"Get a crash kit in here! Officer Benson is hemorrhaging!"

One of the younger nurses picked up one of the Precinct phones. She stared at the receiver, then turned it over and realized there were no numbers to push for a phone call. She followed the curly, somewhat knotted cord to the part of the phone that was on the desk. This part of the phone had a round metal disk with holes along the edges. In each of the holes was a number. She stuck her finger in the hole with the number 9 and pushed. Then she pushed her finger through the hole with the number 1 twice. Nothing happened.

"How do you work one of these?" she asked in confusion.

Smitty entered the Precinct and saw all the commotion. He heard the call for a squad and watched the nurse's confusion as she attempted to use a rotary phone. Smitty bounded over, took the phone from her hand, and barked, "Move it, sister. I got this."

He took the phone and dialed 911. The young nurse watched in fascination as the dial spun around.

"How does that call out?"

Smitty ignored her. "Dispatch, this is Officer Smith from HQ. I need a couple of hospital wagons to the Ol' Blue Retirement Home, and step on it."

Smitty pulled the receiver away from his ear and mouth. He looked at it and yelled, "What do you mean, you don't understand?"

The nurse grabbed the receiver back from Smitty. "I need two squads dispatched to the Ol' Blue Retirement Home at 156th and Maple. We have two elderly males that have collapsed. One is hemorrhaging from the back of his head. Nurses are evaluating at this time."

She attempted to hang up the phone by pushing the underside of the receiver.

"Just hang it there," Smitty said, pointing to the apparatus that was above the spinning dial.

Within minutes, sirens were heard and paramedics and the nurses were feverishly tending to Big Brock and Benson. Agnes could see that the nurses and paramedics were particularly concerned with Benson as they tried to stop the bleeding.

"Get him as stable as possible while we transport. He may need a blood transfusion." From all around the Ol' Blues stood and started pulling up their sleeves, then offering their arms.

"I got some. Take some of mine; Benson owes me five bucks."

The nurse temporarily stopped in amazement to see how eager these men were to help a fellow Blue.

"No, guys, not like that. Just stay back we'll handle this."

Helplessly, the Blues watched as both men were placed on gurneys. Sarge walked over to Boss Nurse Betsy.

"Which hospital are they taking them to?"

She looked over and was about to answer him when she noticed that his mouth had started to slowly open, and then his cigar fell to the ground.

"Sarge, are you all right?"

The Sarge shook his head as if to clear his thinking. "I just need to know... which... hosp..." Sarge's eyes started to roll back in his head.

"Oh, not again!" Boss Nurse yelled.

Sarge started to fall forward, and for the second time Boss Nurse ended up on her back. "Stop that squad, get 'em back here!" she yelled from the floor.

Boss Nurse raised her head off the ground and looked at the Sarge, whose fall she had broken. Lying on top of her, he was breathing deeply, which was a good sign. Emotionally exhausted, she let her head fall back onto the floor.

She looked up at the ceiling, and after taking a deep breath she uttered, "First time in my life two men have fallen for me, and it's just my luck they're both wearing diapers."

⁓

The cleanup crew had finished their work. The tables and desks had been righted, and the glass from the broken window to the Sarge's office had been removed.

Agnes tapped her earpiece. "I'll need all the remaining officers on the special task force to meet in the downstairs conference room."

Thane was at his desk when he heard the summons. "Wonder what that is about?"

Mac had just got back to his desk and started to review the Boomer Butt surveillance tape when he heard Thane.

"What are you saying?"

Thane realized that Mac didn't have a communication earpiece yet.

"Lead Officer Crantz just called everyone on the task force to go to a meeting at the conference room. That's odd; usually the Sarge calls these meetings."

Mac shrugged, "Well, you'd better get going. I've got a lot of surveillance tape to go through yet from the pooch cam."

෴

In the conference room, Pauli and Tony Chelini, Smitty, and Thane were sitting at the large table. Thane looked around and could see the various hidden security video images on different screens mounted high on the walls. By panning from the left to the right, one could see what was going on outside the building, throughout the retirement home and the Precinct. There was also a new screen with blank squares.

Thane touched Smitty on the shoulder and asked, "What is that new screen for?"

Smitty looked up. "That will be the new camera shots we will get once the cameras are hidden on the Health and Human Services and the medical wing. We didn't take them into account when we first set up our security. Once they are set up, it should fill the new monitor with surveillance from those areas."

Thane nodded in appreciation. "That would have come in handy. Boomer Cam seems to be doing a pretty good job for the time being."

Smitty smiled. "Freaking stroke of genius from the Sarge."

The small talk stopped as the sound of the squeaky wheel on Agnes's oxygen tank carrier was heard. Agnes shuffled in, and a trail of cigarette smoke followed her.

"Smitty, did you contact Jake?"

Smitty nodded. "Should be here soon."

"Good, now the rest of you…" Agnes stopped and smiled as she saw that Thane had stood up when she entered the room. Her heart warmed for a second. "Please have a seat, Thane."

She had started to sit down when Tony loudly cleared his throat. Agnes looked over to him and saw that Pauli was pointing to the chair at the head of the table. Smitty verbalized what all the men in the room were thinking: "Lead Officer Crantz, that..." he motioned with his head, "... is your chair now."

Agnes paused and let out a breath. "Thanks, fellas. Hopefully it won't be mine for long." Per her duty as Lead Officer, she took her place at the head of the conference table.

Suddenly everyone stopped moving and put their hand to their earpiece as they heard an unusual tone. Agnes looked confused. "What tone is that?"

Smitty spoke up. "That's Tucker Preston."

In response to the confused look on Thane's face, Smitty added, "Officer Preston is our eyes and ears around the nurses' station. They do a lot of talking, and we learn all kinds of things from their conversations. Preston sits completely still like someone who has had a stroke. The nurses just move him around from station to station. When he has some intel, he lets us know by pushing a button on his watch."

Thane's head jerked back. "I've seen that guy! I've never actually seen him do anything but sit in his wheelchair. I thought I knew everything that went on in this place." There were snickers around the table.

"Tony, could you go get Officer Preston and have him join us?"

Tony nodded and left the room.

"Where is the rest of the task force?" Thane asked innocently.

Everyone at the table realized that Thane had no idea what had transpired in the Precinct an hour ago.

Agnes looked at Smitty, and with the cigarette between her index and editorial finger she motioned to Smitty to fill Thane in.

Smitty began by clearing his throat. "The Sarge, Big Brock, and Benson all collapsed upstairs in the Precinct. They've all been transported to the hospital. We don't know what happened to them yet. Every time I asked the nurses, they said they can't talk about it."

Smitty looked around the table and asked, "What does a hippo have to do with people in the hospital?"

Thane noticed that everyone else at the table shared Smitty's confusion. He explained, "It's not *hippo,* it's HIPAA. Smitty, what is with you and acronyms? HIPAA basically means that the medical staff has to keep information on patients private."

Thane looked at Smitty.

"Hippo! Really?"

Suddenly Thane realized that the person he leaned on when trying to translate modern society to these geezers wasn't there to help him. "Where's Brittany?"

"She is taking care of Amanda for a week or two," Agnes explained. "Amanda spotted another one of the guys that kidnapped her. This one seems to have done something really violent to her. The guy showed up in the parking lot of Health and Human Services. He saw Amanda, and something happened in that moment and she remembered some things that really shook her up. Luckily, Big Brock was there. The guy wanted no part of Brock, then he skedaddled into the government branch offices, probably to the office of Lois and her two goons. Mary in the parking lot got a good look at him and was able to look into his car. She saw a name tag with the name *Monte* on it. She was going to send you the information on the vehicle so could possibly get a lead on identifying this guy."

Agnes noticed that as she spoke about what had happened to Amanda, Thane was gripping his laptop computer as if he was getting more and more upset.

"I'll have that information as soon as we're done here," Thane promised in a very determined tone.

Agnes softened her voice. "Amanda is fine, Thane."

Not knowing his physical reaction was being observed by everyone in the office, Thane loosened his grip on his computer. The Ol' Blues exchanged knowing looks with each other.

Smitty spoke up. "Don't need a hippo to tell us there's a sweet spot for Amanda."

Thane's face blushed red as he placed the laptop on the table, thinking, *Dang, these cops see right through me.*

There was an almost unbearable silence for a couple of seconds until the elevator door chimes announced Tony Chelini and Tucker Preston's arrival. Tucker Preston was wheeled in. He sat with the usual empty look on his face until Agnes asked him for his report. Suddenly he seemed to jerk to life. Thane jumped, saying, "I've never seen you move before."

Officer Preston gestured toward Thane with his thumb. "Who's the ginger?" Again Thane was shocked. "I didn't know you could talk."

Looking at the old officer, Agnes explained Thane's role in the Precinct. Officer Preston seemed impressed.

Thane commented, "I've seen you in the surveillance video of the facility. You're good." Tucker Preston smiled and acknowledged the compliment, then turned his attention to Lead Officer Crantz.

Officer Preston reported, "The nurses said that the Sarge, Big Brock, and Benson are at the Nebraska Medical Center. The doctors at the center are trying to figure out why they collapsed. At first they thought it was just because old people occasionally did those things, but three guys at the same time? Nobody could explain it, and everybody seemed at a complete loss. I figured you would want to know the latest, Agnes, when I heard the announcement on the task force meeting."

Agnes nodded. "Thanks, Tucker. Sounds like they are all right for now."

There was a friendly sounding tone over the intercom, followed by an announcement that was broadcast throughout the retirement home. "Would all the officers that take afternoon medications please come to the dispensary."

Agnes threw her hands up. "Nuts, I forgot about med call." Tony, Pauli, and Smitty looked at Agnes. She realized that she was about to lose all the attendees of her task force meeting. She also knew that if they didn't go, the nurses would come looking for them.

"All right, you afternoon med takers better get upstairs. We will assemble again in an hour right here. Now get up there before you're missed. Don't want the nurses to start snooping around for you."

With that, the men went upstairs for their prescription medication.

⌒

Mac put his headphones on and reviewed the video that had been collected from the dog's poop shooter. He sat up straighter as the video showed Lois and her two men jump at a loud sound and turn towards the office's door.

"What's going on here?"

Mac was intent on finding out what had caused everyone to jump. Then he saw a man walking towards Lois's desk.

"This should be interesting."

⌒

At the medication dispensary, or "Med Shack" as the Blues call it, a line of men were waiting for their afternoon pills. Each received a small plastic cup that contained his pills. Many of the men just popped the pills into their mouths and chugged some water, then went back to their duty stations. The Chelini brothers downed their meds and went about their business.

As Smitty was handed his plastic cup, he inspected its contents and noticed two pills that he hadn't seen before. He turned to the student nurse and said, "These look different."

The supervising nurse responded, "Whatever is prescribed for you, Officer Smitty, is what we give you."

Her explanation didn't satisfy Smitty. "But I haven't seen my doctor for a while. Why would my medications change?"

The nurse started to get a bit testy. "Look, we've got to get to the rest of the patients in line here. If you're refusing to take your medications, I'll have to report it to Nurse Betsy."

Smitty still didn't like what he saw. "Nope, don't like not knowing what I'm taking."

That comment earned him a frustrated look from the nurse.

"Come on, Smitty!" One of the Blues in line said. "I got things to do, and you are not on my itinerary."

Smitty moved off to the side so the other officers could get their meds.

ᔆ

Boss Nurse was sitting at her desk trying to catch up on the medical status of the collapsing officers when her phone rang. The caller was a doctor from the Nebraska Medical Center. After identifying himself, he told Boss Nurse that the bloodwork showed that all three of the patients had strong sleep medications of Temazepam and Zolpidem in their systems which made them very severe falling risks. In addition, there was Warfarin, a blood thinner.

Boss Nurse's eyes widened as she realized that the two prescriptions together had put the men at a high risk of falling, and if injured, at a high risk of bleeding out. Benson had been bleeding profusely. Clearly something was wrong with the medications the Sarge, Brock, and Benson had taken.

ᔆ

Mac reached up and pulled off his headphones. He sprang from his chair, then ran toward the area where he thought the meeting was being held.

Agnes and Thane were sitting in the conference room waiting for the others to return. Suddenly Agnes heard someone yelling in the hallway, followed by various doors being opened and slammed shut.

"Where are you, Thane? Where is this blasted meeting?"

Thane got out of his chair and opened the door. Sticking his head into the hallway, he saw Mac frantically opening doors and yelling Thane's name.

"Mac?"

Mac looked in the direction of Thane's voice. "Thane! Where is everyone in this meeting?"

Thane, still confused, pointed his thumb over his shoulder into the conference room behind him. Mac ran toward him and excitedly yelled, "Move, move, move!"

Mac entered the conference room and saw Agnes. "Pharmacist! The Chemist is a pharmacist!"

Agnes looked at him in confusion. "Okay, that's good to know."

Mac shook his head, realizing he needed to explain. "He was talking to Lois and wanted the names of the old cops. He said if he had that information, he could get access to their medications."

Agnes still looked a bit unsure of the point Mac was trying to make. In frustration, Mac almost yelled, "If he gets their medications, he can add things to them or change the medicine they get."

Agnes started to comprehend what Mac was saying. Finally, Mac flatly stated, "He can kill them."

Agnes's jaw dropped, and she pressed the button on her earpiece.

"This is an all points bulletin. Our medications have been contaminated. Do not take them."

捠

The door to the Med Shack burst open, and Boss Nurse's voice bellowed, "Nobody takes their meds! Stop distributing now!"

Boss Nurse could see that some of the officers were holding empty plastic cups. Other officers had already spit out their pills before she entered the room. Boss Nurse didn't stop to ask why they had done it. The nurses were looking at her with questioning expressions.

"Everyone that has taken their meds sit over here."

She looked at the nurses in the Med Shack and said, "Ipecac syrup now."

The nurses knew what that meant. There was a flurry of activity as emergency kits were torn open and Ipecac was pulled out. The nurses yelled to the students, "Trash bags, buckets, anything you can get your hands on that will hold about a gallon of fluids."

The students knew there was an emergency, and they didn't ask what was going on. All the Blues who had swallowed their medications sat down and were given a drink of a dark syrup. After about a minute, the officers who had taken the syrup got strange looks on their faces. The nurses and students put the buckets in front of the faces of the men. Suddenly there was an explosion of sound as ten men began vomiting.

Smitty looked at the nurse he had previously argued with. She was holding a small bucket that was splashing vomit onto her shirt and neck. She looked around, and when her eyes met Smitty's he held up his clear plastic cup still containing his pills as if he was toasting her. Then he turned and left the room.

Smitty headed back to the conference room. As he entered, Agnes, Thane, and Mac looked at him.

"Tony and Pauli took their meds," Smitty reported. "The nurses gave them something to make them puke. They are probably gonna have a bunch of ambulances here shortly."

Smitty added, "Mac here was listening in on our friend Lois and her goons. Evidently this Chemist is a pharmacist."

Mac spoke up. "I'm not sure that Lois sanctioned this attempt to poison everyone like this, because it seems like this will attract a lot of attention. After listening to this Chemist fellow, he sounds like he is paranoid of people knowing about him. My guess is that this is the guy providing the drugs to Lois and her bald helpers. From what I've learned from this outfit of old cops, the girls were all drugged with heroin. Looks like they were being doped up and addicted for use in the sex trade. A pharmacist would come in real handy. He probably provided something to knock them out when they were originally kidnapped."

Agnes and Thane appeared upset by what Mac was saying. Smitty voiced what all the Blues were thinking.

"That makes sense. This Chemist must have provided the tools that they needed to carry out their little operation."

Smitty put his hands on the table and said what everyone was feeling. "It's gonna be fun taking these guys down."

11

CHAPTER

"What is happening out there? Is there a fire or something?" Lois asked one of the other staff members of Health and Human Services.

"I don't know what's going on, but there must be ten squads over at the retirement home. I've got a friend who's a nurse over there. I'll call her."

As the other staff member called her friend, Lois looked through a window that provided a view of the parking lot and the entrance of the Old Blues Retirement Home.

"Are you kidding me? That's terrible," the staff member said before hanging up her phone. Her mouth was open in reaction to what she had just heard. She looked over at Lois and some of the other staff and announced, "The prescriptions for the patients at the retirement home had been screwed up. A bunch of the patients are sick. They took three to the hospital this morning, and a bunch of the others are sick right now, puking their guts out. How in the world could that have happened?"

Lois cringed, and without saying a word she walked back to her office. Once inside, she closed the door and walked over to her desk. She sat down and calmed herself before speaking.

"That idiot just tried to kill a bunch of the old police officers at the retirement home. He is panicking, and the fool is going to get all of us caught. It won't take long for investigators to figure out what happened."

She tapped her fingernails on the desk and thought for a few seconds. Vladimir and Victor gave each other looks of concern.

"*This may come in handy,*" Lois said in Armenian. "*If the authorities get occupied with our little Chemist friend, that could buy more time for us. Is everything about ready to move?*"

Both men nodded. Victor asked, "*Why do we need all these records, and why do you have to take so long to clean out the computer information?*"

Lois started to tap her fingers in frustration. "*Haven't you been listening to what I've told you? There is an audit going on. If I download too much information it will be noticed. We need to do this right or everything we've done here will be lost. And if we lose everything, we won't have anything to offer the Mexican cartels.*"

Lois sighed, rubbed her temples, and then looked at both men. "*When we're finished, we need to be ready to leave at a moment's notice.*"

Victor voiced another concern. "*What about our own cartel? Don't you think they are getting suspicious? This was supposed to bring them a fortune.*"

Lois nodded and was surprised that such a good observation had been offered by the stupid dunce.

After giving Victor a thoughtful glance, Lois pointed to the boxes that were stacked next to the stuffed dog. "*Load the boxes in the van. I need to make a call.*"

The phone rang. "*Why has it taken you so long to call?*"

There was a short pause. "*Aziz, whatever do you mean?*"

The answer was swift and loud. "*Don't fool with me, Lois. We've been waiting for a call from you. What is going on?*"

Lois pressed the speaker button on her phone and set the phone on her desk. She pressed her palms on the desktop as she spoke.

"*Aziz, the audit is almost over. We will be functioning and ready to transport the girls within the week.*"

There was a moment of silence, as if Aziz was holding his hand over the phone. Lois could still hear, though muffled, a familiar sound. Aziz got back on and told her, *"The leadership has been angry with the lack of communication."*

Again Lois calmed herself. *"Let them know everything will be fine, Aziz."*

The muffled whining sound continued as Aziz covered the mouthpiece of his phone. *"I will let them know. Don't fail us, Lois."*

The line went dead. Lois knew that the last thing her brother had said to her was a threat. She wondered about the muffled sounds she had heard as Aziz covered his phone. Was Aziz speaking to the Cartel leadership while he spoke to her? That would make sense because they were obviously very interested in everything she was doing.

"Still, he said he would let them know. Like he hadn't told them yet." Lois mumbled to herself, "There was something about the sounds during that phone call."

Lois walked to the shipping area where Victor and Vladimir were loading a van with the records, addresses, and general information on the numerous girls who would soon be turning eighteen and aging out of the foster care system. Lois looked into the back of the van and instructed, "Make sure everything is organized. Don't just throw the boxes in there like piles of trash."

Then Lois heard a sound that made her freeze. At the front of the large facility, there was still a flurry of activity due to the medication contamination. The sounds at the main entrance of the large facility were muffled by the buildings. Those sounds were the sirens of the ambulances as they approached and then departed from the retirement home. Lois reached over and held the door of the van to steady herself from the shock as she realized that the muffled sounds of the sirens that she was hearing and the muffled sounds she had heard while speaking to Aziz were the same.

"Aziz is here," she said to herself. *"He is watching us from somewhere outside the building."*

Lois, always motivated to maintain every advantage, decided to keep this information to herself. *If Victor and Vladimir knew that the Cartel's enforcer was nearby they might panic. It's time to tighten up the loose ends and get out of this place… hopefully to new employers.*

⟋

The shock of someone's voice so close to the side of his head caused Aziz to snap his head to the left. This caused him to hit his forehead on the door jamb of his car. It also caused a slight gash through his left eyebrow and broke his sunglasses.

"I said, 'Are you lost, young man?' Oh! Did that hurt?"

The man in the car let loose with a number of curses that Meter Maid Mary didn't quite understand, although she did comprehend the tone.

"Ah! Why you do that, woman?" The man took off what was left of his sunglasses and rubbed his eyebrow. He looked at the palm of his hand and saw blood. He glared at the old woman

"Oh, I saw you sitting here for so long, I thought you might not know where you are going. Do you need any help?"

The man's frustration was intensified by the throbbing above his eye. "Help! What help, old woman? I just sit here."

Aziz decided that he had better not stay and possibly draw attention to himself and this old woman with the huge eyes and purple hair. He closed his car window and drove off.

"You're up to something there, bub," Mary said as she watched the vehicle drive off. She saw the driver looking into his rearview mirror as if to see whether she was still watching him.

"Bye, sweetie," Mary said as she waved.

"Agnes, this is Mary. Do you read me? Over."

Agnes had just wrapped up her meeting in the basement and was on her way back to the Sarge's office. She tapped her earpiece and responded, "Read ya, Mary."

She listened as Mary recounted her interaction with what appeared to be a pretty good-sized man with an accent across the street from the main building.

"Come on in, Mary. I have a photo I want you to look at."

⟋

Jake, Brittany, and Amanda rushed through the Precinct doors and went directly to the Sarge's office. Amanda noticed that her grandmother wasn't at her desk and one of the Sarge's windows was missing.

Jake knocked on the door, and after a second or two they heard a female voice say, "Enter." Jake and Brittany entered the office as Amanda watched the crew cleaning up after the afternoon's events. Jake was first through the door and saw that Mary was handing a photo back to Agnes. Mary flatly stated, "That's him." Agnes thanked her, and Mary quietly turned her wheelchair and with a quick wave of her hand glided back to her post.

Jake spoke first. "We heard what happened on the radio and rushed over as fast as we could."

Before Agnes could say anything, Jake motioned with his head. "Amanda insisted on coming."

Agnes looked past Jake and said, "Amanda, sweetie, come on in."

Once Amanda was inside, Agnes motioned for her to close the door. Then they all sat. Brittany's eyes gave away her question as to why Agnes was sitting at the Sarge's desk. Agnes pointed to the chair she was sitting in. "When the Sarge was taken to the hospital, that made me, as the Lead Officer, Acting Sergeant." Brittany smiled, and Amanda did a little eye roll. Amanda still didn't fully understand how entrenched these Blues were in the structure of command and the need for consistency in an organization like the Precinct.

Brittany said, "We heard that there was some sort of medication mix-up." Agnes nodded and lit a cigarette, making an "Mm-hmm" sound. After taking a drag, she spoke with smoke streaming out of her mouth and nostrils.

"Looks like everyone is gonna be all right. Sarge, Big Brock, and Benson collapsed. Benson got a big gash on the back of his head and was bleeding pretty bad. Big Brock fell right on top of Boss Nurse, and as he was being taken care of, Sarge collapsed. Luckily Boss Nurse was standing close to him. She broke the fall of each of those two. Probably saved them from getting injured as they fell. Good thing she's such a big gal. It wasn't till the afternoon med call that they figured out that there was a mistake in the medications. About ten officers had to have their stomachs puked out. They're all at the hospital for treatment."

Brittany blurted, "My dad takes his meds in the afternoon!"

Agnes raised her hands towards Brittany. "He's fine. That eagle-eyed side squirter spotted pills that didn't belong in his little cup and refused to take them." Brittany rolled her eyes and sighed with relief.

Agnes looked at Amanda. "How are you, dear?"

Amanda replied, "I'm doing fine." Then she smiled and added, "Lead Officer Crantz."

That got a big smile out of Agnes. "Listen, Recruit, there are a lot of old coppers out there that might need some help getting re-focused on their jobs with all that's happened. Do you think you could get out there and help them get this office back up and running? I'll make sure today's annual leave is put back in your books."

Amanda suddenly felt a sense of duty to help out the Precinct. She stood, saying, "I'll get right on it." Out of the office she went, shouting, "All right, ladies! Break time is over. You don't get paid by the hour here."

As the door closed behind Amanda, the three people in the office relieved their stress with a much-needed laugh.

Once Agnes had finished her usual post-laughter coughing fit, she waved her cigarette in the air signifying that she had something important to say. "Before she gets back, this is what you have to know. This was no accident. Our new guy, Mac, was monitoring the Armenian commies and he figured out that they have a pharmacist that works for them. It was the guy that Amanda recognized, and it looks like he recognized her. Mary was able to get the license plate number and look into the guy's car. She saw a name tag on a white medical coat that said *Monte*. Thane is running the license plate. Mac thinks this pharmacist is panicking and tried to poison our guys."

Brittany and Jake tried to process all of the information after Agnes finally stopped talking to take another drag on her casket nail.

Brittany abruptly blurted, "That means he knows she works here! But it doesn't mean he knows she is staying with me. As soon as she is done getting the Precinct in order out there, I'll take her back to my house."

Jake said, "When we get the full name of this pharmacist I'll research our records on him. Have Thane call me with the information."

Agnes nodded. "This sounds like a good strategy for the time being. As soon as I can, I'll get over the hospital and fill the Sarge in on our findings and our plans up to this point."

Jake gazed into Brittany's eyes. She smiled at him, looked over her shoulder toward the Precinct, then turned back to him.

"This is gonna be our lives from now on," she said. "Are you sure you want to step into this?"

He returned the smile, then got up and gave her a kiss on the cheek. "I was starting to think that my life was getting pretty boring. You and this merry band of crazed geezers have added some spice to my life."

Then Jake looked over at Agnes. "I'll get back to my office. Have Thane call me once he gets that Chemist's name."

Jake reached down and gave Brittany's hand a squeeze. "See ya soon."

She squeezed back. "I know."

Agnes seemed to enjoy the love story that was unfolding in front of her. "You've got it backwards, Jake. You've already stepped into this little outfit, and you already have all that goes along with it." Agnes pointed to Brittany. "She is the fringe benefit of working with us."

"I guess that is one way of looking at it. I'll be waiting."

After Jake left, Agnes took a drag from her smoke and looked at Brittany. "As far as partners go, you could have done worse. I gotta say that any man who still wants to be your partner after all this"—she pointed to various directions—"is definitely a keeper, or a nut. You get to find out which."

6∿

"That was easy." The Chemist smiled at the reflection in the hospital's computer monitor as he signed out. To carry out his plan, he had gone to the large pharmacy in the hospital where he worked part-time. There were numerous pharmacists rushing around and lots of computers that could access virtually anyone who had a prescription filled. The pharmacists were rushing to fulfill the medication needs of all the patients who had been admitted to the entire hospital. On top of that, they supplied the medications for the surgeries and the emergency room.

"Hey, Monte, bad time to visit. Things are crazy right now," one of the pharmacists said. "I've got to get up to the E.R.; they are swamped. Two drive-by shootings, and the rival families are fighting in the lounge area." His hands were full of various medications. "Oh, crap. Monte, could you sign me off the computer, please? I've gotta get these upstairs."

Monte smiled. "No problem. I got ya covered."

Monte, the Chemist, had known that someone always leaves their workstation without signing out. Once he had accessed the computer, he simply changed the prescriptions for the names he had received from Lois.

"That will make it very difficult to trace this to me. With all that's going on here, it will be difficult to trace the source to anyone." Monte stood to leave.

"What's going on, Monte?" another pharmacist asked.

"Oh nothing. Just left something here during my last shift, so I had to come back to get it. You guys are getting your butts kicked. Do you need me to help out?"

The pharmacist shook his head. "We're good. Just another busy night. See ya later, gotta get up to surgery."

The Chemist quickly left the hospital and went to his regular full-time job at an Omaha pharmacy. He had purposely left himself signed in at his computer there. It would be difficult for anyone to connect him with a medical mishap at a busy hospital while he was signed on at his other job.

6s

"Monte Kurt," Thane said.

Jake listened intently.

"The guy has a number of addresses listed." Thane read through them. "Oh, that's interesting. One of the addresses listed is in Kennard."

As he listened to Thane, Jake felt the emotional jolt of a break in a case. Only another investigator could understand how a break in a case causes every conscious thought to be focused on seeing the case through.

Jake ran Monte Kurt's name through the law enforcement database. There were a couple of hits, but they were old cases. They hadn't been scanned into the computers yet, but the cases were all assigned to the Sexual Assault Unit. Knowing this, Jake decided to take a different, possibly quicker, approach. He contacted the sergeant in charge of that unit.

"Special Victims Unit, Sergeant Benson."

Jake introduced himself: "Hey, Sarge, this is Jake Mitchell. I'm the PIO for the Chief."

"What can I do for you, Jake?"

Curiosity got the better of Jake. "Did you say your name was Benson? The same as Officer Benson out at the Old Blues Retirement Home?"

Sergeant Benson replied, "Yeah, that's my old man. He retired back in the early nineties. How do you know him?"

Jake paused, wanting to avoid giving out too much information. "We don't know him too well, but I'm the liaison between the Chief's office and the old coppers at the retirement home. They do a lot of community advising for us. I heard he was one of the officers that got sick from some medical mix-up. Is he doing all right?"

"I went over and saw him last night. Looks like he is gonna be all right. Gave us a good scare, but he's a tough Ol' Blue."

Jake sighed in relief. "That's good news. Hope he is up and around soon. Listen, the reason I called is because I was looking through some cold cases and a name popped up that I wanted to check out. Since I'm not in your unit, I couldn't run it down. Could you look it up for me? The name is Monte Kurt."

Sergeant Benson looked into the Sexual Assault database and found the name.

"Oh, that guy's name came up a couple of times a few years back. Looks like he was questioned but we couldn't make anything stick."

The sergeant read a little more. "This Monte Kurt always seemed to be on the fringes of the investigation. Doesn't look like the detectives were able to nail him down to any of the sexual assaults. Why are you asking about this guy?"

Jake knew that the sergeant of the Special Victims Unit would know about the raid on the safe house that Amanda was in.

"Well, his name popped up in relation to that big raid that the F.B.I. did on that house with all the young girls in it. I know it's not our investigation, but I thought I'd see if we had anything on the guy."

Sergeant Benson paused. "Wait, back then DNA wasn't as useful a tool as it is today. There was blood at two of the sexual assaults that did not belong to the victim."

Jake's heart rate quickened. He understood that DNA could convict this Chemist even if there wasn't much more evidence against him. Jake smiled, then snickered as he realized that the reason this guy could get caught was advances in modern police work and technology—something he would be sure to rub in when he talked to those Ol' Blues.

Sergeant Benson added, "Looks like the investigator on this case was Detective Angie Jacks."

Jake hadn't worked long enough with the Omaha Police Department to know a lot of the officers. "Is she still with the Department?"

"Angie? Sure is. She's a short-timer, though. Probably going to retire soon. She still works for Special Victims, but she's involved with Domestic Violence now. Since she was the original officer, it won't be any problem re-opening this case with her as the investigator. I'll contact her and have her call you. Will that work, Jake?"

The excitement Jake felt at the break in these old sexual assault cases caused his mind to race.

"Jake?" Sergeant Benson prompted.

"Oh, sorry, Sarge. Got a bunch of things on my mind. Yes, have her call me, thanks."

⁓

Agnes, Brittany, and Smitty walked into Thane's work area. Mac was still trying to catch up on the surveillance video of Lois's office. He had already provided enough intelligence to be a tremendous asset to the investigation.

Thane informed the others that he had identified the man that Amanda recognized as part of the group that had abducted her.

"I called Jake and gave him the information. Seems this Monte Kurt is the son of the lady that owns the house in Kennard, Ethel Kurt. The pieces are coming together. And thanks to Mac, the Armenian connection has been established."

Mac heard his name and the reference to the Armenians. "Well, looks like there's another player in the mix."

Agnes sighed. "Oh great! This toilet bowl doesn't have enough brown trout swimming around."

This comment drew a subdued snicker from Mac. Since his arrival, Mac had observed that Agnes's masterful use of euphemisms was impressive.

"Well, since this Armenian operation has collapsed, Lois and the goons have been packing up and closing shop. Looks like they are trying to scram. It also looks like this Lois is the clever one. She has a contingency plan. She's trying to offer a similar service to a Mexican cartel."

Mac sat back in his chair, interlocking his hands behind his head. "Lois is smart. If she hooks up with another powerful cartel, she gets protection and is able to continue doing what she does best. I'm guessing that she has some sort of database of young women that she plans to provide her new bosses."

Smitty added, "If there is a Mexican cartel involved, it will be in South Omaha."

Smitty looked at Mac. "That is where a large population of Latinos live. It's an ideal place to blend in and not attract attention." Smitty smiled. "It's also an old part of town where there are lots of tunnels, many of which are being retrofitted as we speak."

Mac held up his index finger. "There is one thing that bothers me—that Chemist, Monte Kurt. He met with Lois and the others. He was pretty upset that the cops had been around his mother's house. Looked like it really shook him up. Lois provided names of the Blues upstairs, but she warned him to keep a low profile or her goons would beat him to death. Then, within twenty-four hours, their medications are tainted."

Agnes lit a smoke and took a long drag, then pulled the cigarette from her lips and stared at the ceiling as she blew the smoke upward. Squinting through the haze, she flatly announced, "He's scared and overreacting. Lois and the others did all the work. I'll bet he liked staying in the shadows. When the cops, even old cops, show up at his house he is exposed."

Mac added, "Yes, to debilitate the cops so quickly was a knee-jerk reaction, an emotional response. A very good move, but strategically premature."

"Shine a bright light on slime like this and they'll panic," Smitty added. "By the way, what has Jake found out?"

Thane looked at Smitty. "I don't know. I'll call him when we're done here and then fill you all in."

Agnes spoke up. "It looks like your other Armenian friend has arrived." Mac gave her a questioning look.

She held up the photo of Aziz. "Our exterior security officer positively identified him. She stated that he has been parking at different locations throughout the day. Seems to be watching the building. We originally thought it might have been the police. We thought they might have connected Lois to the two bald thugs. I showed our security officer the photo you provided to the Sarge, and she stated that it was him."

Mac leaned forward in his chair. "Is she sure about this visual ID?"

Brittany decided to chime in. "If you ever saw that woman's eyes, you wouldn't doubt her powers of observation."

Smitty had been watching Mac as his eyes exposed his intense interest in the man who had been observed outside the facility. After Mac was satisfied that Aziz had been positively identified, he rubbed his left hand and told Smitty, "Remember, they play for keeps."

&

"Public Information Office, Officer Mitchell. May I help you?" Jake said as he answered the phone in his office.

"Hey Jake, Angie Jacks here. Sergeant Benson said you might have some information on some cold cases of mine. He told me that you had a guy named Monte Kurt pop up."

Jake sat back in his chair. "Yeah, he said you interviewed the guy years ago. Were you able to find any case notes on the interview?"

Angie took a breath and then let it out as she scanned the old report notes on her computer screen.

"This was when those date rape drugs were just entering the scene," Angie recalled. "I think this guy was in the medical field. All the girls who had been assaulted were unable to remember what happened. The only reason we figured out they had been assaulted was the presence of someone else's blood at a couple of the scenes. The guy had come in through the window both times and got small cuts as he did so."

"If I remember right, this guy couldn't be pinned down," Angie continued. "He would be at the same bar the victims attended, and he knew them. He was kinda creepy, but in the end we couldn't nail anything to him."

Jake sat forward, excited at the chance to nail a sexual predator. "Do we still have the blood in evidence?"

Angie checked the computer. "Yep, looks like we still have the blood evidence in one of the cases. What makes you think that he's the perp?"

Jake explained, "His name came up in this big human trafficking case the joint task force is working on. I thought I'd check and see if we had anything on him. All we had was your work all those years ago."

Angie's voice became a little more high-pitched as she considered the prospect of a break in an old case. "I'll have crime lab get the DNA and get it over to the lab. Meantime, how 'bout we have that guy come in and see if he'll give us a blood sample?"

⸎

The reflected eyes in the beauty section mirrors in the little pharmacy gave Monte a look that he'd never seen before. There was the recent confidence that he felt as he was able to easily victimize a couple of women and get away with it. There was also a look that gave him pause. *I could kill them all if I wanted. I may have even killed a couple of them today.* A feeling of power rushed throughout his body. Previously, Monte always had a feeling of control. This time there was also power over life and death.

He winked at his reflections and started to strut toward the pharmacy section of the drugstore. As Monte walked, he looked high up on the wall to study the mirrors that the employees used to observe people in the store's aisles. The mirrors gave him a heads up if there were customers waiting at the pharmacy desk.

He noticed a couple standing with their backs to the pharmacy. *That's odd,* Monte said to himself. The closer he got to his workstation, the more familiar the woman seemed. He could not place it, but there was something about her that bothered him. Monte tried not to stare at her as he approached. He smiled and said, "Can I help you?"

"Mr. Monte Kurt, it's been a long time."

Monte tilted his head as he looked at the woman, trying to place her familiar face. There was something scary about her. She didn't look like some sort of crazy person, but he felt nervous as he looked at her. He just couldn't remember why.

"Don't tell me you don't remember who I am?"

Again, Monte tilted his head. "Your face is so familiar. I'm sorry, I just don't... umm."

Monte started to look away from the woman's face to take in her whole appearance. Then he noticed a badge on her hip. A jolt of fear shot through him. Gone was the confidence and power that had propelled his strut. Monte had come to a startled stop physically and emotionally.

"Now do you remember? I'm Detective Jacks of the Omaha Police Department. We spoke a few years back about some women that had been assaulted."

Detective Jacks spoke slightly louder than she usually would. She hoped that it would make the man very self-conscious about what was being said and who could hear it, especially since he was a man of professional standing.

Both Jake and Detective Jacks saw the shock in his face. *Gotcha!* Detective Jacks thought. As she had done so many times before to convince someone to come downtown for an interview, Detective Jacks looked around as if she was concerned about who might overhear their conversation. In a calming voice she suggested, "Perhaps this isn't a good place to talk. Could you come to headquarters with us? We need to talk to you."

Monte's eyes darted back and forth to see if anyone was listening. "Yes, that would be fine. What's this about?"

Detective Jacks again lowered her voice. "We can talk about that at the station. I don't want you to be misunderstood by your customers hearing things. We just have a few questions, so it shouldn't take too long."

Interrogation rooms are pretty much the same from one police department to another. There is usually a table with two or three chairs, and that's it. Of course, everything is recorded.

Monte Kurt was shown to the interrogation room, asked whether he needed to use the restroom, and offered a glass of water. He declined. Jake and Detective Jacks told him they would be right back, and then they left the room. They let him sit in the room for a few minutes and watched his behavior on the monitors in the recording room.

"Look at him sweat," Jake observed. "This guy seems to be really worried about something."

Detective Jacks had printed her notes from the last interview she had with Monte Kurt. "I'll start with the fact that we periodically go through old files and see if people remember anything since the last time they were interviewed. That should settle him down a little, because we didn't arrest him back then."

She continued, "After that, I'll read him his rights and see if he'll talk to us now. These guys will talk if they think we don't really have anything on them...up until they think the law is about to crash down on them. Then they lawyer up."

Jake looked at Detective Jacks. "Well, we don't have anything else on him except possible DNA evidence."

"I know that and so do you," said Detective Jacks, "but he doesn't." She pointed to the monitor displaying the sweating pharmacist.

"Let's see if we can sweat some information out of him."

The longer Detective Jacks spoke to Monte, the calmer he became. *They don't have anything more than they did years ago.* In his mind, Monte smiled.

"Didn't we already talk about this?" he asked.

Detective Jacks smiled. "We sure did. I just wanted to make sure I have everything correct from back then. It's procedure for old cases."

Monte started to look more comfortable and relaxed, right up to the time Detective Jacks said, "Oh, there was one thing—the bloodwork we had on these victims. Back then we didn't know about various date rape drugs. We re-checked the bloodwork for two young girls who had been assaulted. Both of them had some drugs in their blood. That was a preliminary test. The evidence bloodwork has been sent to the state research labs to determine what those drugs actually were."

Detective Jacks scooted her chair a little closer to Monte.

"You are a pharmacist." Detective Jakes paused while scrutinizing Monte for signs of evasion. "Do you know what we'll find when we get the blood work back from the state lab?"

Monte shook his head and answered, "N-No, I'm sure I wouldn't know."

Detective Jacks responded, "Well, maybe not. After all, the DNA could have degraded after all these years, or the blood could have been contaminated. I mean, after sitting around all this time, who knows what might have happened?"

Then Detective Jacks leaned forward. "Would you be willing to clear your name and give us a blood sample?"

Monte looked around the room, then down at his hands. "I think I should consult a lawyer."

Detective Jacks looked toward the hidden video camera and smiled.

∞

"Match the blood type from that many years ago? Do you think that's enough to convict him?" Smitty said. "Honestly, Jake, police procedures have gotten pretty weak since we were on the force."

"What other evidence do you have? Amanda's memory is not enough for even a search warrant. What about witnesses? Did the victims remember anything about this guy?" Agnes asked.

Agnes and Smitty were taking turns quizzing Jake on his approach to the Chemist's case.

Exasperated, Jake tried to explain his reasoning. "You two don't understand. DNA is not just blood type. It is so much more. It is the individual's specific genetic/chromosome makeup. I know you coppers didn't work with this stuff, but it is the latest in crime fighting when it comes to identification. It is also solid in court. If we get a DNA match, then the crook is caught and there's no getting out of it."

Unconvinced, Agnes blew smoke into the air. "I hope these newfangled ideas of yours work, Jake. I'm telling you there is nothing like old school, down and dirty police work. You cops nowadays don't seem to walk away from your computers, smartphones, or even walk a beat. How do you know what's going on in the streets if you don't walk around and find out for yourselves?"

Smitty looked at Jake. "If it's not too much trouble, I'd like to go over all the old reports on this guy."

Jake was impressed by Smitty's grit and desire to dig into the investigation. "No problem, Smitty. I'll get them from the archives and make some copies for you."

Then Jake shook his head. "Trust me on this, you two. We've got him."

13

"I'm gone for a couple days and my window still isn't fixed yet?"

The Precinct doors closed behind Sarge as he took a step into the room he loved, then saw that his window had a piece of plywood covering the broken section.

The big doors opened again, and Big Brock walked in. There were cheers and statements like "Good to see ya. Missed ya, Sarge. Hey, Brock! You both look good."

The Sarge's office door opened, and from inside came an unmistakable raspy voice. "Good thing you're back, that chair was getting comfortable. C'mon in, I've got to update you on some things. You too, Brock."

After Sarge and Brock were in the office and Sarge took his rightful place behind his desk, Agnes lit a smoke and started to speak. "Since you two have finished playing Bouncing Boss Betsy, we've learned quite a bit. The man that Amanda recognized was actually the Chemist. His name is Monte Kurt, and it looks like he panicked once he learned we were sniffing around his mother's house. Our friend Lois provided him the names of the Blues in our home. Then he accessed your medical files and played with your daily prescriptions. Looks like he was ready to take out a bunch of Blues."

The Sarge and Big Brock looked at each other. The realization that they could have been killed came in loud and clear.

"What protective measures have been taken to make sure this guy can't get to us again?" Sarge demanded.

"There has been a lock-down on all medications," Agnes said. "Each Blue's prescriptions are being reviewed. Boss Nurse and the other nurses that have been here the longest and are the most familiar with the Blues are making sure that the medications are correct for each officer."

Agnes cleared her throat. "Now there's the matter of this Chemist, Monte Kurt. Jake tells me that he had been researching records on him, and it turns out that a few years back he was questioned about some assaults on young women, but they couldn't nail him with anything. Today I talk to Jake and he tells me they got some new scientific way of identifying someone's blood. It turns out that when Monte Kurt was questioned they did have blood at a couple of the scenes that didn't belong to the victim."

Agnes waved her smoke around. "Jake tried to explain it. He said that something in the blood called DNA can identify whose blood it actually is. So if they can get Monte Kurt to give a blood sample, they can compare it to the blood that was at the scene. I guess it would be enough to prove that Monte Kurt was the one that attacked those girls all those years ago. I have my doubts, but Jake swears by the DNA stuff. He also told me that they questioned this Monte and when they started to interrogate him and ask him for a blood sample, he refused and wanted his lawyer."

Big Brock stated, "So they think they can collar him with this?"

Agnes shrugged. "I guess so. Seems like a long shot to me."

Brock added, "I saw Amanda's face when she saw that little maggot. I also saw his face when he recognized her. That guy was blinded by anger, and I'll bet we could squeeze a confession out of him, or at least trip him up and have him incriminate himself. By the way, how is Amanda?"

Agnes smiled. "Got the best therapist I know taking care of her. She is staying with Brittany for a couple of weeks. For some reason she wants to keep working here with the Blues. Must have been the thrill of being promoted from Cadet to Recruit."

That remark got a chuckle from Sarge and Brock. "She really does fit in quite nicely here, Agnes," observed Sarge.

"As far as this Monte the Chemist goes, I feel the same way Brock does, but it's a different way of policing now. We've gotta let today's coppers do their stuff."

Agnes let out another breath of smoke. "Anyway, he's lawyered up, and it would be difficult to trip him up now. My guess is that this Monte Kurt will stay low for a while and hope that the heat wears off."

The Sarge let out an exasperated breath and then leaned back and put his feet on his desk. "Well, so everything has been pretty quiet around here, huh?" he said sarcastically. "By the way, anything else?"

After blowing another breath of smoke into the air, Agnes looked over to the Sarge and said, "Oh yeah, one more thing. An Armenian hit man has been seen staking out our building."

The Sarge's cigar dropped from his mouth.

$\sim$

"As your lawyer, I would strongly recommend against this. Volunteering a blood sample? Don't do it. Make the police prove their case against you. From what I've seen so far, it looks like the only solid evidence they are betting on is blood DNA. I say just stay at home and make them prove it."

"I can't do that," Monte said. "I've got responsibilities to my patients. I have my reputation. Once I get this cleared up, I can get back to my life without the cops showing up at my office or harassing me."

Monte Kurt sat back and thought, *I'll trash their case against me, and they'll have no choice but to move on.*

$\sim$

As Detective Angie Jacks hung up her phone, she shook her head in disbelief as if to make sure she understood exactly what she had just heard. She picked up her phone to make another call, and once she heard the voice on the other end she announced, "Jake, you're not going to believe this, Monte Kurt is going to give us a blood sample. We are going to nail this guy. When I interviewed him, I told him that over the years the blood evidence could have become contaminated and may not even be able to be used. He must be banking on that. I'll meet with him and his lawyer at the hospital for a blood draw, then I'll get the sample to the state lab."

Jake couldn't believe what he was hearing. "He fell for the suggestion that the blood evidence could be contaminated or go bad. I'll bet he thinks he can beat the DNA. We're gonna get this guy, Angie. Good work. Please keep me advised as things play out."

⁓

"Take the offer," Monte said to his Realtor.

"I think if we wait for a few more offers we can get a better…"

Monte interrupted her in mid-sentence. "I said take the offer and get the deal wrapped up today. I want the money in my bank account by tomorrow."

The Realtor sighed and then agreed, "Okay, if you say so. I'll call their Realtor and ink the deal."

Monte smiled and hung up. "I'll bank this money and have a sufficient financial cushion in case I have to leave town," he said to himself.

As he drove to the hospital, Monte looked forward to ruining the police investigation. While stopped at a red light, he glanced at the eyes looking back at him from his rearview mirror.

"Those idiots think they got me with DNA. They actually think I believed that stupid line about blood being contaminated. I can't wait to see their faces. 'The DNA might be contaminated,' they tried to tell me."

Monte smiled, then added, *"The DNA won't be contaminated, but it can be changed."*

Then he looked away from the mirror and thought about the names on the list from the retirement home. It had been so easy to get their information and add to their prescriptions. Monte had heard that there were a number of ambulances at the retirement home.

"*That will teach them to mess with me,*" he gloated.

Then Monte looked up again to the reflected eyes. "*Got everyone on that list but the one that caused me so much trouble... Amanda Crantz.*"

After looking up her name in his records, he had recognized an opportunity. "*Epilepsy medications.*"

Then he had learned that she was living at a new address. He vowed, "*I'll take care of her later.*"

His conversation with the reflected eyes was interrupted by a honk from the car to his rear, letting him know that the light had changed. Monte waved to the driver behind him and proceeded forward. Next stop: the hospital.

&

Jake's phone rang. "Hey Jake, Angie here."

Jake felt a tinge of excitement. "How did it go? Did he say anything we could use against him?"

There was a pause, and then Angie responded hesitantly, "He didn't say anything we could use, but..."

She paused as if in deep thought. "There wasn't a hint of nervousness. It seemed like he was anxious for us to take his blood. I'm not sure, but I thought he even smiled."

Jake was taken aback by Detective Jacks' observation. "Really? Well, it will take a while to get the results from the State Lab. We'll just have to see what they find."

Jake hung up. *He was smiling. That's odd.* He let the thought linger for a moment. Then Jake snapped back to his current task. *Gotta get over to the Precinct and see how the Sarge is doing.*

Jake picked up his phone and called his favorite number. As always, he was eager to hear her answer. He wanted to give her a greeting that might make her smile or at least blush.

After the first ring, Jake heard, "Hey," and responded with what he thought would be a smooth yet masculine line.

"Oh, those lips sound like something I'd love to kiss."

There was a short giggle, followed by, "Glad you think so, but I don't think Britz would like it" followed by a laugh.

Jake's smooth, masculine voice tone seemed to drop flat. "What the... Amanda?"

Another giggle. "Yep, Britz wanted me to answer the call for her. I'll get her."

Jake rolled his eyes as Amanda walked to Brittany with the phone while commenting how lucky she was to have such a macho man and telling Brittany what Jake had said. Of course she didn't cover the phone, so Jake had to listen to the emasculating sound of two women laughing at him.

Brittany got on the phone. "Tell me about my lips."

Again the disarming sound of two women laughing at his expense. "I was just about to go and see the Sarge and Brock, then brief them on what's been going on. I wanted to know if you and that little answering machine of yours would like to go with me?"

Brittany asked Amanda if she wanted to go, then got back on the line and said, "Sure, just make sure you don't confuse the lips when you get here to pick us up." More giggling.

Jake let out an embarrassed sigh as he stared up at the ceiling. "I'll be there in a few minutes." He hung up and looked at a photo of Brittany he had on his desk. "What have I gotten myself into?"

Watching this facility was more work than Aziz had anticipated. It took him a couple of days to figure out that Lois, Victor, and Vladimir were not acting as if everything was going to get back on track. Aziz had been forced to change his vantage points numerous times during the day because that old woman in the wheelchair always seemed to eventually show up wherever he parked.

While watching Lois and the others loading up some sort of cargo van, Aziz thought about his next steps. If they had actually failed and this operation was ruined, they would all pay. Out loud Aziz mumbled, *"Her failure will be seen as my failure. I must make them all suffer for this disgrace. One thing is certain— whatever they are putting in that van, it must be important. Wherever that van goes, I will follow."*

As soon as Lois and the others went back into the building, Aziz drove up to the van, got out of his car, and quickly placed a magnetic tracking device under the front bumper. Then he got back into his car to drive away. As he exited the loading area, he looked to his left.

"Ah, there she is again!" Aziz watched as the woman came around the side of a parked car. "The woman has eyes like headlights on a car."

Aziz stepped on the accelerator and drove off to get another view of the building. He also wanted to figure out exactly what Lois was up to.

⟡

Jake, Brittany, and Amanda walked into the Precinct. Jake and Brittany headed straight to the Sarge's office, but Amanda saw Big Brock and went over to him. A huge smile lit up the face of the big man as Amanda ran up and hugged him.

"I'm so glad you're all right, Big Brock. I was sick with worry when I heard what happened."

"I'm fine, doll baby." Brock's deep voice seemed to calm Amanda's nerves. Then Brock started to chuckle as he added, "Luckily Boss Nurse broke my fall."

All the Blues around them laughed. One yelled, "Ol' Brock has had the hots for Boss Nurse for a while now." This drew a scowl from Brock, and the Blue quickly went back to tapping away on his typewriter.

In the Sarge's office Jake and Brittany were being updated by the Sarge. Jake jumped up from his chair.

"A hit man from Armenia!"

Sarge pulled the cigar from his mouth. "Yeah, I had to replace my stogie after I heard that too."

Jake and Brittany looked at each other in mutual confusion.

"Our new guy, Mac, knows all about this guy named Aziz Luka, who happens to be the brother of Lois Luka. According to Mac, the Armenian Cartel must know by now that the operation that Lois and her goons were running has collapsed. He also said that this Aziz is the punisher of the organization. Sister or not, he will kill her and the bald duo."

Jake sat down and looked at the Sarge. Then he said, "I've got to notify the F.B.I. They will want to know about this guy."

Sarge put the cigar back in his mouth. "He has popped up around the facility off and on. It looks like he's watching this little trio. Mac thinks the cartel wants him to find out what is going on. If he determines that they've failed, he will take action. What he doesn't know is that good Ol' Meter Maid Mary has had his number for a few days now. She snuck right up to his window. She said she scared him so bad that he cracked his head on the door jamb. She also put a tracker on the back bumper of his car. Thane told me it works by satellite like Amanda's watch. I still don't know how the satellite knows the difference between a watch and a bumper tracker."

Brittany was about to explain how satellites worked. Then she decided it wasn't worth the effort because Sarge would never get it.

Smitty knocked on Sarge's door and then stepped into the office. He gave Brittany a kiss on the head. She looked up at him and said, "Heard you didn't like the meds you were supposed to take."

Smitty smiled. "I'm picky that way."

Brittany's eyes let Smitty know she was glad he was all right.

⌒

Boss Nurse was at her desk when the phone rang.

"Oh yes, she's here. I just saw her walk into the Precinct. The dog? Yeah, I'll send her over to get Boomer."

Lois walked into her office and pointed to Boomer in the corner.

"Get that thing out to the van. Set it by the open doors. Soon I will send the girl out to get it. There should not be anyone out there at the time. When she gets there, subdue her and get her into the van."

Lois pointed to Victor and said, "Remember to do it quietly, because we don't want any attention."

Victor grabbed the dog and rolled it out of the office, commenting, "This thing really is disgusting."

As Victor left, Lois picked up her phone and called her Mexican Cartel contact.

"Yes, we are ready. I even have one of the girls that was going to Armenia. She will belong to you if we decide to do business." Lois listened to the contact's instructions. Then she hung up the phone and thought, *South Omaha... a large population of Hispanic people and next to that giant Omaha Zoo. Makes sense. The Italian Mafia stayed in their Italian neighborhoods where they could blend in and it was difficult for the authorities to track them. Looks like my Mexican friends know the same trick.*

Once Victor reached the van, Vladimir gasped, "No, no I don't want this filthy thing to come with us. Throw it into the trash."

Victor smiled and explained, "Lois is going to ask for that Amanda girl, then send her out here to retrieve the dog. Look, there's nobody around. Get into the cargo area of the van. I'll get her to the doors. You grab her, pull her in, and secure her, but keep her quiet. I guess she is what we will show the Mexican employers of our product." Victor ended his instructions with a laugh.

"What about this dog?" Vladimir wanted to know.

"I don't know. Maybe Lois wants to dump it in the river or something. Anyway, this dog is what we are going to use to get the girl out to the van."

Carrying his laptop as he usually did, Thane looked into the conference rooms and scanned the large surveillance monitors. He noticed that in the back loading dock there was a large cargo van. The front of the white vehicle had the front portion of a van, but the cargo area was a large square section to maximize storage. That van was the only vehicle in the area, and someone was loading items into it. Then something caught Thane's eye. It was one of the bald goons, and he looked like he was dragging something…

"It's Boomer!" Thane blurted out loud. "Why is he pulling him toward the van?"

Lois sat at her desk waiting for the young lady who had no idea know how much trouble she had caused.

"Hello, I was told to come down and get Boomer," Amanda said, standing in the doorway of Lois's office.

Lois looked up with a fake smile. "Oh, yes, young lady, that dog is.." Lois feigned surprise. "What the… Oh, the loading men must have taken it out back to the loading dock. They must have thought it was supposed to go with all the office equipment. Do you know how to get to the dock from here?"

Amanda smiled. "Yeah, I can get there."

Lois looked at Amanda with concern. "You had better hurry. They may leave any minute."

Amanda turned and trotted out the door, assuring Lois, "Okay, I'll stop them."

Lois's smile was now sinister. "You do that."

Thane was still staring up at the monitor and watching the odd activity. Then, just as he was going to notify the Sarge, he saw something that caused his mind to go blank. "Amanda?" Thane watched as the girl he had a crush on from afar ran toward the bald man who appeared to be loading Boomer into the back of the cargo van.

"Hold on! Don't take that dog!" Amanda yelled.

The bald man had the animal halfway into the cargo van. He stood up quickly, pretending to be startled. "What do you mean?"

The girl came closer, breathing hard. "The lady in the government office told me that you had accidentally taken it." She was still about ten steps away and could only see the back of Boomer. The bald man had his hands under the back legs, but the front of the dog was inside the cargo hold.

"My hands are full. Could you climb inside and grab the front and help me unload it?" the man asked.

Amanda responded, "No problem."

She looked down as she stepped up to the floor of the cargo bay. Then she glanced inside and noticed that the van was loaded with all kinds of boxes and supplies. There was also...

She froze. Her eyes bulged wide as she focused on another bald man that seemed to rip a memory from the back of her mind. He looked at her with a vicious grin on his face that she immediately recognized and associated with a painful blow to her abdomen.

"You!" she yelled, pointing an accusing finger.

The man lunged at her but stumbled on some boxes at his feet. Amanda screamed. As the dog was shoved into the bay, Amanda tried to jump out of the van. The bald man outside the van attempted to grab her in midair. During her time in foster care Amanda had been in her share of fights, and she started punching, slapping, and scratching at the man's face.

Blood rage surged through Thane's neck, and he thought his chest would explode. He ran up the stairs and down the hallway to the rear dock. The door that closed behind him was another "Do not enter" Electrical Servicing Room façade.

Thane bolted onto the loading dock to see Amanda in the arms of one of the goons. As she thrashed at his face, the other man jumped from the back of the van and from behind wrapped his arm around Amanda's neck and squeezed until she dropped limp. Neither man saw Thane charging at them. He swung his laptop, which had an aluminum casing that caught Vladimir under his left eyebrow, cracking the orbital section of his thick skull. The hit was painful but not enough to drop the burly brute.

Victor had felt as though he was trying to hold onto a wildcat. Once Vladimir had choked Amanda into unconsciousness, he glanced up in time to see a shiny movement to his right as the laptop smashed into his head. After throwing Amanda's unconscious body into the back of the van, Victor spun around and planted a solid right punch on Thane's left cheek. Thane dropped to the ground before he even knew what had happened to him. His laptop skidded on the dock. Vladimir was spitting Armenian curses, trying to clear his head from being on the receiving end of a nerd's laptop.

"Throw them both in the back and bind their hands with duct tape. We've got to get out of here," Vladimir yelled.

Victor threw Thane's flaccid body into the back of the van, then partially closed the doors as Vladimir restrained Amanda and Thane. The burns he had suffered from being captured by the SWAT team were still very painful. Now Vladimir's left eye was swelling shut.

"What are we supposed to do with this guy?" Vladimir spat as he kicked Thane in the back.

"Just finish getting them secure. We'll decide what to do with him when Lois meets up with us." Victor's face had numerous bleeding scratches. He used his sleeve to wipe his face, then looked at the blood that soaked it. "These two will pay for this."

Vladimir quickly secured the cargo and the two unconscious prisoners. He jumped out of the rear cargo doors, then closed and locked them. He trotted toward the front passenger door to join Victor. As he did so, he noticed a movement to his right in the parking lot. Vladimir did a double take, unable to believe what he was looking at. Across the lot was a woman with purple hair in a motorized wheelchair, moving fast.

Vladimir opened the door and yelled to Victor, "Go, go! Someone is driving toward us."

Quickly putting the vehicle into gear, Victor yelled, "Where? I don't see a car."

Vladimir had to turn his head farther than usual because his eye was swelling shut. He pointed to the right. "Over there—an old woman in a wheelchair."

Victor stared at his cousin in disbelief. "A wheelchair? What are you talking—" He stopped speaking as he saw what Vladimir was pointing at.

An old woman with purple hair was sitting in a wheelchair that seemed to be racing toward them. Victor floored the accelerator and the van lurched forward. As they headed for the exit, Victor looked into his rearview mirror. "She is following us... No! She is catching up to us!" The van started to speed away. Again, Victor looked into the rearview mirror. Even though the mirror carried a warning that said *Images in mirror are closer than they appear*, he could clearly see the woman's purple hair flapping in the wind. She seemed to be wearing large goggles, but as he was able to get a better look he could tell that those goggles were glasses that magnified her eyes.

"She is chasing us!"

Finally the van was able to pull away from the speeding, elderly pursuer.

"That was the craziest thing I ever saw," Victor commented.

Vladimir stuck his head out the window and looked at the woman as they drove away. He couldn't see her face, but she clearly let him know what she thought of him by flipping him the bird.

◌

Jake stood and announced, "After I get back to my office, I'll put together an intelligence brief. We'll have to get a better explanation as to how we found out that the Armenian hit man was in Omaha."

The Sarge pointed down to the floor. "Why don't the three of you go down and talk to Mac? He may be able to provide some sort of plausible explanation that we can give to the Feds that won't raise a lot of questions."

Mac was just returning to his workstation with a cup of coffee from the break room. When he walked in, he was surprised to see three people there.

Smitty spoke first. "Mac, you remember Jake, our contact at the police department."

Jake acknowledged Mac with a smile and nod.

"And this is my daughter Brittany," Smitty continued. "She is also an Ol' Blue."

Mac cocked his head to the side as he looked Brittany over. "She sure doesn't look like the women I've seen in this cranky old bunch. What on earth do you do here, Brittany?"

"I'm still trying to figure that out for myself," Brittany replied with a grin. "But I wouldn't want anything else. I've got my dad and a bunch of crazy uncles here. I also ended up finding—of all things—a future husband," she said as she pointed to Jake.

Smitty added, "This little daughter of mine helped us break a major gang ring about a year ago. Without her, we would have really been in a fix."

Mac's eyebrows lifted as he was clearly impressed. "Well, if Smitty says you're all right, you must really have this crazy cop stuff in your blood."

Jake grabbed a chair for Brittany and then sat down himself. "Sarge thought you would be able to help us out with something, Mac."

Mac sat and motioned for Jake to continue.

"I need to let the F.B.I. know about this Armenian hit man. I can't just tell them he's been hanging around the retirement home. We need a reasonable story that explains how we know who he is and why he's hanging around here."

Mac took a sip of his coffee and rubbed his chin. "You don't," he calmly replied.

Jake was taken aback. "I have to let them know about this guy."

Mac shook his head. "No, you don't. What I mean is *you*"—he pointed to Jake and then to everyone else in the room—"..don't tell them. That would bring you under close scrutiny. We've got to let the C.I.A. or Home Security know. When I say *we*, I mean *me*. I have some contacts who won't ask questions. I can let them know that the investigation here in Omaha busted what they thought was a drug house until they found out it was part of a human trafficking operation. Once they know about the two bald goons with the green tattoos on their wrists, they'll understand why an Armenian hit man is in the country."

Jake shrugged. "That sounds good, it's less for me to explain."

Then Jake looked over to Brittany and asked, "Where's Thane?"

Brittany shrugged. "Don't know."

"He left about an hour ago, headed in that direction." Mac pointed to the door that led to the conference rooms. "Don't know where he was going."

"Thanks, Mac." Smitty gave him friendly look. "How ya doing?"

Mac smiled, "Fine, Smitty. This place with all its strange quirks seems to be good for me." Then Mac got a devious grin on his face. "It's even provided me a way to get some therapeutic payback."

Mac pointed to the photo of Aziz, then scooted his chair over to his monitor. "Well, I've got some more pooch cam video to review. I'll see ya around, Smitty. Jake and Brittany, I'm sure we'll talk again soon." Mac put his headphones on and keyed up his monitor.

⌒

Sarge's earpiece signaled an incoming call. He responded with "This is Sarge."

There was a short pause and then "Sarge, this is Mary. I just saw something go down at the rear loading dock. I only saw the tail end of it, but it looked like those two bald Armenians were in a big hurry. They loaded something into a cargo van. I tried to get over and see what they were up to, but when they saw me they punched it and flew outta here. I couldn't get close enough to get the plate. Don't know what they were doing, but it sure looked suspicious."

Sarge listened intently to what Mary had to say, knowing that if she thought something was wrong, it probably was.

"Good to know, Mary. Thanks."

"There's one more thing, Sarge. Earlier, I saw our Armenian guy snooping around the same van. It looked like he was putting something in the wheel well. He quickly got back in his car like he didn't want anyone seeing him. Then, as he was driving away, it looked like he saw me. Haven't seen him for a while."

Sarge was reaching for his earpiece button to call Thane when there was a knock at his door. "Come in."

Brittany, Jake, and Smitty entered. Smitty immediately began updating Sarge on what was going on with the investigation.

"Hey, Sarge, Mac is gonna contact his people at the C.I.A. or Homeland Security or whatever other special agency he worked with and tell them about Aziz. That way, we avoid any questions about how we knew about the guy and why he is hanging around an old cops' retirement home."

Sarge nodded, satisfied with what Mac had suggested. "I like it. Sounds like a smart way to handle the situation."

"Oh, Jake, catch me up on the Chemist situation," the Sarge continued. "Agnes told me your boys with their chemistry sets may have a way to collar him without doing any police work."

Jake smiled. "It's modern police work, you rusty copper. We've developed technology that can check DNA that is unique to each person and match it to evidence at the scene of the crime, like blood or other body fluids. Once we get a match, there's no disputing it. We'll get this Chemist for a couple of rapes that happened years ago. Some blood was at the scene, and once we match the DNA of Monte Kurt to the DNA we had at the scene, he's fried."

"I've been in contact with the Detective working the case," Jake added. "She got Monte to give us a sample of his blood. She tricked him to thinking that the blood at the scene might have been contaminated, so he probably thinks giving us his sample will clear him." Jake smiled at the skeptical look that Sarge was giving him.

The cigar came out of Sarge's mouth. "No staking out his house or where he socializes like bars or night clubs. No sweating him in the interrogation room. How about flashing photos of the victims on the desk in front of him and seeing the expression on his face? Then you hit him with the shame he will bring on his mother if she found out that he had done these things, and the only way to restore her faith in him was to come clean?"

Smitty chimed in, "What about going over the daily activities of each of the girls, finding their common traits, and looking for any intersection between this Chemist and each of the girls? That will tell you what's going on in his mind and what his next move might be. It takes a lot of digging, but it's worth it. Might even be able to catch him before he strikes again."

Shaking his head, Jake couldn't resist a little dig at the strategy of the past. "Old school, Sarge, Smitty. Give modern police work some credit. We got this."

Brittany watched her father's expression as he rolled his eyes, gave a slight shake of his head, and then sat back with his arms crossed. *Dad doesn't like it, and I'll bet he'll start his own little investigation.*

The cigar went back into Sarge's mouth. "Seems pretty lazy to me, but if you say so… *Junior*"—giving Jake the poke a seasoned cop always gave a new officer with an attitude, simply letting him know who really had the years to back up whatever point the senior was trying to make.

Smitty asked, "Can you get me the reports of those old rape cases? I'd like to look them over. And any similar sexual assaults recently, Junior."

Jake took the jibes in stride. "I'll get those reports to you, Smitty, and let you know when we arrest him. I've got to get going."

He looked at Brittany. "Are you ready to go?" She was still watching her father, admiring how he would dig and dig until he found something that would solve a case. It had been a hard trait to live with as she grew up, especially as a young girl hoping to get a date with a young man. She thought about how difficult it must have been for a wife to live with a man like him. Took its toll on his marriage to her mother.

"Oh," she responded as Jake interrupted her train of thought, "…sure. Do you know if Amanda wants to stay around here or leave with us?"

Jake shrugged.

There was a knock at the door. "Come in," the Sarge responded.

The door opened, and squeaky wheels let everyone know who was entering Sarge's office. Brittany waved. "Hey, Agnes."

Lead Officer Crantz smiled at Brittany and waved back with a cigarette between her fingers. "I was just at my apartment looking for Amanda. Anybody seen her?"

Brittany looked at Jake. "That's funny—we were just downstairs looking for Thane."

The Sarge smiled. "I've heard Thane got the twitters for Amanda."

Brittany's face lit up as she replied, "Well, she can hang around here if she wants. Let's go. Thane likes Amanda, so maybe they're together now." She smiled at Agnes. "Oh, that would be so sweet."

જ

Lying on a wooden and metal floor in a moving vehicle as it hit bumps, turned, and periodically stopped was extraordinarily uncomfortable. Added to that was a splitting headache after passing out. Amanda thought, *"I don't know where I am, but this sucks."* Then she looked around and realized that she was in the big cargo van that the two bald guys had been loading. She smiled as she remembered *"At least I got my shots on the face of one of them."*

The ceiling of the van was made of a material that allowed sunlight to illuminate the cargo area. She looked to her left and saw boxes and files that had been bound together. Her eyes continued to scan the opposite side of the van. There was other office equipment, including a computer. She continued to focus on each item until she looked down to her knees. She jumped at the sight of the Boomer's face staring at her. The dog was upright and braced against her knees. "Jeez!" She jumped as her eyes met the shiny glare of the stuffed dog.

"Great, I'm stuck here with the dead dog." There was a sound that seemed to come from the back of the dog. Then she heard it again—a moaning sound. Amanda suddenly realized that she was not alone. She popped her head up to see over the dog and saw a man on the floor at her feet.

He moaned again and started to roll from his side to his back. His eyes opened, and he looked around and tried to clear his brain by blinking and shaking his head back and forth. Then he started to look around some more.

Amanda recognized him. "Thane?"

He jumped at the sound of his name. Amanda got a better look at Thane's face. "Ouch," she observed as she looked at his swollen left cheek. The two of them were on the floor, and their legs were touching at the knees.

Thane raised his head and looked over at her. "Amanda, I tried to stop them. I saw them grab you, and I tried to stop them." His head fell back to the floor as he moaned again.

"Thane, Thane..." She nudged him with her feet. Amanda's hands were behind her, bound together with duct tape. She could see that Thane's hands were taped together too. She was able to touch his chin with her foot and try to rouse him. "Thane!"

He started to moan again as he raised his head. "Oh, man, I've never been knocked out before. It really hurts. One of the bald guys clobbered me."

Then Amanda watched as his face started to contort and Thane smiled in spite of the swollen cheek. "I cracked the one that was choking you in the face. I got him pretty good, 'cause blood splatted from the side of his eyebrow."

Amanda asked, "Never punched a guy before, have you?"

Thane spoke through his broken smile. "Better, I cracked his skull with a laptop of my own making. Has a strong aluminum case—solid as a metal brick."

Somehow Amanda managed a smile through her pain. "Good. I remembered that guy from the house where they kept me and those other girls. I also remember what he was trying to do to me before the cops got there. He's a pig. I'm glad you were able to crack him upside his head."

Thane tried to keep his voice down in case the two goons driving the van could hear them. He also started to look around. "What is all this stuff?"

Amanda looked around the cargo area. "Don't know. Looks like a bunch of office supplies, a computer and lots of files." Thane scanned with his eyes as Amanda spoke. Suddenly he looked in the direction of Amanda's face. "I wonder where they're going?"

Thane noticed that he needed to look over something to see Amanda. He was irritated trying to raise his head high enough. He looked at the object and saw that it was fuzzy. Then he focused on the fuzzy object and realized that he was looking at the back side of the stuffed dog. "Boomer?"

Then Thane asked Amanda, "Any idea where we are?"

"No clue" was her reply. Thane started to scoot and grunt in an attempt to turn his head toward Amanda's knees.

"What are you doing?"

More grunts. "I'm trying to get you out of here."

Amanda smiled, but she didn't think Thane was going to be able to do much. She watched as Thane kept scooting and grunting until she couldn't see his face. "Moving around like that isn't going to get us outta here." She sounded a little frustrated.

Thane strained to look over the dog's tail. "I'm gonna make a call." Amanda's eyes widened and she shook her head, doing a double take at what she thought Thane was doing behind the dog.

"Mac! This is Thane. I know you'll be reviewing the surveillance video. Amanda and I have been abducted from the loading dock area behind the buildings. We're in the back of a white cargo—ah, moving-type van. I'm not sure exactly…"

"Thane, you're… ah… you're talking to the butt! To the dog's butt!" Amanda's head dropped to the floor. She stopped listening to what Thane was saying.

"He thinks he can make a phone call through the butt of a stuffed dog," Amanda mumbled. "That guy must have belted him hard. We're so screwed."

"Mac, listen. On my computer my username is Thanerboy." Thane peeked over the dog's rump to see if she was looking at him. "The password is… Amanda." She kept her head on the floor of the van where Thane couldn't see her face, and in spite of the hopelessness of their situation, Amanda heard what Thane tried to quietly say was his password and she smiled.

After peeking past the base of the dog's tail to find out whether Amanda could see him, Thane lowered his face again to the anus cam.

"Once you open to the main menu, look under 'outdoor surveillance/rear loading area.'" Thane lowered his voice. "I'm pretty sure they want to keep Amanda around, but I think they'll get rid of me. I'm not valuable to them." Thane looked around again and with a worried look on his face he whispered, "Please hurry, Mac."

The address was easy enough to find. Didn't look like anyone was home. Driving around the house, he looked for vantage points where he could observe and contrive a means to slither into the mind of the young woman who had dared to humiliate him. Grabbing her throat and squeezing had been so empowering. The thrill of the power and control he had over the girl surged through his body. Before, his satisfaction had been more of a general feeling of revenge against women. This was something he hadn't experienced before, and he liked it. Sitting back in his seat, he looked into the eyes that gazed back at him from his rearview mirror. He vowed, "This woman will pay."

The doors to the Precinct opened, and Boss Nurse pushed the wheelchair into the big room.

"Hey, look who's back from vacation!"

Benson smiled and pointed to the Blue who had extended the greeting. "Has any work been done without me here?"

The rest of the Blues started to chime in with welcomes and well wishes. Boss Nurse told Benson, "No hanging around in here. I want you in your room and resting for the rest of the day. You understand me?"

Benson pointed to the rear doors of the Precinct that led to the residential apartments. "No problem, I'm tired. Please take me to my room."

Brittany and Jake exited the Sarge's office as Benson was being wheeled by.

"Hey, Benson, good to see ya. How ya feelin'?" Sarge gave Benson a wink and pulled his cigar out of his mouth, pointing it at Benson. He added, "About time; those reports aren't going to finish themselves."

Benson smiled. "Boss Nurse says I need to take the rest of the day off. Could you put me down for a sick day, Sarge?"

"Okay, but just one day. I expect you back in the Precinct tomorrow morning, starting your shift on time."

Benson smiled and Boss Nurse shook her head as she wheeled Benson to his room. "When will you Blues figure out you're patients?" she said to nobody in particular.

CHAPTER 14

Opening the door of her car, Lois turned back to look at the large building that housed her office as well as the nursing school, medical facility, and retirement home. The fact that so many agencies were able to function in one facility was indeed amazing.

"It served its purpose," Lois said to herself, then smiled and added, "Well, it served *my* purpose."

She had looked all around the outside of the giant building in an attempt to find Aziz. Lois knew her brother had to be out there somewhere. She picked up her phone and made a call.

"Victor, has everything been moved? Good, and the girl?"

There was a pause. "Victor! What about that girl?"

The answer came slowly, and Lois could feel her frustration build.

"The girl came out as planned, and she asked for the stuffed dog. She must have recognized Vladimir because she tried to run. She fought like the devil when I grabbed her."

Lois raised her voice. "Did she escape?"

Victor tried to use a reassuring tone. "Of course not. We were able to get her bound, and she is in the back of the van now."

Lois knew there had to be something more. "Victor, there is something you're not telling me."

After a slight pause, Victor reported, "Well, some young guy saw us struggling with the girl and ran up and hit Vladimir in the face with something hard. Might have injured his eye socket, because it's swollen pretty bad and there is a large bruise. We ended up throwing him in the back of the van with the girl...after I taught him a little lesson," Victor said with a snicker.

Lois gripped the steering wheel and attempted to stay calm. "You're telling me you have the girl and some man in the back of the moving van?"

"It could not be helped, Lois. If we left him, he would have told someone or been discovered before we were able to get the operation out of there."

"Well, we will have to take care of that problem soon," Lois replied. "Go to the safe house and wait for me. Don't do anything until I get there."

After hanging up, Lois looked around again to see if Aziz was nearby. *Aziz must know something is wrong or he would have made contact with us by now. We've got to get out of here as fast as we can.*

✺

The van with its cargo exited the interstate. This particular exit usually had heavy traffic because of its proximity to one of the greatest animal havens in the country, Omaha's Henry Doorly Zoo. The zoo was constantly undergoing construction of new exhibits, which meant that construction vehicles were always in the area. With so much traffic, nobody would likely scrutinize a cargo van driving around the neighborhood directly behind the zoo.

However, one man was watching them intently. He was furious that he had been lied to and certain that these two men were part of a massive failure that they would soon regret. Aziz could maintain a safe distance from the van while monitoring its location thanks to the hockey-puck-sized magnetic tracking device he had placed inside the wheel well.

"Well, now, where are the two of you going?" Aziz muttered.

✺

Mac's eyes widened, and he stood up so abruptly that his chair shot across the room and crashed into the wall behind him. As he tried to move, his headphones were still connected to the computer and they jerked down onto his face. Cursing, Mac fumbled to get them off his head and neck, then rushed out of the door.

The Precinct was buzzing with activity again. All of the Blues were back and appeared to have recovered from their ordeal.

Boss Nurse walked into the Precinct through the doors that connected it to the living quarters of the Blues. She announced, "Now, I don't want none of y'all disturbing Benson. After a day of rest, he should be good as new tomorrow. That means..."—she started to count on her fingers—"no poker games, no midnight snacks at the cafeteria, and I had better not hear of any....."

With a loud bang, the door behind her was jerked open. Boss Nurse turned just in time for a full frontal collision with a good-sized man. With the wind knocked out of her, she fell backward and landed with a thud as Mac fell on top of her.

Mac jumped up and looked around at the Blues, who were shocked by what had just happened.

"Where's the Sarge?" Mac demanded.

One of the Blues pointed to Sarge's office. Mac ran into the office after looking at the large woman on the ground and telling the Blues, "Take care of her, and don't let her into Sarge's office."

Smitty, Sarge, and Agnes were discussing the shortcomings of modern policing and Jake's misplaced confidence in some chemistry set. The Sarge's door burst open, and Mac stepped in and closed the door behind him. The three stared, knowing something was terribly wrong.

Mac struggled to catch his breath while trying to make sense of what he had just learned. "Amanda and Thane..." He paused to breathe and swallow. "They were kidnapped by the two goons. I didn't watch the whole video, but I ran up here as soon as I realized what was going on. I think I knocked down a big woman in the office out there."

Sarge pushed the button on his earpiece and announced, "This is Sarge. We need to get down to the research lab without Boss Nurse seeing us. We need a diversion."

Boss Nurse started to regain her senses and make some groaning noises. Big Brock pointed to the ground next to her and told the Blues, "Everybody kneel down and block her view of the back doors."

The Blues gathered close together. Those who could kneel did so, and the ones who had walkers or were afraid they wouldn't be able to get up just jammed together as tightly as they could. Big Brock rolled his eyes, saying, "Gotta do this," then got down on the floor and rolled up against Boss Nurse.

Bumping her to get her attention, Brock said, "Boss Nurse, are you okay? I didn't see ya." As he spoke, Sarge, Smitty, Agnes, and Mac walked, tiptoed and shuffled behind the Blue shield and made their way through the back doors.

"Brock, What's wrong with you? You could have killed me. Running in here like that just about knocked me into next week."

"I'm so sorry. I just was in a hurry and tripped right into you."

As Boss Nurse started to stand, Brock grabbed her arm. "Are you sure you can stand just now, Boss Nurse?" He simultaneously looked up at one of the Blues who gave him a thumbs up to indicate that the back doors had closed. Big Brock nodded.

"Okay then, upsy daisy." Big Brock pulled Boss Nurse to her feet.

"You Blues are gonna be the death of me. If I get knocked over one more time..."

"I gotta tinkle," one of the Blues said as he grabbed the front of his gown. I forgot to put my diaper on."

Boss Nurse put her hands on her hips. "No diapers? What did I tell you about that last time? C'mon." She led the Blue out of The Precinct. "Keep this up and it's a catheter for you."

꘡

On the way to his workstation, Mac was peppered with questions about what had happened.

"I only got to the point where Thane told me he and Amanda had been taken by the two bald goons."

Mac trotted over to his desk and tried to find his chair. Finally, he looked behind him and found the chair lying sideways on the floor. He grabbed it and wheeled to his desk, then disconnected the headphones from his computer so that everyone could hear what Thane was saying.

When Thane said that the goons were going to get rid of him, the concern in the room raised to alarm level. Sarge pointed to the computer, saying, "Get the surveillance video he was talking about."

Mac clicked on a folder. After he clicked on the proper video, the room went silent.

"The two men are talking about how they will use the dog to get the girl close enough for them to grab her and throw her in the van." Mac listened intently and translated as quickly as he could.

Once the dog was halfway in the van, Mac explained, "One of them is waiting inside the van." Amanda was seen at the bottom of the screen talking to the one who was holding the back end of the dog in the van. Everyone could hear him tell her to step inside the cargo area and help him unload the dog. As soon as she did so, it seemed like a split second later that she yelled something and tried to jump from the back of the van.

The goon grabbed her, and she started to rip into his face.

"That kid's a fighter, Agnes. We're gonna get her," Sarge stated matter-of-factly.

As Amanda was working over goon number one, goon number two stepped from the back of the van and put a hold on her around the neck. As she dropped into unconsciousness everyone gave a collective gasp. Then Thane appeared, charging with everything he had at the brutes. He cracked one of them with his laptop to the face.

"Yes, Thanerboy, that's how it's done!" Sarge yelled.

Then everyone went quiet as Thane was knocked to the ground with a punch to the face. His laptop skidded on the dock, and both Amanda and Thane were thrown into the back of the van.

The goon with the bleeding face went inside the van. "Probably to tie them up," Smitty observed. Everyone nodded. Agnes's face showed a determined resolve.

After a minute or two, the second man got into the cab. Before he climbed in, he pointed to something behind the camera, then said something that could not be heard. As the van pulled away, the man was still pointing toward something behind the surveillance camera.

Bolting into the screen was Meter Maid Mary, and she was in hot pursuit. Mac sat back in his chair. "Look at her go. She's gotta be doing thirty miles an hour!"

Sarge spoke up. "Mary called me and told me that she tried to catch up to the van. She said she didn't see what was going on but could tell something was fishy. Then when they sped off she knew something was definitely wrong and chased them out of the parking lot."

Sarge stopped for a second, then snapped his fingers. "Mary said that this Aziz character was standing by the white van and it looked like he put something in the rear wheel well. I'll bet it was a tracking device. The guy has been watching this little trio for days now. My guess is he figured out they were packing up shop to get outta here."

Smitty rubbed his chin. "From what I hear so far, both Thane and Amanda are still alive. All we gotta do is find out where that white cargo van went.

"Mary!" Sarge shouted. Everyone in the room looked at him. "She put one of our trackers on Aziz's car when she snuck up on him. If we follow Aziz.."

Agnes interjected, "We'll find my Amanda and that brave Thane."

Mac started to search Thane's computer for a folder on tracking devices. "Once we get that, we'll need his laptop that's on the back loading dock." Mac pointed to the area where the laptop had slid and was against a wall.

Smitty jumped up and announced, "I'm on it."

While Smitty was gone, Mac found the folder. "Holy Moley, that Thane is amazing. A freaking map of the city just popped up. There are a number of stars that are moving."

Sarge walked over to the monitor. Mac pointed to the screen and asked, "Why are there different-colored stars on the map?"

Sarge put his hand on top of the monitor. "Different vehicles... people we like to keep our eyes on."

Sarge pointed to the blue star and said, "Chief of police." Then he started to rattle off others. "City Councilmen, Building Inspector, that idiot Dr. Baggaley from the State Offices. He's a new addition, since he seems to think he can just pop in here whenever he wants. The gold one is the Mayor."

Mac's mouth dropped open as he looked at Sarge and then at Agnes. Holding her cigarette, she turned her palm up without taking her eyes off the monitor and said, "Hey, I'm just as surprised as you. This is new to me."

Sarge tapped the monitor. "The bright orange one would be our suspect, your friend Aziz. He seems to have stopped on South 13th Street."

Mac pointed to a large dark spot on the map. "What is this huge thing here? Looks like some sort of industrial area."

Agnes chimed in, "South 13th? Oh, that's the zoo."

Sarge looked at his watch. "I think the zoo closes about 4:00."

Mac gave the Sarge a questioning look. "What's that got to do with anything?"

The Sarge smiled and picked up the phone. "Let me speak to Ben Mitchell, please. Ben, this is Sarge. We need a special favor..."

After Sarge had finished talking with Ben Mitchell, he hung up and touched the broadcast button on his earpiece.

"This is the Sarge. We will have a special field trip to the zoo for after-hour tours. I'll need at least forty officers—some for the zoo and others for a search mission in the surrounding neighborhood. Those who are searching the area must be mobile and dressed in civvies. Those with wheelchairs or walkers, make sure you are on the zoo tour and look like patients. That's gowns and police shirts."

The Chelini brothers were already dressed in civvies, and they were among the best surveillance officers in the precinct. Sarge added, "Tony, Pauli, I want you two to head over now and scout out the neighborhood south of the zoo. We will follow up soon. I need some eyes over there."

൭൶

Boss Nurse hung up the phone, shaking her head and saying, "I don't believe it."

Another nurse gave her a questioning look.

Boss Nurse explained, "The owners of this house of crazy cops have arranged a special tour of the zoo. We'll need about ten nurses and students to go with them."

One of the student nurses asked, "How do you know they'll want to go?" Boss Nurse closed the folder in front of her and walked to the Precinct doors. She motioned to the student to follow her. As she opened the door, she gave the student a *watch this* look.

Boss Nurse held the door open and yelled, "Who wants to go on a field trip?"

From the Precinct came shouts of "Ooh, me! Me, me! Field trip!"

Boss Nurse pointed into the room for the student to look inside. When she did so, she saw a bunch of old men raising their hands like a class of second-grade children. Some were trying to hold their hands higher than the others. She didn't know that they were already aware of the trip but enjoyed toying with the nurses.

Boss Nurse asked, "Does that answer your question?"

The student laughed. "These guys are hysterical."

In a satirical tone, Boss Nurse agreed. "Oh, yeah, they're the joy of my very existence."

$\sim$

"Can I get a taste of those lips now that your roommate isn't here?" Jake asked Brittany as they stopped outside her house.

With a smile, Brittany acted like Jake was asking for a favor. "Well, I suppose so. You can't come in for a while?"

Jake shook his head. "No, gotta get back to headquarters. Soon, though, I won't have to take you home."

She smiled. "We'll be home."

She leaned over and gave Jake a taste of sweetness, then followed up with a short kiss and smile. "Call me when you get some free time, babe." She caressed his cheek with her hand, and he gazed into those eyes of hers.

"What was I doing again?"

She tweaked his nose with her fingers. "Headquarters," she said with a smirk.

"Oh, yeah. I just can't think straight when you look at me like that, Brittany."

She opened the door and gave him a final look. "You better get used to it, because you'll be seeing these eyes for the rest of your life, buddy." She blew him a final kiss and closed the door.

Jake waved and smiled, saying to himself, "I'm a lucky guy."

As Brittany walked to her front door, she noticed a puddle of water on her walkway. The garden hose faucet was slowly running.

"Did I leave that on? I don't remember watering." She shook her head, stepped through the puddle, and slipped, coming down on her knee and getting muddy water on her pants.

"Just great!" she blurted in annoyance, then shut off the faucet and went into her house.

From half a block away, a man lowered a pair of binoculars and looked into the rearview mirror with a satisfied smile. He commented, "Well, someone else also lives there, probably a roommate."

The vehicle that had dropped her off drove by. The eyes in the mirror widened at the sound of the vehicle approaching. Monte quickly looked down in an attempt to become inconspicuous.

Jake glanced at the parked blue PT Cruiser as he drove by. He noticed that the man sitting behind the steering wheel suddenly looked down, which immediately got Jake's attention. He could not see the man's face, but as he drove by, the man stepped out of his car and started to walk toward the nearest house. Jake gave the guy one last look in his rearview mirror, thinking that he looked a little suspicious. If Jake was in a police cruiser, he would have pulled an old police trick.

"I would have turned on that guy," Jake said to himself, which meant pulling a U turn in the middle of the street. If someone is up to no good, they usually scram because they think the cop knows it and is coming after them. "Ah...well, gotta get back to the office," Jake said to himself.

&

"So now we have two people in the back of the van instead of one," Lois said. "Have you checked on them since you arrived?"

Vladimir shrugged. "You said 'pack the van,' so that is what we did. Victor did bash the head of that man pretty good."

The bleeding near Vladimir's left eyebrow had stopped, but the bruised and swollen eye would eventually have to be seen by a doctor. Vladimir didn't know it yet, but Thane had cracked the outside of the orbital area of his skull. The injury was small but painful.

Lois didn't bother to calm herself down this time. "Fool! For all you know, they could be dead. Get out there and make sure they are all right."

Vladimir walked outside and looked around. The house at the end of the street had been selected because there were few people around, and across the street was the zoo. Vladimir looked up and down the street but saw nothing unusual. Very quiet. He smiled at the thought of seeing the face of that stupid girl again. "I'm not through with the other one yet," he said out loud.

Inside the van Amanda and Thane were still lying on the floor. Amanda didn't bother telling Thane to stop talking to the stinky end of the dog. He continued talking to a guy named Mac.

"We are at a stop now," Thane reported. "They've kept us in the cargo bay of the van for a while. Not sure what is going on or where we are."

As a set of keys jangled outside the latched door, they looked at each other. Amanda whispered to Thane, "Play like you're unconscious still or he will probably belt you again." Thane nodded, then stretched out on his back and shut his eyes.

Amanda could hear the lock pop open as the latch turned to the open position. The door slowly raised about two feet. As the door opened, Amanda could see Vladimir's fingers curled under the door. Amanda kicked at them. Vladimir let loose with Armenian curses as his fingers got kicked against the door. His eyes were large with anger. He looked over at Amanda and saw an equally angry pair of eyes.

"What do you want with me, you pigs?" she spat.

"You will shut your mouth, stupid girl, or I'll finish off your friend here." He kicked Thane's legs out of his way as he stepped into the cargo area and closed the door. Amanda was able see the giant sphere landmark at the zoo as she quickly stole a glance past the bald goon before the door closed behind him.

Vladimir checked Amanda's hands to make sure the duct tape was secure.

"What do you want with me?" she begged.

"You will see, girl."

Amanda was slammed onto the floor of the van.

"Now for this one."

The goon smiled, then turned and raised his foot above Thane's face.

"No!" Amanda yelled, kicking the inside of Vladimir's knee. It buckled, and he fell to the floor with a thud, which caused the burns on his shoulder and neck to flare into searing pain. Furious, he punched Amanda in the stomach and knocked the wind out of her.

The punch brought back Amanda's memory of Vladimir punching her the first time she was abducted. The fear in her eyes was exactly what the big man wanted. He was about to pounce on the girl when Lois's voice interrupted him.

"What are you doing in there, idiot?" Lois spoke in Armenian. The door of the van opened, and Amanda was shocked to see the woman from DHHS.

Lois looked at Vladimir and hissed, *"Don't you dare damage the merchandise."*

"She needs to be taught a lesson," Vladimir protested.

Lois pointed to the ground by her feet.

"Get out of there, fool. We will contact the Mexican Cartel once everything has settled down."

Vladimir took a step toward the back door and kicked Thane once for good measure.

Thane had braced himself for being hit again. *"I've got to keep my eyes closed and not respond to anything this guy does,"* he thought. Thane heard the man getting yelled at by a woman, then heard the man take a step toward the back of the cargo bay. Vladimir glanced down at the young man on the floor, then kicked at his chest sending him against the wall of the cargo space. Vladimir looked for a reaction. Satisfied that the man was still unconscious, he turned and jumped out of the back door, which was immediately closed and locked. Amanda tried to scream for help but couldn't make any sound because she was still recovering from Vladimir's punch.

Lois pointed to the side of the house. "Park the van over to the side there, away from the street. We still have a lot of work to do, and I don't want anything disturbing me."

Since this was the last house on this street, and the zoo was the only thing across from the house, Lois was confident that their cargo would not be discovered.

Amanda looked around as the van's engine started. "Thane, we're moving."

Thane opened his eyes, groaning from the pain of being kicked in the chest. "I've gotta let 'em know," Thane said as he belly-crawled to the back of the stuffed dog. With his face as close as possible to the hidden microphone, he announced, "Mac, we're moving again. I'm not sure where we are, but…"

The van stopped moving after about twenty seconds and the engine was shut off. Thane looked around. "Wait, we've stopped. I think they just moved the van a short distance, probably to hide it. They've shut the engine off."

Amanda rolled her eyes. "How hard did he hit you?"

Thane looked up from the base of the Boomer's tail. "Huh?"

Shaking her head, Amanda repeated, "How hard did that guy hit you? You've been talking into that dog's butt since we got into this mess."

Thane couldn't explain that he had been using the anus cam to communicate with the Precinct. "Oh, yeah, um, sorry," he said lamely.

♋

Looking into his monitor, Mac observed that Thane wasn't looking too good.

"Thane has taken quite a beating," he commented. Having suffered multiple beatings as well as torture, Mac empathized with Thane's predicament as few others could. He thought about the bunch of old guys who were organizing to attempt some sort of rescue operation. "I don't know what these guys are gonna do, but I'll go with them. Hang on, kid."

♋

The school bus was full, with more Blues wanting to go on a field trip than usual. The student nurses seemed to be the most excited.

"I heard of this zoo when I came here for school, but I haven't had time to visit it," one of the students commented.

"You'll freak! There are places in this zoo where the animals are walking around you. They have an overhead chairlift that takes you from one side of the zoo to the other. You can even feed the giraffes," another student responded.

A shuttle bus was transporting those who needed extra help traveling. Meter Maid Mary was locked into the wheelchair spot next to Officer Tucker Preston, who was sitting motionless and staring forward. Once the staff was busy making sure that the other Blues were strapped in safely, Mary spoke out of the side of her mouth.

"Try anything fresh with me and I'll crack ya a good one. Ya follow?"

Tucker Preston remained motionless. His face was as still as if he was in a comatose state, but he released a fart that was loud enough to be heard by the staff at the back of the bus.

Mary rolled her eyes and commented, "Disgusting."

The right side of Preston's mouth twitched with a slight smile.

One of the staff looked toward the front of the bus. "Whoa, there, Officer Preston. You all right?"

Inside the school bus Boss Nurse began lecturing the Blues. "I know y'all know how to conduct yourselves, but I'm gonna give you a few reminders."

She started to count on her fingers. "One, the zoo staff does not need to be frisked. Two, they do not need to be interrogated, questioned, or asked to provide fingerprints for your records. Three, just because someone resembles a suspect from the 1970s doesn't mean you can collar them and hold 'em for the detectives at Central."

Boss Nurse put her hands on her hips. "We've been through this before— wolves are not K-9's. Don't try to bring one back."

She started to shake her finger like an elementary school teacher. "You are not going to make any arrests." After completing her warnings, she raised her right hand and pointed all around the bus. "Do you all understand?"

"Yes, Boss Nurse Betsy," came the childlike reply.

One student nurse said to another, "Aren't they just the cutest little old men? They remind me of my grandpa."

When the school bus and shuttle bus had headed for the zoo, a few nurses had stayed behind to care for those who were still at the facility. They were pretty much involved in their administrative duties, which made it easy for the other group of Blues to take the tunnels to transport vehicles that would bring them to the nearest access point for the network of old tunnels near the zoo. It turned out that there was only one tunnel along D Street that could be utilized. The rest of the Blues would have to walk and search as best they could. They all knew that Thane's life depended on them finding him and Amanda as soon as possible.

The Blues were giddy with anticipation. "I haven't been on a man hunt in decades," one of them said to another.

The Sarge sounded off. "I want everyone to pair up. From what we've been able to figure out, they are close to the zoo. There are old neighborhoods with a lot of trees. The van we're looking for is one of those box cargo vans. It's white with no markings. We should be able to find it pretty quick. Once it's located, just observe and call it in. Don't forget that the two goons are gonna be close. There is also an Armenian hit man whose car we've been tracking. We figure he is in close proximity and trying to figure out what Lois and her henchmen are doing. Our latest intelligence is that Amanda and Thane are being held in the cargo area of the van."

⚬

"While they are locked in the van, I want to make sure there is no chance of escape. Keep them locked up. I need to meet with our new contact from Mexico. I will also see about getting the heroin we need to prepare the girl. Maybe they can take care of that man for us. Just keep things quiet here. When I get back, I'm sure we will have a plan for our operation, the girl, and that man."

Lois had previously arranged to meet with her Mexican contact in south Omaha at one of the numerous Mexican restaurants in the area. The contact gave her directions to the restaurant, and she was expected to have something that she could offer.

As Lois drove to the meeting, she gripped the steering wheel tightly. She had tried to make sure the transition to the new cartel would be seamless. However, she had not anticipated that Aziz would be involved so soon.

"*I've got to get this deal done quickly. Aziz must know that we've left that government facility by now.*"

She looked at her phone. "*Perhaps I should call him and try to figure out what he is up to.*"

Then she shook her head. "*No, I need to first meet with the new cartel, then contact Aziz.*"

"*Where is she going?*" Aziz wondered as he watched Lois leave the house. "*She has stored the cargo van at the side of the house. Why on earth would she leave if everything she stored is in that van? Hmm.*"

At the table Lois met with a representative from the cartel. The man was wearing an expensive suit, and his thick black hair was combed straight back. He escorted Lois to a table in the far corner of the restaurant. Undoubtedly there would be bodyguards nearby.

After confirming all of the information Lois had provided regarding the scheme that she had organized in Nebraska, the man seemed impressed.

"So you have everything ready to start," the man said.

"Yes, we had to make a rather hasty exit from my previous location. As we discussed before, all we will need from you is a safe house, protection, and…"

She scanned the other tables in busy restaurant to make sure nobody could hear her, then continued, "… the injections to make the girls addicted and, well, willing to do whatever you tell them." She smiled.

"Once we are established in a safe residence, I and my associates will be able to start picking up the girls that are aging out of the system. I even have one of them with us that you could look at as a… umm…a deposit."

The man seemed satisfied. "I will call my superiors, and what you need will be provided." He paused for a moment and then added, "You already know about our cartel's activities, Lois. Make sure you can deliver, or we will finish what the Armenians didn't."

Lois cleared her throat. "There is one more thing I need to mention. It could not be helped."

The man looked at her in a questioning manner.

"A man tried to stop my associates from taking the girl. He was quickly knocked unconscious by my men, but they had to secure him and throw him into the cargo van with the girl. They were able to get away from the government building without being seen, but they had to take the man with them. Can you assist in disposing of this fellow for us?"

The man's lips tightened. "This was not part of our agreement, but we will see what we can do… as long as you can produce what you said you could."

"Excellent," Lois stated with some relief. "I'll head back to where our operation is waiting."

After drinking the last of his water, the representative flatly stated, "You will have a safe house soon."

The meeting was over. "Everything is working out better than I had hoped," she said to herself. "Now to call Aziz and keep him from knowing what we are doing. Soon the Mexicans will be able to keep him and the Armenians away from us."

She cleared her throat and dialed her brother's number.

"What has taken you so long to contact me? The Cartel does not like to be kept waiting. You know that, Lois."

Lois took a slow breath to calm herself. *"Of course I know, Aziz. As I told you, there were complications due to the audit. But now everything is in order. Tell the leadership that everything is back on schedule. We are preparing the girls now. I anticipate they will be on their way to you tomorrow."*

There was no response. *"Aziz, did you hear me? Tell the leadership the girls will be on their way tomorrow."*

Lois wanted to put Aziz on the defensive. If he were in Armenia, he would have called while being close to the leadership of the Cartel. She wanted to tell him, *"I know you're here somewhere, Aziz."* But not yet. The longer he thought he still had the upper hand, the longer Lois could use that to her advantage. She wanted to see if she could get him to slip and say something that would give her more information about his whereabouts.

There was silence from the other end of the phone. Aziz tapped a finger on his steering wheel, thinking *What is she up to?*

Finally, Aziz broke the silence. *"I will tell them. They are meeting just now. I'm sure they will be pleased, Lois. I expect they will want to speak to you. Do you have need of anything? Oh, what about this audit? Were there any problems?"*

Lois smiled. *He's stalling.* "Everything was fine, Aziz, just as I told you it would be. If the leadership has any other concerns, let me know."

"Very well, Lois. Goodbye."

Aziz sat for a few minutes, deep in thought. *What is she doing? She seems to have some sort of plan. Lois is far too intelligent to slip up. But Victor and Vladimir are something else. Vladimir is the real idiot of the three. Maybe the right kind of pressure will lead to some information.*

Aziz raised his binoculars to see if anything was going on at the safe house. The van had been moved to the side of the building. *Victor and Vladimir must still be inside. I will watch and look for some sort of opportunity.* With the help of his binoculars, Aziz could see Victor and Vladimir through a window. They were drinking what appeared to be vodka.

∽

"Thane?"

No response.

"Thane, can you hear me?"

Amanda nudged Thane with her foot, then rolled and squirmed until she was able to get her face next to his. "Hey, Thane, are you all right?" She was answered with a groan and mumblings that were hard to understand.

"What?"

This time the answer was clearer. "I said it hurts to talk. He kicked me so hard my face hit the sidewall of this bay. My shoulder also hurts."

Thane opened his eyes, and when he was able to focus he saw Amanda's face close to his. Surprised, Thane shook his head to clear his thoughts.

"Hi," Amanda said with a worried look. "I'll say this about you, Thane, you can take a hit. That bald thug kicked you pretty hard."

Thane tried to smile at a compliment he'd never heard before, but his smile only worked on the right side of his mouth. The left side was too swollen to move. "Maybe now they'll make me a recruit like you."

That comment brought a smile to Amanda's face.

Suddenly she remembered something. "The zoo! We're close to the zoo. I could see the big Desert Dome sphere when that bald guy opened the door. I kicked him once when he opened the door and again when he was about to smash your head by stomping on you."

Thane's eyes got wide. "You're really tough," Thane mumbled, "and really nice."

Amanda had always heard guys talk about her in terms of being really hot, pretty, and other terms for a good-looking young woman. This guy, she had to admit, spoke in way that was so sincere it went right to her heart.

She could not understand the attraction she felt toward this computer nerd. He wasn't at all like the guys she had known all her life—men who only talked about her like she was a centerfold from some magazine.

"You are a different kind of guy, Thane." She started to look around at their surroundings. By scooting toward the side of the bay where Thane was lying, she was able to get a different vantage point. She could see the opposite side of various boxes and office equipment. Then she saw something that caught her interest.

"Thane! There's one of those things that take staples out of paper. Looks like a little set of jaws with fangs."

Stating the obvious, Thane replied. "You mean a staple remover? We're not stapled to the ground. Just a bunch of duct tape. Those things don't cut."

Amanda's tone matched Thane's sarcastic note. "I know that, but those sharp parts can be used to poke a bunch of holes in the tape and weaken it. We can rip it ourselves once there's a bunch of holes in it."

Thane thought for a second and then said, "Worth a try."

Amanda scooted closer to the staple remover, and with her hands behind her felt around until she grabbed the little instrument. Then she crawled back to Thane.

"Roll over," she instructed.

She then rolled so that they were back-to-back. "Here, take it."

There was a little fumbling, but Thane was able to grab it and reach the area of tape that was between Amanda's forearms. The sharply pointed staple remover started to easily pierce the tape.

Getting excited, Thane said, "This might just work."

༄

The empty glass was plopped back on the table.

"*You're right, this American vodka is piss.*" Victor scratched his face, and the sound of his nails against the day's beard growth make a loud scratching noise. "*But there is nothing else here, so pour some more.*"

Vladimir smiled as he poured. "*Worse yet, we will have to start to drink Tequila from now on.*"

Both men laughed. Vladimir held up the bottle like he was making a toast, and with an Armenian accent tried his best to say, "Si, senior!"

Both men laughed again as Vladimir sloshed down two large gulps.

"*Ah, get some rest, Victor. I'll check on our cargo outside.*"

Victor smiled. "*Good idea. After Lois is finished with her Mexican contact we'll probably have to pack up and leave at a moment's notice.*"

Vladimir smiled and mumbled to himself, *"I have some unfinished business in the back of that van."* He walked out the front door, stumbling a bit over the threshold. The vodka had slowed his reflexes and thrown off his balance. He stood outside the door, looking around to make sure there were no prying eyes in the neighborhood. Directly across the street was the large wall of the zoo, at least 15 feet high. Nobody over there. Then he narrowed his eyes as the sun was setting and the shadows from the trees in the neighborhood began to merge in preparation for nightfall's dark blanket.

He noticed a slight movement to his left on the sidewalk. *What could that be?* he wondered. The strange, slow-moving shadow seemed to weave back and forth in a way that caused Vladimir to stare. Then the mysterious object seemed to separate. It wasn't one shape but two—a pair of old men walking close together. Both held canes and had locked arms for support. They shuffled their feet as they walked. It was their interlocked arms and the shadows from the trees that had created a peculiar shape.

Vladimir let out a breath with a chuckle at the realization that it was only a couple of old men taking a walk together. *Nothing to worry about. Now back to my business with that van.*

⌒

"I can wiggle my wrists, Thane. It's working." Amanda was also able to move her arms up and down as she rubbed her forearms together. Little by little, the staple remover was eating through the tape.

"I can't see what I'm doing, so I'm just gonna keep poking holes 'til it rips," Thane said.

Suddenly Thane froze. Simultaneously Amanda raised her head off the floor and stared in terror as a set of keys jingled against the large sliding door of the cargo area.

"Oh, no!"

15 CHAPTER

The first shuttle van containing the less than mobile Blues pulled up in front of the famous Henry Doorly Zoo. A group of tour guides had been hurriedly assembled from the zoo staff. One of the newer employees stood alongside the others who were waving and smiling at the special guests. She leaned over to her supervisor and tried to inconspicuously ask, "Now, how did this group of people get this special tour?"

Her supervisor responded matter-of-factly, "When two of our largest contributors call and ask us to provide a tour for the residents of their retirement home, they get the tour. This tour is for our special guests. We take them to parts of the zoo that other people don't see—behind the scenes, so to speak. Just show them around the feeding areas, and don't let them get too close to anything. Most of them are in wheelchairs or they use walkers or walking canes to get around. Shouldn't be too difficult to keep up with them."

The Blues were divided into small groups, with each staff member taking a group to a different part of the zoo.

Outside the zoo walls, other Blues were being dropped off to search the neighborhood. Each Blue was equipped with some type of geriatric weaponry. Some of the Blues preferred ordinary-looking canes or umbrellas that dispensed pepper spray or even wireless taser darts. Others preferred the less sophisticated but highly effective weapons known as *piss packs*. After a catheter bag was full, the owner would keep it around for a couple of weeks. This allowed bacteria to grow until the fluid had darkened to create a stinky, slimy substance that caused complete disorientation in human targets when the projectile splatted like a water balloon. Occasionally one of the targets would experience a gut-churning vomiting reaction. Piss packs had a devastating effect on the punks and also provided unsurpassed entertainment for the Blues.

Benson and Brock had been instructed to join the less mobile Blues even though Benson could get around easily with his walker and Big Brock didn't need one. The Sarge had insisted on this assignment because he knew that both of them were still recovering after their medications had been tampered with. As quickly as possible, they slipped away from their tour group and began walking around on their own.

"Hey, look at that," Benson said, gazing up at the Skyfari, an overhead ride that resembled a ski lift. "Maybe we can get on it."

Benson pointed to the seats where passengers could wait to board the ride.

"Ain't no way; it's been stopped," Brock snorted, still miffed about not being assigned to search for Amanda.

Once they reached the loading area, Benson spotted a control panel with two buttons, one labeled *RUN* and the other labeled *STOP*.

"Don't do it," Brock said, half smiling.

Benson pushed the RUN button. The large cable with dozens of hanging seats started to turn, and the seats began to move. Benson pointed to the line on the ground where people would stand to get on the ride, and the two giggled like mischievous little boys. A lift seat glided up behind them, and they leaned back into it and were scooped up.

Once airborne, Benson laid his walker across his and Brock's laps. Up they went. They started swinging their feet and were surprised to see that they were only about thirty feet above animals in outdoor pens. The Blues were mesmerized by how close they were to them.

On the far side of the zoo, one of the zookeepers had finished his work for the day and was walking along one of the many pathways that zig-zagged throughout the sprawling complex. With his uniform shirt tossed over his shoulder, he was heading for the parking lot after a long day of feeding animals and cleaning up the end product of his feeding chores. He approached the place where the Skyfari comes back to the ground to discharge riders and load new ones.

"What is that machine doing on?" he commented out loud, walking into the hut where the control box was located.

Big Brock was looking toward the west where the sun had just set. Beautiful orange and pink hues filled the horizon. Suddenly Brock and Benson were surprised when the Skyfari stopped abruptly. Their combined weight caused the chair to swing. Both men gripped the safety rail and looked down at the ground.

They were sitting above an open animal compound and had caught the attention of three large birds that were standing directly under them. The animals were looking up in a manner that made Benson laugh, but Big Brock yelled, "Vanilla Rafters! They're gonna try to eat us. Stay still."

Benson tried to calm him down. "Brock, that was a movie. What is wrong with you?"

Sweat was beading up on Brock's forehead as he pointed downward. "They're getting ready to jump. Hold your feet up. I know they're gonna try to pull us down!"

Brock held Benson's walker down in an effort to fend off the monsters.

"Brock, those are not turkeys!" Benson said. "They're ostriches! They are just looking at us. I mean, we're hanging right above their heads."

"I said stay still; they ain't eating my face."

᠍᠍

The lock popped open, and as Vladimir was getting ready to enter the van, he thought he heard a noise from inside the cargo bay. Then from behind him he heard someone saying, "Scusi."

Turning quickly, Vladimir was ready to spring onto whoever had snuck up on him.

"Scusi, Signore. You help-uh me and my brother?"

"What you want, old man?" Vladimir realized there was no threat; it was just those two old men he had seen earlier walking through the neighborhood.

"He's talking to someone. Keep ripping holes in the tape," Amanda whispered frantically to Thane. She moved her arms back and forth and forced her elbows in opposite directions to loosen the duct tape. Finally the tape started to rip.

"It's working!" she said, ripping her forearms free so there was only the tape around her wrists. "Okay, stop."

Thane watched Amanda as she pulled her knees up and worked her bound hands down the back of her thighs. Then she rolled over onto her back, pulled her knees up to her chest, and worked her hands from behind her to the front. "Give me the staple thing." She took the device from Thane's hand and started ripping into the tape. She was quickly free.

The voice outside seemed to be yelling something that Amanda could not quite decipher. She desperately jabbed the pointed staple remover into the tape on Thane's arms.

"Try working your arms up and down. It will pull the tape so it starts to rip," she said.

Thane followed Amanda's instructions. Her panicked ripping into the tape had cut him a few times, but he didn't say anything.

"Sorry," she said as she saw blood welling up on Thane's skin from her quick poking and pulling. She scanned the cargo bay, and when she looked toward the cab area she noticed that on the wall sticking out from a box was a portal window. "Keep working at it, Thane."

Amanda sprang to her feet and moved closer to the boxes that were piled in front of the window. She tried to quietly move them. The first was no problem. Amanda set it on the floor. The second was much heavier. She tried to pull it away from the wall. As she did so, the full weight of the box plopped onto her chest and stomach. She fell with a thud. The man outside the van suddenly stopped talking.

"The zoo, *signore,* we go into the zoo."

From behind the large bald man there was a loud noise inside the cargo van. His eyes widened, and he turned and looked at the door, making sure the latch was secure. It was.

"Zoo… there." The bald man pointed. "Go away, no speak English good."

The old man smiled and asked "Parle Italiano?"

Vladimir recognized that the man was speaking Italian. "No, no Italy. You go now."

Whomp! Another sound came from behind Vladimir. He hurriedly moved his arms at the old men as if to shoo a cat or dog away. The two Italians put their hands out in front of them as if to say they were sorry for the intrusion, then started to walk back the way they had come. Vladimir tried not to make any sudden moves that might cause the old men to look back at him.

"That looks like the guy and the moving van," Tony said to Pauli. "Call it in."

Another pair of eyes was watching the confusing scene unfold. Aziz saw two old men walk up behind Vladimir and start talking to him. Then it looked like he was telling them to leave, and they turned and walked away.

"What is going on over there?"

Amanda knew the sounds she had made had given her away. Now the window was exposed, and it was big enough to easily crawl through. She forced the window to slide open, then looked inside the cab of the van. There were no keys in the ignition. She looked around the cab and then at the sun visor, where some keys were partially visible.

"Yes!" She easily worked her upper torso through the window. She looked into the passenger rearview mirror and could see the big bald man waving his arms at a couple of old men. Had she looked closer at the old men, she would have recognized them as the Chelini brothers. She heard a noise from the front of the house, which was visible from the passenger side window. The other bald man was standing outside the front door yelling something to the other guy.

Thane had worked his forearms free, and with his wrists still bound he tried to do what he had watched Amanda do. He stood, bent at the waist, and started to work his bound hands down his legs as she had done. He raised his right foot and was able to work his thin leg between his arms. "Halfway there."

Suddenly the latch that secured the sliding back door popped open. Thane jumped up in surprise while his bound wrists were still between his legs. This caused him to straighten up and then come to an abrupt stop when his wrists jammed into his groin. "Owaagh" was the only sound he made as he fell over in pain. He landed on his back with his feet toward the door as it slowly began to rise.

Vladimir remembered that the girl had kicked him the last time he opened the door, and he stopped for a moment when he heard the sound of someone falling onto the ground. "Not this time, stupid girl," he said with a smirk.

Victor's voice bellowed, *"What are you doing, Vladimir?"*

In response, Vladimir looked around the side of the cargo area to his cousin. *"Only checking on our cargo. A couple of old Italian men walked by and asked about the zoo."*

The door was opening as Vladimir spoke. *"I sent them off, and I'm checking on..."*

The sound of the engine starting caused both men to look at the van in shock. Victor locked eyes on Amanda at the wheel. The sight of his gaze shot fear through her body. Vladimir heard the sound of the engine and felt the exhaust hit his knees. He looked down for a second, and as he looked back up he saw the bottom of Thane's shoe as he used all the strength he could muster from his pretzelled position to kick the goon in the face. Thane popped the goon in the same eye that had been injured at the loading dock.

Vladimir let out a bloodcurdling scream as Thane's foot hit the cracked orbital bone and sent pain shrieking through his body. Thane strained to sit up, then turned to the access window at the front of the bay. Amanda's head was visible on the driver's side. Thane figured she had started the van. He could not stand straight up and was still in a lot of pain as he tried to walk but could only shuffle.

"Go, Amanda! Get us out of here."

Hearing Thane and simultaneously gazing at the very angry goon outside the house, Amanda shifted the van into Reverse. Her foot hit the accelerator before the van popped into Reverse. When the teeth in the transmission locked into gear as the engine was revving, the cargo van lurched backwards.

Thane's eyes popped wide open as his painful shuffle turned into an Olympic triple jump. The window seemed to be rushing toward his face. Somehow he had the wherewithal to point his forehead toward the opening, then through the opening he went. The crown of his head hit the framework of the window.

Bending at the waist, Thane fell the rest of the way through the window, landing on the steering wheel and Amanda's right leg. Thane's feet were pointing to the roof of the cab as his face bounced on the floor.

The sudden jolt caused Amanda to floor the accelerator, and the racing engine turned the vehicle into a large, backward-sprinting, uncontrollable square missile.

Vladimir's eyes widened in shock as he saw and heard the van's tires spinning on the ground as the vehicle raced directly toward him. He rolled out of the direct path of the van, but the rear tire rolled over his left foot. He yelled in pain, and the van quickly passed.

Everything was happening so quickly that Victor was frozen in a dumb stupor. He stood transfixed, watching the van race backwards. A screaming girl was trying to control it, and the feet of the man who was with her were bouncing off the dashboard and the windshield.

Vladimir was yelling and cursing. Luckily for him, the lawn cushioned his foot as the van rolled over it. His foot was throbbing with pain, but he didn't feel any bones crack.

6∿

"Pauli, repeat yourself. You think you found the cargo van. What is your location?"

Pauli and Tony were also staring and trying to make sense of what they were seeing.

"We're on D Street, and the van is currently moving backwards at a high rate of speed."

Sarge and everyone else on the channel put their hand to their ear to make sure they had heard the broadcast correctly.

"It's taken out three full-sized bushes and a small tree. Oh, one of the bald guys got his foot run over. I don't think that was part of their plan."

Sarge looked over at Agnes and shrugged.

"The two bald goons are just watching the van," Pauli added.

Agnes looked at Sarge and said with glee, "They're trying to get away!"

6∿

"What are these fools doing?"

Aziz almost dropped his binoculars, then fumbled as he got control of them and put them back up to his eyes. He watched as the van ripped bushes from the ground and clumps of shrubbery got stuck under the rear bumper. The van kept going faster as it hit a small tree, then bounced onto the street from the curb. Its path of destruction finally came to a sudden stop as the bush-covered rear bumper smashed into the huge back fence of the zoo. A cloud of dust that had been chasing the van caught up to it and engulfed the vehicle. There was so much dust that Aziz lost sight of the van for a few moments.

6∿

The van's tires were lifted off the ground as the rear bumper was elevated by the fence. Amanda tried to put the van into Drive and realized that it would take time to work the van free of the fence—time they didn't have. She looked up and saw that one of the bald guys was helping the other up and frantically pointing at the van and yelling. She knew the two men would capture them soon if they didn't find some way out. She pushed Thane's hips toward the passenger door and pulled him by the shoulder so that he sat upright.

Thane was completely disoriented but was able to get his bearings just in time to see the Armenians running toward them. Amanda looked to the right, then left, then forward. There didn't seem to be any way to outrun the two men. Then she looked back through the access window.

"Thane, back out the rear window. We can get out from the back of the truck." Amanda climbed through effortlessly and pulled Thane's shoulders while trying to figure out what was wrong with him.

She pulled him into the rear cargo area and the two ran to the back door and stepped out onto the zoo fence. It had bent backwards. They were able to make their way to the top of the fence but had to negotiate the barbed wire at the top. They both fell over, getting multiple cuts on their arms and legs. Thane landed with a bit more of a thud than Amanda, but luckily they were on a grassy area.

"Come on, Thane, they'll be here soon. You've gotta get up and run."

The shadows were growing as it was getting darker. Amanda could not immediately figure out why Thane ran so funny.

After about a hundred yards they stopped next to a building.

"I kicked that guy again, right in the face!" Thane told Amanda with pride, looking at her with blood streaming down his forehead and over his swollen cheek. He smiled through the pain. "That felt so good. I got him in the eye again."

Amanda shook her head, then looked at the rest of him as he stood in front of her. He was slouched forward, and his hands were in front and behind his pelvis.

"Sit down."

She helped him down, then guided his wrists around his leg so that they were in front of him. "That's better."

Thane stood up straight. "Thanks. Umm, where did you learn how to get out of having your hands tied behind your back?"

Amanda shrugged. "In foster care you learn a lot of things."

She reached into her pocket and pulled out a tissue. She put one hand on Thane's cheek, and with the other she wiped off the blood that had dripped down the swollen side.

"Thank you for trying to stop them. Sorry your face got smashed up."

Thane smiled. The touch of Amanda's hand had caused all the pain to disappear for a moment. He closed his eyes and was lost in her comforting gesture.

"Thane!"

His eyes opened, and he looked at Amanda.

"I said let's go! We've got to keep moving. They've probably figured out we're somewhere in the zoo by now. It's getting dark. This place is huge."

Thane started biting at the duct tape. It began to rip, and soon he was free of the binding adhesive. He showed his free hands to Amanda in an effort to impress her. "Used to bite my nails a lot as a kid," he explained.

She smiled and said, "Where do you think we are?"

Thane looked around. "This must be the far end of the zoo. The main exhibits are near the front entrance. This is where they have the big enclosures where the animals roam around."

There was a loud sound about a hundred yards from where they stood. It came from the area where they had climbed over the fence.

Vladimir's sore foot got caught in the barbed wire as he tried to step over it. The barbs ripped into his calf and lower leg. As his leg got caught, he fell forward and his shoulder and head hit the ground. Vladimir let loose with a string of Armenian curses.

Victor stopped, turned around, and yelled, "Stupid! What are you doing?"

Vladimir looked up from the ground, grunting, "Shut up and get me out of this." After a chorus of curses and threats, Vladimir's leg was finally worked free.

"We need to find the girl and get her back or Lois will be furious," Victor said. "Kill that skinny guy. This has gone on long enough."

Blood was dripping from Vladimir's leg. He pulled a knife from his pocket and thought about killing that red-headed man. "I am going to enjoy this."

෴

The young staff member was perky and loud.

"Hello, everyone! We are so excited to have you with us for our special tour. Not only will you see the wonderful animals here, but we'll bring you to the places that the public is not allowed to see. Are you ready to have some fun?"

The Blues stared at her in silence. The nurses started cheering, trying to get the Blues excited.

"C'mon, let's go!" the zoo employee said. "We'll break up into groups and take you all around this wonderful place."

෴

"Sarge, this is Tony. Amanda and Thane are making a break for it. They crashed their van into the zoo's fence, and it bent the fence down. It looks like they climbed over the broken fence. We think the two goons just figured out what they did and went into the zoo after them. We'll follow them."

෴

The binoculars were dropped onto the floor of the car.

"*How did we ever trust this operation to these imbeciles? I'll have to report this as soon as I know what is going on. Where is Lois while all this happening? Now there are a couple of old men walking around the truck. This is a mess.*"

෴

"Tony, just put your cane over the barbed wire and push it down."

It took some work, but the Chelini brothers eventually got into the zoo. Tony surveyed the grounds in front of him. For years he had been involved in numerous nighttime stakeouts. Working the shadows was his specialty. The zoo was not built to have visitors in the evening. As a result, its lighting was minimal.

Tony asked Pauli, "Did you get a look at which direction they went?"

Pauli glanced to his left and then his right. "Ahhh, I'm not sure."

Tony shook his head. "I don't like splitting up when it's getting dark, but I don't see any other choice."

Suddenly Pauli bent over and looked at the ground. "We got a blood trail. I don't know whose blood it is, but it's a trail."

Tony looked down. "It don't matter whose blood it is. We'll find someone if we follow it. Let's go, but stay in the shadows."

"Hello, Sarge," Pauli reported on his earpiece. "Me and Tony are in the zoo now. We picked up a blood trail. Not sure whose blood it is, but we are on it. We'll check in when we find something."

The Sarge pushed the small button on his earpiece. "Got it. Keep me informed."

Sarge looked around to make sure nobody was near enough to hear him. "I want the radio channel kept clear—no unnecessary chatter. Monitor, and we'll respond as conditions warrant. Sarge out."

∽

"How big is this place? I don't even know if we're heading in the right direction. I never came here as a kid," Amanda whispered.

"My head is throbbing." Thane touched the swollen side of his face. "We've been running for a while. Let's get out of the light and look around. Maybe we can figure out where we are."

Amanda saw that Thane was struggling to keep moving. She moved over to him and lifted his arm onto her shoulders so she could give him some support.

"I'm sorry, Amanda. Let's just stop for a couple of minutes so I can catch my breath."

She looked into Thane's face and listened to his labored breathing. He might have a broken rib from that goon's kick. Looking at his bloody, swollen face and remembering the beating Thane had taken for her pierced her heart. Out of sheer appreciation and growing affection, she hugged Thane.

"When we get out of this, we're gonna go to this great place I know in the Old Market for some ice cream."

The eye that wasn't swollen opened wide. "You mean a *date*?"

She pulled him a little closer. "Haven't you ever had a girlfriend before?"

Thane shrugged. "I've never even been on a date before."

Amanda was touched by Thane's honesty. "Well, you better believe we're going on a date after this. Not every girl gets to go out with a guy who got his face mashed for her."

With all that was going on between the two of them, the young couple momentarily forgot about the fact that two very angry men were trying to find them.

"Let's go over there by that fence."

Thane looked in the direction where Amanda motioned with her head. "Umm, yeah, that should be good." Thane was so focused on the girl that he'd had a crush on from a distance that he had forgotten about the pain he was suffering… for a moment.

They stood next to a large fence. Amanda released her hold on Thane and let him lean against it. She was careful to stay in the shadows and to look back to where they had come from to see if they were being followed. She held her breath as she peered through the darkness. She heard a quiet sound behind her head and figured Thane had moved closer to her. She grinned for a moment and then felt his breath on the back of her neck. It was really hot. She didn't want to make any sudden movements but reached her hand back, feeling for Thane. Then the breath against her neck became louder.

"Thane, what are…"

Suddenly there was a rubbing sound by her ear. She felt what she thought was a hot, wet piece of long sandpaper wrap under her ear and beneath her chin. She turned and found herself looking into two huge nostrils as an animal sucked its foot-long, tree-grabbing tongue back into its mouth.

"Thane...waaleechaa!" Amanda involuntarily shrieked. The giant giraffe was startled, and its head jerked upward. The surrounding animals were also alarmed by the noise. Shrieks, squawks, and other strange sounds filled the air.

Amanda realized that she had started an avalanche of noise. "We gotta get outta here." She grabbed Thane's arm and wrapped it around her shoulders again. Off they went, into the darkness.

Big Brock's eyes widened as a horrible sound was followed by other noises. "What was that?"

Benson made a muffled sound and pushed at Brock's chest. The big man was so scared that he had pulled Benson's face into his chest as a small child would grab its mother for security.

Benson extracted himself from Brock's grasp. "What's wrong with you, ya big palooka?"

Brock seemed embarrassed, then remembered what had scared him in the first place. "Did you hear that animal scream? What on earth could have made that noise?"

"Did you hear that scream, Victor?" Vladimir asked.

Victor laughed. "Maybe they walked too close to the lion's cage."

"Tony, what kind of animals they got in here?"

Shrugging, Pauli pointed toward a semi-lit area. "It came from over there. Do you think it was Amanda and Thane?"

Tony whispered, "We got no other leads." He pointed to the ground. "I can hardly see the blood trail now. Maybe we should head that way. If those two bald guys heard that noise, I'll bet they will be heading there too."

16 CHAPTER

Smitty and Mac had quickly become friends during Mac's sojourn at the Ol' Blues Retirement Home. Most of the other Blues were at the zoo or doing surveillance outside it, but Smitty and Mac were monitoring the situation from Thane and Mac's office.

"Gotta hand it to that young lad Thane," Mac said, leaning back in his chair. "That kid has taken a beating and was still trying to give us information. Throughout all my years in the crazy work I've done, there's always one lesson that sticks out in my mind."

Smitty looked at Mac and inquired, "What's that?"

Mac sat back up. "Bravery comes in all sizes and shapes. I've seen the biggest, meanest men break down and cry in a fetal position during a firefight, and unassuming guys like our Thane here..."—he pointed to his monitor—"...just rise to the occasion and become freakin' heroes."

Smitty nodded in agreement. "Maybe we should get over to the zoo and see if we can help out."

Mac looked over at Smitty and shook his head. "We don't know where Aziz is. If he recognized me, he would know that a lot of heat was about to come down on him."

Smitty gave Mac a questioning look. "How so?"

"One of the rules of being captured: If you're being tortured, tell them something before you go past your breaking point."

Mac held up his left hand. "After the beatings, I could tell I was starting to lose it. Then my friend Aziz decided to work me over another way. Once he finished ripping the fingernails off my left hand, I knew I wouldn't make it if he started on my right hand. I told him that I worked for the American government as an agent. My mission was to keep track of the old Soviet KGB agents in this area."

Smitty could see that Mac's eyes were looking past him into a painful memory.

"Looking back, that's probably what saved me," Mac continued. "The Armenians hated the KGB just as much as the other countries in the Soviet bloc did."

"I was also spying on the Armenian underworld, including Aziz and his cartel. I just didn't tell him that part," Mac added with a smile. "That bought me some time. They didn't kill me because they thought we were fighting against a common enemy. You see, the old KGB officers didn't really have any legitimate way of making a living once the Soviet Union broke up. They were taking advantage of the political instability and joining rival gangs. This Armenian group only believed in having true Armenians in their cartel. I was treated a little better and kept around until they decided what to do with me. Luckily, back then the Turkish government was a little more friendly to the United States. The Special Forces guys were able to use military bases in Turkey as rallying points, and they infiltrated Armenia from those bases. They located me and got my keister out of the country."

Mac pointed to a photo of Aziz. "Some of my friends at the CIA want to take particular interest in that man's discomfort. I would like to get a little payback myself." Mac flexed his fingers by opening and closing his left hand.

"Maybe we can help you there, Mac," Smitty said. "There is one good tunnel in the area. It hasn't been upgraded yet. By using it we can still get a good look-see, and it would be hard for our friend there"—Smitty pointed to the photo of Aziz—"to get a look at you, and maybe we can figure out a little payback of our own until your buddies in the CIA get here. I'll get one of our utility vans and a driver. When we arrive at the access point, the driver will set up a fake utility work area and we'll scoot down the tunnel and see what we can find out about our friend Aziz."

A smile slowly grew on Mac's face.

6∽

When Jake returned to his office, the light on his phone signaled a new voicemail. Jake picked up his phone to retrieve the message. He looked at the messages on the readout and saw that the caller was *Detective Angie Jacks-Special Victims Unit.*

"Excellent!" Jake said, then called the number. "Angie, this is Jake. I saw you called. Any news on the DNA yet?"

Angie sighed, "Not yet. I'm heading over to the State Lab. They've been really backed up lately. I know the lab techs over there, so sometimes I can get the results a little quicker. I just wanted you to know I was going over there today."

After a pause, Angie added, "Gotta tell ya, Jake, I get a strange feeling from this guy. Seems like he should be a lot more nervous, but since giving us his sample he seems really calm."

Jake knew that when an expert like Angie was concerned about something, it wouldn't be smart to disregard her misgivings.

"I'm not sure why he's so calm," Jake said. "It looked like you had him riled up when you interviewed him. Let's just see the lab results and go from there. Thanks for the update, Angie."

Jake hung up, then rubbed his hands together. "It's gonna be so good to arrest this guy."

He sat back in his chair. "It's about quitting time. Think I'll call the Sarge and give him an update."

After dialing the number, Jake put his feet up on his desk and loosened his tie. "Hey, Sarge. Got some news. Hopefully we'll have some information about the Chemist, Monte Kurt, soon. I...what?...The zoo?" Jake listened with his mouth open. "I can get a rapid response unit there in minutes."

"No! We've got Blues outside the zoo and inside. If we need you, we'll call," Sarge said.

Jake stood up. "What do you mean, *you'll call?*"

Sarge explained, "We've got CIA or some other federal unit heading our way, thanks to Mac. This way, we won't have to explain what we're doing to the Omaha Police Department. Mac's friends won't ask questions."

Jake started pacing back and forth as Sarge told him about the tour, the Blues doing surveillance outside the zoo, then the mystery of Mac's friends. Amanda and Thane were in the zoo somewhere, as well as the two bald Armenians.

"Oh, and also the Armenian hit man is running around."

Jake froze. He tried to say something, but nothing came out of his mouth. Finally he uttered, "Are you sure about this, Sarge?"

Jake looked around his office to make sure nobody could hear his end of the conversation. "A bunch of geezers against the likes of these guys."

There was a snicker on the other end of the phone. "We got this, Jake."

Jake wiped his forehead. "I've gotta tell Brittany. I'll stay in touch."

When Brittany answered the phone and heard Jake's voice, she tried to give a cute greeting but was cut off immediately. What Jake told her made Brittany gasp in shock. "The zoo! Jake, get over here and pick me up now!"

She hung up, breathing quickly and involuntarily looking out her living room window. There seemed to be a movement by the bushes in the front yard, but she dismissed it. She dashed through her house grabbing shoes, a sweater, and anything else she might need, then stopped and wondered aloud, "Just what are we going to do when we get there?"

Watching Brittany through a side window, the man in the bushes spoke to his reflection. "What is she doing?"

She ran by a doorway and briefly went into the mud room where the window from which she was being watched was located.

"My hat, where's my hat?" She looked around quickly and thought she saw something outside the window, but dismissed it as her own reflection. "Oh, there you are."

She grabbed a blue baseball cap and quickly pulled her ponytail through the opening in the back while she headed for the front door. She took her phone from her purse and called Jake.

"Hey, it's me. How far away are you? Okay, I'm outside."

Realizing that someone was about to pick Brittany up, Monte Kurt crept away into the darkness.

◊◊

"How long have these things been around?" Mac asked Smitty as they worked their way through the eerie dark tunnel and sewer system.

"They go back to the days of the bootleggers and even before that. Nobody really knows. The old neighborhoods are full of them. Our finance guys, The Bureau, have been finding and upgrading the tunnels as they discover them. Some are very short and have caved in on themselves. Others..."—Smitty pointed at the walls of the tunnel they were walking through— "go on for blocks. This one is pretty old, based on the walls and the smell."

As the men got closer to where they thought the cargo van was located, they stopped frequently to look through the sewer drains that opened onto the streets. Each opening was about twelve inches high and six to eight feet long. When the Midwest gets a heavy thunderstorm, the rainwater flows like a river down the streets. Large sewer intake drains are a must. The openings also allowed some of the illumination from the streetlights to provide visibility within the tunnel.

"There!" Smitty pointed as he looked out an inlet. "Does that van look familiar to you?"

◊◊

Aziz glanced around quickly to make sure the coast was clear, then parked his vehicle two houses from the safe house. There were no people around, the dust had cleared, and the van seemed to have settled back down onto the base of the fence. The fence was still bent inward, providing easy access to the zoo.

Again, Aziz scanned the area to confirm that there were no people about. Earlier he had observed a lot of old men walking about, but they were gone now. He walked up to the wheel well that held the tracking device, reached in, and found that it was still attached. Then he decided to find the two imbeciles. With an angry glare, Aziz thought, *These three have been a monumental failure to the Cartel. Lois's lies have deceived the Cartel, and she tried to fool me. This is an insult to my honor. Now she seems to be packing up her operation into this van.*

Gritting his teeth, Aziz closed the large door and then started to work his way up the bent fence. After he jumped over the barbed wire and landed inside the zoo, he heard a strange scream followed by the sounds of many other animals. *Kill those two idiots, then break Lois's neck.* Into the darkness he ran, heading toward the sound that would surely have attracted the attention of Victor and Vladimir.

$$\sim$$

Smitty watched as Mac glared at the man who had tortured him and had been the cause of many a nightmare over the years. Smitty noticed that Mac's hands were both clenched in fists.

"Not the time yet, Mac. If this guy is the trained killer you say he is, we'll have to keep cool heads and plan very carefully."

Mac relaxed his fingers. "You're right. With guys like this we can't go looking for him. He's too tactical. Once he knows I'm here or that my friends from the dark places know he's here, he'll disappear."

Smitty agreed, then asked, "Will he leave if the three people he has been following are not punished?"

A small grin started to form on Mac's face. "No, he would never leave without accomplishing what he was sent here to do."

Smitty nodded. "Good, that intel will come in handy."

They watched from their street-level vantage point as Aziz looked around and then walked to the rear wheel and reached in like he was checking the tire. Then Aziz looked around again and closed the cargo bay door of the van.

"What is he doing?" Smitty said out loud.

Mac rubbed his chin. "He has a job to do. If he is satisfied that Lois and her two bald helpers have screwed up, he'll run them all down and kill them....Wait, look."

Both men watched as Aziz stepped onto the bent fence and jumped into the zoo.

Now it was Smitty's turn to smile. "I've got an idea. We've got to get to that truck. But first we gotta let Sarge know that Aziz has entered this corner of the zoo."

⌒

"Are you the Sargie-wargie?" the perky twenty-year-old girl tour guide asked the Sarge. She spoke as if she was talking to a child. This got a glare from the Sarge. Without listening for an answer, she continued, "This is going to be so much fun. Let's have everybody stay with your buddy so that nobody gets lost."

The student nurses joined in as if they were teachers leading an elementary school outing. "C'mon, everyone, buddy up, this will be fun!"

The Blues smiled and pretended to be excited, then started to have some fun.

"I don't want to hold his hand," one of the Blues complained.

The guide said, "Well, that's okay as long as you stay close to your buddy." She commented to one of the student nurses, "Aren't they the cutest!"

Sarge's earpiece sounded a tone. Someone was trying to reach him. He could not respond with the students and guides around. He raised his hand to get the guide's attention. "Oooh, oooh," he said like a little boy.

"Yes," the guide said with a smile.

"I have to go tinkles," the Sarge announced.

Her eyebrows went up. "Oh, yes, of course, right over there." She looked at a student nurse. "Does he need help?"

Shaking her head, the nurse in training said, "Nope, Sarge can go all by himself. Can't you, Sarge?" Her question was answered with a smile and a nod of the head.

Once the restroom doors had closed behind him, Sarge tapped his earpiece. "Sarge here."

"I was wondering if these communicating things worked out here. This is Smitty. Me and Mac have been watching the white cargo van that hit the fence. While we were watching, the Armenian hit man Aziz pulled up and walked around the truck, closed the back door, and acted like he was checking things out. Then he climbed over the broken fence and jumped into the zoo. He came in through the southernmost part of the zoo. Thought you would like to know."

The Sarge paused, then responded, "That is good to know. Now we have two bald Armenians and the hit man along with Thanerboy and Amanda running around the zoo."

Smitty keyed his earpiece. "Okay, Sarge, me and Mac are working on something for Aziz. I'll brief you when we're ready."

Sarge answered, "Good. I'll let everyone else know what's going on."

As he was about to head back out to the tour, Sarge stopped abruptly. *Oh! I really do have to tinkle.*

⟶

Sarge hit the button on his earpiece twice to make a general announcement.

"This is Sarge. Amanda and Thane are currently somewhere in the zoo. The two bald goons are trying to find them, and the Armenian hit man is trying to find the bald goons. Everyone with weapons, work your way free of the tours. For those of you who are just entering the zoo from the manhunt, go ahead and walk through the gates. They are open for our tour. Spread out. Once Amanda and Thane are located, I want to know exactly where they are. We'll deploy accordingly. Sarge out."

⟶

"They're jumping, they're trying to get us!" Brock shouted.

Benson rolled his eyes. "Brock, what are you talking about?"

Brock's eyes were wide as he pulled his feet up, then reached back and grabbed the large pole that connected the chair to the cable above them.

Benson yelled, "What are you doing?"

Brock kept squirming around until he was able to raise his feet and pull himself up so that he was standing on the seat of the chair.

Benson was leaning to the left in the chair, which was bouncing up and down with Brock's panicked movements. Benson suddenly realized he could fall out. Again he looked at Brock, whose eyes stared downward at what he was sure were giant, ferocious turkeys.

"Jumping at my face," Brock kept saying to himself. Benson looked down and to his surprise the ostriches were indeed jumping up and down. They were also flapping their wings and stomping their feet.

Benson pulled his feet up, then pulled at Brock's leg with one hand and grabbed his walker with the other. Brock reached down and helped Benson stand up. Now both Blues were standing in the chairlift and holding onto the main support pole with one hand while hugging each other with the other.

"I don't think they can fly," Benson said in a voice that betrayed his sudden fear.

⚬∫

The lights in this part of the zoo were so far apart that there were plenty of shadows where Amanda and Thane could conceal themselves as they moved through the huge animal park.

"Where are we?" Thane asked, looking around with the eye that wasn't swollen. "Well, we know where the giraffes stay."

The bit of comic relief helped Amanda clear her head for a few seconds. "This is the first time I've been to the zoo. I don't even know if we're heading in the right direction. The main entrance has got to be around here somewhere."

Thane commented, "I'm not from Omaha, and I've never been to the zoo either."

Amanda looked to the right and then to the left. She saw paths going in various directions.

"Let's just keep moving," she suggested.

⁂

Thousands of years of instinct cannot be removed simply by transferring a wild animal to a new habitat. The lion exhibit had recently acquired a new inhabitant, a young male that was adjusting to living among lions accustomed to captivity. The newcomer constantly paced around the compound, paying special attention to the moat that was designed as a natural barrier for containment of the animals. Natural barriers allow the public to look at the animals without having to do so through bars or fences. All of the other lions had been raised next to moats and seemed to accept that they could not traverse the water. They knew they would be fed soon enough.

Suddenly something caused the predatorial aspects of the young male's DNA to jump to attention: the scent of fresh blood. The odor was also noticed by the other lions but didn't have the same effect on them. They all put their noses into the air as they realized that something was wounded.

The young male was almost full grown but didn't have a full mane yet. Nevertheless, every sensory nerve in its body had burst into hundreds of thousands of impulses that tensed the lion's muscles and caused it to sit down facing the moat, planting its front feet on the edge and its back paws by the front ones. The lion's entire body started to shiver, with muscles twitching. The large cat slowly leaned forward and at the point where it would normally fall face-first into the moat, its mammoth legs sprang upwards and brought it almost to the other side of the moat. As the lion's trajectory started to descend, it instinctively stretched its front paws forward.

Its claws extended, and one of them caught the edge of the moat. The lion's lower body splashed into the water, but it quickly reached up with its other paw and its claws took hold. Straining to pull its massive weight forward with its front paws, the animal started to fall back into the water. The heavily muscled back legs curled upwards, and with claws scratching against the smooth cement, the lion was able to pull upward. Once its body began to move upward, the lion quickly retracted its front claws and then extended them to catch itself before it fell. A final lunge brought its body halfway out of the moat. The beast thrashed and clawed until at last it was out of the water. Then it quickly cleared the smaller fence designed to keep human spectators from getting too close to the exhibit. No longer restrained by man-made confinement, at last the beast was free to hunt.

⌒

Jake's car skidded to a stop outside the main entrance of the zoo. While Jake was driving, he had filled Brittany in on the information he had gathered up to that point.

Brittany reached into her purse and grabbed a pink, key-sized container of pepper spray. She clicked the spraying mechanism off the safety position. Brittany explained, "My dad makes me carry the stuff. I've never had to use it, but I'd love to burn the eyes out of those two goons."

The gruff and determined tone of Brittany's voice shocked Jake into stunned admiration. She put her purse under her left arm and reached for the door latch. Catching Jake's look, she stopped moving and stared back at him. "What?"

Jake came out of his amazed stupor and mumbled, "Nothing."

Brittany's voice was commanding and clear. "Then move it. Amanda and Thane are in there." Jake shut his mouth and got out of the car.

⌒

"I've got an idea," Mac said, smiling. "Can you get me over to that cargo van?"

Smitty shrugged and said, "Sure." Then he pointed upward to the circular manhole cover above their heads. "I can push you up through this hole."

Mac's smile revealed that there was a definite reason for his request. "A little more," Mac grunted as Smitty pushed him until he was out of the hole and standing. Mac stepped over the storm drain, gave Smitty a thumbs up, and ran over to the van. He walked around it, giving it a once-over. Suddenly Smitty spotted headlights approaching from a distance. He yelled to Mac, "Somebody's coming. Hurry up and get back here."

Mac was already on his way. He pulled on the manhole cover and dragged it as he lowered himself. Smitty helped him maneuver the heavy cover over the hole. Just as it fell into place with a clank, Smitty looked up and saw headlights illuminate the house. The car stopped, and the engine was shut off. The headlights, however, were left on as someone opened the driver's side door.

Smitty elbowed Mac. "She's gonna blow her stack!" Both men looked at Lois as she took a few steps from the car and noticed that the van was gone. She hurriedly trotted to the house.

"She's probably looking for her two bald helpers," Mac said. "I'll bet she's running all through the house now yelling their names."

Sure enough, Smitty and Mac could see one room window after another light up as Lois went from room to room.

"She should figure out those two are gone any minute now," Smitty flatly stated.

Mac added, "She's gonna come flying out of that house." Right on cue, the door was flung open and Lois appeared on the front porch. She looked over where the van had been parked, then looked around.

"She should see the van any second now," Mac added, with an elbow to Smitty. Lois had her hands on her hips as she looked around. Then it happened. She could see the damage to the grass, and her eyes followed the path of destruction where plants, bushes, and even small trees had once stood.

"Any second now." Smitty was almost giddy with anticipation to see Lois's face. "There it is!" he almost yelled.

Lois's eyes got wide at the sight of the cargo van across the street. She frantically looked about, then ran over to where Mac had been just moments before she arrived.

"What did those idiots do?" Lois asked out loud. Vladimir and Victor were nowhere to be seen. She ran to the back of the van and opened the rear door. Everything was inside except the two prisoners.

"Gone," she noted. "They must have escaped somehow." She stepped back and looked at the van again, then announced, "They are on their own. I don't need those fools anymore."

Lois climbed into the van, started the engine, and put it in gear. After a few tries she was able to break free of the fence. Then off she went. She looked around as she drove. "As long as Aziz doesn't find me, I'll be safe." Satisfied that she was not being followed, she smiled and drove away.

Smitty told Mac, "She's getting away. I gotta call the Sarge."

⌒

Sarge listened intently to Smitty through his earpiece.

"She's gone, Sarge. She climbed into the van and took off. She left her two bald goons. I'd say she's taking off on her own."

Sarge's voice became serious. "We'll take care of that later. Right now, Thane and Amanda are on the run through the zoo. The two goons are after them, and from what we can figure out Aziz is after them."

"We're on our way, Sarge. We'll be there soon," Smitty promised.

Meanwhile, a few Blues had managed to sneak away from their private tours and were making their way through the zoo.

"I see some Blues," Benson said. He pointed in the direction of his gaze and nudged Brock to get his mind off the killer giant turkeys below them.

Brock looked in the direction where Benson was pointing. "I see them," Brock said. He gripped the supporting pole harder, then looked toward the southern part of the zoo. His eyes caught sight of a man and woman in the distance running from the shadows of some trees across the lighted pathway and into the shadows on the other side of the path. The woman seemed to be helping the man run. It had to be the recruit and the computer nerd.

"Look over there! It's Amanda and Thane. Gotta be them. Way off yonder. Look."

Benson looked where Brock was pointing and said, "I don't see them."

Brock realized that he wasn't holding onto the support pole with both hands and quickly put his hand back on the pole. "Way off yonder, I saw them. Had to be them. They are staying in the shadows. Looks like she has to help Thane run. He must be hurt."

ᏽ

Benson keyed his earpiece. "Sarge, this is Benson. Brock just saw Amanda and Thane in the southern part of the zoo. He only saw them for a couple of seconds, but it looked like they were heading east. They are staying in the shadows, and Thane seems to be hurt."

Sarge listened and then wanted to get an idea of where Benson and Brock were in relation to the sighting.

"Roger that, Benson. Where are you?"

There was a pause.

"I need to get some sort of reference where they are, Benson," Sarge explained. "Where are you located, Benson?"

Another pause. Sarge looked around to make sure nobody could hear him, then raised his voice. "BENSON! Where are you?"

This time there was no pause. Benson figured he'd better come clean.

"Umm… we're above the ostriches."

Sarge shook his head to make sure he was hearing correctly.

"What do you mean, above the ostriches?"

Benson and Brock looked at each other like two boys whose mother had just caught them with their hands in the cookie jar.

"Um, me and Brock got on the Skyfari ride and came to a stop above the ostriches. Brock thinks they are giant turkeys."

Sarge rolled his eyes, then thought for a second. "Stay right there. I need you to keep a lookout and give us updates on what you see. That's a great idea you two had. Keep me informed."

Benson gave Brock a look of surprise. Brock looked back in relief, like they had just gotten away with something big.

"Should we yell to them and let them know where to run?" Benson asked.

"If we do, the others will probably hear us too. Let's just watch for a bit and see what…"

Brock was cut off by the sight of the two goons walking down a lighted path. They were obviously looking for Amanda and Thane but a good distance from where the two were last seen.

"Sarge, we've just spotted the goons. They're walking up a lighted path heading north. The way they are walking, it doesn't look like they have a clue where the recruit and Thane are. The two of them are just walking fast and looking in all directions."

Benson paused, unsure of what he was seeing in the distance, about 300 yards from where he saw the goons.

"Lion! That's a lion!"

Brock looked in the direction Benson was pointing. Under one of the pathway lights, a lion had stopped and was sniffing the air.

"Sarge, you ain't gonna believe this."

The Chelini brothers were walking down one of the many paths. Tony looked up and saw the Skyfari overhead.

"Hey, Brock and Benson are on that somewhere."

Pauli spotted a stack of zoo maps by one of the exhibits.

"Look, on the map this Skyfari goes from one end of the park to the other. Benson said they are above the ostriches."

Pauli pointed the ostrich compound. "He said the computer guy and the recruit were last seen south of the ostriches heading east."

࿇

"Thane, I need to rest. I can't keep helping you unless we stop for a minute," Amanda whispered urgently.

Thane pointed to a small cement wall that was the bottom of a much bigger building. All of the buildings in this area had large bars on them, and it was quiet. About ten feet from the wall were a small fence and bushes that seemed like a good place to hide.

It was very dark, and after catching her breath Amanda stuck her head out of the bushes to try to locate their pursuers. The immediate area seemed clear. She then looked back the way they had come and the two bald men walking on the lighted pathway they had recently crossed. She ducked down again and crawled over to Thane as he sat against the base of the building.

"I saw them," Amanda said. "They're on the walkway we ran across. They seem to be staying in the lighted areas."

Thane rubbed his face and tried to move his shoulder. The blood was drying on his face, and with every deep breath he took, there was a piercing pain near his ribs. Sitting still felt good, and he let his hands rest on his thighs. His khaki pants were filthy. His left hand started to drop from his thigh to the ground. Suddenly, he felt something that made him open his eye wide.

"Phone! I forgot that my phone is in my leg pocket."

Amanda gave him a startled look. Thane tried to unzip the pocket on the side of his left leg, but moving his arm caused him to wince and struggle with the zipper.

"Let me do it," Amanda blurted out in a frantic whisper.

She pulled the phone from his pocket.

"Really, you forgot you had your phone?"

Thane shrugged. "I usually just communicate through my headset on my computer. I don't really talk on the phone much."

Amanda looked at it. "What's the password?"

Thane shifted his weight, and after a short, uncomfortable pause he quietly said, "A-M-A-N-D-A." She responded by looking at Thane and holding the phone to her heart. Then, with the awkwardness typical of a young couple trying not to talk about their relationship, Amanda clumsily dropped the phone. The phone's flashlight came on, illuminating both of them and causing something to jump in the cage behind them.

"Shut it off! Shut it off!" Amanda fumbled as she tried to hand Thane the phone.

Once Thane had a grip on the phone, the light beam was facing the small fence and bushes. Thane froze in horror as he saw two large green eyes fully aglow reflecting the beam of light and staring straight at him. With his other hand he grabbed Amanda and pulled her against his chest. Despite being in agony from his ribs, he raised his feet and started to kick at whatever was starting to lurch over the fence and bushes. The air was filled with a horrible roar that brought terrified screams in response.

&

Aziz's phone buzzed in his breast pocket. He had to stop his searching and answer the call from his superiors.

"*What is happening, Aziz? We have not heard from you all day.*"

Aziz used as harsh and unemotional a tone as he could muster. "*They have failed. The entire operation appears to have been ruined by these three failures.*"

There was a pause. Aziz knew that he was probably on a speaker phone in the conference room. In the background there was an angry outburst of curses and threats. Aziz decided he had waited long enough for a response. "*There is more.*"

The room went quiet.

"*I have not been able to figure out what has happened to all the girls yet, but Victor, Vladimir, and Lois appear to have collected their entire operation and attempted to flee the area. I am currently chasing the two men. I will then take care of Lois.*"

"*How could this have happened?*"

The question came from someone in the Cartel.

"*The entire shipment gone and we don't know what happened?*"

There was the sound of a fist hitting a table. "*Wait,*" one of the leaders said, and his statement seemed to silence the room. "*You said that they have collected their entire operation and are attempting to flee?*"

Aziz answered, "*Yes, that is how it appears at this time. They have loaded a moving van with all kinds of supplies. When Lois spoke to me she tried to say that everything was fine and that they would be able to resume operations now that the audit was finished. I watched as they loaded up the van with what appeared to be all of her operational records. I have been following them all day, and for some reason a man and woman were mixed up in their plans. Both have escaped from the cargo van, and Victor and Vladimir are looking for them in the zoo that is in Omaha.*"

There was a short pause that was undoubtedly the result of the leadership looking back and forth at one another. "*The zoo?*"

Aziz was getting tired of explaining, but he knew he had to let them know everything they needed before he hung up.

"*The two people that were locked in the van escaped and got over the fence into the zoo which was next to a safe house they were using. I am currently looking for these two fools. Once I learn what I need from them, I will kill them and find Lois.*"

Around the table thousands of miles away, there were nods of acceptance. "*Very well. Call us when you have more information.*"

Aziz hung up the phone and resumed his search. At the table one of the leaders asked aloud of nobody in particular, "*Are we all sure Aziz will kill his own sister?*"

The answer came from the head of the table without hesitation. "*He will not only kill her, he will make sure everyone in the organization knows it. This will cement his status as our enforcer and possibly earn him a place at this table.*"

᷍

"Hey, the zoo is closed!" a staff member yelled to a man and woman as they were trotting through the main doors. Jake had a flashlight in one hand and put his other hand on his chest.

"I'm so sorry. We are with the old police retirement home," he explained. "We just found out about the tour and rushed over to be with them. Are they still here?"

The staff member smiled. "Oh, yes, they were broken up into a few groups and taken to various places in the zoo. I'm sure if you walk to any of the exhibits you'll find one of the tour groups. There is nobody else here."

Jake and Brittany smiled and waved.

"Okay, thanks, I'm sure we'll find them," Brittany said. "Sorry to just run through like that."

The staff member waved and then turned and walked back into the main ticket office.

Brittany and Jake watched as the zoo worker walked away. When the coast was clear, they looked at each other and bolted into the semi-lit zoo.

While Smitty and Mac were on their way to the zoo, Smitty noticed that Mac was looking at something small, but Smitty could not figure out what it was. Then Mac put it in his pocket and pulled out his phone.

"Now we let my friends who *don't exist* know where we are and what's going on." Mac dialed a number and put the phone to his ear. "This is Mac. Aziz is at the zoo in Omaha. It appears that the operation I told you about has collapsed and he is here to punish those responsible. Two of the cartel members are in the zoo and Aziz must be after them. The zoo is closed. How soon can you get here?"

Mac listened for a moment and then informed the other party that a bunch of retired police were in the zoo for a tour and that a couple of folks might be injured. After hearing the other person's response, Mac's mouth opened. "Oh, that fast, huh? The zoo is not well lit. Good, talk to you later."

Smitty looked at Mac as he hung up, then said, "Well?"

"They are located down at Offutt Air Force Base. They'll be flying in by helicopter. They have to get the pilots and helicopters ready for launch, but once they're airborne it shouldn't take them too long to get here."

Smitty asked, "So what are they going to do?"

Mac grinned.

⌢

"Only a hit man would walk around like that by himself," Pauli said with his heavy Italian accent. The two brothers watched as a large man methodically walked, keeping in the shadows and looking around him with each couple of steps.

"Oh, yeah." Tony agreed. "That guy is lookin' for those two goons. Bet he is furious about what happened to their whole operation."

The brothers watched Aziz as he spoke to someone on the phone, then put the phone in his pocket. Aziz went into a careful jog, staying in the shadows again. Tony and Pauli could not keep up with the hit man, but they could keep him within sight.

"Hey, Sarge," Pauli spoke quietly.

"Sarge here; go ahead."

Pauli tried to speak while he walked. "We have eyes on the hit man. He is working his way eastward. It looks like…." Then the air was shattered with a roar followed by screaming.

⌢

The green illuminated eyes of the lion were transfixed on Thane and Amanda while the beast was in mid-air. Amanda covered her head and buried her face in Thane's chest. Thane was kicking into the air before the lion had even leaped.

At that point, everything seemed to go into slow motion. Thane's eyes were locked onto the bright green eyes of the beast. While the lion was in mid-lunge, Thane watched as its gaze moved from him and Amanda to something above them.

Thane's brain had blocked the screaming for a few minutes, but his hearing came back when he realized that the huge lion was no longer focused on him. Suddenly there was an earsplitting roar from just above Thane's head. He and Amanda were sitting directly in front of the Siberian tiger exhibit, which consisted of an indoor and outer cage. The tiger instantly responded to the aggression of the lion outside its cage. Thane looked up as the huge tiger slammed into the cage bars, biting and reaching at the lion with teeth and claws. Having lost interest in the young couple, the lion sprang upward in response to the other roaring, snarling predator.

Thane and Amanda lay paralyzed near the lion's back feet as the two beasts snarled, bit, and clawed at one other through the bars of the tiger's cage. The roars were deafening. The couple were frozen with fear, but the blood and saliva and fur raining down seemed to free Thane from his temporary paralysis, allowing him to think clearly for a moment.

Thane yelled, "Run! Run! Run!" and he and Amanda scooted away from the fighting frenzy. They made an adrenaline-fueled sprint to get as far as possible from the jaws, claws, and roars that would be the source of nightmares for the next couple of months.

The initial screams and roars of the two alpha predatory beasts were heard throughout the zoo. Blues, goons, the hit man, and even Jake and Brittany froze. The night air was torn by the horrible, almost prehistoric sounds of the two beasts in combat.

Brock and Benson both jumped, which caused the Skyfari to bounce up and down. The bouncing of the lift chair added to the fear Brock was already suffering.

"Did you hear that? What was that?" Brock asked.

The initial shattering sounds were followed by the horrible fighting of the great cats.

"*Jeez, Victor! What is that?*"

"*Mio Dio! Pauli!*"

Aziz drew his gun, as did Jake.

"Take the flashlight, Brittany, and stay close. Something is really wrong," Jake cautioned.

"Sarge, this is Benson, there are some horrible screams, and it sounds like animals are fighting." Benson looked around. "There! I see Thane and Amanda. They are running and... Oh, the goons! They seem to be moving in the direction of all the noise."

Then Benson caught a movement from the corner of his eye. A man emerged from the shadows, crossed a lighted path, and moved back into the darkness again.

"I just saw someone else—might be our hit man. There is lots of movement going on all around us."

There was a pause, then Sarge said, "Good to know, Benson, keep me informed."

The Chelini brothers chimed in. "We see the hit man and will stay on him."

⁊

Smitty looked at Mac and commented, "It sounds like the zoo is going crazy."

Mac looked up into the sky. "In a little while it will get crazier."

Smitty followed Mac's gaze upward. "Don't see any helicopters yet."

Mac smiled and said, "Don't worry, they'll be here soon."

Then he looked at Smitty and said, "Tell me about some of the weapons you guys have."

Smitty shrugged. "There's a bunch of them here right now. Every Blue you see with a walker, cane, or crutches—especially crutches—is holding a weapon that fires pepper spray, taser darts, or even a bean bag round."

Mac thought for a minute, then said, "Do you think you could get a couple of those canes or walkers? We might need them. We'll also need a place where Aziz won't be able to maneuver well and people won't be in the area in case things get out of hand."

Smitty smiled and said, "I know just the place."

⁓

Brittany and Jake had been running down one of the many paths that wound throughout the zoo. They paused for a moment to look, listen, and see if they could locate Thane and Amanda.

"Why don't we just start yelling for them?" Brittany asked.

Jake shook his head. "If they answer and give away their position, those two goons who are looking for them will know where they are too. We don't want them found by the Armenians before we reach them."

"That's good thinking." Brittany heard the familiar voice of Big Brock. She looked around with her flashlight and saw nothing.

"Up here."

Brittany pointed her flashlight upward and saw Big Brock and Benson standing in one of the Skyfari chairs. Brock's hospital gown was bunched up, and his diapers were illuminated by the beam.

"Why does this always happen to me?" Brittany asked nobody in particular.

Jake looked at her and said, "What are you talking about?"

She explained, "I got stuck under Big Brock's robe hiding from Boss Nurse at the Precinct. It wasn't a good experience. Then I'm in the zoo, and I look up and what do I see?" She pointed to Brock's big backside. Clutching the pole, he looked down at them and smiled.

"Why are you two standing on that chair?" Jake asked.

Brock looked directly under him and said, "Vanilla Rafters." Jake looked underneath the dangling duo and saw three ostriches that seemed to take an intense interest in the two Blues.

Benson pointed to the last place they had seen Thane and Amanda. "They were running over there, and then some horrible roaring and screaming was coming from where they ran from."

Suddenly there was more roaring.

"What is that?" Benson asked.

Back at the tiger exhibit the two beasts had separated, but neither was backing down. Both animals were bloodied and still furious. The lion had backed off a step or two, and both were growling and snarling at each other… staring and baring fangs, giving fake charges, and roaring. Each time one would start to pace to the left or right, the other would match it. Neither turned as if to run. This gave Thane and Amanda plenty of time to get away.

"How did you two get up there?" Brittany asked Benson and Brock.

"We saw one of the ride buttons and turned it on," Benson explained. "When the seat came around we both got on. Then someone shut off the ride and we got stuck up here."

Brittany used her flashlight to look around in an effort to figure out where the Skyfari ride ended. She couldn't see how far it went, but the drop-off location seemed to be where Thane and Amanda had last been seen.

"We'll head to where the ride ends and see if we can turn it back on," Brittany said. "Keep a watch for Thane and Amanda. Does Sarge know what's going on?"

Benson nodded. "We're keeping everyone informed. We're the lookouts in this rescue operation. It appears that the drop-off end of the ride is the same way that Thane and Amanda were running a couple of minutes ago."

Brittany and Jake looked at each other. Then Jake said, "Let's follow the Skyfari." He looked up at the dangling Blues. "We'll turn the ride back on at the end of the line."

⚓

"Sarge, this is Smitty. Looks like Mac's friends are gonna be dropping in at any minute. Mac says they'll be coming in from Offutt Air Force Base. We gotta get Thane and Amanda outta here soon."

Sarge responded, "We're trying. There's a number of Blues in the zoo area away from these tours. Oh, I don't know if you heard yet, but they think a lion got loose and is running around."

Smitty looked over at Mac and said, "You better call your friends. There's more than human animals running around the zoo right now."

Mac gave Smitty a questioning look.

17 CHAPTER

Two special operations Black Hawk helicopters were heading north from Offutt Air Force Base in Bellevue, Nebraska, about ten miles south of the zoo. Special clearance had been granted, and as they started to approach the zoo they slowed and gained altitude.

The leader of the strike force was in one helicopter, and the covert operations agents were in the other. One of them felt his phone vibrate in his pocket. He looked at it and found a text from Mac: "I know you wouldn't be able to hear me in the chopper, but be advised—along with Aziz and two of the other male cartel members, somehow a lion has gotten loose and is running around. Might want to let the guys know if they end up rappelling into the zoo."

After reading the text, Mac's friend yelled out a string of curses and signaled to the pilot that he needed to get a message to the other chopper. Then he asked over the intercom, "Do you have infrared abilities?"

The pilot answered, "Affirmative, and an array of other tools at our disposal."

The pilot was instructed to circle the zoo using the various search tools that they had, and Mac's friend provided descriptions of the subjects.

"Roger that" was the cool, professional response.

The choppers circled from a distance in order to get a good look at what they were getting into, determine if there was an area to land, and see if they could spot the targets.

The search technician was looking through the camera, and over the intercom he asked, "Is there some sort of party going on down there? There are two guys standing in an overhead ride, and a bunch of what look like old men are walking around. I see two big guys, and according to the infrared camera one of them appears to be bleeding from his legs."

Mac's friend said, "The two big guys are two of the three targets. See if you can locate one pretty good-sized man. Probably alone."

"Yep, their heat signatures are pretty obvious. They seem to be moving in the same direction."

The technician almost yelled, "I think there's a..." There was a pause, as if he wanted to make sure of what he saw before he finished his sentence.

"... lion! It also has bright cuts on its back and around his neck, like it's been in a fight." Then the tiger's heat signature glowed as it jumped against the bars of its cage. "Looks like the lion and a tiger in a cage have been fighting. Wow!"

"Let the rest of the team know what's down there," ordered the operational commander.

"*What are we supposed to do with a freaking lion?*" The commander wondered, keeping that thought separate from his mission at hand. "First things first: chopper #2 will fly low and slow to the north end of the zoo to create a diversion. Chopper #1 will drop the extraction team on the opposite or south side of the zoo. We'll guide them to the targets. Once the targets are captured, bring them back to the landing zone and return to base."

From chopper #1 came the reply "Roger that, on your signal."

The pilot of chopper #2 looked at Mac's friend, the commander, who gave him a thumbs up. "Execute!" was his command.

Chopper #1 dove to just over tree level and moved from the southern part of the zoo to the northern part. This maneuver was designed to attract attention and be a diversion as the extraction team was unloaded and made their move on the ground.

Aziz was the first person to notice the helicopters in the distance. He was familiar with tactical maneuvering, and when he observed the copters engaging in what appeared to be a search or recon pattern, he knew that these were no ordinary helicopters. *They will be searching with night equipment*, Aziz thought. He looked around for a building that could shield him from the searching that undoubtedly was taking place.

How did they know to search here? Aziz clenched his fist as he answered his own question. *Lois has set us all up! She somehow knows Victor and Vladimir are in the zoo, and I must assume she knows I am here as well. She called the police and told them about each of us.* Aziz gritted his teeth and vowed in Armenian, "She will pay."

Aziz pulled out his phone to call his sister, but he noticed an alert from the tracking device announcing that the van had changed locations. *She took the van and left the other two to fend for themselves.* Aziz noticed that the location of the van was no longer by the safe house. *Lois must have taken the van and moved it...*

Aziz looked again at his phone. Out loud he said, "She parked it on the north end of the zoo?" *What is she doing?* Then Aziz guessed that she must have been in touch with Victor or Vladimir and made plans to pick them up. Aziz couldn't know for sure, but it was as good a guess as any.

Perhaps she didn't abandon those two fools yet... but that doesn't sound like Lois. She must have some need for them still. Usually she is willing to sacrifice anyone to get what she wants.

Aziz heard the sound of a helicopter flying low. "I will find Lois, and the other two will soon show up. This works out nicely," Aziz said quietly to himself.

Smitty looked at Mac and asked, "Are you sure about this?"

Mac clenched his left hand a few times and looked at the scar tissue where he used to have fingernails. "Yep. I have to do this."

Smitty added, "You said these guys play for keeps. I don't know if this is such a good idea. This Aziz is a killer."

Mac stared straight ahead as if looking into the past. "So was I."

∼

One of the premier attractions at the Omaha zoo is its incredible aquarium equipped with huge transparent walls that are strong enough to contain water. In addition to fish and other underwater creatures, animals that are exhibited behind these barriers include species that live both on land and at sea, such as penguins and sea lions.

"You can see them swimming underwater and watch as they shoot out of the water and land on the dry part of their home," Mac observed. "I'll say one thing for you Omaha folks— you really know how to build zoos. I've never seen anything quite like this."

"Wait," Smitty stated. "There's more."

After walking past a few other beautiful aquariums holding various types of aquatic creatures, they came to a dark hallway. Mac noticed a bright blue glow emanating from around a corner.

Smitty stopped and let Mac go in front of him. As soon as he stepped out of the dark hallway, Mac found himself inside an incredible tunnel of clear plexiglass. It went on for about twenty-five yards.

"The walls of the tunnel are so clear," Mac said out loud. "It's like I'm in the water with them."

"What's more important is that Aziz will actually be in the tunnel with us," Mac continued. "He's going to be faster, but there's not much room to maneuver in a tunnel."

Mac had to force himself to stop gawking at the incredible array of fish, sea turtles, sting rays and …sharks! The ceiling of the exhibit was designed so that if one looks up, it appears that the tank is thirty to forty feet deep.

Mac reached in his pocket and pulled out an object that made Smitty tilt his head in curiosity. He watched as Mac looked around the tunnel, no longer distracted by the amazing living scenery. He placed the small hockey-puck-like object on a bench midway through the amazing walkway.

Mac pointed to the far end of the tunnel. "We had better wait over there. Wait a minute—I thought there was a tour with the Blues in these buildings."

Smitty pointed upward. "There is. They are above us. On this tour they get to see the places that the public usually isn't allowed to visit. In the aquarium, the area above us is where they feed the fish and do whatever it is that they do."

Mac looked up and said, "I don't see them."

Smitty pointed above the tunnel entrance. "The shape and coloring of this place is genius. People can't see it, but there is a feeding deck above the entrance of the tunnel. I got to take this tour once."

Touching his earpiece, Smitty asked, "Any Blues in the aquarium feeding deck?"

There was a short pause. "Yep, we're here," Meter Maid Mary responded. "Me a few others and this worthless lump Officer Preston."

Smitty smiled. "Good to know. We are in the tunnel. Mac thinks he can get that hit man in here. Keep an eye on us."

Mary responded. "Roger that."

The low-flying Black Hawk made a noise that was deafening. Everyone including Vladimir and Victor looked up at it. As a result of this distraction, nobody noticed the second chopper as it unloaded the special ops crew on the southern section of the zoo.

The first chopper, code-named "Eyeballs," completed its low distraction run and then pulled up and gained altitude to continue the surveillance and guide the boots on the ground to the targets.

"Striker One, this is Eyeballs, back at surveillance altitude. Continue northbound. Two of the primary targets are together and moving northbound as well. Be advised that we are unable to locate the third target at this time. Also be aware that we are unable to locate the lion. Will continue searching and advise."

The second chopper stayed in the area for a quick evacuation.

∽

"How are we supposed to get away from a lion? A lion! I've never been so scared in my life. Thane, we gotta keep running."

Thane stopped for a quick breath. "Adrenaline dump," he explained to Amanda. Thane's arms were shaking, and his hands were trembling. "I read about this. When the body senses a life-or-death situation, it dumps adrenaline to help us fight or run. Immediately afterwards, this is what happens."

He raised his hands, which were shaking uncontrollably. "My hands remind me of one of the Blues at the Precinct. My legs are shaking too."

Amanda looked back from where they had just run. "I don't see the lion, but it sounded like it was fighting with that tiger. Do you think it's trailing us?"

"I have no idea, but I hope not. I can hardly stand up, Amanda. I need to sit down for a minute."

Thane almost collapsed. Amanda grabbed his arm to ease him to the ground, then she helped him lay back. As he looked up at the sky, the stars seemed blurry. Amanda cradled Thane's head for a few minutes to help him relax. Thane was breathing as if he was completely exhausted.

Amanda stood and started to look around to see if the four-legged beast was nearby. She put her hands on her knees and spun around slowly, hoping not to see those horrible huge green eyes attached to fangs and claws. She had practically turned a complete circle when she heard "*Barev, aghjik.*" Amanda jerked her head to the sound and saw the two bald men they had desperately tried to escape. She stared at the one whose face she had been able to claw when they grabbed her.

"What is wrong? He just said *hello girl.* Can't you show good manners and say hello back?"

Amanda stood up straight and lunged at the man, trying to scratch his face again. Victor grabbed her arms, laughing. "Not this time. You have been enough trouble." He looked to Vladimir and said, "Let's get out of here."

"Not yet," Vladimir said. "I have something to settle with the piece of red-headed trash."

Amanda tried to break free of Victor's grip but she didn't stand a chance against the big man. Victor turned and started pulling Amanda with him back to where they had entered the zoo. "Just hurry and catch up" he told Vladimir.

Victor left with Amanda trying in vain to break free as she was practically dragged by the big man.

Through the fog of exhaustion, Thane could see Amanda being pulled away by one of the goons. He tried to sit up, then saw the other goon take three quick steps at him. Thane tried to lift his legs to kick at the man, but Vladimir easily pushed his legs to the side, then grabbed Thane by the hair and spun him around on the ground. He kicked Thane to the side, then bent Thane's head back so that he had to look up into Vladimir's face. Thane could hardly breathe as he looked up.

"Now I finish you, boy." He slapped Thane's face, then slammed his head to the ground. Vladimir stood up straight and smiled as he usually did when he felt in complete control of his victims.

Phifft—Phifft.

Vladimir let loose with a high-pitched scream as pain shot through his body. Fifty thousand volts from two darts shocked the large muscles from his right shoulder where the first dart hit, to the back of his left thigh. Every muscle tightened, convulsed, and cramped simultaneously.

Vladimir fell forward like a stiff board, slamming onto the ground face-first.

Pauli kicked the brute in the head. "Hi ya, tough guy." The taser darts stopped their torturous impulses after about five seconds. Vladimir rolled onto his back and placed his hand on his forehead where Pauli had kicked him.

"Who are you?"

Tony spoke up. "You're under arrest, hood. Reach for the sky."

Vladimir didn't understand the statement from Tony. Since he didn't follow Tony's order, Tony decided to reintroduce him to the taser darts. He pushed the button on his walker and the darts immediately pumped additional convulsion-causing volts into the Armenian's body. Again he let loose with a scream and rolled on the ground. As he rolled back and forth on the ground, the darts were ripped from his back and leg.

Vladimir was able to roll away about six yards, but the movement caused the cuts he had received when falling through the barbed wire to start bleeding again.

He stood up with both fists clenched, furious at the two old men who had caused him so much pain. He glared at them and was surprised to see that they were glaring right back at him. The old men's fearless stare unnerved Vladimir, who decided to leave and catch up with Victor. After a few choice Armenian curses, he turned...

Then the brute froze. In front of him, not quite twelve feet away, was an enormous crouching lion. Blood fell in large drops from its head. The fully grown tiger had been able to rip five to six huge gashes in the juvenile lion's face. A lion is terrifying enough to see, but one with blood, cuts, and gore on its face is even more horrifying. Involuntarily, Vladimir peed himself.

*

"There are two men stranded on the overhead cable ride," the soldier manning the infrared camera radioed to the ground team. "You're approaching the small hut where the ride begins. Might want to see if you can get that ride moving and get them off."

One of the special ops men looked at the sergeant who was his team leader. "Seriously?"

The sergeant looked toward the hut. "Just go inside, and if there is a switch just hit it and we move. Don't waste any time."

The soldier looked inside and saw some buttons. The closest one to him was labeled "Reverse." He pushed it, and the massive turning wheel came to life. There was an initial jerk, then it ran smoothly backwards.

"Those dangling guys are on their own now. Let's go," ordered the team leader.

The sound of the Skyfari moving caused Victor to look up. "I don't remember that moving" he said as he stopped and gazed up at the chairs swaying above his head.

Amanda had been trapped in the big man's clutches, but when he stopped she was moved from his side to a step in front of him. She saw that the bald man was looking up at the ride above their heads. She also realized that she was in a perfect position to…

"Bawaah!" was the sound that came from the brute as Amanda pulled her knee from his groin. He collapsed face-first onto the cement pathway. Amanda, knowing that the other goon was probably following, could not run back the way she had just come. She started to run along the path that the cable ride was moving. Then she stopped and said, "Thane!"

Big Brock let go of the chairlift pole for a moment as he swung his shoulders to scan the area. The helicopter had startled him and Benson so much that they had almost jumped out of the chair. Suddenly the chair jerked backwards. Brock was thrown off balance, and his feet slipped from the seat. He let out a yell as he started to fall. The backrest of the ride provided him something to hold onto, but he was hanging from his stomach down.

Benson grabbed Brock in a leg lock around his shoulders and head. He was able to hold onto the connecting pole.

Brock looked down and noticed that the ostriches were so excited that they were jumping and actually coming close to his feet.

"Aaahh! Rafters! Aaahh!" Brock yelled as he tried to pull his feet up as best he could.

"Don't you let go of me Benson!"

"Don't worry! I got ya, I think."

They were now moving at a pretty good pace and away from the ostrich exhibit.

"Can't get myself up," Brock grunted.

Benson kept repeating, "Hold on, I got ya, we can make it."

⌒

"Striker One, this is Eyeballs. Looks like there is a female being held by subject #1. They stopped about fifty....whoa!"

The team leader keyed his microphone. "Eyeballs, this is Striker One...repeat, over."

There was a brief pause, then "Striker One, the female just kneed subject #1 in the nuts and dropped him. She started to run but appears confused. At twelve o'clock your point, about twenty yards."

Amanda knew that she couldn't run directly back to Thane, so she decided to try to avoid the second goon by doubling back. She smiled with satisfaction at the pain that she had caused the big man, then started to run, thinking she could loop around the other goon.

She was looking back at the groaning man on the ground and smiling when—"Ooooff!"—she ran face-first into the chest of another huge man. She fell flat on her back and looked up, screamed, and started kicking. This man was joined by about six others standing around her. Amanda kicked at each of them. She couldn't initially hear what they were saying, but she saw that they had their hands up, palms facing her.

"Easy, ma'am, easy. We're American Special Forces."

As she started to comprehend what they were saying, she slowed down her kicks. She was still on her back with her knees up to her chest, ready to kick out again.

"Where's Thane?" she demanded.

The leader of the men got down low and calmly said, "We're here to help. If I reach over to help you up, are you gonna kick me?"

There were muffled snickers from behind the big man. He smiled.

"May I help you up, young lady?"

⌒

Vladimir tried to avoid the animal by running to the right, but the lion leaped and grabbed his leg with its front claws, then clamped down on the back of Vladimir's thigh with its teeth. He let out a scream that could be heard throughout the zoo.

Pauli and Tony looked at each other.

"Should we help him?" Pauli asked.

"All I got left is the pepper spray," Tony said. "It's supposed to work on bears, but..."

He gestured toward the lion. The beast had pinned Vladimir onto the ground and had a horrible biting grip on his leg. Vladimir screamed over and over.

"Here goes nothing," Tony said, using the trigger on the other side of his walker. He held the walker up, aimed the bottom of the front leg toward the lion's face, and fired. A large stream of orange, burning fluid hit the lion, dousing its face with three million Scoville heat units. The corrosive fluid burned the lion's eyes, mouth, and the huge gashes in its face. The resulting pain and blindness startled the beast into releasing Vladimir's leg. It jumped upwards, clawing at its own face, and when it landed it started to rub its face on the ground. Each time the lion tried to look at the still-screaming man and the others present, the pain shot through its eyes and facial cuts.

It was too much, and the lion turned and started running. As it did so, it made strange sounds of pain and anger. Shaking its head, it ran in a confused yet determined way as it tried to escape from the chemical heat that was burning its eyes and face.

"My leg broke!" Vladimir said. He was still bleeding heavily. Pauli took the man's belt off and wrapped it around his thigh for a tourniquet. The pepper spray had also gotten onto the bald man, and the chemical burning added to the pain from his broken femur.

Both Pauli and Tony stood over the man. "Where is the girl, Amanda?" Pauli asked.

The goon looked at the old men. "Nothing, I tell you nothing."

Suddenly Vladimir recognized the two men as the ones he had talked to at the safe house.

"That's right, you commie pig. We're the two old men. Remember now?" Pauli asked again, "The girl?"

The big man was accustomed to pain. "Nothing, she is gone, you get nothing… Arrgggh!" he screamed. Tony and Pauli stepped back as Thane approached and put one foot on the man's thigh. Pauli tried to hold the man's arms down as he tried to resist and pull away. This time Thane put his full weight on the man's thigh.

"Aaaargggh! No more, stop! Stop!" The man put both his hands behind his back. "No more, stop."

Thane's eyes burned with anger. He no longer felt the pain of his injuries. "Where's Amanda?" he demanded, then kicked the man's leg. Again a scream, then Thane lost control and started repeatedly kicking the man's back and head.

"Thane, stop!" a woman's voice shouted. Thane looked up as Brittany and Jake ran toward him.

"The other one took off with Amanda," Thane said, with saliva dripping from his mouth.

Brittany put her hands on Thane's arm and said, "It's all right, Thane calm down."

Thane's second adrenaline dump had caused him to start shaking uncontrollably. Pauli and Tony helped him sit down while Jake cuffed the Armenian.

⏎

The team leader pointed toward the man moaning on the ground. With thick plastic zip ties, he was secured at his hands and feet. The Armenian was dragged over and sat down on the ground.

As Amanda was being helped up by the team leader, she said that there was another Armenian man "that way" as she pointed in the direction where she had last seen Thane. Then she turned at a moaning sound and saw that Victor was seated behind her. "You!" Before any members of the striker team could react, she bolted at the goon and kicked him in the face. Then she punched and scratched, demanding, "Where's Thane?" over and over again. One of the team members picked her up from behind with his arm around her waist. She was still kicking and yelling.

"You better cooperate or I'll let her beat you to death," he said with a sadistic smile.

"Eyeballs, do you read?"

"Loud and clear, Striker One."

Looking at the helicopter high above him, the team leader knew the camera could see him. He pointed in the direction where Amanda had stated that Thane was located and said, "The woman here states that the second target is in this direction a couple hundred yards. Can you confirm?"

The response was "Stand by, wait!"

This alarmed the team leader, and all the members of the striker team pointed their weapons outward, looking for a possible threat.

"Inbound to your location, there's a…"

A pause caused the team leader to look around at the members of his team. Each shrugged in answer to his unasked question.

"Eyeballs, there's a what?"

The reply was a simple "At your twelve." The men all aimed their weapons directly in front of them, pointing where Amanda had come from. The camera tech saw what the team was doing and corrected himself: "No, your twelve o'clock high."

The entire team looked up to see a man's legs dangling from a lift chair. He was wearing shoes, socks, no pants, but some sort of gown, and diapers. Another old man was holding on to him with his legs wrapped around his shoulder and head. The second man was holding onto the connecting bar for dear life.

"What the…" Amanda suddenly spoke up. "Big Brock, Benson! What are you doing up there?"

Brock cranked his head to a position where he could look toward the source of the familiar voice. "Oh, hey, doll baby! We've been looking for you. Looks like you found some friends."

Amanda looked up at the cables to the hut where the ride started. "Only about twenty-five yards left. Can you hold on?"

Benson briefly let go of the connecting bar with one hand, said, "No problem," and then quickly grabbed it again.

The voice on the radio sounded a warning. "Incoming fast at your twelve... on the ground. Looks like... ah, ah—"

The team leader cut him off and blurted, "Freakin' lion!"

The beast was running erratically, snorting and shaking its head. It ran by the strike team. The team leader pointed to three of his soldiers and said, "Head back up that direction and locate the second subject. Advise me when you've secured him."

With a quick nod, the men took off at a trot and headed in the direction where Amanda had pointed.

"Get her off of me!"

The team leader turned and saw that Amanda was again beating on the secured subject and yelling, "Thane better not be hurt, you filthy pig."

Again a large arm wrapped around Amanda's waist and picked her up, still kicking and yelling.

After a few minutes, the team leader was contacted by one of his team members. "Sergeant, the second target has been secured by an off-duty Omaha cop and some old guys."

"Clear on that." Then the team leader gazed over at Amanda, who was waiting for news about Thane. He realized that this was very important information. He held his finger up to Amanda.

The team medic was dressing the Armenian man's wounds. "Never seen a lion bite before," he commented.

Then the team member who was talking to the team leader put his hand to his ear, listening to a communication from the team leader. "Stand by."

He looked up and announced, "Listen up. Who is Thane?"

Brittany wasn't sure how to address the special forces man, so she just pointed to the young man sitting on the ground. Thane looked up and raised his hand.

"That's me, sir."

The medic looked at him and asked, "Are you all right?"

Brittany spoke up: "We'll take care of him." She looked at Jake, who responded with an affirming nod.

"When we get out of here, it's straight to the E.R. for you, buddy."

Thane replied, "Good idea."

The medic listened again to the team leader, then smiled and said, "There's a young lady that is beating the snot out of the other Armenian because she thinks you're hurt."

Thane smiled…sort of. He still had some swelling on one side of his face.

"This guy was doing the same to this bald pezzo de merda," Tony said, then spit at the goon.

"Tell the young lady that he is here and fine. These two are quite a pair. This Thane had been beating all over this guy once the lion let loose of him, demanding to know where she was."

The team leader had unplugged his ear microphone so that Amanda could hear the answer. Once she heard that Thane was okay, she let go of a breath she had been holding. Then when she heard he had been beating on the other goon, she held her hand to her heart. "What a sweet guy."

Amanda looked at the team leader. "The lion bit the goon… Yesss!"

The team leader shook his head. "You two are made for each other." Then he got back on the radio. "We will meet you there. Stand by."

The response was, "Clear on that."

"Strike Team to Eyeballs, do you have the third subject in sight?"

The reply was "Not at this time. Still searching."

Aziz looked at his phone in confusion. The small map he was looking at indicated that the cargo van was located at the building where he stood. He looked up and saw signs for fish and water exhibits.

"This is odd. Victor and Vladimir were probably supposed to meet Lois."

He decided that there must be some sort of shipping or loading dock on the inside of the building. The doors were open due to the tours being conducted.

Aziz made his way past various exhibits and eventually walked into the large underwater tunnel. As he entered, he was momentarily surprised by the magnitude of the experience. He stopped and cast his eyes upward at the large fish swimming directly over his head. There were even sharks. The wall was so clear that Aziz reached up and touched it. This is a common reaction among people entering this exhibit. Visitors feel like they are actually among the incredible animals.

Aziz's eyes followed a shark as it swam away from him toward the far end of the tunnel. He looked down at the end of the tunnel where a man was standing and staring at him. Surprised, Aziz tried to quickly jump to the left and inadvertently thumped his head on the sloping wall of the tunnel. This caused a loud thud, and the fish all jumped, just as their smaller cousins do in home aquariums around the world when children tap on the glass to see the fish dart around after being startled.

"It's been a while Aziz. I thought you would have gotten smarter, but as most thugs, you just do what your green star masters tell you to do," the man said in fluent Armenian.

Aziz looked at the wall of the tunnel, which was no longer clear. There was a small blood splatter from a cut on his forehead. He staggered back toward the middle of the tunnel and tried to clear his head. He focused on the man who was about ten yards in front of him. There was also another man behind him.

Aziz focused on the first man and asked, *"Who are you?"* Then he looked at Smitty. *"And you, I don't know either of you."*

There was a grunt from the first man, who took two steps towards Aziz and then held up his left hand and wiggled his fingers. *"You ripped my nails from my hand. Now I find that you are taking young girls and women and destroying their lives by addicting them to drugs and prostituting them. You make me sick."*

Aziz stood up straight and gave Mac a long look. In Armenian he said, *"The American?"*

Mac nodded. *"I owe you."*

The tension immediately rose. Mac started to take a step toward the younger and stronger man.

Smitty said, "They play for keeps" to remind Mac that just rushing this hit man was probably not a good idea.

"This is who you brought to even our score. An old man?" Aziz jeered.

Smitty could tell that Aziz was talking about him. With his two fingers he gave a mock salute to Aziz and smiled. Then Smitty touched his earpiece and asked, "Are they caught yet?"

Pauli answered, "Both of them are tied up, and the special forces guys are arranging for the pickup with their helicopter. Thane and Amanda are bruised up a bit but are fine."

Smitty told Aziz, "Your bald goons have been captured. Who knows what they will tell the homeland security about your little operation."

Aziz didn't understand, so Mac translated. The expression on Aziz's face brought satisfaction to Smitty, who reached into his pocket and pulled out a piss pack. Then he touched his earpiece and said, "We need that diversion in the aquarium."

Officer Tucker Preston leaned forward slightly in his wheelchair and discreetly looked around as the young tour guide described various points of interest in the giant service area of the aquarium. The service area is located above the tunnel/ main aquarium and out of sight of visitors in the tunnel. This invisibility is accomplished by painting the ceiling black and using other architectural strategies that make it difficult to see the staff from the tunnel. However, staff in the service area can clearly see visitors who are in the tunnel.

The nurse pushing Tucker's wheelchair wasn't really paying attention to him because he rarely moved. Up jumped Tucker, who could see that there was a man facing Smitty and Mac. He plunged into the aquarium above the man's head.

The fish that surrounded the three men in the tunnel suddenly darted in different directions. The flashes of silver and the bubbles above Aziz's head gave an almost blinding display. It was as if there was an explosion, but once the bubbles cleared the fish started swimming around normally, except for one animal that definitely didn't belong there.

Aziz took a step backward and stared up into the underskirt of a robe. As the bubbles cleared, he could see black loafer shoes and black socks that were held up by small, strap-like suspenders that were wrapped around Tucker Preston's calf. His wrinkled white legs were kicking as he tried to keep his head afloat. Then his catheter broke free from the strap around his thigh.

The combination of the shoes, socks, flowing hospital robe, and piss pack bouncing about behind the white boxers worn by Officer Preston created an engrossing scenario that provided Mac with a small window of opportunity. He charged at Aziz, and before the hit man could react, Mac delivered a straight right punch to Aziz's stomach. This surprised the big man, who bent forward as the wind was knocked out of him.

Mac's momentum allowed him to bull rush right into Aziz. This caused the big man to fall backward and hit his head on the tunnel. As Aziz fell backward, Smitty saw a hand gun drop from his waist. It was a good initial blow, but not enough to debilitate the likes of the hit man.

Aziz kicked his feet upward so that Mac's momentum was used against him. As Aziz rolled backward, Mac was propelled into the wall behind Aziz. Mac hit with a thud, and pain shot from his neck to his shoulder. He also received a nasty gash on his cheek.

Aziz attempted to spring back to his feet, but having the wind partially knocked out of him slowed his movements. Mac seemed to take the impact against the wall pretty well. He was able to get back to his feet more quickly than Aziz and charged back at him. This time Aziz saw him coming and was ready as

Mac tried to dive at his legs. Aziz slammed his fist onto Mac's back, causing him to slam down on the ground. Aziz kicked Mac in the side, and he yelled out in pain. As Aziz lifted his foot to smash down on Mac's head, Smitty rammed him from behind with his shoulder. Since Aziz was standing on one leg, he had no way to brace himself and ended up falling to the ground.

Mac thought he had felt a rib break. He forced himself up to face Aziz again. This time Aziz quickly reached to his waist for his gun. His eyes quickly looked down as he grabbed and patted at his waistband, then instinctively reached behind him and pulled a nasty-looking dagger from a sheath at the lower part of his back. With the dagger in his hand, he looked at Mac and smiled. Mac was not quite ready to defend himself as Aziz started to lunge, but Aziz's charge was cut short by a projectile that struck his chest and released thick, brownish, vile-smelling goo all over his chest, neck, and face. Aziz's mouth got a small splatter, which caused an almost immediate gag reflex. The slimy liquid spread all around his face and chest as Aziz jerked back in reaction.

This distraction gave Mac an opportunity to land a solid right punch to Aziz's jaw. The punch even surprised Smitty as he watched and heard the impact of a blow that sent Aziz wheeling on his heels. Mac's face was rigid with determination as he ignored the pain of his ribs and let loose a flurry of jabs and punches to Aziz. This time the big hit man was not able to simply absorb the blows, and each of Mac's punches found their mark. Aziz was knocked back against the tunnel wall, and Mac rammed a final jab to his chin, breaking the big man's jaw. Aziz dropped face-first onto the ground.

Mac put his hand up against the tunnel wall for support. He was exhausted. He turned and leaned against the wall and looked over at Smitty.

"What is that smell?" Mac was confused at the sight of Smitty grinning. "What are you smiling at?"

Smitty shrugged and held up Aziz's pistol. "I was only going to use it if you weren't able to come out still standing. Plus, I'm not sure if shooting a gun in here is such a good idea. That is why I used another one of the weapons we sort of cultivate at the home. I'll tell you about it later."

Both men looked around and then stared at Officer Preston, who was still swimming around. He was now able to touch his feet to the top of the tunnel.

Then Mac noticed one of the sharks swimming up behind Preston. "Smitty! Call him and tell him to get outta there!"

The shark appeared to be curious about the pack of fluid bouncing around behind Preston's legs.

"Tucker, get out of the water now!" Smitty screamed over his communicator. Everyone heard it, but none of the other Blues knew what was going on and each of them had their hand to their ear making sure they had heard what Smitty was saying.

The shark nudged the bag, which burst open and created a yellowish cloud. Both Smitty and Mac watched what appeared to be the slow disbursement of the contents of the piss pack. The shark didn't seem to like the contents of the pack. With a quick thrash of its tail, it bolted away.

"Well, that's a new application," Smitty said with his eyebrows raised in amazement.

Mac shook his head and pulled his phone out of his pocket. "This is Mac. Aziz is in the aquarium building. We have him on the ground unconscious now, but he may come around any minute. Get your guys over here pronto."

Mac hung up and looked at Smitty. He spit out some blood that was in his mouth. "You know you could have ended this sooner if you would have at least pointed the gun at him."

Smitty shrugged. "You needed to pound out some demons."

Mac smiled as he looked down at the big Armenian. "I have five more I have to get rid of."

"Entering the aquarium now, Eyeballs," the team leader broadcasted. "The two other targets are secure, and it appears that the old people are leaving. The lion is still loose, but it ran to the south part of the zoo. Looks like it's rolling around on the ground and pawing at its face."

The Armenian began to stir. He made some strange sounds, and as he tried to move his arm, his left hand suddenly shot stabbing hot pain through his arm. Aziz let out a yell, then started getting up to his knees. He looked at his left hand and was shocked to see that all of his fingers were broken and pointing in grotesque angles.

Aziz gritted his teeth to keep from screaming. He looked around until his eyes met Mac's gaze. Mac gave Aziz a smile revealing bloody teeth. The hit man stared at the disjointed fingers of his hand in disbelief, then back at Mac, knowing the smiling man had got his payback by breaking each of his fingers. Mac held up the hockey-puck-shaped tracking device, showing Aziz how he had lured him to his capture.

Aziz gave Mac a vicious glare, then with a yell tried to jump to his feet. His yell was cut short by a cracking pain in his jaw. He was determined to make Mac pay for what he had done.

Mac crossed his arms and continued to smile. His insulting smirk enraged Aziz even more. He got one foot under him and was ready to spring at Mac when he was kicked between the shoulder blades by a size 12 boot. The kick sent the big man into the wall of the tunnel, giving him another gash to his face. His left hand slammed onto the ground, which shot searing pain up his arm.

Aziz screamed in agony as three men drilled their knees onto him, then wrenched his right hand behind his back. One of the soldiers grabbed his left hand, not knowing about its current lack of connected bones and tendons. While attempting to get the zip ties around the left hand, the soldier commented, "Whoa! That's gonna mess up your handwriting."

Once Aziz was secured, he was jerked to his feet and marched out. "Oh, man!" a soldier exclaimed. "This guy smells putrid."

Aziz and the other two goons were never going to see the inside of a courtroom. Instead, they would be transported to a different country where America keeps international criminals who have information that needs to come to light.

"Ts'tesut'yun," Mac said.

Smitty asked, "What did you say?"

Mac smiled and translated, "Bye-bye."

Suddenly Smitty remembered something. He hit his ear communicator. "Preston! Are you all right?"

The answer came from Meter Maid Mary. "He's fine. The idiot didn't know there were sharks in the pool when he jumped in." Then Mary laughed.

"When they pulled him outta the water, the nurses and the staff screamed at him that a shark was taking an interest in his keister! His piss pack tube shot pee like an over pressured hose! 'Bout scared him into a real coma!"

She snickered again. "Serves him right for thinking he could get fresh with me."

Smitty smiled, looked at Mac, and said, "Let's get outta here."

"Sarge, this is Smitty. I suggest we pack up and scram."

Sarge answered, "We've been able to neutralize three of the suspects. We still have some more work to do. We will wrap up our little tour and debrief back at the Precinct."

The tour guides were informed that the tours were going to be cut short. The Ol' Blues Retirement Home staff started to escort the Blues from the zoo, and they were joined by other Blues who had been walking around the zoo without any guides. The zoo staff were confused at the number of old men walking out of main gate.

"I don't remember this many walking into the zoo when we started," one of the staff said to the manager of the main ticket office.

"Oh, some came late," she replied. "I remember a man and woman from that home running in and trying to catch up with the tours."

Jake approached the manager of the ticket office and said, "I really like the fact that some of your exhibits have animals running around the inside of the giant buildings. It was a great experience."

The manager said, "Oh the Lied Jungle—that's one of our main attractions."

Jake then asked why there was an animal outside the exhibit building. This brought a confused look from the manager. "What do you mean? We don't allow animals outside their building complexes."

Jake pointed toward the southern part of the zoo. "We saw a lion over by the tiger cage, and it didn't look like the two of them got along very well."

The manager, again looking perplexed, responded, "The lions are not that close to the tigers."

Jake explained, "The lion was not in a cage; he was running loose. Thought you should know."

The manager looked terrified. "Is everyone out of the zoo?" she said into a walkie-talkie. While waiting for her staff to check in, she looked at Jake and offered a fake smile. "Thank you. I have to get back to my office."

The manager turned and ran. Once in her office, she grabbed her radio and issued an alert. "Someone reported a lion walking outside of its cage in the southern part of the zoo." She then started to frantically look through a procedures manual.

Jake turned back and motioned to Brittany to bring Thane and Amanda out to the parking lot. As Jake drove to the hospital, Brittany said, "Remember, you two, you were driving and hit a deer, then went off the road and struck a tree. That's your story. Amanda, I'm your roommate and you called me to pick you two up. We decided to have both of you checked out when we saw the swelling on Thane's face and he told us about the pain in his ribs."

At the E.R. Brittany smiled as she watched Thane and Amanda in the examination room. Amanda reached over and took Thane's hand.

Brittany turned to Jake and said, "Our little precinct just got a bit more complicated."

CHAPTER 18

"How can a man who is almost comatose jump out of his wheelchair and dive into a shark tank?" Boss Nurse thundered.

The young nurse who was pushing Officer Preston's wheelchair shrugged. "I don't know how. I don't know what. I don't even know when. All I know is he was his usual self, just sitting in his chair—you know, like he always does…"

She demonstrated by cocking her head to one side and staring straight ahead with a blank expression.

"The next thing I know," she continued. "I feel the chair move, and Officer Preston is doing a swan dive into the drink! I… I just froze. It was kind of graceful, and time seemed to stand still."

Boss Nurse watched in disbelief as the nurse described the incident as if it had been some sort of life-changing event for her.

"Are you outta your mind? All you had to do was watch someone who doesn't move. Just push him around in his chair, maybe point him at something shiny and tell him how pretty it is. Now you're back here at the home with a soggy police officer who is not moving."

The nurse perked up. "Maybe it's a breakthrough. I mean, maybe there was something at the shark tank that triggered his mind, and what we saw was some kind of miracle."

Boss Nurse stared at the nurse in disbelief and said, "Get him back to his room and into some dry clothes."

Not wanting to prolong the conversation with Boss Nurse, the younger nurse quickly took Officer Preston out of the reception area of the Precinct and back to his room. Before the door closed, she heard Boss Nurse mumbling, "Crazy old men gonna be the death o' me, I just know it."

6~

The Sarge broadcast a message to all of the Blues in the Precinct: "You did a good job at the zoo. Get some shut eye, and we'll convene the task force in the morning. We are gonna stop by the hospital and see Amanda, and we'll brief everybody tomorrow."

Sarge and Agnes walked into the E.R. and were met by Brittany, who announced, "They hit a deer while driving, then went off the road. Me and Jake picked them up and brought them to the hospital. Got it?"

Sarge and Agnes stepped into the room where Thane and Amanda were being treated. The doctor had listened to their story about hitting the deer and seemed to have a problem matching some of the injuries with their explanation.

"Cripes, Thane, I let you use my car to take my granddaughter on a date and you kill a deer and plow into my willow tree."

Thane and Amanda looked up and in waddled Agnes with smoke billowing out of her mouth and nostrils as she spoke. The doctor quickly forgot about quizzing the young couple about the accident and shouted, "Whoa, no smoking in here. This is a hospital!"

Acting surprised, Agnes pulled the cigarette out of her mouth. "Oh, I'm sorry, Doctor, he wrecked my car on the far end of our farm. Some friends brought them in. I forgot all about your no-smoking rules here. Lucky for Thane it happened on our property or the cops would have given him a ticket. Are they all right?"

Amanda realized where Agnes was going. "We're fine, Grandma. Thane might have a cracked rib or two and a swollen jaw, but we should be coming home soon. Right, Doc?"

Thane just sat quietly and let Amanda and Agnes finish telling their little story. The doctor was satisfied. He had wrapped Thane's ribs and prescribed pain medication and something to reduce the swelling.

"Well, looks like your grandmother will take care of you from here on out," the doctor said. Then he looked at Thane and said, "You'll be fine in a week or so, young man. Next time, keep your eyes on the road, not the cute girl." The doctor smiled and left the room.

"Whew, I didn't think he was gonna believe us there for a second. There was no police report or anything. Thanks, Grandma," Amanda said with relief.

Agnes gave her a wink. Then she looked at Thane and said, "You're slipping. You didn't stand when this lady entered the room."

Thane looked at her and tried to smile, but it hurt. Agnes gently patted Thane's chin and said, "Thank you for taking care of my Manda Cakes."

Thane forced a half-smile on the side of his jaw that didn't hurt. "She took care of me, too." He looked at Amanda with admiration and said, "She's really something."

Again, Amanda was taken with Thane's simple and kind demeanor. He had such a sincere way of speaking to her that she had no defense. The nerd had won her heart.

"I think some cold ice cream will help the swelling," she suggested.

Thane smiled and looked at Sarge, who had just entered the room. "We're going on a date," Thane announced, as it was a really unusual event.

"Oh, really?" Sarge replied. "As long as you finish your work. From what I'm looking at right now, it looks like I'll have to put the Chelini brothers to work at your station."

Thane's eyes widened at the thought. "I'll be in first thing in the morning," he half mumbled.

Sarge got a big smile on his face and took the cigar out of his mouth. "I'll give you a couple days of sick leave, and then I expect you back at your station. Sound good to you, Agnes?"

Lead Officer Crantz crossed her arms and commented, "You're getting soft, Sarge. In the old days Thanerboy here would be required to be in bright and early. But since it looks like he may be going on a real live date, I suppose we could give him forty-eight hours."

"We'll get them home," Brittany said. Everybody smiled.

As Sarge and Agnes left the room, Sarge didn't look back but just said, "Forty-eight hours, Thanerboy, then back to your computer games. Don't know why we keep this guy around."

Jake understood the statement as an old copper's way of telling the young guy that he was glad to have him back.

"Okay, Sarge," was Thane's muffled reply.

Jake dropped Brittany and Amanda off at Brittany's house. Brittany looked puzzled.

"Why are the lights on in the house?" she asked. "I thought I had turned them all off when you picked me up, Jake."

Jake agreed. "I seem to remember that, too."

Amanda broke the strange quiet. "Well, just remember to kiss the right lips there, Jake," referring to the phone call where Jake had mistaken Amanda for Brittany.

Brittany smiled and said, "Here." She gave Jake a kiss and added, "I don't think you'll mix that up with someone else."

Amanda laughed, then looked at Thane and gave him a kiss on the cheek. "Don't forget that cold ice cream helps swelling."

Thane touched his cheek. "Thanks, that made the pain go away."

Amanda smiled, and she and Brittany got out of the car.

"Talk to you tomorrow, babe," Brittany said to Jake. Amanda smiled and gave a small wave to Thane.

Thane looked at Jake and then looked up at the ceiling of the car. "Wowie!"

Jake smiled and said, "Let's get you home, Thanerboy." Then he thought, *This poor kid isn't gonna know what hit him.*

&

Once inside, Brittany and Amanda walked through the house, shutting off the lights in rooms they weren't using.

"I must have run out in a hurry when I heard what had happened," Brittany said.

Once everything was back to normal, Brittany opened the refrigerator and grabbed a pitcher of orange juice.

"Just like you do every night." A pair of eyes were looking at Brittany and Amanda through binoculars. *"She likes her juice. Oh, now she is making Amanda drink a glass, too. That is good to know."*

Monte Kurt looked at Jake's car as it pulled away from the house after dropping the girls off. This time Monte wasn't sitting in his car, so he was unconcerned about being noticed. He had parked a block away and walked into a wooded area where he could watch Brittany and Amanda from a distance.

"That Amanda is really quite a girl, Thane," Jake said. "She's sharp, so you will have to be extra careful what you do around her. The secrecy of The Precinct is too important."

Thane looked at Jake and replied, "Don't I know it. All I think about is how to talk to Amanda without her finding out something that she's not supposed to know."

Suddenly Jake noticed something as he continued to drive. "Hmm."

Thane responded, "What?"

"That Blue PT Cruiser. I've seen it parked around here before. There was something about it the last time I saw it. A guy in the car looked like he was hiding his face from me as I drove by."

Jake shrugged. "I can't put my finger on it, Thane, but I know when someone's being evasive. If I was still in a cruiser when I saw him, I would have turned on that guy."

Thane asked, "What do you mean?"

Jake gestured with his hand. "If something about a car bugs us cops, we do a quick U-turn so the crook will think we're coming after him. If the guy is up to no good, he will run or hide. When we make a U-turn, it scares them into doing something that shows they were up to no good. It's a simple trick that works."

Jake pointed over his shoulder with his thumb. "That PT Cruiser bugs me." They continued driving.

Observing the girls in the house, the Chemist noted, "Well, now, while you're drinking your juice, the two of you talk for a bit, then it looks like you're going to bed."

Monte checked his watch. "Between nine thirty and ten o'clock each night. That's a routine." He smiled. Watching them closely was giving him the information he needed in order to entertain himself by messing with their minds.

⁘

The following morning, Jake walked into his office and sat down at his computer to read the morning reports of the previous night's activities. There was one from the overnight district that included the zoo.

"Requested for outer perimeter around zoo due to a possibility that some llamas had gotten loose. Per the zoo security, the animals were located inside the facility and placed back in their cages."

Jake smiled. "Llamas, huh? They were afraid that if the truth got out, it would have caused a mass panic." Then Jake added to himself, "Can't blame them."

Then he looked at his phone and noticed a blinking red light signifying a message. The number belonged to Detective Angie Jacks at the Special Victims Unit.

"Oh, good." He listened to the voicemail.

"Jake, this is Angie. You're not gonna believe this. The DNA was not a match. We've got nothing on Monte Kurt."

Jake sat back in disbelief. "I was sure we had him."

Then he remembered that Smitty wanted all the reports related to the serial rapist. He called Detective Angie Jacks.

"Hey, Angie, I can't believe it's not a match on the DNA. Listen, I'm going to need all the reports on those cases that you worked when Monte Kurt's name popped up as a suspect. There's a cold case guy who wants to take a look at them. Could you get them for me?"

"Sure, Jake, I'd take help from anyone at this point," Angie replied.

Once Jake had a compilation of all the reports that were available, he called Sarge and asked for the task force to meet so he could update them on his findings on Monte Kurt.

Everyone was in the Sarge's office when Jake arrived. He sat down, looked at each member of the group, then announced, "The DNA test did not identify Monte Kurt as the rapist."

The Blues looked at each other in disbelief.

Jake added, "Smitty, I've compiled all the reports we had on the guy." He handed Smitty the stack of reports. "The detective told me that she would appreciate any help at all."

Smitty's excited gaze signaled his eagerness to work on the case. He looked at the Sarge and said, "I'd like to get started."

Sarge gave him a nod, and Smitty left the office.

Agnes took a drag from her smoke and decided to give modern policing a bit of a jab.

"So all that scientific policing that is so popular didn't really work out after all?"

Jake just gave her a frustrated look.

Sarge interjected, "Let Smitty look things over. He usually finds something. Right, Agnes?" Sarge was trying to keep Agnes from deflating Jake further by criticizing the accuracy of DNA testing. She rolled her eyes, crossed her arms, and then leaned back against the wall.

The doors of the elevator opened on the underground offices of the Precinct, and Smitty walked out with his arms full of reports and photos from various crime scenes. He was on his way to one of the conference rooms so he could utilize the big tables to spread out the reports and get an overview of the big picture.

Smitty walked past the room that contained Thane's office and heard a familiar voice. He stuck his head in the office and saw Mac talking on the phone.

"Really, they were jumping from one cartel to another. Hmm... well, when the ship is sinking, the rats abandon it quickly." Mac sat up straighter. "It also makes sense. Her enterprise had collapsed, and she knew the Armenian bunch was going to punish them. Why not join another team that could offer them an opportunity to do what they did best and provide some protection?"

Mac looked up, saw Smitty and motioned to the chair next to him. He looked at Smitty with a big smile on his face as his contact in black ops briefed him on their findings so far with their interrogation of the goons, then filled him in on Mac's old friend Aziz.

"He's complaining about his hand, is he? Well, find a cross-eyed orthopedic doctor to match up all those little bones in his hand. Let me know what it looks like when he's done."

Mac laughed and hung up. He put his phone down and told Smitty what he had just learned. "Looks like Lois joined a Mexican cartel. Aziz isn't talking much, but that will change with a little time and persuasion. The two goons, Victor and Vladimir, are only brave when they are beating up women. It also helps when you play a recording of a lion growling and roaring down the hall."

Smitty lifted his hand to ask a question: "What are you doing here? You should be at home resting." Smitty pointed to cuts and bruises all over Mac's face and arms.

Mac shrugged and winced. "Yeah, I'm a little sore, but the job ain't finished yet. Little Miss Lois is still out and about. I've taken a real interest in her discomfort." Mac then looked at the stack of papers and photos Smitty was carrying. "A little light reading before chow?"

Smitty smiled. "I'm gonna rip into all these old reports and see if I can make some sense of them. The guy who provided the chemical knockout juice after the girls were kidnapped is still out there."

Mac's eyebrows went up. "You mean the Chemist?"

Smitty winked, "That's the guy—this... uh... Monte Kurt. The Omaha coppers thought they had a DNA match on him with these old rape cases. I think this chemical knockout method is what he used when he was attacking women before he joined the Armenian bunch."

Mac scratched his chin. "So now that the Armenian operation is out of commission…"

Answering Mac's unfinished question, Smitty said, "My bet is that he's going to go back to his old ways. I'll leave you to find Lois. Right now I'm gonna work on this Monte Kurt and take an interest in his discomfort."

Smitty smiled and took his pile of reports to the conference room table to begin a detailed analysis. Before leaving Thane's office, he turned to Mac and said, "Oh, give Sarge a call and brief him on what you found out about the Armenians from your friends."

Mac gave Smitty a "thumbs up" and picked up his phone.

⚬

"What do you mean there's been a change of plans? We had a deal."

Lois kept her voice under control as she tried to put the best possible slant on her current predicament. "The change has nothing to do with you. It's just that those who were my assistants are no longer with me. Perhaps they just wanted to go back to Armenia. I don't know, but I have the information and equipment to set up my operation just as before. The only difference is that the money will go to your employer, not to Armenia."

"The last time we spoke, you asked for help in removing an unwanted individual. Do you still need our assistance?"

Lois saw an opportunity to give some reassurance. "No need to bother. We took care of the problem so that you and your employer won't have to worry about it."

She paused, then added, "I like to keep things simple. I would think your superiors would appreciate that as well… no?"

Her contact paused, then responded, "We are still working on an acceptable safe house and proper security. It is not ready yet." Internally Lois screamed at the thought of continuing to drive the cargo van full of her equipment. It was just too big to keep around. She exhaled slowly to calm herself.

"No problem at all. When your employer has established our new base of operations, let me know." Lois thought to herself, *What am I going to do with this van for a couple more days?*

⌐∿

The Sarge looked around at the group of people in his office: Brittany, Jake, the Chelini brothers, Agnes, Benson, and Big Brock.

"The next items on this case will be the Chemist—Monte Kurt, and Lois—the ringleader of this little outfit," Sarge announced. "Smitty is on assignment going over some old reports and trying to put together a case on the Chemist."

"Our friend Mac is looking for information on Lois," Sarge continued. "He says that her two goons have been talking to the Feds. She has packed up her outfit and is currently trying to join a Mexican cartel. Once she gets established, she will continue kidnapping and drugging young women, only this time she will be supplying them to the Mexicans instead of the Armenians."

Agnes stood up and announced, "I say it's time we go after this guy old-school."

The Sarge took the cigar out of his mouth. "The Chemist? What do you have in mind?"

Jake said, "At this point I'd be open to anything."

Agnes shuffled to the middle of the room where everyone could see her. She tidied her hair and straightened her stance to the point that everyone in the room started to give each other questioning looks.

Sarge repeated himself, something he didn't like to do. "Agnes, what did you have in mind?"

Agnes reached up and pulled her robe with her right hand, exposing her Vicky's Secret bra strap and right shoulder. The questioning looks had turned to expressions of confusion and concern. In what she thought was a seductive tone, Agnes explained, "Bait."

The room fell absolutely silent in disbelief. Tony leaned over to Pauli and said, "Well, that should scare him out of town." Brittany quickly crossed her legs once again to keep from peeing.

Meeting adjourned.

᠁

After the meeting, Jake and Brittany were walking toward the exit of the Precinct.

"Hey, you two." Agnes's unmistakable voice caused them to stop and turn.

"What do you need, Agnes?" Jake asked.

She pulled a cigarette from her mouth. "I was wondering if I could catch a ride with you to see Amanda for a short visit?"

Jake looked at Brittany and shrugged. "Sure, when can you be ready?"

Agnes pulled out a compact mirror and looked at herself. She adjusted a few curls, then shrugged. "About as good as it's gonna get. Let me change into something a little less cop-like. Umm… twenty minutes?"

Brittany smiled. "No problem, Agnes. We'll wait here."

After Agnes had shuffled out of the Precinct to change, Smitty hustled in. He scurried toward the Sarge's office, but before he got there he spotted Jake and Brittany nearby.

"Hey, Jake!" Smitty said. "Glad I caught you. I've been going over the reports, and there's plenty of information on the victims. However, since we have a good idea who the suspect is, I'd like to get more information on our little pharmacist prick. Criminal, medical, educational… anything else you can find."

Jake shook his head. "I can get criminal information, but for what you want we'll need Thane."

Smitty thought for a second. "We've got his laptop downstairs. Can you bring it to him?"

Jake nodded. "Sure. This will give Thane something to do besides think about Amanda."

⁓

Brittany opened the front door and motioned for Agnes to go in first.

"Hey, Manda Cakes!" Agnes said with her arms open for a hug.

Amanda smiled, then winced as she stood up to hug her grandmother.

"A little sore still, huh?" Agnes asked.

Amanda nodded, "I guess stealing a truck, jumping over a fence, running all over the zoo, and almost getting eaten by a lion can make a girl a little stiff."

Agnes smiled at being reminded of all her granddaughter had gone through over the last twenty-four hours.

"What an amazing young woman you are." Agnes hugged Amanda and then gave her an extra squeeze.

When she let go, Amanda took a step back. "Grandma, you look really different."

Amanda gave her grandmother a once-over. "No uniform? I've never seen you wearing anything but the uniform shirt and indignity bottoms."

She pointed to her grandma. "A nice blouse, kinda wide at the neck." Her voice dropped as she added, "And the indignity bottoms."

Agnes shrugged. "Hey, when a look works for me, I keep it."

Brittany smiled at the interaction between Agnes and Amanda. "Hey, you two, I'm gonna make a sandwich. Do you want something?"

Both declined.

In the kitchen, Brittany opened and closed drawers. "Amanda, did you put the silverware away?"

Amanda looked toward the kitchen. "No, I think the dishwasher is actually still running."

Brittany took a step away from the silverware drawer. "The forks, spoons, and knives are all in different slots. If you didn't change them around, who did? I swear I'm losing my mind. The other day I must have left my water running outside. There was a puddle when I came home. I'm really losing it."

Amanda shrugged. "I swear I didn't touch anything in the drawers."

Brittany shook her head. "This is so weird."

The three women talked for a while. Agnes let Amanda know that each of the goons and an extra Armenian had been taken into custody. She also filled her in about the latest developments at the Precinct.

"Oh, and we have surveillance video of those two bald goons grabbing you at the shipping dock. The video also got a nice young computer guy trying to fight those two off of you."

This comment brought a smile to Amanda's face, and her countenance lit up. She asked, "Is there any way I could go visit Thane?"

Agnes said, "Oh, Brittany, call Jake before he gets too far. He's going over to visit Thane. I'm sure he wouldn't mind bringing you with him."

Jake answered his phone. "Hey, Britz. What's up?"

Brittany explained what Agnes had suggested.

Jake smiled. "Well, I think that would help Thane feel a lot better. I'll turn around and pick her up."

Before doing so, Jake called Thane. "Hey, buddy, how ya feeling?"

The answer was a flat "Awful. I guess the day after getting a complete beat-down is when the pain really hits."

Jake sympathized, then explained what Smitty needed and mentioned that he was bringing Thane's laptop to him. Jake also told him that Monte Kurt's DNA didn't match the blood found at the scene. Jake added, "We really thought we had him. But DNA doesn't lie."

Thane responded, "So much for a couple of days off."

Jake chuckled and added, "I'm bringing some medicine that might make you feel a little better."

Thane answered, "I've already got my prescription meds."

Again, Jake chuckled. "Not that kind of medicine. I'm going to pick up Amanda. She wants to come and see you."

Thane's tone of voice brightened. "I've gotta clean up. How long 'til you get here?"

Jake laughed. "I can probably stretch it out to about forty-five minutes."

"That should work."

Jake added, "She said something about picking up some ice cream for you on our way to your apartment. But remember, Thane, she's a sharp girl. Don't let her know what you're doing."

Thane was already tidying up his living room as he talked. "Yeah, no problem. I've gotta go."

6∽

Once Jake had picked up Amanda, Agnes asked Brittany to drive her to a pharmacy. "I just need to pick up some new eyelashes," Agnes explained.

Brittany shrugged. "No problem, let's go."

The pharmacist who was on duty at the drugstore handed a customer her prescription. "Do you have any questions? All right, have a nice day."

The pharmacist looked up to see an older woman in an unusual stance with a hand on her hip. Her collar was pulled over her left shoulder. She stood with her chin down on her chest, but her eyes were looking directly at the man standing behind the counter. Then she reached down and started to pull up her hospital gown, revealing a knee-high stocking slightly rolled at the top just below her knee.

Then a young, red-headed woman walked up behind her. This woman didn't even seem to notice the man behind the counter, but he recognized her and immediately started to run her nightly routines through his head. At the moment, she just appeared to be standing behind the old lady who didn't seem to know how to keep her clothes on correctly. Agnes looked up and noticed that the pharmacist's name tag said "Monte."

His eyes were fixed on the woman over the old lady's shoulder. Agnes looked up and thought Monte's eyes were locked on her. In her mind she said, *Got ya, slime ball!*

Brittany listened to Agnes talk to the man at the desk. Her eyes widened as she realized that Agnes was trying to seduce the pharmacist.

"Hey there, big boy, could you show me where the beauty products are located?"

Brittany looked from Agnes to the pharmacist's name tag. Suddenly Brittany realized he was "The Chemist." She locked eyes with the man and felt his cold stare. Fear shot through her.

His eyes shifted to the old woman with the loose blouse. "The beauty products are over on aisle three."

Agnes smiled and put a piece of paper on the counter which read, *I'm Agnes, call me!* Under the invitation was her phone number.

Brittany stepped closer to Agnes and turned in the direction the pharmacist was pointing. As they started to walk toward aisle three, she noticed that he was staring at her and smiling. Brittany felt instant disgust. Her spine shivered as she walked away. As she did so, she looked up at one of the circular mirrors near the top of the wall. He was still staring at her and smiling.

As they got out of hearing distance from the pharmacy counter, Brittany stated, "It's him, isn't it?"

Agnes smiled. "It sure is, and he just went for my bait. Did you see how that was done, sweetie?"

♋

Sarge popped into Thane's office and saw that Mac was reviewing video from the Boomer cam. Mac shook his head, said "Nothing," and sat back in his chair.

The Sarge commented, "Doesn't look like there has been any luck tracking down Lois."

Mac invited Sarge to have a seat. "I called my contacts who are trying to get information from our Armenian friends. It looks like Lois doesn't trust anyone but herself. All her two bald helpers know is that they were supposed to join up with a cartel from Mexico. Lois wouldn't tell them anything about the deal. Gotta hand it to her; it makes it hard to track her down. I checked the Boomer cam, and the mutt is still in the van. The good thing is that when she moves that van we'll be able to listen in and hopefully figure out where she is."

Sarge smiled in appreciation of Mac's work. "You're proving your worth around here, Mac. Keep this up and I'll put you in for a permanent transfer."

Mac smiled back and replied, "I don't know. For a retirement home, a guy can really get busted up with these characters. Oh, please pass my thanks to the nut that jumped into the shark tank. He provided the distraction I needed. I'm pretty sure I couldn't have beat that hit man without the help of those rogue geezers."

Sarge pointed to Thane's computer. "Ol' Thanerboy is at home and doing some research into Lois's Chemist friend. Gotta admit that young guy had some mettle I had not expected."

Mac agreed. "You never know about men. I've learned not to judge a man until I've seen his full measure, not just a few instances here and there. This Thanerboy of yours is something special."

෨

"You actually look worse than when the lion got through with you," Amanda said with a smile.

Thane tried to rearrange his thick red hair with his fingers. "Well, they told me the bruises would show up today and I would be pretty stiff."

"You don't look so bad. I heard you gave that bald goon quite a beating," Amanda said.

Thane tried to smile but winced at the pain.

"The soldiers told me you were beating on the other brute, the one I really hated," Amanda added. "Was it true that the lion broke his leg?"

Thane nodded. "I heard it snap. Pauli and Tony sprayed the lion with pepper spray."

Amanda tilted her head. "Must have taken a lot of pepper spray. Where did they get enough to douse a lion? I've only seen those little keychain canisters." Amanda used her thumb and forefinger to show how small the keychain pepper spray cans were.

"Shot it with their walker..." Thane started to explain, then caught himself. "Tony had it in a bag on his walker. I guess old cops like to carry some sort of weapon all the time."

"The stuff really worked. Anyway..." she looked at Jake, who realized that it was his cue to leave these two alone.

"Oh, I've got to get going. When should I pick you up?"

Amanda waved into the air. "Don't worry, I'll call Brittany. You probably have to get back to work, right?"

Jake smiled and agreed. "Thane, Smitty will need those records as soon as you can finish."

Thane patted his laptop. "I'll call him as soon as I've got the information."

Jake waved and closed the door.

"Are you serious? They asked you to do some work in your condition?" Amanda asked in disbelief.

Thane tried to smile but couldn't. "Don't worry, Amanda. Those guys do a lot for the community. I'm glad I can help out."

"Well, you're not going to start working until you get some of this ice cream I told you about. Since we can't go on our date, I thought I'd bring the date to you." She opened three small containers of different flavors. "Chocolate, Peanut Butter Fudge, and Mint Chocolate Chip."

She helped Thane sit back on his couch, then she pulled up a chair and scooped up some Mint Chocolate Chip. "Taste this." She put a spoonful in his mouth. Thane had a difficult time putting his mouth around the spoon. Amanda scooped the ice cream dripping down his chin.

Thane closed his mouth. That was the best-tasting ice cream he had ever had. "That is so good."

Amanda smiled. "Told ya. This stuff is the best."

Thane strained to swallow. After a few spoonfuls he said, "I don't think I can eat any more, but thank you, Amanda, it is really good."

Again she smiled, "I'll put this in the freezer compartment of your fridge so you can have it when you feel better."

Amanda walked over to the fridge and opened it. After seeing its contents, she looked at Thane. "I take it you didn't have much notice we were coming."

Thane could not lean his head upward to where she was standing. "Why?"

She opened the refrigerator the rest of the way to reveal all the dishes that had previously been in the sink. She pulled them out, and the sound reminded Thane where he had tried to hide the dirty dishes.

"Sorry, I was going to get to those." Thane stretched out on the couch. "This is embarrassing." The prescribed painkillers were taking effect, and he started to doze off.

Amanda loaded Thane's dishwasher and cleaned up the rest of his kitchen, then called Brittany. "Hey, Britz, can you come pick me up? Thane needs to sleep for a while. Okay, I'll see you soon."

After sitting down in the chair next to Thane, Amanda watched him for a while. She thought about what they had been through during the last couple of days. She had only seen and talked to him a few times since she started working with these crazy old cops. Then there was the fact that he had made her name his password, which was sweet in a nerdy kind of way. Her grandmother liked him, and that spoke volumes.

"What an interesting guy," she said. With the back of her hand, she lightly stroked his face. His eyes opened and he tried to smile. She could not help herself; she was really attracted to this man who had taken such a beating for her. Smiling, she leaned over to give him a kiss. After planting a sweet little smooch on Thane's upper lip, she sat back.

Thane let out a frustrated sound.

"What's wrong?" Amanda asked.

Thane let out another disheartened sigh. "The first time I get to kiss a girl and I can't pucker up my lips."

Amanda laughed. "I think there will be plenty more where that came from once you're feeling better."

Thane gave a half-smile. "I hope so."

Brittany's knock on the door signaled the end of their time together. "The faster you start feeling better, the quicker you can work on that pucker of yours," she teased.

The door closed and Thane waited until he heard Brittany's car drive off. Once he was sure they were gone, he popped open his good eye, forced himself up, and looked around for his laptop. "I'm gonna get that guy."

With the information he had received on Monte Kurt, Thane started drilling into his background: schools, criminal history, addresses, and medical background.

"I can't believe I'm doing this. Amanda was right here and wanted to be with me, but I had to act like I was dozing off so she'd leave." Then Thane thought about what those men had been planning to do to her. Something inside of Thane burned with those thoughts. "I'm gonna know everything about you, Monte. You're not gonna get away with this."

After a few hours on his laptop, Thane had gone through all of Monte's educational records, places he had lived, and the very few entries on his criminal history and his records with the Department of Motor Vehicles. Then he started on Monte's medical history. Thane looked for Emergency Room visits and medical procedures. Then he paused. "Lymphoma?" A few years back Monte had been treated for lymphoma, a type of cancer.

Thane saw that Monte had received a bone marrow transplant, which is not unusual in treating that condition. Under that category of treatments was the asterisked statement "See side effects." This piqued Thane's curiosity. As he read about the side effects of a bone marrow transplant, he suddenly looked up.

Thane slammed his laptop closed and called Jake. "I need you to come pick me up as soon as possible. Call the Precinct and tell everyone to meet in the conference room. Twenty minutes? That's fine; see you then."

Thane sat back, looked up at the ceiling and in a disbelieving tone said, "He's a freakin' Chimera!"

&

Smitty stuck his head into Thane and Mac's office. "Hey, Mac."

Taking off his headphones, Mac turned.

"Sarge wants all of us in the conference room," Smitty said. "Thane is on his way here with Jake and says he found some information that will help us with the investigation into this Chemist character."

Mac shrugged. "Okay, sounds fun to me. Hey, Smitty, how do I get one of those ear communicators?"

Smitty smiled and leaned against the door frame. "Well, now, we don't just give them out to any top secret, black ops, nobody knows what he really does guy that walks through this door."

Mac folded his arms. "Well, Ol' Sarge asked me about staying on here."

Smitty smiled as he looked toward the supply room. "Well, I'll have to take you to the supply room supervisors," he said with a mischievous smirk.

CHAPTER 19

Her phone rang. "Finally," Lois said out loud. She answered, and without any exchange of pleasantries she listened.

"The safe house has been established, and a security detail has been assembled. You will have four assistants. You will train them so that they can perform the same functions as your previous associates."

Lois listened as her contact provided directions to the location of her new base of operations.

"You will be there tomorrow at noon. My employers do not want any more delays. Do you understand?"

Lois cleared her throat. "Of course. I will see you tomorrow."

After she hung up, she looked over to where the van was parked. "I'm stuck with that thing for one more day."

෴

Sarge contacted the task force to meet in the lower level after dinner but before med call. At that time it would be easy for the officers to slip away unnoticed.

Jake called Thane to offer a ride, explaining, "The way you look, we better bring you in through the tunnels." Then Jake picked up his phone again and called the Precinct to make the arrangements.

After driving down the utility road at the rear of the facility, Jake parked next to the maintenance garage. As he and Thane walked into the building, an Ol' Blue was sitting next to the door and reading a magazine. He looked up and said, "Hi ya, Junior."

Jake smiled and said, "Two going down." The Blue turned an oil can and the hissing of the car lift soon revealed the elevator. Jake shook his head and said, "That is so cool."

When Jake and Thane got off the elevator, another Blue in a golf cart was waiting for them. "Hop in... Whoa there, Thane what happened?"

Jake answered for him: "You should see the other guy."

Once in the conference area they went to the room where the meeting would take place. They took one step in and then stopped. Smitty had taken over the big table with photos, divided the reports of sexual assaults into categories, and had lined up the reports in chronological order.

"Smitty is amazing," Jake observed.

Thane walked to the far end of the table where there was a small section that Smitty had not covered...yet. He was setting up his computer as the other members of the task force walked in—Sarge, the Chelini brothers, Big Brock, Benson, and finally Agnes, whose arrival was announced by the squeaking of her oxygen tank holder. Smitty was already waiting for everyone.

Once the task force had gathered, everyone's hand went to their ear. "Testing one, two, three... testing."

Agnes inquired, "Who's the yutz playing with the communication earpiece?"

Smitty smiled as Mac walked around the corner with his hand on his earpiece. He was so wrapped up in using the communication device that he didn't notice that the conference room was full of people who were staring at him.

"Can anyone hear me?" Mac asked.

Sarge spoke first. "Take your finger off the transmitter button!"

Mac looked up and found that he had become a source of annoyance to everyone in the room. Then he realized that he was also speaking into the earpieces of everyone upstairs. He stopped in his tracks and said, "Oh, sorry. Um, these are really cool communication gizmos."

Sarge took his seat at the head of the table. "I'm glad you like them. We like them, too... especially when they are used correctly."

Mac replied, "Sorry, Sarge, I had to get back here for this meeting and could not get fully trained by those two with the electric spark show in Supply."

This comment put a smile on Sarge's face. "Yeah, those two don't get out much."

Then Sarge got down to business. "Now for the purpose of this meeting. Looks like our Armenian friends are guests of the U.S. Government...somewhere only Mac knows."

Mac smiled and said, "The two bald goons are singing like birds. The hit man, Aziz, is going to be harder to break."

Smitty spoke up. "His penmanship probably won't be quite up to par for a while, either."

Mac and Smitty shared a private laugh.

"The only remaining pieces of business are Lois and the Chemist, Monte Kurt," the Sarge said.

Jake spoke up. "Sorry, folks, we thought we had him. DNA is a slam dunk nowadays."

Agnes gave a sarcastic cough accompanied by a snide remark.

"All right, Agnes, that's enough," the Sarge responded.

"No problem, Sarge, I've already started the beginning stages of my old-school investigation."

Agnes looked at Jake and announced proudly, "I gave Brittany her first lesson."

Jake gave her a questioning gaze.

"Looks like he sold the house in Kennard," Thane said, typing and looking at the screen of his laptop.

Smitty commented, "I'd say he's cashing out. My bet is he's building up some cash and about to skedaddle." There were nods of agreement from around the table.

"Your DNA evidence didn't fail you, Jake," Thane said.

Everyone looked at Thane for an explanation. Agnes was surprised that he was present for the meeting. "Cripes, Thane!

You look terrible. Shouldn't you be at home recovering from all..." She pointed at Thane's face and arms: "that."

Thane looked up at everyone, then down at his computer and muttered, *"That Chemist done wronged my woman, and I'm gonna make him pay!"*

Every mouth in the room dropped open in disbelief at what they had just heard.

Mac looked at Sarge and then quietly said, "What did I tell you? It's often guys like this that surprise you."

Thane ignored everyone in the room and kept tapping away on his keyboard. "The reason your DNA test didn't fail you was because it didn't fail you."

Jake spoke up. "That doesn't make any sense, Thane. If the test didn't prove it was his DNA, it failed."

Thane smiled. "It didn't fail because it revealed someone else's DNA." Thane smiled... sort of.

Pauli leaned over to Tony and asked, "How hard did they hit this guy?"

Thane stood up and announced, "The Chemist is a Chimera."

Big Brock asked, "What's his religion got to do with it?"

Benson added, "I think I heard of them. Aren't the Chimeras the ones that don't believe in blood transfusions?"

Thane rolled his good eye. "No, you're completely wrong about Chimeras being a religion. A Chimera is a mythical creature made up of different attributes of other beings—like a person with a human upper torso, but a goat's legs. One of the reasons they exist is bone marrow transplants."

Mac spoke up this time. "In English, Thane."

"I looked through Monte Kurt's medical files and learned that he had a bout with lymphoma that resulted in a bone marrow transplant a couple of years ago," Thane explained.

Everyone looked at each other as if trying to determine whether anyone comprehended Thane's point.

"Blood cells are made in bone marrow," Thane explained. "The DNA in your blood is linked to your bone marrow. If you put someone else's bone marrow in your body with a transplant..."

Jake finished Thane's sentence: "It will change the DNA in the blood! That sneaky, slimy pig! No wonder he gave us the blood sample. He knew that his DNA was not the same as it had been when he had assaulted those women."

Jake slammed his fist on the table. "He's been laughing at us the whole time. He acted like he was nervous and so we would think he was guilty. When he initially declined to give us a blood sample, we were sure we had him. Then he decided to give it to us, knowing his DNA had changed after the transplant."

Thane summed up Monte Kurt's condition: "He's one person with two different DNAs."

"This guy is very slick, but now we're on to him," Smitty said. "Now that I know more about this guy, I can tell you about his victims. Each of the women who were assaulted told the investigating officers that they had thought they were losing their minds because things at their house or apartment were missing or moved around. Lights were turned on while they were away, and something was always just slightly wrong when they returned home."

"These women had all kinds of self-doubt." Smitty rubbed his chin. "It sounds like this guy enjoys playing with his victims before attacking them. Afterward, they can't remember what happened. They called him the Chemist for a reason. I'll bet he gets a kick out of watching the girls think they are going crazy. He drugs them up and assaults them while they are defenseless."

Mac said, "Now that the Armenians are not in the picture, he's probably going back to his old ways. Jake, I'll bet you'll have some cases real soon with young women who think they are going crazy and can't remember what day it is."

Jake replied, "I'll check it out when I get back to Central. Thane, do you need a ride home?"

Thane waved the question off. "I'm here now, so I might as well get over to my office and see what else I can dig up on this guy."

Jake looked at Sarge and asked, "Anything else Sarge?"

Shaking his head, the Sarge answered, "Not that I can think of. Anybody else?"

There was no response.

"Okay, then. Smitty, Jake, and Thane—keep digging. The rest of you, it is end of shift so go and get some rest. I think we are really going to be busy over the next couple of days."

Benson turned to Big Brock and said, "I could go for something to eat. How about you?"

Big Brock smiled and said, "You know it."

∽

As Agnes shuffled to her apartment, she reflected on what Smitty had said about Monte Kurt. *This animal likes to torment the girls before he assaults them. He's afraid to confront them directly, so he stays in the shadows. He enjoys making them feel like they are losing control of their minds.* She entered her apartment, and as she closed the door she said out loud, "What a sick piece of—" Her sentence was interrupted by her phone ringing.

The caller ID told her it was Amanda. "Hi ya, Manda Cakes. How are you feeling?"

They exchanged pleasantries and Amanda told Agnes about her visit with Thane. "He is the sweetest man I've ever met. The guy has been so wrapped up in his work that he's never had a girlfriend."

Agnes listened and smiled as her granddaughter spoke. She knew that Amanda had never had someone she could talk to about her life since she was taken from her mother as a small child.

"I'll probably stay here a couple more days and come home," Amanda said. "Oh, Brittany just walked in." There was a pause as Agnes heard Amanda say, "Hey, Britz."

Agnes could hear Brittany in the background as Amanda said, loud enough for Brittany to hear, "I think I better come home; I think I'm driving Britz crazy." She laughed as she spoke. "Brittany must be getting nervous about getting married. She went into her living room earlier and swore that her collection of little figurines that she keeps on her shelf had all been turned and faced a different way."

Brittany walked closer to the phone and spoke so that Agnes could hear her. "Between the squad of saggy diapers over there and this granddaughter of yours, I'm losing my mind!" They all laughed.

"Anyway, Grandma, just wanted to say goodnight to you."

"Okay, luv. I'm gonna shower and call it a night. Bye."

A few minutes later, Agnes stood in her shower and let the warm water help her relax. Suddenly she realized she had forgotten to take off her makeup and eyelashes. The right side of her face was purple and blue, and her extra-long eyelashes were stuck on her cheek.

"Ah, cripes!" She groaned. Agnes stepped out of the shower and looked at herself in the mirror. Her purple curls were drooping over her face. She smiled at the sight of the eyelashes on her cheek. "They don't belong there," she said out loud. She started to peel the lashes from her cheek and had them about halfway off when she froze.

"It doesn't belong there?" Suddenly she realized that Brittany had said the same words a couple of times in the last few days. Then she remembered something that Smitty had said during the meeting. All the victims thought they were losing their minds. Things had been moved around...

"CRIPES!" she screamed. "He's going after the girls!"

She grabbed her hospital gown and tried to put it on as quickly as possible. At the same time, Agnes was trying to figure out how the Chemist had found the girls. She said out loud, "Amanda was at Brittany's house. There's no way he could have found her. We didn't plan it in advance; we just decided to have her go that day. She packed up and..."

Then Agnes realized how the Chemist had found the girls. "Her prescription—we put Brittany's address on Amanda's prescription for her seizure meds. That pharmacist slimeball got the address from her prescription."

Without thinking about what she was—or was not—wearing, Agnes shuffled out of her apartment. She was still dripping wet, with makeup dripping from her face and the extra-long eyelashes still dangling from her cheek.

6o

"Blueberry pie. I saw it in the kitchen," Big Brock said while rubbing his hands together.

Benson added, "I had some at dinner. The thought of the deep blue juice from that pie is making my mouth water."

Suddenly around the corner shuffled Agnes. She almost plowed face first into Big Brock. The two men took a step back as she looked up at them and shouted, "Outta my way I gotta get to the Sarge."

Both men looked at the bluish-purple liquid trailing down Agnes's face. Their initial shock at her appearance caused both men to look at each other in disbelief. As she scooted by, they were presented with an appetite-suppressing view of Agnes's wrinkled posterior. Both men looked at each other and simultaneously shook their heads.

"She did it again," Benson mumbled. "I'll never eat another raisin as long as I live."

Big Brock added, "From now on I'll see a giant eyelash in the blueberry pie."

"The Chemist is going after the girls!" Agnes yelled as she moved away. As she approached a corner, the combination of dripping wet feet and a tile floor caused Agnes's feet to slip out from underneath her.

Boss Nurse heard the commotion and watched as Agnes slid around the corner. "Oh, no!" she yelled as Agnes's walker flipped into the air and Agnes's feet followed and she landed flat on her back. Agnes was motionless on the floor, dazed and confused by what had just happened to her.

Boss Nurse called for help from other nurses in the area. "Fall! We have a fall by the cafeteria entrance!"

Within seconds nurses were running to Agnes's aid. A brace was placed around her neck, and she was checked for bleeding. The wind had been knocked out of Agnes's lungs, which held very little air in the first place because of her emphysema.

Boss Nurse saw that Agnes was struggling to breathe. "Oxygen!" she yelled into her radio.

"It's on the way" was the response.

Agnes was placed on a gurney and wheeled back to her apartment with an oxygen mask over her mouth and nose. With panic in her eyes, she looked at Brock and Benson as she passed them, frantically waving her hand and pointing toward the Sarge's apartment. Both men nodded, and Benson tried to contact Sarge via his ear communicator. No luck.

"He must have taken it off to go to bed," Benson said to Big Brock as the two men rushed to Sarge's apartment.

By the time they knocked at the Sarge's door, Agnes was in her apartment. The nurses were trying to comfort her. Slowly Agnes started to breathe, between coughing fits.

"Sarge, she was dripping wet when she scurried by us," Benson said. "Agnes told us she needed to see you. Must have been important. She slipped on the floor and fell pretty hard. You better come and check on her."

Sarge immediately put down the photo of his departed wife and pulled on a bathrobe. "Let's go." Once they arrived at Agnes's apartment, they saw Boss Nurse and three other nurses trying to help Agnes recover. She was conscious but gasping for air between coughs.

"Wait outside," commanded one of the nurses.

Boss Nurse straightened up with her hands on her hips. "I don't like how much she has to struggle to breathe. Call a squad."

Sarge knew Agnes needed to see him for an important reason. She was desperately looking at him from the gurney. Sarge said to Big Brock and Benson, "She has something to tell me."

Benson told the Sarge, "When she went by us, she said that the Chemist is after the girls."

"We already know that he's after girls," Sarge responded. "There's something more."

⸎

Thane had gone through various aspects of Monte Kurt's background. He had already learned about the Chemist's bone marrow transplant and how he had fooled the investigators with the DNA test. There was nothing suspicious about his educational background. The house in Kennard had been sold. Thane leaned back in his chair, rubbing his sore temples.

"What else is left?" Thane said out loud, then looked at a category he had not explored before. "Traffic and motor vehicle information. Hmmm." Thane shrugged. "What could it hurt?"

"No tickets, no accidents. The guy's clean as far as traffic is concerned." Then Thane clicked on vehicle registration.

⸎

Brittany's phone rang. It was Jake.

"Hey, Babe, how was the meeting?" Brittany looked around to make sure Amanda was out of earshot. She listened as Jake told her about Thane's findings on Monte Kurt's DNA.

"Are you kidding? Agnes asked me to take her to a pharmacy and was trying to seduce the guy at the pharmacy counter. I looked at his nametag and realized he was this Monte Kurt guy. Jake, my skin crawled. He seemed to be watching every step I took. I even looked into the aisle mirror and he was still watching me."

As Jake listened to Brittany, he gripped his steering wheel more tightly. "Does that guy just stare at pretty women? Doesn't sound like what he normally does. He would not be so obvious about it. If he looked at women like that, he would be noticed, and from what Smitty had to say about him, this guy doesn't like to be noticed. I don't know what to tell you, Brittany. We're working on a case against him, but at this point it's weak."

Jake thought to himself, *Brittany is sharp. If something bothers her, she's probably right to be concerned about it.*

&

The paramedic squad from the Omaha Fire Department arrived and attempted to get Agnes to cooperate. When she slapped the blood pressure cuff away, they knew that starting an IV would be out of the question. The firemen firmly but gently kept her on the gurney and wheeled her out of her apartment.

As Agnes was transported down the hallway, Meter Maid Mary rolled up to see what was going on. Agnes was still having coughing fits, and her face was turning a light shade of blue. The oxygen level in her blood was getting low.

Agnes locked eyes with Mary and pulled the oxygen mask off her mouth long enough to blurt out, "Stop 'em."

The firemen repeatedly told Agnes to calm down and to try to take deep breaths.

"Let go of me, you stinking hosers!" Agnes protested.

Mary zipped through the cafeteria, recruiting Blues as she went.

The fireman finally got Agnes to the ambulance. She was lifted up into the back and her gurney was locked into position. It took three firemen to hold her down.

"Now, ma'am, don't make me strap you down. We do need to put at least one belt around you to keep you from falling off the gurney."

The driver started the engine. As the emergency flashers came to life, the driver put the vehicle into gear, then he froze. Through the windshield he saw a woman in a wheelchair staring at him with the biggest eyes he had ever seen. He hit the brakes and put the vehicle back into Park.

The rear doors had not been closed yet. Agnes's breathing was getting better. She was in pain from her fall but breathing on her own now. She pointed to the mask and told the fireman, "You can take this off now."

He looked at her and smiled. "I don't think so, ma'am. How are you feeling?"

Agnes tried to use her sweetest little-old-lady voice. "I just got the wind knocked out of me, young man. Could you please help me sit up?"

The fireman said, "No problem."

After Agnes was sitting up, she smiled and said, "Oh, that's much better. I'm a little sore, but I feel…"

She was cut off by the driver yelling through the portal into the bay of the ambulance.

"Hey, guys, there's a lady in a wheelchair and four old men on the ground in front of us."

Agnes looked at the two firemen who were attending her and told them, "Oh, I'm fine. Get out there and help those people that collapsed."

The driver put the vehicle into Park, and all the squad members ran to the people in front of the ambulance.

Agnes looked down and unlatched the seatbelt holding her in the gurney. Once free, she grabbed nearby equipment for support and shuffled through the portal into the driver's seat.

The flashing emergency lights were already on. Agnes put the vehicle into Drive and turned sharply to the left. The firemen let out a string of curses when they realized that their ambulance was leaving without them. Agnes hit the gas, steering clear of the Blues on the ground.

The firemen tried to chase the vehicle on foot but were unable to catch up. They stood dumbstruck, watching the ambulance depart in a cloud of dust. They looked at each other in disbelief as they realized that the old people who had been lying on the ground were gone. The woman in the wheelchair was watching them. She pointed to the three stupefied men and at the ambulance leaving the parking lot, commenting, "Your Chief ain't gonna like this."

The 911 dispatch center was a picture of modern technology. Both the police and fire department communication units were housed in the facility. Whenever an emergency call was received, it was quickly processed and sent to the proper unit for response. Then the police or fire dispatcher would get the needed information and pass it along to the responding units. This procedure has been refined and streamlined to reduce response times. Proper police and fire protocol is a must to keep the radio channels from being tied up with anything but professional communications.

Suddenly the fire dispatcher's headphones blasted the voice of a female. "HQ, HQ! Officer Agnes Crantz calling, over. HQ, do you read? Over. HQ, do you read? Over."

The dispatcher turned on the speaker phone so that the other dispatchers could hear. "This is the Douglas County Emergency Communications Center. You are not authorized to utilize this radio channel. Get off this channel immediately."

"Negative, HQ. Patch me through to Jake Mitchell in the Police Chief's Office, over."

The Fire Dispatch Supervisor got on the radio. "This is Fire Department Dispatch. You are not authorized to be on this radio. Discontinue this transmission immediately."

"Clam it, bub! This is Lead Officer Crantz of the Old Blues Precinct with a priority radio call. Now patch me to Jake Mitchell in the Police Department, over."

The supervisor almost fell out of his chair. He yelled over to the police dispatchers across the hall. After filling them in on what was occurring in the fire dispatch, the supervisor decided to dump this on the police dispatch supervisor.

"Omaha Fire Dispatch to Lead Officer Crantz, you are being transferred to Omaha Police Dispatch. Uh, over."

As the Public Information Officer for the Chief of Police, Jake always had his radio with him in case of urgent business. His radio jolted his attention.

"Chief's Office Radio Three, Chief's Office Radio Three."

Jake answered, "Radio Three to dispatch, go ahead."

After a short pause, Jake heard, "Radio Three, stand by for a transmission." Jake looked at his radio. "That's odd." At the same time his phone buzzed with a text message. He glanced at his phone while waiting for the transmission. The text was from Thane: "Monte Kurt drives a blue PT Cruiser!"

At first Jake didn't understand why he was being told what Monte Kurt drove. Then his radio transmitted "Officer Agnes Crantz to Jake Mitchell, do you read? Over."

Jake was stunned to be talking over the radio to Agnes. He wanted to make sure Agnes understood what she was doing.

"Officer Crantz, this transmission is being monitored. Do you understand?"

The answer was short. "Roger that, Jake. Manda Cakes and Britz are next for the Chemist. Do you understand? Over. I am heading that way right now. Over."

Jake understood that Agnes was going over to Brittany's house.

"That's clear. Agnes, let's stay off this radio channel. Chief's Office Three out. Radio resume normal air."

The staff at E.M.S. Dispatch was dumbfounded. "Well, if the Chief's Office knows about it, I guess it's all right," the supervisor concluded with a shrug.

After the radio exchange, Jake contacted Dispatch for a wellness check and provided Brittany's address. Officers were dispatched and advised to contact Jake upon determining a disposition.

⁓

Thane contacted Sarge and the rest of the task force.

"This is Thane. I've discovered some information that should be helpful. Jake told me that he has noticed a Blue PT Cruiser around Brittany's house at various times. Once he said that the occupant hid his face from him as he drove by. Jake said that if he was back in a cruiser he would have *turned on him*, whatever that means."

Sarge listened and said, "So the person in this PT Cruiser was suspicious. Does that relate to what you've found?"

Thane keyed his headpiece and replied, "Definitely does. Monte Kurt drives a Blue PT Cruiser."

The Sarge announced, "I'm calling Jake. He can get someone to Brittany's house faster than we can. I'll advise when I'm finished. Until then, everyone get ready to respond to Brittany's house if needed."

Jake answered his phone. After hearing what Sarge had to say, he replied, "Yes, Thane texted me and I have a couple of officers heading over to Brittany's house right now. Do you know where Agnes is? I just got a radio transmission from the Fire Department."

Brock filled the Sarge in on recent developments while Jake waited on the other end of the line.

"She may have borrowed the Fire Department's ambulance. My guess is that she is heading to Brittany's house now. We stopped the ambulance from leaving and we thought she was going to get out, but she... ummm... took it."

The cigar fell from Sarge's mouth.

6⁷

Brittany was unaware that she was being scrutinized closely as she and Amanda were getting ready to drink their nightly glass of juice. From his vantage point, Monte Kurt smiled as he watched the two of them engaging in some silly talk. They were laughing, and Amanda turned the television on.

He watched more intently as Brittany filled both of the glasses and put them on a tray. It was the same pitcher of juice to which he had added his knockout cocktail in the early morning hours after turning Brittany's figurines in different directions. Later that afternoon he had smiled and watched as Brittany put her hands on her hips, looked at her little collection, and then returned the figurines to their original positions.

"Any minute now," Monte said to himself. He watched as Brittany carried the tray with the drinks and pitcher into the living room where Amanda was waiting. Monte rubbed his hands together in anticipation.

Suddenly red and blue lights were flashing in the windows. Both Brittany and Amanda looked out the living room window. They screamed and Brittany dropped the tray, spilling the pitcher and glasses. An ambulance left the road in front of the house and slid on the grass and driveway, then rolled to a stop on the front lawn, five feet from where they stood.

Brittany pointed and said, "Is that…"

"Grandma?" Amanda cut her off.

They ran outside. Agnes was sitting in the driver's seat of the ambulance, looking around frantically until she laid eyes on the girls.

"I was worried sick! I totally pissed off some firemen after I borrowed their ride," Agnes said.

Amanda was trying to understand what she was looking at. *The ambulance with the lights on, the red and blue lights lit up the dust all around the ambulance that had stopped on Brittany's lawn. Oh, and Grandma was driving!*

"Grandma, what are you doing here in that…" She pointed to the ambulance.

Agnes was struggling to answer her question as two police cars drove up to the house. One of the officers got out of a cruiser and walked up to the trio. "Umm. What's going on here?" The other officer was on the radio as his partner was talking to the women.

"I'm sorry, Officer, I must have gotten confused," Agnes said in her sweet-little-old-woman's voice. "I thought I could use the car since I was a police officer."

The other officer walked up and heard her explanation. They looked at each other and rolled their eyes.

"The Fire Department wants their ambulance back. Would it be all right if we had them come pick it up?" The officers spoke to Agnes as if she was just a confused old woman.

She played along. "Oh, that would be fine. Would you thank those nice firemen for me?"

Once the officers had called in the location of the Fire Department's missing ambulance, they walked over to the women. One of the officers asked, "Is this your house?"

Brittany answered, "Yes, I live here. Hey, I didn't tell her to take that ambulance."

The officer shook his head. "Nope, we were sent out here for a wellness check. It looks like you're... well. Um, is there any problem here besides an old lady who can't park?"

"No, Officer, everything is fine. Why?"

Just then Jake's car could be heard speeding up to the house. He got out, ran to Brittany, and hugged her.

"Jake, what is going on?"

Jake spoke to the officers. "I'm from the Chief's Office. We got a call informing us that there may have been a disturbance here. Must have been because of this lady taking the ambulance. She got on the radio and caused all sorts of problems at the communications center."

The officers laughed, and one of them said, "Well, I'll call Dispatch and have them send the firemen to pick this up."

"Thanks, guys. I'll take care of this." He pointed to Agnes.

The officers gave a thumbs up and returned to their cruisers to wait for the firefighters and give them a good bit of jibing for having their vehicle stolen by an old lady.

"Come inside. We need to talk," Jake said.

Once they were inside, Jake explained that they had been able to determine that the Chemist, Monte Kurt, had found out where Brittany lived and somehow figured out that Amanda was here, too.

Agnes chimed in, telling Brittany, "Her prescription—I had you fill it and gave the pharmacy your address. That must have been how he found it." Outside, things seemed to be settling down.

Putting down his binoculars, Monte was paralyzed with disbelief as he realized that his well-thought-out plan had completely unraveled. He turned, made his way back to where his car was hidden, and then drove away into the night. In his rearview mirror he could see the commotion at the house. He was glad he had parked his car at a different spot. Since he was planning on going after the girls tonight, he wanted the car parked where it would not be spotted from the street.

"What was an ambulance doing there, and the police?" The eyes in the mirror shifted from the house to stare directly at him. "This could not have been some coincidence. Somebody figured out what was going on, but who?"

⌀

Lois heard her phone ring. "Well, now, this is a pleasant surprise," she said to the caller.

"What's going on? I've been staying low for a few days and have not heard anything from you. Did you ever get together with the new cartel?"

Lois replied, "Yes, and I have been given control to set up my organization as I see fit. The Mexicans are very accommodating. They are in the process of setting up a safe house complete with a staff and security team. I should be moving in later today. Can you meet me at the safe house?"

Monte thought for a second. This last experience of working on his own had given him a bit of a scare. It would be nice to have some sort of security detail involved.

"Yes, let me know when it is ready."

CHAPTER 20

The countryside of Nebraska is beautiful, and there are plenty of farmhouses that can be purchased by those who want privacy and enough space between houses to ensure seclusion. With these features in mind, the Mexican cartel had selected a house that would serve as an ideal base for Lois's operations.

"I am texting you the address. Bring your equipment and be here in about two hours. Is that a problem?"

Lois was relieved to hear that the safe house was going to be a reality. "I will be there. I will also have the Chemist that I told you about. He is essential to the operation and has served us well."

"Don't make us wait."

Lois hung up. "Finally," she said out loud. Then she looked at the moving van. "Soon I will be finished with that thing."

⌾

The task force was meeting in Sarge's office.

"I'm at a loss. We don't have any leads where Lois or Monte the Chemist are. They have just disappeared," Sarge said.

Smitty spoke up. "My guess is that he was watching the other night when Agnes made her grand entrance with the stolen ambulance. Then the cops showed up. If he was watching, that would have put a real scare into this cockroach. Once the lights

416 | DA BROAD SQUAD

turn on, he disappears. Now that he has the money from selling the house in Kennard, he could go anywhere."

Pacing around the room, Smitty tried to predict the most likely behavior of Monte Kurt. "Then again, it may have scared him back to looking for protection. From what Mac said, Lois was establishing ties with a Mexican cartel. She would be foolish not to keep her Chemist. That guy provided quite a service to them."

Sarge added, "Lois could provide that protection again if her new bosses were helping her set up her little women's trafficking outfit in a new location. The two of them could get the ball rolling again really soon. We've got to find out where they are and figure out how to stop them."

The communication devices in everyone's ears blared, "Hey, Sarge, this is Mac. Can you hear me?"

Sarge answered, "You're loud and clear, Mac. What do you need?"

Mac announced, "I don't know where they are going, but the van looks to be moving. I can see that the pooch cam is bouncing, and shadows are moving like the van is in motion. Our friend Lois may finally be moving her operation."

The Sarge looked at each person in the room. "That's the first piece of news that could help us locate Lois. We'll wrap things up here and I'll be down in a couple of minutes, Mac."

Sarge asked the task force, "Anything else?"

Frustration was evident on the faces of everyone in the room. Agnes took a puff of her cigarette and said, "Unfortunately, there's nothing else."

Jake shrugged. "At least we stopped him from doing what he wanted to do."

Smitty stopped pacing, then turned and faced Jake. "Exactly! He didn't get to do what he really wanted to do. My guess is that he's not going to let this go. Remember how he was in the parking lot. From what Big Brock said, the guy had fire in his eyes. I'll bet Brittany and Amanda haven't heard the last from this guy. In his mind they are unfulfilled business that he doesn't want to leave."

Sarge closed the meeting. "We'll keep that in mind, Smitty. Thanks."

Then Sarge rubbed his chin. "Lois will be harder to catch, but if we don't, a lot of young women's lives are at stake."

❧

Thane looked at Mac and said, "She's gonna get away, isn't she? I mean, we have no way of figuring out where Lois and her Mexican buddies are located."

Mac sat back in his chair. "All we can do is see what's on the pooch cam. If they throw Boomer in a ditch somewhere, there's not much we can do."

Then Mac reached over and tapped the monitor. "She does seem to be doing quite a bit of driving. My guess is she will be somewhere in the country. That would make sense. Some of those country houses are very secluded. She could do a lot of damage in the middle of nowhere and never be noticed."

"That's my fear as well," Sarge said as he walked into Thane and Mac's work space. "She has received protection from the new cartel, a new base of operations, and we have no clue how to locate her. Once she gets started, nobody will be able to stop her."

❧

The dirt road leading to the farmhouse was difficult to find.

"This is perfect. The nearest house is at least two miles away."

Lois was clearly impressed with the effort that the Mexicans had made to get her a base of operations.

"Nobody will be able to find us out here," she said out loud, smiling in satisfaction.

Eight men were standing on the porch as she took the van up the long driveway and then parked it. Six of the men walked over to her door and opened it, motioning for her to get out. When she did so, they checked her for weapons.

"Just a precaution; I'm sure you understand."

Lois nodded. "Of course, and I'm sure that once we get our joint operation up and running, these searches will not be necessary."

"I hope you will be able to back up what you've said. We've spent a great deal of money to provide this little private office for you."

Lois recognized the voice as the one that she had spoken to so often on the phone.

"You are Miguel?"

The man smiled. "These men will unload your van and set you up in the house."

6✧

Mac's monitor brightened, and the change caught his eye.

"Hey, looks like the door to the van has been opened." Mac checked to make sure the video was being recorded.

Thane looked over and asked Mac, "What's going on?"

Mac tapped the monitor. "Looks like Lois has arrived at wherever she is going to set up shop."

In the monitor the cameras from Boomer's eyes were facing the sliding door of the van. The door opened to reveal four to five Latino-looking men. All of their faces flinched in shock at the sight of Boomer staring at them.

"Aye! Que es esto?" The men looked back and forth at each other.

"Don't have to translate that. Ol' Boomer scared the crapola out of those guys," Mac said with a laugh.

"Can you see anything?" Thane asked.

Mac tried to look past the men. "Nothing but cornfields."

Then he added sarcastically, "That should narrow it down in Nebraska."

The men went to work unloading everything in the van and putting it in the house. Thane watched and said, "I don't see anything—no landmarks, nothing that would help us figure out where this house is."

Boomer was placed in the living room of the house and the office supplies were placed in a large room that had been renovated with additional electrical outlets and cable lines for Lois to use.

"This will do nicely," Lois said to Miguel.

She pointed to the man who seemed to be watching everything that was going on. "I take it he is your employer. Tell him that this will work well. I will have young women for you within the week."

Miguel translated what Lois was saying into Spanish for the man that was obviously the boss. He smiled and answered in Spanish. Miguel turned to Lois and explained, "He says that would be acceptable."

"Sarge, I can't make out anything that would help us place her on a map," Mac said. "She's about to start grabbing those girls and we can't do a thing to stop her." Frustrated, he started pacing back and forth.

"I wouldn't even know what section of Nebraska or Iowa to point a satellite. I mean, we've got absolutely nothing."

Mac pointed to the monitor. "All we can do now is hope she doesn't throw out Boomer, then helplessly watch her as these girls are doped up, dragged to this house and pumped so full of heroin that they can't think straight."

Sarge touched his earpiece and said, "Shakey, come down to Thane's office."

After a few minutes the elevator opened. Out walked Shakey with his quivering hands. As he came into the room, Mac and Thane looked at each other and then at Sarge.

"Is Lois in that big room now?" Mac looked at the monitor. "Yep, she's talking to a couple of the cartel guys."

Thane added, "One of them doesn't seem to be moving very much. He looks like he's the boss."

The men all listened to the conversation between Lois, the interpreter Miguel, and the mysterious boss.

Lois looked around and commented, "This house is really large. It's much larger than we'll need."

Miguel smiled and agreed, "Yes, it's very large. This operation will be bigger than you can imagine." He looked at his boss for approval to tell Lois the big-picture plans for the operation. The man nodded his assent.

"Lois, this house will be part of a much bigger operation. We already have a network of people in central and south America. Many parents will give us their daughters if we tell them that they will be taken to the United States for jobs. The families are told that when the girls are paid, monthly payments will be sent to their parents. These families are so poor that they will give us their daughters without asking too many questions. There are approximately one hundred young women in the process of being smuggled from various countries to the United States. Once they arrive, we will need this part of the operation to prep them to work in the sex industry. It will be an excellent contribution to the cartel."

"Did you hear that!" Thane yelled. "These Mexican banditos will destroy them just as the Armenians did, but on a much larger scale. Once they're no longer useful, they're dead."

Thane asked, "Seriously, we can't do anything about this?"

Mac threw his hands in the air. "A bunch of girls are about to die a slow, painful death, and all we can do is watch."

Shakey reached into his pocket and pulled out a cell phone. Then he looked over at the Sarge.

"Make the call," Sarge said.

Mac and Thane looked at each other, trying to figure out what was going on.

"Who is he going to call?" Mac asked.

Sarge said, "Boomer." Then he nodded at Shakey.

Mac quickly realized what was about to happen. He sat up and yelled, "No!" Sarge and Shakey froze and quickly looked at Mac, who warned, "Don't cross that line, Sarge."

Thane could not comprehend what was happening, but he knew something important was taking place before him.

"I know about that code of the Old Blues. Smitty told me all about you guys. 'Protect and serve.' I've heard it all." Mac pointed back and forth to Shakey and Sarge. "This is not you. If you cross this line, you can't go back."

Mac stood up and quickly moved closer to Shakey. "Give… me… that." Mac tried to get the phone from Shakey's trembling hands. After three or four unsuccessful attempts to grab it from his wobbly and jittery grasp, Mac finally gripped Shakey's wrist. Mac took the phone from him, then looked around at all of the men in the room. Mac's voice became stern as he pointed the phone back and forth at the men as he spoke. "Clandestine operations… locate… observe… engage and destroy the enemies of our country. That has been my life for as long as I can remember. I don't even remember what it was like to be a normal human being. Adhering to those Old Blue values makes all of this so special and keeps you Blues to dedicated to your mission."

Mac pointed to the phone and said, "Make this call and you lose all of that."

Then he looked at Shakey. "Electric triggering mechanism?" he growled as more of a statement than a question.

Shakey understood Mac's attempt to protect the integrity of the Old Blue Precinct and answered, "It's the logical choice to initiate the fulminant device."

Mac spoke with quiet resolve: "I'll make the call."

Thane could not restrain himself any longer. He yelled, "Who are you calling?"

❧

"He wants to know what is the purpose of that disgusting dog?" the interpreter said after his boss whispered something under his breath.

"That? Oh, it is a little trophy that reminds me of the foolish people who stood in my way."

Lois turned to her new associates and smiled. "I think this is going to turn out to be very profitable for us. My Chemist is on his way here. We will be ready to resume operations within the week."

Taking a quick look at her reflection in a mirror on the wall, Lois thought about her future and the money she would make. A satisfied grin made its way across her face. She stepped back and widened her view of herself. The grin left her face as she noticed over her shoulder that the stuffed dog seemed to be moving… no, it was vibrating and lightly bouncing.

Miguel and his boss also noted that the stuffed animal was vibrating and making a strange sound. They both stepped toward the critter to get a closer look.

Lois walked over to them and said, "One of my men swore that the dog's eyes followed him around the room."

As she approached the head of the dog, she noticed that its eyes actually did follow her. She bent over to get a closer look. The last thing Lois saw during her pathetic sojourn on earth was the eyes of Boomer as they blew from the dog amid an explosion.

❧

Mac looked at the monitor and sat up as the screen suddenly glared white, then went blank. Immediately he knew what had happened. He looked at Sarge, who said, "There was no other choice."

Mac nodded. "I agree. That dog was full of surprises." Then he sat back and gave a hearty laugh.

Thane looked around the room at Sarge, Mac, and then at Shakey, who announced, "The implantation of C-4 into a canine is another application that I had not previously considered as a viable delivery system. To my surprise, it appears to have been successful."

Thane jumped up from his chair and almost screamed, "BOOMER WAS A BOMB! Why didn't anyone tell me?"

Mac leaned over and in a matter-of-fact tone asked, "Would you have talked into Boomer's butt if you had known he was a bomb?"

Thane sat back down and said, "I guess not."

There was a knock on the door of Thane's office. Officer Charlie poked his head in and asked, "Has anyone seen my dog?"

~

Monte Kurt was driving down the same dirt road that Lois had taken about an hour earlier. In the distance he observed a mushroom-shaped cloud of black smoke emerging from part of a house about a mile away. As he came closer, he could see a couple of men running about. They had a hose and were trying to put out a fire that had started on what was left of one side of the house.

"What happened here?" He checked his GPS to confirm that it was the location where he was supposed to meet Lois. Now the black cloud would immediately draw attention from people who were miles away.

"I don't know what happened, but I'm not staying around to find out," he decided. The PT Cruiser did a three-point turnaround and left the area. Again Monte looked into the rearview mirror. Smoke was now billowing hundreds of feet into the sky. Soon the vicinity would be crawling with emergency vehicles. His eyes met those in the mirror.

"It looks like Lois's new enterprise has gone up in smoke. So much for a new partner."

Then Monte thought about the thousands of dollars he had acquired from the sale of his mother's home. She had given him Power of Attorney, so there were no problems selling it.

Now a smile crept onto Monte's face as he looked at the eyes in the mirror.

"The police can't touch me, and I can still move freely about. It's time to move on," he announced to the reflected eyes with confidence.

Down the road he drove, relishing the freedom to do as he pleased. Nothing to worry about, only a feeling of frustration about the two women who had gotten away. Then he looked back at the reflection in the mirror and said, "Or did they?"

~

Brittany and Amanda had just begun to feel somewhat normal again. Brittany kept the lights on in the living room as she and Amanda went back to their routine.

After spending so much time together, the two young women had become like sisters. Amanda's relationship with Thane was blossoming into something really special. Brittany told her about the perils of falling for a guy who worked with all those lovable geezers.

"To tell you the truth, though, Amanda, it's gotten to the point where I can't remember what it was like without these old coppers making my life an adventure. I've been sucked in with their continued sense of duty at that precinct of theirs."

Amanda stretched her spine and yawned. "I've really never got to know my grandma until now. We moved around so much. Then when I went into foster care I lived in a lot of different homes. I think I know what you mean about what kind of life I would have without them. I just really like being with these old cops. Of course having Thane pop up to see me is really nice, too."

Amanda stretched once more, then announced, "I'm heading to bed. 'Night, Britz."

Brittany walked around the house making sure that all the doors were locked. She closed all the curtains and gave the living room a once-over before calling it a night herself. She wanted to make sure everything was still in its proper place.

Once the lights were off and Brittany settled into her bed, she was finally able to relax. Amanda was in the other room, fast asleep.

"After all the things that girl has been through, she can go right to sleep. Amazing," Brittany marveled to herself.

The moon rose slowly on its nightly glide across the evening sky. A window in the utility room emitted a slight squeak as it was pushed open. A couple of weeks earlier during one of his sojourns to the girls' residence, Monte had moved various things around and put some black electrician's tape over the latching mechanism of this window. It opened with only a slight noise that was unlikely to betray his presence.

Once the window was pushed open, Monte Kurt slithered through it into the house. He was not there solely to dominate chemically incapacitated women. This time he was planning to take revenge. Somehow these women had played a role in exposing him, and they were going to pay.

He made his way through the dark hallway. The silence was so complete that he could hear both women breathing as they slept. Rubbing his hands together, he thought to himself, *"I have a choice—the pretty one who came into the pharmacy with the old woman who was trying to seduce me, or the one who laughed..."*

Suddenly the burning embers of revenge burst into flames of anger. "The one who laughed at me," he whispered through gritted teeth. He pulled the thin leather gloves tighter on his hands and made his way to Amanda's room. He remembered the look of terror on her face when he'd had her by the throat at his mother's house. The feeling of power was something he had craved ever since.

The bedroom door was slightly ajar. As he pushed it open, there was a slight creaking. He stopped as the sound pierced the silence. He froze, stopped moving the door and turned sideways so that he could step into the room without opening the door any further. Again he adjusted his gloves. The form of the woman's body under the blanket caused him to focus like a predator that was about to pounce on its prey. A shallow, hissing sound could be heard, but that was of no consequence.

I've been waiting for this for a long time, Monte said to himself, wanting to see that look of absolute fear on the girl's face once again. He smiled and took hold of the blanket that covered her face. He had readied himself to jerk the blanket with his left hand, with his right hand cocked back like a boxer delivering a straight jab, ready to grab her throat. This would keep her silent by strangling her ability to breathe or scream.

In his mind, he prepared himself, tightened his grip on the blanket, and... *FLOOM*, the jerking motion made a peculiar sound, revealing a pair of eyes that were not fearful at all, but *furious!*

"What's wrong, sweet cheeks, your chemistry set not working?"

The Chemist jumped backwards and tripped. He fell against the bedroom wall and slid into a sitting position. Agnes clapped her hands twice and the lights came on.

Monte's eyes darted back and forth, trying to focus as the unexpected brightness momentarily left him unable to see. He quickly regained his sight but not his comprehension.

"Couldn't resist, could ya, lover boy?" Agnes asked in an accusing tone.

Suddenly he recognized the woman who was standing in front of him. She popped a cigarette between her lips and flicked her lighter to life with her thumb. She kept her eyes on Monte as she lit her smoke.

"You don't scare me, ya little puke," she rasped.

"Me either," said Amanda as she walked into the room. She reached into her pocket, and pulled out a small keychain pepper spray can, then used it to spray both of Monte's eyes. The pain that shot through his body felt as though his eyes were being burned from their sockets.

Agnes looked at Amanda, who smiled and explained, "I got some after I heard it worked on lions."

Monte started to thrash around on the floor, yelling and cursing. Then a pair of large hands grabbed him by the collar and jerked him onto his feet. "Worthless punk," Big Brock said as he pulled Monte's face up to his and glared at him. Each time Monte could get a flicker of sight, all he could see was Brock's angry eyes. The big man shoved Monte with such force that he smashed into the wall on the opposite side of the room, breaking the drywall.

The burning of his eyes didn't dim his fury at being caught and exposed. He tried to stand and run.

Phift! Phift! The taser darts struck him in the chest and groin. The electric pulsating shock of fifty thousand volts jolted through Monte's body. The irony of Monte's groin being zapped did not go unnoticed by Big Brock. As Monte screamed and thrashed on the ground, Brock chuckled, "Now there's some justice."

After five seconds the jolts stopped. Monte tried to sit up and fell back after a splat in the chest by a piss pack. The splatter sent the nauseating fluid onto the walls and floor of Amanda's room. No words could describe the shock, pain, and discomfort Monte was experiencing at that moment. Every sensory nerve in his body was overwhelmed with pain, smell, and anguish. He vaguely perceived that he was being handcuffed.

"We'll talk tomorrow. Don't tell the coppers that we were here. Boss Nurse would be furious." Big Brock smiled, and Amanda ran over and hugged him. "You're fine, doll baby. Remember, don't tell anyone we were here. We're supposed to be in bed."

Detective Angie Jacks arrived with two police cruisers after the police received a 911 call of a break-in and the caller informed them that the suspect, Monte Kurt, was being held until the police arrived.

Jake Mitchell also showed up. He looked at Detective Jacks and noted, "This was a long time coming for you, Angie."

She smiled and said, "Sometimes I love my job."

She and a uniformed officer grabbed Monte by the arms and lifted him to his feet. The pungent odor was overwhelming. Detective Jacks stepped back and looked at Brittany and Amanda.

"Pepper spray is great stuff," Amanda said with a smile.

The uniformed officer looked in disgust at Monte. "These women must have worked you over pretty good, ya perp. Did you piss yourself?"

With an even bigger smile, "Pepper spray is really great stuff!" Amanda announced again with excitement.

Monte was marched outside. Detective Jacks looked at Brittany and Amanda. "You two got this guy while he was breaking into your house?"

Amanda was almost giddy. "I love pepper spray!"

Once everyone was gone and Amanda decided to sleep on the living room couch, Jake and Brittany sat down and told

Amanda that they needed to talk to her about her grandmother and the Ol' Blues.

Jake began, "Amanda, all of those Blues care very much for you. I'm sure you're wondering why they were so involved in your case. I'm also sure you don't understand exactly what they are doing." Jake looked at Brittany, who nodded encouragement for Jake to continue.

Jake took a deep breath. Amanda sat on the edge of the couch and listened intently to every word Jake was saying.

"Amanda, your grandmother, Sarge, Big Brock, and all those old cops at the Precinct are not just a bunch of retired cops. They are a special breed of people who have known nothing but going after those who victimize the innocent and protecting people, all their lives. When they retired, it was like their reason for living was ripped from them. When they see something suspicious, they check it out."

Brittany added, "They can't help themselves. It's really annoying."

Jake continued, "If the public, the police, or even the staff at the home were ever to find out what these old coppers were doing, it could destroy their reason for living and could even hurt the police work in the city."

Amanda cut Jake off by holding her hands up. "Say no more."

Jake gave Brittany a worried look.

"I figured it out a while ago," Amanda said.

Brittany spoke up: "We weren't sure how or if we could tell you. I hope you're not upset."

Amanda had a tear in her eye. "To tell you the truth, I'm proud of how they're still old fighters. I think it's cool."

Brittany questioned, "Cool?"

Amanda started listing on her fingers, "That crazy police precinct set up, the uniforms, the Sarge, and the way they still act like they are cops. It's pretty obvious."

Jake got really uncomfortable at the thought that Amanda had been able to discover the secret of the Precinct despite all the precautions.

Amanda sat back and said, "I can't believe they've been able to pull this off."

Brittany said, "It is pretty amazing. It's such a relief to know that I don't have to keep this secret from you anymore."

"To think..." Amanda started to laugh. "My grandmother and all those geezers are... the best-ever neighborhood watch group."

Brittany and Jake exchanged a quick glance of surprise.

"If Boss Nurse found out that they were being so active in the community without her okay, they would really be in trouble," Amanda said.

Jake smiled. "Well, you two get some rest. I've gotta go."

Brittany walked out to Jake's car with him. After a hug and loving kiss, Jake gave Brittany's hand a squeeze. "I'll talk to you tomorrow, babe."

"Jake, she still doesn't know about the Precinct. She thinks it's a neighborhood watch club. Oh, and lest I forget, she is falling in love with Thane."

With a shrug of his shoulders, Jake said, "Let the Blues deal with it. Those geezers never cease to amaze me."

Two months later…

A shiny vintage 1960 police cruiser with a single rotator on the roof was parked at the loading area of the Precinct.

"It's gonna be donated to the Precinct," Sarge told Agnes. "Ain't she a beauty? Look at the size of this thing. The trunk alone in these cars could hold all kinds of emergency road cones and equipment."

Agnes and Meter Maid Mary moved around the classic police car.

"Brings back a lot of memories, Sarge. I think it would be great to have it parked in front of the home," Agnes said.

Meter Maid Mary added, "Sarge, could you call Benson and Smitty up to take a look at this? I believe they used to be partners when we used this model of cruiser."

Amanda stood nearby and wondered at the nostalgic gazes the Blues were giving this old car. The car was backed up to the elevated loading dock. One could literally step out onto the top of the trunk.

Smitty and Benson walked out and froze at the onrush of memories of those old cruisers.

The Sarge said, "Remember how we used to joke about the size of the trunks of these old boats?" They laughed.

Agnes stood by the driver's door, and Meter Maid Mary was next to the trunk.

Amanda said, "Open this trunk. I wanna see how big it is."

The trunk was opened, and as the Blues had said, it was huge. Amanda said, "Oh, Smitty and Benson, sit down in the trunk and let me take a picture of you. The guys in the Precinct will love it."

They all laughed. "Good for morale," Sarge added.

Smitty and Benson looked at each other and shrugged, saying, "Why not?"

Everyone cheered as they stepped down into the trunk, smiled, and waved.

Amanda exclaimed, "It's unreal. You two could almost lay down in there."

Smitty and Benson were laughing as they bent over to lie down while waving to the camera. Suddenly Meter Maid Mary reached over and slammed the trunk shut. Agnes got in and popped the car into gear. She floored the accelerator, and the large engine roared and the tires burned into the ground.

Trapped in the trunk just as Agnes and Meter Maid Mary had been half a century earlier when they were new to the force, Smitty and Benson screamed in terror. The sound of the two men yelling caused Agnes to laugh and cough as she did donuts and slammed on the brake, causing them to bounce around. This went on for a few minutes until Agnes felt she had shelled out sufficient payback for what Smitty and Benson had done fifty years ago.

Once she came to a stop, Agnes got out and in front of everyone, pulled out her keys to open the trunk. What she saw was enough to induce another wave of cough-laughing.

Smitty and Benson sat up, and the result of Agnes's donuts and braking became evident. Smitty's crap catcher had exploded, and both men were covered with the mostly digested contents of the Blues' previous day's dinner.

Speechless, they stared at each other in shock. Their faces were covered with brown, runny excreta. Agnes held her cigarette between her index and editorial fingers as she looked at the men and explained, "That video is for the Christmas party."

She put the cigarette back in her mouth, took a drag, and while turning to walk away said, "Touché."

Dear Reader,

Thank you for taking some time out of your busy life to read about some of the antics of these Ol' Blues. I really appreciate it. For those of us who self-publish, there are no financial advances or other means to help us get these stories out to be enjoyed.

Every time I talk to a retired officer or Ol' Blue, I learn a lot about how things were done in the old days. Suddenly the Ol' Blues find another avenue to my mind, and they refuse to leave me alone until I put their stories to paper. Hopefully, after reading about them, you will begin to look at the folks we call "geezers" in an entirely different way.

May you come to realize the value of the experiences and stories that they want to share, if you'll only listen. Or, in my case, read.

Otherwise, the Blues won't leave me alone. The only way I can get them off my back is to tell you about them. Once they are in your memory with their stories, you're stuck with them. So when life beats you down, grab your inner geezer and beat it back.

Sincerely,
Chris LeGrow
Over and out.

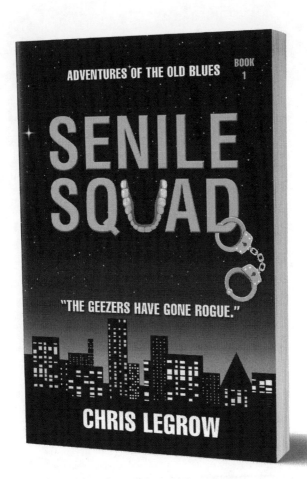

Book 1 Available at Amazon.com
in paperback, ebook and audiobook.

DETECTIVE CHRIS LEGROW, badge number 1557, is a retired member of the Omaha Police Department's Special Victims Unit. He investigated domestic violence cases that included everything from destruction of property to sexual assault and crimes against vulnerable adults. Formerly he worked for nine years as a Family Teacher at Boys Town. He and his wife, Kara, have nine children and a whole precinct of grandchildren.

Made in the USA
Middletown, DE
11 July 2022

69017527R00265